GLEAM OF CROWN

THE WALLKEEPER TRILOGY BOOK 3

GLEAM OF CROWN

CAREN HAHN

To Cori, who was one of the first to be invited into the Wallkeeper world, and whose love for it pulls her to return.

Books by Caren Hahn

Find Caren's work on Amazon.com

ROMANTIC FANTASY:

THE WALLKEEPER TRILOGY

Burden of Power

Pain of Betrayal

Gleam of Crown

THE HATCHED TRILOGY

Hatched: Dragon Farmer

Hatched: Dragon Defender

Hatched: Dragon Speaker

CONTEMPORARY SUSPENSE:

This Side of Dark

What Comes After

THE OWL CREEK SERIES

Smoke over Owl Creek

Hunt at Owl Creek

Visit carenhahn.com to receive a free
copy of *Charmed: Tales from Quarantine
and Other Short Fiction.*

GLEAM OF CROWN

THE WALLKEEPER TRILOGY BOOK 3

CAREN HAHN

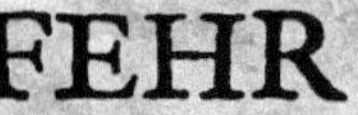

FEHR

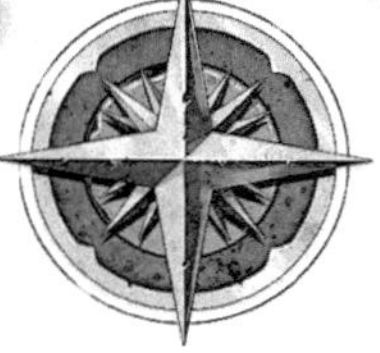

KINGDOM OF RAHM
CILLITH
YANETH
DELL

BRANVIK
ARDANIA
HALDIN
ENDVAR
VALDIRK
ALBON
BERSETH
LORIN

ONE

Aiya pulled her cap down tighter around her ears. The first part of their journey had been warm, with abundant sunlight warming their backs as she and Dan rode north. But as the forests thickened around them, the air's bitter chill reminded her of how late in the year it was.

It felt good to be on a horse again, and Aiya was pleased the skill had come back to her so quickly. The Rahmish saddle was too large, but that was to be expected when using a horse meant for a soldier. At least the animal was disciplined and intelligent, and Aiya soon felt at ease with her.

She did not feel at ease with Dan. He'd been very quiet since they left the army camp. Aiya watched him for signs of pain, wondering if he would tell her if he had trouble. He hadn't fully recovered from the wound that had cost him his arm, sustained when he fought to save Endvar from the invading Ardanians. This journey to the northern village of Haldin was as much to give him a distraction as it was to deliver an important message to Captain Falbrook.

Coming out of one forest, there was a break in the trees as they headed down a small rise toward another.

"Is all the rest of the country like this?" Aiya asked.

Dan glanced up, blinking as if just remembering she was there. The sun glinted off his fair hair the color of summer grass. He looked across the valley at the forested hills that piled one on top of another in the distance. Against the far reaches of the horizon were large peaks that marked the mountains of Branvik.

"It will be more of this the rest of our journey. Typical for the north."

"But the rest of Rahm is not so…" Aiya searched for a word to describe the overwhelming sense of closeness she felt under the thick forest canopy.

"Dense? Forbidding?"

"Wild," Aiya decided. "As if we're intruders whose presence is barely tolerated. I feel as if the very air here is full of ancient secrets that will outlive us all."

Dan shot her a look. "I don't know why you lived in Endvar so long and never ventured out to see the rest of the country. It's not all like this. In the areas surrounding Albon there are wide valleys good for farming that stretch all the way to the coast."

"And the coast? Tell me about it. I should like to see the ocean someday." She continued to keep Dan talking for some time, but as the daylight waned, his mood grew sullen.

When they stopped to make camp, Aiya busied herself gathering wood for a fire while keeping an eye on Dan to see how he managed his horse with one arm. He loosened the girth and lifted the saddle, but it was a laborious process, and some of the saddlebags slid to the ground.

Aiya hurried to help him, but as she bent to pick them up, he growled at her.

"Don't! I can manage."

Aiya stopped, startled by his sharp tone. But she obeyed, returning to the kindling and tinder she had gathered. It took all her attention to coax a small flame using a stone and flint, and she didn't realize until she finished that Dan was watching.

Her own smile of satisfaction died when she saw his scowl.

Without a word, Dan moved away into the darkening forest. He started chopping small branches one-handed with a hatchet, the motion fierce and impatient. Aiya sat back on her heels and watched. If this was what he needed to work out his frustration, so be it. All his racket would likely frighten away any bears or wild things in the area, so that was good, wasn't it?

Still, she was troubled by his agitation and felt at a loss to know what to say.

Dan returned to camp carrying a load of evergreen branches and arranged them in strips over a fallen log. *He's making a shelter*, Aiya realized. She moved to help, then thought better of it and let him finish on his own. When he was done, he stood back and admired his work with a gleam in his eye. One side was open to the fire, but the rest was enclosed by thick branches.

"How brilliant! Now we shouldn't freeze tonight," Aiya said, delighted.

Dan just grunted wordlessly.

Aiya sighed, reaching for her saddlebag to see what the cooks at the army camp had packed for them to eat.

She sat at the fire, chewing on the stringy meat that had been overly peppered, and hummed idly. The horses snuffled as they grazed nearby, a soothing sound against the popping of the fire. She felt a sense of adventure that the evening chill couldn't dampen.

Dan had been quiet for so long that she almost forgot about him.

"What is that tune?"

Aiya stopped and looked up, realizing what she'd been humming. "It's an old Khouri song. A lullaby or nursery tale."

Dan frowned. "I've heard it before, I think. It seems… familiar somehow."

"Hmm. Maybe you heard it at one of those festivals you went to in your youth. I'm sure you must have seen people from many countries in your travels." Aiya didn't say that it was one of the tunes she sang the night he lost his arm. They hadn't spoken of that night, and she didn't know what he remembered, delirious as he'd been with pain and medicine. But she couldn't bring herself to sing again.

After a time, Dan stood and wandered into the forest. Aiya let him go, wishing she knew how to make him stay. He hadn't returned by the time she curled up in her bedroll under the shelter and went to sleep.

· · ✳ · ·

Dan's mood did not improve with the daylight, and Aiya's worsened. She couldn't remember a time when she'd been so cold. She'd spent much of the night in a stage somewhere between sleeping and wakefulness where she was poignantly aware of how much she was shivering. But the shelter had helped, or so it seemed. The open areas of the forest had a coating of glittering ice, but under Dan's ceiling of branches the ground was free of frost.

Saddling his horse proved to be harder than unsaddling it the previous night had been. Dan struggled with the girth for some time until Aiya came and gently intervened, taking the big leather strap from him and holding one end in place while he pulled it tight.

She tried to catch his eye and smile, but he resisted looking at her.

"Dan," she said quietly, holding out her hands to him. "You have another pair of hands anytime you need them. "

Dan looked down at her outstretched hands. "I don't want your pity," he said tersely and stalked away.

Aiya stiffened. "Very well," she called after him. "I will stop pitying you when you stop pitying yourself."

"I don't pity myself!"

"Oh yes, you do. You've been moping since we left the army camp, and every day you sink further into despair."

He glared at her. "Well, forgive me if I'm trying to adjust to my new life. It's a little more difficult with only one arm."

"Adjusting? Is that what you call it?" Aiya crossed her arms in irritation. "This is not adjusting. This is pining for what you once had and being angry at those who care for you. I don't pity you, Dan, but I do want to help. If you don't let me, if you insist on wallowing in your misery alone, then it will take you a very long time to adjust to your new life. And quite frankly, we just don't have that kind of time."

Dan looked Aiya over, and his mouth turned up in a sad smile. "I suppose you think I should be grateful to have you with me, helping with those things I can't manage alone."

"I don't want your gratitude," Aiya replied, picking up her own saddlebags and hoisting them over her shoulder, "but I'll take a smile now and then."

Dan moved to help her with her own saddle. Aiya let him, feeling a tenuous truce of sorts. His mood didn't improve, exactly, but at least he didn't snap at her again.

They passed through a village that day where Aiya had hoped to find a hot meal, but Dan squirmed under the villagers' stares and pushed onward. In truth, more of the stares were for her than his missing limb. Aiya guessed that most of them had never seen a Khouri woman before. It was a strange sensation. She hadn't felt so foreign since her early days as a refugee in Endvar when she and Imar had struggled with the language and customs of the Rahmish people.

As evening approached, however, Aiya insisted that they ask a farmer for shelter in his barn. The wind was picking up, and she cringed at the idea of spending another night exposed to the weather.

The barn was little more than a shack, but it was warm. After a coin from Dan, the farmer brought them a hot stew made with some unidentifiable meat. Dan pronounced it as rabbit, but Aiya suspected that was only for her benefit. It was easier to imagine eating one of them than a bushy-tailed squirrel or fox.

Aiya reclined against a haystack and ate the bland mixture of vegetables swimming in a thin broth, trying to ignore the sharp smell of cow manure from the stall on the other side of the wall. The stew was hot, and her empty belly welcomed it.

Dan settled across the room on a burlap sack stuffed with grain. The gloom that had become his constant companion hung low over him, worsening with twilight.

Aiya welcomed a little distance, as she'd had little enough privacy in recent days. She leaned back and let her thoughts drift to the open rafters above, hung with thick cobwebs that seemed decades old.

She didn't realize Dan was watching her until he asked, "What are you smiling about?"

Heat warmed her face. "It's nothing."

"Please. I could use some amusement."

"If I tell you, you will be disappointed in me. I will no longer be the fair lily you imagine me to be."

He grunted and went silent. She'd meant it tenderly—remembering how he'd once described her—but realized he might think she was mocking him. Everything seemed to settle on him the wrong way these days. There was nothing for it but to set aside her pride and give him something else to think about besides his wretched future. Even if his opinion of her suffered at the telling.

"There was once a pair of thieves," Aiya began. "A young man who was reckless and alive with adventure, and a young woman who was carried away by the aura of excitement that surrounded him. They made a good pair. She grew up with the craft; it was a family business and she learned young. The young man was recruited by her father and sometimes ignored the rules that governed the family. This also attracted the young woman, as she wished for freedom from the tight hierarchy that always placed her father and his family subservient to her uncle. Any glory they earned was chipped away to raise her uncle's status."

This was not what she'd intended to share. She was in danger of becoming too introspective.

Aiya cleared her throat and continued, "As I said, they were a good team. One night they took a small item from a visiting dignitary at the royal palace itself. A bauble, really, it seemed. But her uncle wanted it, and that was that. Unfortunately, the young thieves didn't get away quickly enough and found themselves hiding in the rafters of Prince Lahri's stables. Waiting for the guards to weary of the chase and the palace grounds to quiet with the night, they each clung to a narrow beam in perfect stillness, trying not to disturb the beautiful beasts in the stalls beneath them.

"The young woman's heart raced with the fearful anticipation of discovery, but the young man was easily distracted and soon his mind wandered to other things. The danger didn't seem so great, and after a time, he fell asleep, lost his hold on the beam, and fell."

Dan snorted in quiet humor.

"The young woman's heart nearly leaped out of her throat as she saw him fall. As fate would have it, he landed right on the back of a beautiful mare the color of sun-baked sand. And so—whether it was instinct or dreaming, the young woman couldn't tell—he decided to ride the mare to freedom, making of her an even bigger prize than the small ruby pendant. The stable boys wasted precious time trying to stop him, so by the time they drew the attention of the guards, the young couple had burst free of the stables, jumped the low fence, and were on their way to an elder where they were married that very night while sitting upon one of the prince's favorite steeds."

A smile tugged at the corners of Dan's mouth. "And what happened to the young woman after that? Surely that was not the end of her story."

"Ah, but a wedding is always the best place to end a story, don't you think?" Aiya smiled. "The end of one great adventure and the beginning of another, full of promise and a future yet unwritten."

Dan leaned forward. "Then you must share how she became an outcast in a foreign land. What happened to the impetuous young man?"

Aiya's smile faded. "He died. He made the wrong enemies and got himself killed. The young woman lost everything, so she fled. Left her home and family and all that was familiar to come to a strange place where the men were hairy and the women were loud and bossy, speaking in a foreign tongue so coarse to her ears that she was certain her mouth could never shape the sounds." Aiya marveled at the memory of herself all those years ago. It seemed like another life.

Dan was quiet for a moment. "I've been unfair to you," he said at last. "I thought you couldn't understand my pain, the loss of my old life—that you couldn't know what I suffer. I see now that wasn't fair. Forgive me."

Aiya was taken aback, and she felt a warmth in her chest at his words. "There's nothing to forgive, Dan. You're a fighter and I admire you for it. When I came to your country, I thought I was starting over. But I didn't start over. I retreated into myself, keeping life at a distance out of fear. For years *I* did not own my life, my grief did. But what I see in you is a strength that says you will not give up without a fight, and I'm glad to have you by my side."

Dan grunted, and the deepening shadows made it difficult to see his expression. But after a few moments, Aiya heard a soft sigh. Whether it was a sigh of satisfaction or mourning, she couldn't say.

Two

The following morning, Aiya was pleasantly surprised to feel a warm gust of air as she left the barn. Gone was the chill of recent days. The wind had picked up during the night, but it was a warm wind that reminded her of spring.

She and Dan had worked out a routine to prepare the horses for traveling. Though some of the tasks would have been faster with two hands, Aiya stepped back and let Dan complete them with one. She wanted to help, and it made her ache to watch him struggle with things that would have ordinarily been simple chores. Her own words of the previous night echoed in her ears. He *was* a fighter, and she would respect him for it. Even if it slowed them down.

"At least it's much warmer today," Aiya said cheerfully as they set out down the road. Barren trees arched overhead, their leaves stripped during the night by the wind now carpeting the road in bright colors.

Dan looked up at the clouds chasing across the sky. "Warmer, yes, but it won't last."

"You don't think so?"

"This is the warm that comes before snow. A big storm, I'd bet."

"Snow!" Aiya laughed. "That's impossible! With this warmth it will surely only rain."

"It won't last," Dan repeated. "There will be snow before the day is through."

Aiya didn't like the idea of being on the road in a snowstorm. Dan must have sensed her apprehension.

"We may reach Haldin tonight if we push hard today," he added.

And so they pushed hard. The forest around them grew dense, and Aiya kept an eye on the wind-whipped trees. Small branches and clumps of moss floated down onto the road, and Aiya wondered what it would be like for one of those great swaying beasts to give way and crash into their path.

Fortunately, their horses were steady animals and didn't shy away from the debris littering the road. Aiya's only complained once—skittering forward and snorting nervously—when a branch brushed against its flank.

By midday, Dan's prediction came true. The wind gusted with just as much fervor, but the temperature plummeted, and the icy blasts made Aiya think longingly of finding shelter. The day darkened early with storm clouds, and by the time the air swirled with snowflakes, Aiya already felt frozen through.

She wanted to ask Dan if they were nearing their destination. She wondered if snowstorms were common in the northern forests. She worried how the cold might affect Dan's arm and if he was in pain. But she voiced none of these things because she had pulled her muffler up over her mouth and nose. Speaking would mean exposing them again to the wind and frozen granules of ice that pelted her skin.

It was nearly nightfall when two dark shapes broke away from the trees and startled Dan's mount. Dan shouted as one of the men seized his horse's bridle.

Something heavy thudded against Aiya's back as a figure dropped out of the tree above. She yelped in surprise and grabbed for the knife she kept in her boot, but the man was too quick. He grabbed her, pinning her arms at her side and hoisting her out of the saddle.

Aiya twisted and kicked to try and free herself, but to no effect. She let loose a string of curses in her native tongue, and the man responded by barking something back at her in a language she didn't know. She froze. This was no Rahmish villager. With surprising strength, the man pitched her out of the saddle.

Aiya fell hard onto the cold ground. She cried out from the sharp pain in her tailbone. Nearby, Dan had drawn his sword in an attempt to fend off the two other strangers, but his movements were slow and awkward with his left arm, nothing like the smooth skill she'd seen with his right.

Aiya gathered her legs under her, but she winced with each movement. A fine fighting companion she was. If she could just distract one of the shadowy figures, perhaps Dan would have a chance.

As she got to her feet, Aiya saw her horse returning. The stranger on its back carried a large tree limb. He rode straight toward Dan.

"Dan!" Aiya shrieked.

Dan looked up and saw the rider advancing. He ducked just in time, and the branch swung harmlessly in the air, but the moment of distraction was all the other two hooded men needed to seize him and drag him to the ground.

Aiya ran forward, her knife drawn, afraid for Dan. But the thieves didn't waste time with him. They were only after his horse. They galloped off into the night, leaving Aiya and Dan behind on the road with nothing more than the clothes on their backs.

Dan knelt on the road amid the swirling snow, clenched his fist, and bellowed up at the sky.

"Does it help?" Aiya cried. "Do you feel better now? I wish I could roar like that because I would—" She broke into a stream of Khouri that rushed out of her like an angry tide. Her voice rose into a shout as she poured every curse she could think of onto the heads of the thieves.

Her words died away into silence, and she stood still, breathing heavily with the echo of her own tirade ringing in her ears. Suddenly she felt ashamed at her outburst. It was childish and did nothing to improve their situation. They were still without horses or provisions, far from civilization, with night and a snowstorm descending.

But Dan grinned at her.

"Well. That's something you don't hear every day."

He jumped to his feet, his eyes bright for the first time in days, and Aiya's anger melted away at the sight.

"Keep that inner fire burning," he said over his

shoulder as he led the way down the road into the forest. "It may be the only warmth we have for a long time."

THEY WALKED FOR WHAT SEEMED HOURS IN THE DARK WITH the snow thickening in the air around them. At first it blew aimlessly rather than settling onto the ground. Aiya was grateful for this, as it took a long time to cover the road. Once the road had a small layer, however, it accumulated quickly, slowing them down.

After a time, the road narrowed and became little more than a path. Aiya's feet were like blocks of ice in her boots, and she hugged herself for warmth. She didn't know when Dan had noticed her shivering, but at some point he removed his own coat and draped it over her shoulders.

"No, you will freeze." She cringed at the sight of him in his light shirtsleeves.

"It's not so cold to me," he insisted, "and we're nearly there. Soon we'll have a fire and a hot meal to warm us inside and out."

Aiya sighed hopefully at the tantalizing image. It was the only thing that kept her moving. When the forest parted at last, revealing a small shack set against the giant stone wall, she nearly sobbed.

The shack—the guardhouse, Dan had called it— looked abandoned, as cold and black as though it had never known the warmth of a fire and a hot meal.

"Are you sure this is it?" Aiya asked.

Dan moved forward to inspect the little building

cautiously. She waited while he listened at the window then carefully opened the door.

When there were no cries of alarm, she followed.

The inside of the guardhouse was cold and empty with few signs of recent occupation. Dry wood was stacked by the fireplace, and a few personal items lay scattered about the room—a hat hanging from a peg, a book resting near a chair.

Through a door at the back, Aiya caught a glimpse of a cot with neatly folded blankets stacked on the end. Suddenly she felt so tired that she didn't care if this building was now the den of the very thieves who had attacked them in the forest. She was staying.

Dan searched both rooms but returned with no answers. "I don't understand. No one has been here for some time. Days. Perhaps weeks. The village of Haldin isn't far from here. Are you..?"

He trailed off as he took in Aiya's expression.

"I'll build a fire first, shall I? And then we'll decide what to do."

With a sigh of relief, Aiya collapsed into a chair. Dan started a fire in the hearth, and she watched him work through a haze of exhaustion, vaguely aware that he was already compensating for his lack of a right arm far better than he had a few days before.

When the fire was crackling merrily, she crouched before it and removed her gloves, holding her hands before the flames. The heat stung her skin but seemed slow to warm the rest of her. She hadn't noticed Dan leave until he returned, bringing a blast of cold air with him as the door swung shut.

"This should hold us through the night."

He carried a stack of wood with his one good arm, the stump of his right doing little more than providing balance. Aiya wondered how many tries it had taken to figure out how to gather wood with one arm. She thought about bringing in a load herself, but the thought of going back outside in the storm chilled her.

"You should have your coat," she said, taking it off her shoulders. "Thank you. I'm warm enough now." But she still couldn't feel much of her legs and feet. Her trousers and stockings were soaked through and clung to her skin.

Dan brushed the snow from his light hair and sat beside Aiya on the hearth. Almost close enough to touch, but not quite, they sat in silence, watching the flames lick the wood and dance in the draft coming down the chimney.

After a time, Aiya finally felt warmed through, and her eyelids sagged. As if reading her mind, Dan moved to stand.

"There's a cot in the next room. Why don't you rest for a while? I'm going to see if I can find out where the soldiers are."

Aiya's eyes snapped open. "You're leaving? Now?"

"Haldin is close. A few miles at most. If I can't find any soldiers on the wall, the villagers will know where they've gone."

"In this storm? Are you mad? Wait until morning when it's light."

"The storm may be worse then, the paths impassable. I won't be able to rest until I know what happened."

Aiya sighed. There was no sense arguing. When had he ever listened to her before? She didn't understand his great sense of duty. Obedience, yes, she understood that. Performing a task with perfection—even artful flair—that was something she valued. But this deep sense of duty was beyond her comprehension.

"Stoke the fire when you come back," she grumbled. "I don't want to freeze halfway through the night."

Dan tousled her hair in response, a playful gesture that made Aiya feel very small. She opened her mouth to protest but shut it again. It was a sign of his improving spirits, and she wouldn't dampen them. But she made a mental note to have a sharp elbow ready for him the next time he tried it. He was her companion, even a friend, but he was most certainly *not* her brother.

THREE

Ria shivered under the gray sky, a fine cold mist dampening her hair and skin. She missed her heavy cloak. She wished for a fire. She wished for Merek's warm arms around her.

A wry smile tugged at her lips. She was less likely to get that than the others. Despite the change in their relationship, Merek wasn't particularly demonstrative in public. And since living in an army camp meant almost every moment of every day was public, there was little outward change between them. Ria would have to use her imagination if she wanted to be inspired with warm thoughts of Merek.

Really, she was glad that he wasn't here to witness this humiliation. Merek had made her promise to learn some basic defensive skills in case she found herself in trouble when she met with Artem. She didn't look forward to seeing the Ardanian prince, but hoped that it would provide the distraction needed for a covert squad of climbers to seize control of Endvar's gates, giving them the opportunity they needed to storm the city. So she watched dutifully as Captain Eldar demonstrated some movements using her own knife.

"Are you ready, Your Highness?" Captain Eldar asked, inviting her to step forward. He wore no beard, and underneath the wrinkles and unsmiling eyes she suspected he might have been handsome once.

Ria shuddered with the cold. "I still don't understand why I must be out in this chill wind without a cloak."

"You'll warm up quickly enough once you begin. Now, if you'll hold the handle like this..." He demonstrated before handing it to her.

Ria suppressed a sigh. These exercises were meant to give her confidence in the blade, its weight in her hand, and her own body's response to it. He claimed that she needed to be more comfortable with the blade before she could properly use it.

But as Ria copied his movements, she felt like a fool. Her left shoulder was stiff, and if she tried to move her arm too much, her old injury complained. Even her right arm didn't move as fluidly as the captain's. She felt like a marionette trying to mimic life and half expected the grizzled captain to laugh at any moment. Except, he didn't seem the sort who ever laughed.

He was right about one thing, though. Her body warmed with the motion, and soon she didn't mind the cold as much.

Ria moved to pass the knife behind her back from her right hand to her left, but her fingers fumbled and the blade sliced her thumb. She gasped, dropping the knife. Her thumb bled freely, but the cut wasn't deep. That was a mercy.

"If you can relax a little, Your Highness, it will feel more natural."

Biren was at her side in a moment, wrapping her thumb to staunch the bleeding.

Ria glowered at the captain. "What about this seems natural to you? This is ridiculous. I'm no soldier."

Eldar waited patiently for Biren to finish then jerked his head in dismissal. Biren cast a reluctant glance over her shoulder as she obeyed.

"I'm sorry to waste your time, Captain," Ria said, annoyed at his brusqueness. "It's unfortunate that Strong assigned this hopeless task to you."

"General Strong wouldn't have requested it if it were hopeless."

"Turning me into a fighter in a matter of days?" Ria scoffed. "If Artem wishes me harm, there will be nothing I can do to stop him. My guards will have to be protection enough because if I get into a situation where I have to save myself, the fight is already lost."

"It may not be a matter of needing to save yourself. It may simply help if you're not such a liability when your guards are trying to protect you. Give them the best chance of defending you by not making a foolish mistake."

"Thank you, Captain," Ria said flatly, stung by how incompetent he thought she was. And how true his assessment.

"Shall I show you some defensive moves, then?"

"I think not." Ria looked beyond the captain to where a young man stood watching them. His light blue uniform was that of a royal messenger, and Ria recognized him as one of Galinn's runners. "I see that word has arrived from Albon, and I'm anxious to hear it." She motioned to Biren to follow her and turned her back on the captain.

"I'd be happy to work with you this afternoon, if you wish," Eldar called as she walked away from the practice field.

"I don't think so. Perhaps tomorrow," she returned.

Her smile was much warmer for Galinn's courier.

"What news from Albon?" Ria asked as Biren joined her, draping her winter cloak about her shoulders.

The young man bowed, his long hair falling in front of his face, and retrieved a folio from his satchel. "Good afternoon, Your Highness. Master Galinn sends his greetings and hopes that you're finding success here. He asks that you review a few matters at your convenience and includes some personal letters that may interest you."

"Thank you. I'll read them immediately. Biren, see to it that he gets a hot meal, please."

Ria couldn't resist opening the folio while she walked. She recognized Galinn's formal handwriting immediately and set those papers aside. The king's steward shouldered more weight these days now that her father had locked himself away in his tower. Whatever business he had for her would need to wait until she had time to give it her full attention.

There was a letter from Lotta next, and she immediately scanned its contents, knowing that it would be the first of many readings. Lotta missed her, worried about her health in the cold exposure of a winter camp, and hoped that she was behaving herself with so many soldiers who must be setting an appalling example.

Ria smiled as she thought wistfully of writing to Lotta and telling her of her newly discovered affection for Merek. It was unfortunate that she couldn't speak of it openly to her old friend, but she couldn't risk fueling any rumors that might be finding their way to Albon—not until she had dealt with her father upon her return.

There was no word from the king, though she hardly expected it anymore. She wondered if he had heard yet about Grammel's death. What would he do when he learned that she had named Merek as his replacement? Worse yet, what would he do when he learned of their fictitious betrothal? Her insides twisted at the thought. She was fighting a war on two fronts, and the one which pained her the most was the one she could do nothing about.

A letter from Count Orlin was brief and full of affected humility. The Ardanian ambassador assured her that he was doing all he could to reach King Idan but as yet hadn't confirmed that his emissaries were successful. In the meantime, as he was proving himself to be a friend to Rahm, could she relent and allow him to move freely about the city again?

Ria sighed and turned to a small envelope with writing that she didn't recognize. Curious, she glanced over the short note.

It was from Captain Drenall, First Captain over the Royal Guard who had escorted Ria on her wall tour over the summer. *Odd*, she thought. The note was brief and to the point, much like the good captain himself.

Your Royal Highness,
The king has barred himself in his room and rejects food

and water. Master Galinn has asked that we defy his orders and force him to eat if need be. If this is your will, I will comply. But I shall not act without your consent.

Your willing servant.

Ria stopped in her tracks. A moment earlier she had been picturing her father as a vengeful threat to be appeased. But this. This image of a man starving in his madness could not be the same person. Questions flooded her mind, and she cursed the captain's brevity and lack of detail. What had caused this change? When was the last time her father had eaten? Of course she would demand that Drenall do as Galinn asked and force the door open. Beyond that, she wasn't sure what they could do. If her father was determined not to eat, what hope was there that they could compel him?

Ria looked up and was surprised to find herself in front of the command tent. Her feet must have carried her here without thinking. But of course. When she was troubled, where else would she go?

But Merek wasn't inside. She found him instead on a practice field at the edge of camp where he was sparring with Captain Firl. Ria waited, watching for an opportunity to interrupt, but as she watched, she became engrossed in the contest.

Neither of the men were armored, and sweat soaked the backs and fronts of their shirts. Steam rose off their warm bodies in the cold air as they met time and time again, practice swords ringing. Firl was an accomplished swordsman, but he was no match for Merek. Firl moved quickly around the field, trying to gain the upper hand, but Merek never faltered in his pursuit, keeping him on the defensive.

There was no pattern or rhythm to their movements, but Ria was awed nonetheless at how they anticipated each other's moves and responded in kind. As she watched, Firl began flagging, and he was a little slower to parry Merek's blows. Eventually, he found himself flat on his back with Merek kneeling at his side, the tip of Merek's blade pointed at Firl's chest.

"Orri!" Firl shouted.

Merek jumped to his feet as another man rushed him from behind. It was Orri, the youngest of his first captains.

"What—" Ria began, indignant at what she saw. But it was clear that Merek expected this, and he met Orri's attack with equal strength. Firl grabbed his own sword but scrambled off the field instead of joining the fight. Ria's protest died on her lips.

Rorden stood nearby in a ring of watching soldiers. She moved closer and spoke without taking her eyes off the field.

"I don't understand the rules of this contest. Why did Captain Firl not yield?"

"They're sparring as partners. When one's in distress, he calls for his partner to spell him."

Ria watched in silence for a few moments, gasping when Orri's swinging blade nearly grazed Merek's ear. Dull edge notwithstanding, she'd spent enough time in camp to know that even the practice swords could cause painful injuries.

"And where is Strong's partner?" she asked.

Rorden grinned sheepishly and raised his own sword

in a mock salute. Ria took in his appearance. His brow was dry, his clothing neat. Clearly he had yet to join the fray.

"When will he call for you?"

Rorden shrugged. "He may, or he may not. It depends on how much he wants to exert himself today."

The wonder Ria felt increased. Orri was rested, yet still he could not gain the advantage over Merek. As they sparred, Orri's face grew increasingly red—whether from effort or frustration, Ria couldn't tell. But while Merek looked tired, he didn't weaken. She felt a surge of glowing pride.

Rorden looked at her expression and snorted. "Impressive, isn't it? I expect I won't even step foot on the field today."

Ria blushed a little that she had been so transparent. "I need to get that man on a dance floor."

"Now *that* I'd like to see."

"He claims he doesn't dance, but look at him move, the way he anticipates what Orri is going to do. Just think what I could do with him if he had some proper dancing instruction."

Rorden laughed. "I don't know of a soldier in this camp who can best him. But you..." He shook his head.

Ria's lips twitched at the compliment.

Captain Orri was younger than Merek, and this contest was more physical. Soon both men were bleeding: Merek from his knuckles, and Orri from his nose. Orri called for Firl and left the field with blood running down his face.

The sight made Ria squirm.

"How do they know who wins? It seems this could go on for hours."

"Strong has already won. The first pair who rotates three times loses. They've already done that. The goal now is to see if they can get him to call me. That will be as good as a win."

For as much as Ria was curious to see how long Merek could hold out, she was becoming chilled standing still in the wintry air. She stepped onto the field and waited to be noticed.

As surely as if she'd called his name, Merek looked up. His eyes brightened, and his focused expression softened at the sight of her.

It was only a fraction of a second, but Firl took advantage of the distraction to swing his sword at Merek's head. This time, Merek was slow to respond. He dodged, but the blow struck him hard on the shoulder. He grimaced and staggered for a moment. Then, in a twisting move that Ria couldn't quite follow, he stripped Firl's weapon so quickly that Firl stood dumbfounded, looking at his sword in Merek's hands as if he didn't know how it got there.

Some of the gathered soldiers laughed or cheered while others groaned. Ria smiled. It was good to see Firl humbled, but more than that, it was good for the men to see their commander shine.

Her smile widened as he approached. She couldn't help it. She felt more…whole with him. And the way he looked at her…Well, it was no wonder that her heart beat faster as he drew near.

She placed her hands on her hips and declared, "You, sir, are a frightful show-off."

"Don't listen to her," Rorden piped up. "She nearly swooned when you broke Orri's nose."

Merek raised an eyebrow, and Ria's cheeks warmed.

"Sergeant, you are a vile betrayer." She laughed. "Though I do hope Orri won't be too disfigured. It would be a shame to ruin his handsome face."

"He's too old for such a handsome face," Merek said, wiping his brow with his sleeve. "At his rank, he should have scars, missing teeth, and a crooked nose like the rest of us."

Ria squinted as she looked him over. "If he wears it as well as you do, then he shan't suffer a bit."

Merek grunted uncomfortably.

Rorden stayed behind at the field, so for a few precious minutes, they were alone as they walked through the camp.

"I received word from Captain Drenall that troubles me," Ria said, handing over Drenall's note.

Merek read its brief lines silently. His expression darkened, and when he finished, he returned it with a frown. "Your father's madness is worsening, then?"

"I don't know if this is a sign of his madness or if this is how he's chosen to fight it. Perhaps it's the last sane part of him that chooses death over being imprisoned in his own mind. He came to me before I left Albon. Did I tell you?"

Merek glanced at her sharply. "He left the tower?"

"He did. He came to my room late one night and made me promise never to visit him again. For my own safety."

"That sounds more like the Sindal I know." His words filled her with a mixture of grief and pride.

"I feel torn in two," she admitted. "A part of me wishes to rush home and tend to my father. But I also can't bear the thought of sitting uselessly at his side when I could instead help you thwart Artem and put an end to this conflict."

Merek said nothing.

"You don't rush to advise me?" she said wryly. "Oh how things have changed."

Merek frowned. "This is your decision. You know I'd rather not put you at risk, but I support whatever you choose."

They walked in silence for a bit as Ria sorted out the conflicting emotions driving her indecision. She was a little disappointed that Merek didn't just come right out and ask her to stay. With that realization, she understood what she really wanted.

"I'll stay then," she decided. "Let's continue with our plans. If all goes well, I'll be returning home soon anyway and can tend to my father then."

"True," Merek said. "Is it selfish of me to hope it isn't too soon?"

Ria smiled, feeling a warmth with his words. Merek offered her his arm as they walked, and she took it gratefully, clinging to this one form of public affection that he would allow. There was so much more she wanted to say, but she needed more privacy than was to be found out here in the open, and they were nearly to the command tent.

At the entrance, Captain Eldar waited, his face grim. As usual. But next to him stood someone she did not expect to see.

Ria paused, her stomach plummeting. For there stood

Captain Talen, the very man whom she had deceived to save Merek's life.

Her feet slowed, and she let her arm slip from Merek's as he strode forward to meet their unexpected visitor. Why was Talen here? Suddenly she was seized by an irrational fear that he was there to arrest Merek again, and she felt an urge to call Merek back, to tell him to beware. But that was ridiculous. Talen wouldn't dare arrest him now that he was General Strong, leader of the entire Rahmish army. Would he?

But *why* was he here? Pasting a smile on her face and hoping it looked sincere, Ria followed Merek to greet their unwelcome guest.

"Good day, Your Highness." Talen greeted her with a bow and a strained smile.

"What a delightful surprise!" she answered cheerily. "Strong, did you know that Captain Talen planned to visit?"

"I was unaware of it myself. You're a long way from Albon, old friend." His tone was light enough, but Ria sensed an underlying tension. Good. He was as wary as she.

Talen glanced at Ria and ran a hand through his black curls. "Might I have a word alone, Strong? There's something we need to discuss."

Ria's smile froze as she watched the two men disappear into the tent. She would have to wait to have her questions answered, and that was the worst uncertainty of all.

· · ✳ · ·

MEREK WAITED UNTIL HE'D DISMISSED HIS FIRST CAPTAINS and their aides. He waited until he and Talen had settled around the table, drinks poured and resting in both men's hands. Finally, he asked the question that had been burning in his mind since seeing Talen at Eldar's side.

"What's going on in Albon, Talen? You and I both know there's no reason for you to be here unless something is seriously wrong."

Talen reached in his satchel and withdrew a folded sheet of vellum.

Merek opened the document, feeling Talen's keen eyes on him, and the blood drained from his face when he saw what it was. Ria's forged pardon was skillfully done. Paired with Sindal's seal, the signature looked genuine enough. He doubted that he would have recognized it for what it was if she hadn't told him. But if Talen had brought it to the camp, that didn't bode well.

Merek finished glancing over the pardon and laid it on the table between them. He kept his expression neutral, hoping to hide his accelerated pulse. "Why do you show me this?"

Talen regarded him for a long moment. "You know I've always held you in the highest regard, Strong. I didn't feel comfortable arresting you, and I suppose that made me too eager to see you freed. It was wrong that you were never given a chance to properly defend yourself, and I won't let that happen again. So instead of going to the king with my suspicions, I came here. And now I ask, did you conspire with the princess to commit this act of treason?"

The only sound in the tense silence was the snapping of the fire in the brazier.

"What do you expect to learn here, Talen? That a crime was committed? That Ria and I conspired against the king for our own selfish aims? Is that what you think?"

"It does look suspicious now that you're rumored to be betrothed."

"You know me as well as any man. Do you really think I'm the sort to prey upon an innocent young woman for my own gain?"

Talen shrugged. "So it's more complicated than that. I'm listening."

"Why should I say anything to you? What do you plan to do? Arrest her? Throw the whole kingdom into chaos because she took a great risk to save a friend who was unjustly condemned?"

"Would you rather have her begin her reign flouting the rule of law that preserves order in our land?"

"No," Merek admitted. "No, I wouldn't. But with the king a victim to his madness, she was arguably the only one with the authority to right a serious wrong. How is that not just?"

Talen leaned forward in earnest, his voice rising. "Heir to the throne or not, she does not have the right to usurp the king's power and forge his hand, acting in complete opposition to his will!"

"Tell me, Captain," Ria's voice rang out clearly from the doorway, "does the king not also answer to the law?"

Merek started, and Talen jumped from his chair. Ria stood just inside the tent, the color heightened in her cheeks but her eyes cold.

"I would ask that you keep your voice down, Captain.

These canvas walls are ill-equipped to keeping such damning conversations to themselves."

Talen had the good grace to be abashed. "Forgive me, Your Highness," he said with a slight bow of his head. "It's not my intention to start rumors. That is why I wished to speak with you both privately, to hear your testimony directly without fear of scandal."

"To what purpose?" Ria asked quietly as she moved closer, her posture erect. "What do you hope to gain? Why abandon your responsibilities in Albon to come here now? If you expect me to trust you, I must know your motives."

"It seemed more prudent to handle this particular matter myself rather than involving anyone else."

"Your discretion is noted."

Talen shifted uncomfortably. "My duty is to uphold the laws of your father. I only seek to know the truth."

"So, you wish to judge if my actions violate the law. But what if they were required in order to uphold the very essence of law in protecting the people from a gross abuse of power?" Ria folded her arms and looked at Talen as if daring him to contradict her. "How do you think the people shall judge when they learn that a man was imprisoned unlawfully by the king? Might they not see my interference as an act necessary to preserve the laws which protect a man from such offenses—even from the crown—and therefore fulfilling the very duty which the future heir is bound to perform? It's not merely my king whom I am bound to serve but also the people of this country. If I must answer to my people for my actions, then I do so with a clear conscience, for even the king himself ultimately exists to protect and serve them."

Merek was stunned. Somehow, Ria had turned her deception into an act of justice and honor. Even sacrifice. Standing defiantly before Talen, she couldn't have appeared more regal if the queen's crown had even then rested on her brow. It thrilled him, even as he felt grossly inadequate by comparison. He was seized with a desire to explain to Talen that he knew he could never be her equal, that he would never presume to stand by her side as husband and king. But he held his tongue.

Talen seemed shaken by her words. "I don't mean to suggest that your intent was not worthy. Indeed, I've always admired—" He cleared his throat. "There are those who would use this information against you, and I'm afraid their influence at court is growing. For the time being, you may be assured that I will keep it between the three of us."

"For the time being?" Merek asked pointedly.

A look of stubbornness hardened Talen's features. "I reserve the right to act in accordance with my duty as my conscience demands. But," he added, his tone softening, "I swear to you both that I won't do anything without your knowledge."

"Well, that's something," Merek said, but Ria fumed as she bade Talen good night. Poor Talen. He was a good man, and Merek trusted that he would yield to Ria's keen intellect and persuasive nature. After all, no one understood her power better than Merek Strong himself.

FOUR

Aiya awoke to a profound stillness. After weeks in a noisy army camp, and several days on the road sharing her eating and sleeping quarters with two horses and a man, the silence was disorienting. She sat up and looked around at the log walls, pausing to let her mind filter out dream from memory.

The guardhouse in Haldin was just as empty as it had been the previous night when they'd arrived. And cold. So cold. Wrapping a quilt around her shoulders, Aiya shuffled into the other room. The fireplace held nothing but ash.

There was no sign of Dan.

Aiya sighed. The man was proving to be as hard to keep up with as Tupin had been. She went to the window and rubbed the quilt against it with her forearm to brush away the ice that had crusted on the inside of the glass.

She caught her breath. The world had been transformed under a pristine blanket of white. The snow had stopped, but continued to drop in showers from tree branches shedding their load as the morning warmed. Clouds the color of pewter hung in the heavy sky, the whole air thick with the silent expectation of more snow to come. Aiya had never seen anything like it.

There were no tracks in the snow near the small cabin. What if Dan had gotten lost in the night? What if he hadn't found shelter from the storm? Aiya shivered. She was weak with hunger and couldn't bear the thought of going out into the cold. She offered a curse for the thieves who'd stolen their horses and supplies.

Turning back to the fireplace, she was cheered to see another pile of wood that hadn't been there when she went to bed. Dan *had* returned sometime during the night, but the falling snow must have covered the signs of his passing. Well, wherever he was, he would look for her here, so she would just have to wait.

Aiya set about building a fire, which was difficult with her fingers frozen stiff. The cold air pouring down the chimney mocked her first attempts, but the ashes held a few warm embers, and the stacked wood was covered in dry moss. It took some time, and her lungs were full of smoke before she was done, but eventually she coaxed some heat out of the embers.

While flames nipped at the wood, she searched the guardhouse more thoroughly than she had the previous night. It appeared that the previous occupants had left in haste, and she only found some scraps of moldy bread and cheese to eat. Sniffing it made her gag. She was instantly reminded of months of starvation as she and Imar fled their home country. For a time, they'd lived on the streets of Endvar until Imar finally gained a place as a porter and began earning a few coins. Those were dark days she would just as soon forget.

Aiya left the moldy food where she'd found it. She may be hungry, but she wasn't that desperate. Yet.

A moment later, Dan burst through the door, bringing a blast of cold air with him.

"Good! You're awake!" he said. "Come with me. There's hot porridge waiting if you hurry. Here, take these." He handed her two heavy mufflers, a woman's shawl, and a pair of knitted gloves.

Aiya blinked. "Where did you get these?"

"The captain's wife. You'll want them, it's a bit of a walk," he said apologetically, moving to stand in front of the fire. He sighed in contentment as he bathed in the heat.

Aiya felt a twinge of resentment as she wrapped the two mufflers around her head and neck then covered it all with the shawl. What right did he have to be so cheerful after all his days of silent gloom? Then she realized his eyes were alight with purpose, not joy. He was needed.

"Where have you been? Why did you not come back last night?"

"I found the soldiers. They're guarding a section of wall that collapsed a few weeks back, trying to rebuild it during the day."

"And Captain Falbrook? Did you find him too?"

"Yes, he was there. They've been guarding against bandits day and night for weeks, and he was happy for an extra pair of hands. Or, one anyway," he said with a hint of humor.

Aiya glanced at him sharply. This *was* a change. "So you were fighting bandits all night then?"

"Nah." Dan shook his head, turning to warm his backside against the blaze. "The weather kept them away last night. Which was a fair bit of luck since most of Captain Falbrook's men are worn through and needed the rest. You should thank me. I earned us a hot meal this morning at the captain's table. He invited us to sleep there too, but I told him we didn't mind staying at the guardhouse. Unless," he paused. "If you don't want...if it makes you uncomfortable..." he stammered, looking at the floor.

Suddenly, under all her layers, the fire felt uncomfortably hot. Aiya feigned nonchalance. "Dan, after all we've been through together, are you suddenly worried about propriety?"

"No! Well, I mean, yes. I'm not some brute. But Captain Falbrook's house is already pretty crowded. If you'd rather stay there, you can, of course—"

"I'll stay with you, Dan. I don't mind taking my chances with the one-armed soldier. But I get the cot." The truth was, Aiya was feeling so displaced in this strange land with it's harsh weather that it gave her a sense of unease to think of straying too far from the one person she knew.

They closed the door on the guardhouse and stepped carefully along the path Dan had made on his way there. The cold air bit Aiya's face, and she was grateful for the extra muffler and gloves.

They trudged through the forest for a while longer, the snow working into Aiya's boots despite her best efforts to walk in Dan's footsteps. Her feet were wet through before they reached the small cottage in the forest. Two children played in the snow, so bundled by hats and wraps that it was difficult to discern their gender.

They stopped burrowing as Dan and Aiya entered the yard, staring openly at the newcomers. Then one of them said loudly, "Look at that one! His skin is as dark as mud!"

"It's not a he, it's a she," the other child said. "I heard Mor and Far talking about her. Do you think she's got magic like the dark witch in our book?"

Aiya suddenly wished she'd stayed at the guardhouse. Dan, however, didn't miss a beat.

"Watch what you say, or she'll cast a spell on you." Just for good measure, he scooped up a handful of snow, balled it against his leg, and pitched it in the direction of the children.

The children weren't the only ones who'd never seen a Khouri woman before. A few minutes later, as they sat around Captain Falbrook's rough-hewn table with steaming bowls of cooked grain, Aiya felt as if she had a greater disfigurement than Dan. The younger children stared openly. The older ones avoided looking at her directly, shooting her surreptitious glances when they thought she wasn't looking. Even Veln, the captain's wife, blushed if Aiya happened to catch her staring. Only Captain Falbrook seemed unaffected by the sight of a foreigner sitting at his table. He was far more concerned about the instructions Dan had brought from General Strong.

"You've seen what it's like, Sergeant," he argued. "With the wall breached, we're struggling to keep the bandits at bay. Rebuilding will take months. How can I take away a third of my men when I don't have enough men as it is? These orders couldn't come at a worse time."

Dan spoke calmly but with determination. "I assure you, sir, the need for your men is great. Their specialized skill could save the entire city of Endvar, possibly even the whole of Rahm, if the war spreads. General Strong wouldn't have asked if it wasn't truly necessary."

"*General* Strong." Falbrook chuckled, shaking his head. "After all that, he ends up general anyway. I can't wait to tell his mother."

"You know his mother?" Aiya blurted.

"I do. She lives here in Haldin with her daughter."

"Of course. Yes, I should have realized." Aiya squirmed at the captain's look. "I've known the general for some years and have heard a few stories about his mother."

"You're a friend of his?" Falbrook leaned back in his chair and regarded her appreciatively. "Tell me more. I've been trying to get him to settle down with a nice girl for years."

Dan frowned, and Aiya's face grew warm.

"I'm afraid I can't help you there, Captain. He merely rented a room above my brother's shop. Until recent months I've been little more than his cook."

"And recently?"

Aiya briefly recounted her assistance in trying to uncover the plot to attack Endvar. It made her feel important to remember how Captain Strong had relied on her, and her admiration for him colored her words. Those days had changed everything, and she was grateful to him.

"Fascinating," Falbrook announced when she'd finished. "We're honored to have you in our home. Both of you." He looked to Veln for confirmation.

"Of course," his wife said, leaning over the table to wipe away the remains of porridge. "Friends of Merek's are always welcome at our table. He dines here infrequently enough as it is. I suppose when one has no family of their own, it's easy enough to forget their roots."

"Don't listen to her," Captain Falbrook said with a smile. "She hoped years ago that Merek would come home and marry her sister and our children would grow up as one happy family. She hasn't forgiven Merek for destroying her dream."

"I'm not the only one!" Veln protested. "You've complained more than once that he'll die alone without the comfort of a wife or children by his side."

"Then you don't know that he's betrothed?" Dan asked, looking back and forth between the two of them.

They stared at him.

"Betrothed?" Captain Falbrook repeated blankly. "After all this time? To whom?"

"Likely some aging widow." Veln nodded sagely. "Too old to bear children of their own."

Dan grinned. "Oh no, I daresay he'll be bouncing babies on his knee before too long. She's young and healthy and full of noble blood." His eyes twinkled at their expressions of dismay.

"Do we know her?"

"Not likely if she's noble."

"I don't believe it."

"Are you sure this is Merek we're talking of?"

"What's her name?"

"Doesn't matter. We're not likely to know her."

"Oh, you know her name all right," Dan affirmed. "She's none other than the heir to the throne, Princess Honoria Thorodan."

Captain Falbrook sat bolt upright in his chair and swore, making the children gasp. Veln's eyes widened as she swatted her husband with the towel in her hand.

"Betrothed to the princess!"

"Imagine that!"

Aiya watched their reactions with a mixture of humor and jealousy. It was foolish to be jealous of the princess. They weren't rivals. Still, she couldn't think of her without feeling the sourness of envy in her stomach.

"But how?"

"It must be her father's idea," Veln said. "You said they're the best of friends, Stefan."

Stefan nodded. "But that means...by Harr's own sword...he's going to be the next king!"

Veln's face went white. "King! Well, he'll definitely be too high and mighty to sit at this table again!"

They both laughed and peppered Dan with questions.

"When did this happen?"

"What is she like? Do they seem a good match?"

"What does it matter? She's a princess!"

"But you don't want him to be miserable, do you?"

"I believe there is genuine affection between them," Aiya said. Veln nodded at her husband satisfactorily.

"King! From right here in Haldin!"

Their excited conversation was cut short by a knock at the back door. Veln ushered in a motherly figure trailed by two adolescent boys.

The woman's voice was gentle when she spoke. "The

boys and I came to see if your roof needed clearing, what with Stefan—Oh, Stefan! I didn't see you! I thought you'd be at the wall."

The woman seemed flustered to see strangers in the captain's house. Her cheeks grew pink and her words trailed away.

"I should be heading there now," Stefan said, pushing back his chair and standing. "Sergeant, you're welcome to join me unless you need to rest after keeping watch last night."

Dan stood with him, and Aiya was suddenly struck at how short he seemed next to the captain. His strong build had diminished since his injury, and she hadn't even noticed. She wondered if she looked changed to him as well.

"I'd like to see it during the light," Dan said, reaching for his winter wrappings.

Aiya thought about joining them, but Veln had been speaking with the newcomer, and she suddenly heard her own name.

"And this is Aiya, a friend of Merek's. You won't believe the news she brings."

"Oh?" The woman's face was open and honest, and Aiya liked her immediately.

"You'd better sit, Marga. You'll be quite shocked." Veln shooed the boys out the door with the men.

"Does it concern my brother?" Marga asked, an edge of worry to her tone.

His sister! Aiya stayed in her seat, deciding not to follow Dan just yet.

"Oh yes! Don't fret; it's good news. But it's very shocking indeed!"

Veln looked at Aiya expectantly. Gone was the embarrassed uncertainty about the dark-skinned woman with the accent. Instead, they were now co-conspirators. Aiya smiled. Apparently the need for gossip knew no borders. It was the truth traveling minstrels had survived by for generations: If you wanted to be welcome at a stranger's hearth, start with a good story. And so, Aiya looked at the two women with their bright, eager expressions and began.

FIVE

Rorden reached for his waterskin to soothe his throat. Again. The cough which had plagued him for weeks had finally passed—mercifully without progressing into the raging fever that some in camp had suffered—but it had left behind a constant dryness.

The waterskin was already half empty. If he wasn't careful, he would have to relieve himself before he reached the enemy camp. He grimaced, thinking of the scouts who were watching to make sure he arrived safely and imagining their taunts about being so scared he nearly wet himself.

Ironically, just thinking of it created the sensation of need.

Rorden tried to push the feeling away and focused instead on what lay ahead. He approached the enemy camp from the west, passing over the Hoggen bridge that had been recently reclaimed by the Rahmish, then following the Vifar river south. His was a mission of diplomacy, not combat, but it was best to avoid as many enemy soldiers as possible all the same.

Wind whipped the white banner mounted to his saddle, making a mournful sound that accentuated his solitude as he rode. But he wasn't frightened. Anxious, yes. Excited, definitely. But not afraid. This would be a contest of wills and words, not strength or steel.

Perfect.

The city of Endvar rose in the distance behind the Ardanian camp, its gray walls dwarfed by Danvir's Wall on the eastern border. He'd been spotted. Two Ardanian soldiers rode toward him, their armor the color of burnished pewter, their faces obscured by heavy helms.

One of them called out in heavily accented Rahmish, "Halt!"

Rorden obeyed.

"State your business!"

"On behalf of General Strong of the Rahmish army, I seek an audience with Prince Artem of Ardania," Rorden called out in clear, deliberate speech. He considered whether or not to speak the sentence again in Ardanian but decided against it. If these soldiers spoke Rahmish, he would let that be enough. Better that than to make himself a fool by inadvertently complimenting their dog or some such nuisance. He had very little skill with their language.

The soldier who'd spoken before responded with one word. "Follow."

His companion moved to Rorden's rear, and Rorden followed the lead soldier toward the enemy camp. Although they weren't visible to him, he knew that somewhere in the distant trees scouts would be returning to report to Strong that the first step in his mission had been achieved.

As he rode through the camp, Rorden tried not to gawk at the foreign soldiers in unfamiliar armor speaking a strange language. After a few minutes, he realized that when one stripped away the outer differences, there were a lot of similarities between this army and the Rahmish. The soldiers seemed disciplined and adhered to order and structure. Some looked at him curiously, but no one displayed open hostility.

They stopped before a large tent with a pitched roof that reminded Rorden of a church steeple. The decorative embroidery on the golden canvas seemed more suited to a tapestry fit for a noble hall than a war camp. Was the Ardanian prince here? Rorden's heart skipped a beat.

But no, when he was invited to enter the tent, there was no prince waiting for him, only a white-haired man with intelligent eyes. His demeanor, and the respectful postures of Rorden's guards, made it clear that he was a high-ranking officer in the Ardanian army. Rorden straightened his shoulders under his frown.

"What message do you bring from the Rahmish?" the man said, his accent more fluid than the soldiers' had been.

"I bring a message for Prince Artem from my commander, General Strong."

"Do you see any prince here? You will give me your message."

"The general wishes to meet with the prince."

"He refused your former general. Why should he agree to meet with this one?"

"Because this general commands not only the armies, but the attention of the crown as well, in a more intimate manner than General Grammel ever did."

"Intimate? In what way?"

"A betrothal exists between General Strong and the Crown Princess. He will be Rahm's next king."

The white-haired captain narrowed his eyes at Rorden, then turned and spoke to one of his assistants in his native tongue. The man approached Rorden and stood expectantly.

"Leave your weapons," the commander said.

Rorden handed his sword and long knife to the waiting soldier then followed the Ardanian captain outside to where his horse was waiting.

They rode to the city in silence: the white-haired captain, Rorden, and a guard escort flanking him on either side. As they rode, Rorden cleared his throat, wishing again for his waterskin. But he didn't dare reach for it with armed soldiers so near.

The gates of Endvar loomed before them, their weathered wood looking almost as gray as the stone which made up the city wall. They still bore the scars of the failed attack where Grammel had fallen, with cracks and splinters running the length of the wood. Rorden clenched his jaw at the sight of the Ardanian flag flying above the gate, its violet and gold out of place in this stark winter landscape.

When Rorden had last left Endvar, the city was ablaze with autumn colors, but now, as they rode through the streets, all seemed lifeless. The trees stood bare in the chill air. Frost clung to paving stones lying in the shadows where the weak sunlight never ventured.

Melting ice hung from gutters and dripped into puddles on the street below.

The faces Rorden saw were mostly Ardanian—predominantly soldiers, but also merchants seeking an early foothold in the newly conquered city. As they advanced through the streets, Rorden was surprised by the number of Rahmish citizens who mingled with the foreign tradesmen. Though on reflection, he supposed that an enemy in war could become your ally if he has goods for sale and you are desperate.

If the Ardanians had been dressed in Rahmish clothes, they wouldn't have looked that different from his own countrymen. Some of the women were even quite pretty, if a little too wide in the shoulders for his taste. He watched as an Ardanian woman dropped a heavy sack to the ground, the force of the sudden weight blowing a cloud of dust into the air.

He tried to envision Biren carrying a burden like that, and smiled to himself. Yet, she'd seemed at ease in the saddle with a pair of trousers; a position that was decidedly unladylike. There seemed to be a disconnect between the openness of the woman he'd rescued after the princess was ambushed and the prim lady's maid who was so guarded and reserved in the army camp. His efforts at wooing a woman had never failed yet, but it seemed the more he used his polished craft, the less interested she became. Conversely, in moments when he was tired and spoke to her as a friend rather than a prize to be won, suddenly she was all smiles and attention. It was baffling.

Not at all like the coy silversmith's daughter who worked in the armory. Ana flirted with him openly, and he responded in kind as naturally as breathing. But he felt uneasy when he left her company, and had been struck with shame the next time he saw Biren. What had seemed harmless at the armory felt instead like a betrayal when he caught Biren's eye later in the command tent. There was no understanding between them, but somehow he knew that losing Biren's trust would be devastating.

The grinding of stone on stone brought Rorden's attention back to the present and he realized they were approaching Lord Ogmun's gate. The heavy gate dragged against the ground in an age-worn groove.

Lord Ogmun's estate was ordinarily a beauty to behold. Even in winter, when summer foliage receded and branches became barren, colorful lanterns would be placed strategically amongst the plantings to divert the eye from the lack of life as one proceeded to the main house. But this was not Lord Ogmun's estate any longer, and the drab courtyard had an air of forlorn abandonment.

The eagerness in Rorden's belly grew as he walked up the stone steps to enter the house. Would he meet the architect of this invasion? Or just an advisor? He hoped to at least lay eyes on the prince, to affirm that he was indeed in the city.

In this, he was not disappointed.

A large fire burned in the great hall where a feast was being laid—by Rahmish maids, he noted. The soldiers led Rorden past the richly appointed table and through a side passageway into a softly furnished room whose small walls were filled to the ceiling with books. Too small to be a grand library, Rorden guessed this must have been Lord Ogmun's personal study.

The man sitting at the large desk didn't look like a heartless conqueror. His feet were propped up on the shiny surface, and his strong jaw and fair hair curling about his shoulders gave him the look of a mythical hero. His eyes, fixed upon the man who stood at the window, were intelligent and discerning. And his voice, when he spoke, didn't carry with it the sound of doom and destruction. But rather wit and intimate humor.

"I daresay you didn't read it right, Do. Read it again."

Rorden recognized the pale man named Domar who had inserted himself as Lord Bolen's steward. Domar looked Rorden over briefly, but didn't register recognition, for which Rordan was profoundly relieved. Domar raised a book and began to read.

"From heights of silver mist and river's depth..."

As Domar's voice filled the room, Rorden's mind wandered to the shadowy night Domar had discovered him and Yulda in Bolen's kitchen. Yulda had surprised Rorden with a kiss, then protected him by keeping Domar's attention focused on her. The girl was far more clever than Rorden had given her credit for.

"But that makes no sense. You," the prince said, turning his head to look at Rorden. "You are Rahmish. Explain what it means."

Rorden started. He glanced at the book in Domar's hand, but couldn't make out a title, and searched his mind for the words Domar had just read.

"I believe it's a riddle, Your Highness. Not meant to be taken literally."

"Of course it is." The prince took his feet off the desk

and sat up. "It speaks of the moon gazing at her own reflection in the water. That much is obvious."

It hadn't seemed obvious to Rorden, but then again, his attention had been elsewhere. His parched throat burned.

"What I don't understand," the prince continued, "is what the sow has to do with it."

Rorden hoped his expression wasn't as blank as his mind felt. Was this some sort of test?

"Might I read it myself, Your Highness?"

Domar handed the book to him, and Rorden quickly scanned the lines, aware of the prince's scrutiny. His frown relaxed as he read the flowery script.

"Ah, here's your trouble. It's not 'sow,' it is 'low.' This character, it's written in the old Rahmish style which makes it look like the word for sow, but it's actually an embellished 'low.' In this instance, it refers to the lowing of a herd. So it reads, 'No murmur nor low disturbs my slumber but with the silent arc of eel I quake.'"

"Ha!" The prince looked triumphantly at Domar. "After all this time in this country, you still haven't mastered the language!"

Domar's thin mouth twitched. "I confess that I haven't spent these months in academic study."

"You're useless, Domar," the prince said good-naturedly. "Perhaps I will retain him as my advisor instead of you. What is your name, soldier?" He stood, and as his fine robe settled into perfect lines, his casual air was instantly replaced with one of poised presence.

"Sergeant Rorden, Your Highness. Formerly of the Wall Guard and aide to General Strong of the Rahmish army." Something about the prince commanded a bow or salute of some kind, but Rorden resisted the urge.

The prince didn't seem to mind. "Are all Rahmish soldiers educated in the arts as you are, Sergeant? I confess I have a weakness for your Rahmish poetry. The paradox of the poet-soldier fascinates me, and in this library I have found an abundance of both."

Rorden felt a surge of pride. "Our kings have long valued a honed intellect over bloodshed. Our wars are fought not out of lust for power or greed but to defend our lives and homes, our families and freedom. Is it any wonder that men who have been compelled to war might turn to the pen to voice the humanity for which they fight?"

The prince's blue eyes sparkled. "Do you hear that, Do? He even speaks like a poet. Come, sit." He gestured toward two finely carved chairs near the fire, with thick cushions that looked luxuriously soft.

Rorden shook his head. "Thank you, sir, but I'm quite comfortable standing." The prince's charm was disarming. Only Domar's presence in the corner—quiet and watchful—reminded Rorden that he was not among friends.

"And the soldier wins out," Prince Artem murmured with a smirk. He stepped behind the desk and reached for a crystal decanter. Pouring the honey-colored liquid into a goblet, he presented it to Rorden, then leaned against the desk and poured another glass for himself. His proximity and posture were open and friendly, nothing like the shrewd despot Rorden had imagined.

Rorden longed for a sip of the amber liquid, but he resisted. Until this moment he had never understood

Strong's preference for water and diluted wine, but now, in the presence of his enemy, he didn't dare risk dulling his judgment.

"Well, Sergeant," Prince Artem said, "I have another riddle for you. Why would the charming and brilliant Princess Honoria, full of youthful humor and intelligence, marry a commoner so much older than herself? The young woman I know never would have agreed to such an arrangement."

"I believe that is a question best directed at the princess herself," Rorden said carefully.

"Oh, come. That's no answer at all. You would be a poor aide indeed if you didn't at least have a theory."

"And I wouldn't be an aide for long if I indulged in gossip."

The prince chuckled. "I know it can't have been pressure from her father. He dotes on his daughter shamelessly, so who else might have coerced her into agreeing?" He smiled, but his eyes were sharp. Intent.

"I have no reason to think that there was any coercion. The general is regarded with great respect by the people, and I believe the princess is quite fond of him."

"I was quite fond of my old childhood nurse, too, but I wouldn't have invited her into my bed."

Domar snorted. "That didn't stop you with your tutor."

The blond prince laughed heartily, showing perfect teeth. "In my defense, she looked much younger than her true age. And I was very, very drunk."

The two men shared a laugh, and Rorden offered a strained smile.

"You've met the man, haven't you?" the prince said to

Domar. "What were your impressions? Was he truly ancient?"

"Not at all. I'm afraid you underestimate him."

"Of course I do! Otherwise I might be jealous." Prince Artem winked at Rorden. "So what are you, then? Something of a pet, meant to distract the princess when she tires of her aged husband?"

Rorden's smile faded. "I'm nothing of the sort, Your Highness."

"Ah. Do you serve as a diversion for the general, then?"

Domar snorted a laugh, and the prince grinned wickedly. Rorden swallowed hard and wished the goblet in his hand held water. He set it on the desk and clasped his hands behind his back, waiting.

Prince Artem attempted to rein in his grin. "Forgive me, I meant it as a compliment. You are clearly a man of many talents."

Again, Domar snickered.

"Sir, it would be best to see the princess for yourself. She wishes to speak to you in person. I believe your questions would be better satisfied by her than by myself."

"This letter you brought is signed by the general, not the princess."

"It is the princess who insists on meeting with you. I'm sure you can guess that the general acts at her bidding." *Appeal to his vanity,* Honoria had said. *Flatter him, but be sincere.*

Prince Artem raised an eyebrow. "What do you think, Domar? It might be interesting to see her again."

"I think you are getting bored," the other man said drily.

Artem raised the letter to the watery sunlight from the window, then fixed his eye on Rorden. "Tell Ria that I will meet with her. If she wishes to bring the general, I suppose she may. It would amuse me to see what sort of a man she has chained herself to."

"And the terms? Are they acceptable?"

The prince frowned and tugged at a silk sleeve. "It seems awfully inconvenient to meet out in the elements. Why not come here, and we can visit in comfort?"

Flatter him. Appeal to his pride. But the princess wasn't here, and it was vital that the prince agree to leave the city. Rorden took a risk.

"I'm afraid that will not do, sir. The princess warned me that you were an arrogant laggard. She insisted that you leave your fireside to experience for a day what the rest of us have endured for months."

Honoria had said none of this, but Rorden suspected that it would sound enough like her to convince the prince.

The color in Artem's face heightened. "An arrogant laggard? She called me an arrogant laggard? Well, then. She left out, 'finely dressed, clever, and incredibly hand-some.' It's time we remind her that there is much more to this prince than arrogance and indolence." He grinned. "Tell the princess that we agree to her terms. In three days, we shall meet at the Hoggen bridge with a guard of one hundred."

One hundred. Not the numbers they had hoped would leave the city, but it was a start.

Rorden bowed respectfully to give his leave, but as he reached the door, the prince stopped him.

"And Sergeant, tell the princess to bring a couch so that I may recline in comfort rather than exerting myself."

The sound of his golden laughter followed Rorden all the way through the hall.

Six

The collapsed section of wall was as long as a city block in Endvar. A wall of trees and mud loomed over Aiya like a raging brown river frozen in time. Where the mudslide had already been cleared, men with bowed backs worked to clear away the fresh snow that had accumulated during the night. Stones lay nearby like broken teeth where the landslide had swallowed them up and spit them out again. There were far more stones than men.

Aiya picked her way along a trail, following the path of Marga and Veln before her. Dan was with the soldiers working to dig out the stones. It was dangerous, not only because of the unstable ground but also because they were outside the wall's protection and vulnerable to bandit attacks.

Veln and Marga found their husbands working among those relaying the stone. The rebuilt portion of wall was only a few feet at its highest point. In some places it was barely past the foundation stones. The sheer volume of work to be done was overwhelming. The men's movements were slow as if exhaustion and despair were their taskmasters.

All except Dan. He scrambled down from his perch and bounded toward Aiya with a smile on his face.

Aiya couldn't help smiling in return. "Have you good news, then?"

"The climbers leave in the morning. Captain Falbrook will escort them himself."

Veln won't like that.

"Well done. I wasn't sure he would come around."

"Nah, he just needed some time to get used to the idea. To be honest, I feel guilty asking him to leave his family at a time like this."

Aiya looked around at the men and boys with faces red from the cold, breath streaming out in clouds of mist.

"I'd like to stay and help," Aiya said. "We may not be able to replace the men who are leaving, but I can't just leave, not when they've been so kind to us."

Dan didn't laugh at the idea of a small woman and a one-armed man helping rebuild a towering stone wall. Instead, he just grinned.

"And here I've been wondering how to convince you to stay. I thought for sure you'd be angry with me if I suggested it."

"I'm not as heartless as you think I am." Aiya sniffed, rubbing her nose on her sleeve. "I even brought you lunch, though I confess that Marga provided the sweets. I may have let slip how you lost your arm in a battle where you saved her brother's life."

Dan groaned but took the lunch gratefully.

Aiya left him to his meal and moved to the pile of

stacked stone. She grasped one with both hands and heaved. It wasn't large, but she still doubled over with the weight. It rested against her middle, and she worried with each step that she was going to drop it. The men working at the wall looked up in surprise. Some chuckled a little. By the time she returned with her next load, they had all stopped to watch.

"Miss Aiya," a voice said kindly behind her. It was Captain Falbrook. "Here, let me take that."

"No," Aiya said sharply, fearing that if she tried to give it to him she would drop it on her toes.

He watched in bemusement as she placed it on the wall next to the first, the stone grinding as she worked it into position.

"What do you think you're doing?" Captain Falbrook asked when she had finished wresting the stone into place.

Aiya looked up at him and said in all seriousness. "I am building a wall."

"But you can't—"

"Go. Save my city. Dan and I...we will build your wall." Without another word, she walked back to the pile of stone.

The air was heavy with cold when Ria gave up on the restless half-dreaming state that counted for sleep these days. Ever since Rorden had returned with confirmation from Artem, she'd spent her nights staring at the tent ceiling with a weight on her chest. Now the brazier gave off neither heat nor light, so it was very late indeed.

Biren snored softly against the opposite wall. Unable to sleep, but too cold and dark to do anything else, Ria lay on her cot, waiting for and dreading the dawn.

One more day before she would meet Artem. One more day before she would provide the diversion that Merek and his climbers needed to seize the gates and take back the city. The camp had been relatively quiet, as all fighting had ceased awaiting the outcome of their parley. The command tent, however, had been bustling with activity. She and Merek hadn't had a moment alone, and she'd affected an air of confidence for him as much as for herself. But in the dark hours of the night, her mind raced in anticipation of what was to come.

At last, she sat up, throwing the blankets off her. Instantly regretting it, she reached for a quilt and a heavy fur. The thick nightdress, dressing gown, and heavy cloak she wore to bed didn't provide enough insulation against the current of icy winter air that leaked in under the tent walls.

With her body heavily padded, Ria laced her boots with stiff fingers and slipped out the door. Two soldiers stood on watch at a respectful distance, and she stepped in the opposite direction so as to not draw their attention. They would try to convince her to go back to bed, and she would have no good reason why she shouldn't. So instead, she scurried around to the back of the tent where the shadows of the forest hid her.

Since Sergeant Brandel's death, Ria had been guarded by nameless strangers. She missed the trust she'd had with Brandel and hadn't found someone to replace him just yet. She shuddered at the memory of how he and the other soldiers had died protecting her. Scouts had found his body days later, caught on a snag in the Vifar river, already food for the fish. The others were never found.

The frozen grass crunched quietly underfoot, the cold of the hard ground creeping through her feet as she wound her way around the edge of the camp. She didn't want to draw attention. She didn't want to speak to anyone. She just wanted to clear her head, to shake off the feeling of unease that permeated her dreams.

The moon was only the faintest scrape of light in the sky as she walked. The stars were absolutely brilliant, but looking up exposed her neck to the cold, so she kept her head bowed and focused instead on picking her way through the darkness.

As she walked, the perfect stillness of the night brought with it a calm that unwound the tightly coiled spring of her mind. Perhaps she could even return to bed. But as she turned, she realized that she was nearly to the command tent. There was a faint light visible inside, making the walls glow in the darkness.

Merek was either still awake or had fallen asleep with a lamp or brazier still burning. Her own tent seemed very cold and far away, and she moved quickly toward the light.

Approaching from the forest side as she did, the guards didn't see her coming until she was upon them. Their surprise made her feel foolish, thinking of how she must look with her unkempt hair loose down her back and her body formless under the thick blankets. But then she heard the low murmur of voices coming from inside the tent and knew that Merek was not alone.

Curiosity drove her forward, but the soldiers moved to block the door.

"I'm sorry, Your Highness. The general has asked not to be disturbed."

"It's too late for that, Corporal. Or do you deny that he already has a visitor?"

When she spoke, the murmur of voices inside the tent ceased.

The soldiers shifted uncertainly. "Please, Your Highness. It really would be best if you returned in the morning."

Before Ria could protest, the tent door opened and Merek ducked out. He was still dressed in his uniform from the previous day, but his collar was unbuttoned and his cravat hung loose about his neck. The weariness in his eyes told her that he hadn't yet slept.

"Are you alone?" His breath streamed out in a cloud between them. "Come in, but keep your voice down."

He stood aside, and Ria slipped past him into the tent. Inside she found not one visitor but a whole unit of soldiers seated around the table. They stood as one when she entered. All wore the blue of the Wall Guard.

"Ria, do you remember Captain Stefan Falbrook from Haldin?"

A thin man with a rust-colored beard and pronounced laugh lines around his eyes stepped forward and bowed.

"And these are his wall climbers."

As Merek introduced each one by name, Ria became increasingly self-conscious about her appearance. These men were lean and trim with an air of hard strength, and they were all young, most no older than herself. She nodded her head graciously and hoped they weren't disappointed by the heir to the throne appearing disheveled and stuffed like a New Year's goose.

"I dare not risk bringing them to camp in the daylight," Merek explained. "Not if we're to maintain secrecy."

"Then please, continue. The night is far spent as it is."

She settled into an empty chair next to Rorden. "How many of these secret meetings have I missed?" she whispered as Captain Falbrook began speaking to the group.

"They came last night too," Rorden said, yawning. "I think the general didn't want to disturb your rest."

"And what about *his* rest?" she asked, noting Merek's bloodshot eyes. "How long can he go like this? Does the man think he has no limits?"

"Ah, but you forget who you're talking about. General Strong? Limits? That's blasphemy!"

They shared a quiet chuckle, which earned them a glance from Merek. Ria swallowed her mirth and tried to pay attention.

The discussion followed the finer points of the climbers' attack on the northern and eastern gates. The northern gate was the least defended as the Ardanian army camped nearest the western and southern sides to best position themselves for a push further into Rahm. Captain Orri and his men would storm the city after the climbers secured the northern gate. Gaining control of the eastern gate was equally important; the timing critical so that no additional troops could be alerted from the Ardanian side of the border.

Ria had little to contribute to the conversation. After a time, she became drowsy, her eyelids heavy. She half considered lying down on Merek's cot in the corner but didn't even have the energy to leave her chair.

Then her ears perked up.

"Will the princess be capable of keeping the enemy occupied? Our success depends on him not returning until nightfall."

It was Captain Falbrook who had spoken. He'd directed his question at Merek, but all eyes turned to Ria. She straightened up in her chair.

"I can assure you, Captain, that I will engage his attention as long as you need. I'll bring a pack of cards just in case."

Rorden snorted beside her, and Merek's lips twitched in a tired smile.

Captain Falbrook did not smile. "My men's lives are in your hands, Your Highness. This is a very delicate plan that could easily be upset by something as simple as the prince returning earlier than we expected."

"Or not taking as many troops with him as we expect. Or the northern gate being more guarded than we anticipate, and Captain Orri not getting through. Or the troops encamped on the Ardanian side of the border being alerted before your men can close the eastern gate. There are many things upon which your men's lives depend. This is the one matter for which you needn't worry. I shall play my role well, and Prince Artem's attention will be far from Endvar when you attack."

Captain Falbrook looked skeptical, but he turned back to Merek.

"Are you certain that you'd rather join us than meet with the prince yourself?"

Merek nodded, looking around the table. "You've

trained well, but you don't know the city as I do. If things don't go according to plan, you'll want an insider's perspective. Captain Eldar will accompany the princess in my place."

"Captain Eldar!" Ria objected. "I do wish you had chosen someone else to stand in your place. Like Captain Orri! He's young and handsome. It wouldn't be such a sacrifice to pretend to be fond of him."

"The prince is expecting someone older than you," Merek said flatly, "not someone young and handsome. Eldar will give him what he expects while defending you as well as I."

"But he's so old! A woman has to consider her reputation." She winked at a pair of soldiers who must have been brothers. They blushed and looked away, hiding matching grins.

Merek stifled a yawn. "Thank you, Captain. The night is waning, and it'll be light soon. Rest well today. It's nearly time to put your training to the test."

As the soldiers stood, the one nearest Ria spoke to her. He was a young man with ears that jutted out comically from his head.

"So it's true that you and General Strong are betrothed? My older brother is husband to his sister. She'll be in a shock when she hears the news."

Ria smiled. "How is sweet Marga? I should like to see her again."

As the soldier replied with word about Marga and her family, Ria's attention was caught by a murmur of conversation between Merek and Captain Falbrook.

"I don't know, Merek. You really think she can manage it?"

Feigning interest in the young man's story, Ria strained her ears to hear Merek's quiet reply.

"I trust her, Stefan. She's earned it. I don't doubt that she'll do all we ask and more. My only fear—"

"Yes?"

"I only worry what price she'll have to pay to do it."

The young soldier asked her a question, and giving him her full attention cost her the rest of the overheard conversation.

She glowed with pride at Merek's words about trusting her, but his fear troubled her. The tent couldn't empty soon enough for her liking.

When the last of the soldiers filed out wordlessly, Ria held Merek's gaze for a long moment. "I don't think he likes me much."

"Who? Stefan? He's just worried about his men. Your flippant attitude wasn't particularly comforting."

"I see. So should I have told him of my nightmares instead? Would he have *more* confidence in me if he knew how afraid I was?"

Merek frowned, and she instantly regretted the words. "What are you afraid of?"

Ria sighed. "It's difficult to say."

Merek moved around the table and sat on the edge nearest her. She had to crane her neck to look up at him, so instead she looked at her hands tracing patterns in the heavy fur.

"Do you believe you're going into danger?" His tone was grave.

"Not as such, no, but I do wish that you were going to be with me. I'm not asking you to join me; I know why you cannot. But when I'm with Artem, I feel small and lost. When I'm with you...I feel strong. Powerful. I should like to feel that way when I see him."

Merek reached for her hands and pulled her up to face him. The blankets slipped from her shoulders, and she felt exposed in spite of her many layers of clothing. She became very aware of his nearness and the fact that they were—at last—truly alone.

"You are the most powerful woman I know," Merek said simply. "He's no match for you." He kissed her gently, then pulled her close in a warm embrace that made her forget the bitter cold. Ria relaxed, resting her head against his chest. Closing her eyes, she listened to his beating heart as he gently stroked her back.

"Merek?"

"Hmm?"

"There is one thing that would help."

"What's that?"

"Marry me."

His touch stopped.

"I mean it. Marry me today. Right now, even. Surely there's a priest in this camp whom we can wake to perform the ceremony."

"What would that accomplish?"

Ria frowned. "What would it accomplish? Well, to begin with, I wouldn't have to go back and sleep in my cold tent tonight. That alone would make it worth it."

He snorted. "Be serious." He started to loosen his embrace, but she clung to him.

"I mean it, Merek. If you marry me now, then if something happens to either one of us, the throne is secure. There will be two heirs, not just one."

"How could any marriage between us be validated

without your father's blessing? Without proper witnesses?"

"We have nearly ten thousand soldiers in this camp. I'm sure we could find plenty of witnesses."

"Your father would never forgive you. And neither would my mother, come to think of it. If she heard that I married you in a dirty old army camp and didn't even invite her..."

"You're looking for any excuse instead of listening to your heart. Do you want to marry me?" Ria reached up and pulled at his loosened cravat. "Somewhere beneath all these buttons and insignias you must have a heart that says as mine does that we belong together."

He smirked, his eyes sparkling in the dying firelight. "Aren't you the one who told me that marriage is not a matter of the heart?"

"Are you punishing me then? Is that what this resistance is about?"

"No, I'm not punishing you." The humor in his eyes died. "But now isn't the time to speak of such things. We both have work to do. For now, you are a princess, and I am a general. We can speak of this later."

"But I want to marry you as a woman, not just a princess," Ria insisted. "I want to wake up next to you each morning. And I want to do it now, so that no matter what comes, no matter what the future holds, we have these moments to be man and wife. I want to take that knowledge with me when I go to meet Artem, that I'm not just me any longer—that I am *us*, something bigger and better than what I was before. A glorious future with children and grandchildren and nurturing the life of this kingdom with you by my side."

In answer, Merek kissed her longingly, his fingers entwined in her loose hair. Her hands rested on his chest, and she felt his heart beat faster, at the same time her own raced hopefully. But when he pulled away, his eyes were sad.

"As long as your father objects to our union, it can never be. Some might say I commit treason just to hold you like this, that every moment we spend together is a crime against him."

"So you'll let a madman get his way and keep us apart?" she whispered angrily, her throat tightening.

"I didn't say that." He raised her hand to his lips and gently kissed the inside of her wrist. Her skin tingled pleasantly with his touch. "We'll continue with our plan to take back Endvar. Then, you'll return to Albon and work on turning your father toward me. I'll drive the Ardanians out of our kingdom and win back your father's good favor. And in the spring, when the trees are blooming and the flowers are breaking forth from their winter sleep, we'll have a wedding. A wedding fit for a princess, acknowledged before the king and all the people with a grand parade, three days of feasting, and all the public celebrating that you deserve and which I absolutely detest."

Ria smiled in spite of herself. "With dancing?"

Merek groaned. "I suppose there shall have to be. I'll choose a few of my men who will make good partners for you."

"You'll do no such thing! If you can require me to learn a few silly tricks with a knife, I can most definitely expect you to dance with me at our wedding."

He chuckled and drew her close again. "Eldar tells me you haven't been practicing."

"I practice. I just practice poorly because I'm not a soldier, and he's not used to teaching noblewomen."

"Well, keep at it. Even if it's not necessary when you face Artem, I don't want my wife to be utterly defenseless whether she's in the most humble of villages or the finest of ballrooms."

"What do you think goes on in a ballroom that I would need to defend myself?" Ria scoffed, but she felt a little thrill at him calling her his 'wife'. She relaxed in his arms, melting with exhaustion and reveling in the private moment. It was all too short.

"Come. I'll escort you back to your tent."

Ria groaned, her voice muffled against his chest. "Must you? It's so far away, and this is the warmest I've been in days."

"It'll be daylight soon, and you and I both need our rest."

"I confess I was eyeing your cot earlier," Ria said with a yawn, "but I decided that if I laid down it might be impossible to wake me. And what would Biren think if she found me sleeping here in the morning?"

"Best not let that happen." Merek reached to gather her discarded blankets and steered her toward the tent door.

"No indeed. My reputation would suffer, my maid would have a fit, and I wouldn't even enjoy the benefits of what everyone would think I'd done," she said lightly over her shoulder and was rewarded with the sight of Merek's blush before she passed into the night.

SEVEN

An icy rain pelted Merek as he watched Ria's company disappear over a distant hill. The group of hooded figures could have been a religious caravan, with his vision obscured as it was by the rain.

He pulled his hood lower in a vain attempt to shield himself from the stinging pellets, but the wind drove the frozen rain sideways so there was no escaping it. Merek had traded his uniform for the forest garb of the climbers, and he missed the extra layers.

What a miserable day to attempt such an onerous task.

When the last of the riders disappeared from view, he turned his own horse north. Orri's men were hidden in the forest outside Endvar's northern gate, waiting for the signal from Stefan's men. Once they confirmed that the Ardanians had left the city, they would climb the wall and secure the gate in a covert attack, allowing Orri's men to flood the city from the direction least expected.

Merek had stayed behind until Ria's party departed,

watching them safely on their way. It was a sign of Ria's own nervousness that she hadn't teased him about being overprotective. Instead, she'd been unusually quiet all morning. It was difficult not to worry about her, even though Merek knew that Eldar would defend her if needed. It felt wrong not to be there with her when she was putting herself at risk.

Merek tried to put these thoughts out of his mind. With Ria at his back and Stefan's climbers ahead of him, he spurred his horse to move faster. He stayed far from the main road, making a wide arc around the city to avoid Prince Artem and his retinue coming from the opposite direction.

When he was deep within the woods, Merek slowed. The canopy overhead sheltered him somewhat from the storm, but the sleet clattered noisily on the trees and viney undergrowth. Above the sound, he heard a small bird cry. It sounded natural enough, except that it was the middle of winter and no bird would be out in this weather.

Merek reined his horse to a stop. He looked about him, but saw nothing out of the ordinary until a man dropped out of the trees in front of him, landing solidly on both feet.

His horse whinnied and shied away. Merek swore as he tried to calm his horse and his own pounding heart.

"Taking to the trees now, Gyll? Where's your captain?"

The young man's grin looked clownish with the way his ears stuck out from his head. "Follow me, sir."

Merek dismounted and followed the young soldier to a little hollow where Stefan was waiting. Three of his soldiers slept curled up against a rotting oak log. The others saluted as Merek approached.

"I don't like it, sir," Stefan said candidly in a low voice. "The wall is going to be slicker than a greased hog in this ice."

"The city wall is much shorter than what your men have trained on," Merek reminded him. "Stop worrying, Stefan. Climbing the wall is the least of our worries. When we get in the city, that's when it really gets dangerous."

"If you even get a chance. Prince Artem still hasn't left the city."

"Hasn't left? Are you sure?"

"I've had two men watching. There's been no activity, not even so much as a small riding party."

Merek frowned. What was the meaning of the prince's tardiness? Was he amassing a larger force than expected? Or was he simply trying to make Ria as miserable as possible while she waited for him in the cold? Merek felt a twinge of worry as he thought about her. Surely she could manage things without him.

He hoped.

THE WIND WHIPPED THE FLAMES BURNING IN THE BRAZIER, stealing the warmth away before it could properly warm Ria's chilled fingers. Her toes were numb in her boots, and it was only with great effort that she kept her teeth from chattering. She should get up and walk around, but the shelter from the temporary canopy was so meager that if she wandered even a few steps from where she sat, she would be exposed to the driving rain and ice.

On the other side of the brazier sat an empty chair. Artem was late, unusually so. The longer Ria sat in the cold waiting for him, the crankier she became. Biren too seemed to feel the strain. She sat stiffly, her face beneath the light freckles paler than usual.

Ria glanced at Captain Eldar who stood just outside the canopy with his men. "You might as well come in and sit, General," she offered. "Prince Artem isn't using the chair, and it might be nice to have some conversation while we wait."

Eldar was too stoic to grimace outwardly, but his reticence was clear. "I prefer to stand, Your Highness."

"Then at least come stand next to me and block this frigid wind. I mean it. Come, stand right here, and put yourself to use."

After a moment's hesitation, he obeyed, ducking under the canopy and standing as a sentinel beside her.

"Hmm, not enough. You three." She nodded to the nearest group of soldiers standing guard. "Be so kind as to form a windbreak."

The soldiers joined their commanding officer, and Ria immediately felt a lessening of the chill. "Ah, that's much nicer, don't you think, Biren? Thank you, gentlemen." The heat of the brazier was noticeable now that the flames were not being tossed about.

After a moment, she addressed Eldar again. "It does you credit that you wish not to dishonor the general through pretense, but if you cannot imagine yourself to be General Strong, you shall never convince Prince Artem that you are."

"I beg your pardon, Your Highness. I don't feel comfortable with the title as it is, and do not care to begin the pretense prematurely."

"If it helps, I too would prefer that he were by my side instead. But I shall call you General Strong now, so that when Prince Artem arrives you can hear it without cringing."

"Yes, Your Highness."

"And stop calling me 'Your Highness.' Merek only calls me that if he's angry with me."

Eldar shifted uncomfortably. "What should I call you instead?"

"Do not fear; I won't ask you to address me by my name. If you must address me, and I expect you will spend most of the time silent, a simple 'my lady' will suffice."

"Yes, my lady."

"Very well, General," Ria said, but inwardly she sighed. Merek had been so certain that Captain Eldar would be an adequate stand-in for himself, but Ria found his company as discomfiting as something distasteful stuck between her teeth. She just hoped she could capture Artem's attention well enough that he didn't pay much attention to the false general.

If Artem ever arrived.

Ria felt a mixture of irritation and relief that he was late. As much as she'd pushed for this meeting, she dreaded it. The longer the afternoon wore on, the more she just wanted to give up on the whole thing and retreat back to camp.

She'd thought carefully about what she would say to Artem when she saw him. She was prepared for his thinly veiled insults. She would be unflappable: gracious and poised no matter how he might try to unnerve her. But it was becoming increasingly difficult to be poised when her extremities were in danger of frostbite.

"General Strong." This time, Eldar's reaction was more subtle. *Better.* "I'm in severe need of rousing conversation. Pray engage me in something more interesting than the accumulation of ice on that tent pole."

Eldar thought a moment before asking, "Have you been practicing the defensive techniques I taught you?"

Ria grimaced. "I asked for something interesting. Reminding me of my inadequacy is of no interest to me."

The deep creases around Eldar's eyes deepened in something akin to a smile. "You're not inadequate, merely unpracticed. We could practice while we wait, if you like."

"I have a better idea. Answer me this: What are your thoughts about our future king?"

Eldar glanced at her, a small crack in his exterior. "I'm afraid I don't understand the question."

"It's not so difficult. I need a distraction, and this is one subject that I believe we can converse quite readily on. I've already gathered that he's earned your loyalty as a soldier. But you come from a noble family, do you not? Your perspective is more than that of a common soldier. So I ask you, what are your thoughts about my choice for the future king?"

Eldar frowned, his expression darkening.

"You may speak frankly. I won't hold your words against you this once. I understand that serving with him as long as you have, you must know his faults more than most."

"Not at all, my lady. It's not the question of the crown that gives me pause. I'm confident that he will perform those duties well. It is simply the question of—" He glanced at her and caught himself.

"Yes?"

"It's nothing, my lady. Rest assured that, noble blood or not, I will be his faithful servant in whatever calling."

Ria eyed him closely. "Come, Eldar, you must say it. I asked for rousing conversation, and you've almost distracted me from the icy draft blowing about my ankles. Now you must tell me what lurks in that head of yours. I demand it."

Captain Eldar cleared his throat. His discomfort was far more engaging than his actual conversation.

"It's more of a personal nature, Your Highness. I expected that if Captain Strong—forgive me, *General* Strong—ever married, that it would be to a woman of his status and maturity, his equal in all things."

"You worry that our marriage will be unequal because I am a princess and he is a commoner?"

Captain Eldar looked away. "I....yes..."

"Goodness!" Ria sat up straighter in her chair. "I've got it backwards, haven't I? It is *I* who doesn't measure up in your esteem, isn't it?" She laughed.

Eldar straightened his shoulders. "I didn't say that, my lady. I have no complaint against you. You're as fine a princess as I could hope to meet—"

"And yet that still seems like a lackluster compliment somehow." Ria's laughter dimmed and left a sour taste in her throat. "Well, I won't argue with you. There may be many fine women who would make a better companion than I, especially in matters of domesticity. But he chose me, so that counts for something, doesn't it?"

The aging captain regarded her a moment before nodding. "Of course, Your Highness. It must count for a great deal." He didn't seem inclined to say more, and Ria didn't press him further as she too had lost her appetite for the subject.

· · ✴ · ·

A SHOUT STARTLED MEREK AND STEFAN. ONE OF STEFAN'S men sprinted down the embankment toward them. He slipped and stumbled but managed to keep his feet, all stealth abandoned in his haste.

"What is it, Borth?" Stefan demanded.

"Soldiers," Borth gasped. "Leaving the city."

"Is the prince with them?"

"No, sir. They aren't with the prince. They're moving toward the forest. Right to Captain Orri's men."

"How many?" Merek asked in alarm.

"At least a thousand, maybe more."

Merek swore. They would easily overwhelm Orri. "Wake up your men, Stefan. Captain Orri needs us."

"But sir, the attack—"

"There will be no attack. They know about Orri's men. Can we be certain they don't know about yours? Send two of your men to alert Captain Firl that we need reinforcements. The rest of you, come with me."

As Merek moved toward his horse, Stefan followed him, speaking with quiet urgency. "Merek, this isn't what I brought my men here to do. It's one thing to carry out a careful assault they've specifically trained for. But this...this is not our fight."

Merek frowned at him. "Do you not wear the crest of the king?"

"Of course we do, but these boys shouldn't even be here. They should be facing unskilled bandits in Haldin, not a thousand trained Ardanian soldiers. Don't do this to them, please," he begged. "We came when you asked, but it wasn't for this."

Merek gritted his teeth against the desperation in his friend's eyes. "Thank you, Stefan, for showing me the coward I could have been had I sought a life of quiet in the forest as you did."

"Merek—"

"*Captain* Falbrook," he interrupted, his voice hard. "If you cannot follow my orders, then you may go. You're of no use to the king and certainly no use to me. But your men will stay. If you have any honor at all, you won't ask them to share in your disgrace."

Stefan swallowed hard, shame darkening his eyes. "Forgive me, sir. We'll stand with you, of course."

Merek nodded curtly and watched Stefan turn away to give orders to his men. He wasn't unsympathetic to Stefan's plea. He himself had spent many a night after battle thinking of the men he'd lost during the day, unable to sleep despite crippling exhaustion. So it was that as he swung up into his saddle he called to his friend. "Stefan," he promised, "I'll keep watch over them if I can."

Eight

It was difficult not to feel like she'd failed as Ria and her party rode away, leaving the canopy to be disassembled and loaded onto a wagon by Eldar's men. She hoped that Merek and the other climbers hadn't attacked as planned. They were supposed to wait until Artem's retinue left the city, but Ria worried that Artem's absence meant that something had gone wrong.

The sleet had shifted to snow, and it gusted about them in white currents that reminded her of a long cold autumn spent in the mountains of Branvik. Rahm was close enough to the ocean that snow wasn't a serious threat during the winter, but these reaches in the north were more vulnerable to severe weather than Albon.

Biren rode next to her in silence. Usually her quiet companionship was a comfort to Ria, but she seemed unusually distant, and Ria hoped she wasn't feeling poorly. More of the camp had been falling to fevers of late, and it would be like Biren to continue with her duties even when her health was poor.

Ria was struck by a sudden desire to be home, sitting by the fire with her father, warm in the safe embrace of Thorodan Hall with not a care for the storm outside. Her throat constricted at the thought, and she realized that even if she were home, that scene would exist only in her imagination. Instead, she would be weighed down by many cares, not the least of which was her father's absence. His tower fortress cast a dark shadow across her mind, a symbol of his madness and abandonment. Those carefree days of her youth were over.

But there may yet be better days ahead. In a desperate attempt to fight off the gloom that pressed on her as persistently as the oncoming dusk, Ria envisioned another scene. Children—her children—gathered around the hearth. A boy lost in the pages of a favorite book, and a girl lying on her stomach near the hearth, solving a puzzle of wooden blocks.

Immediately the gloom eased, and Ria imagined the great hall filled with shouts of laughter as two more little ones played a game of chase. And in the middle of it all was Merek: swinging the littlest one over his head, ruffling the boy's hair affectionately by the fire, scooping up the girl into his lap with one arm around Ria and a soft kiss on her temple.

Yes, they would have many children. Thorodan Hall would once again be filled with the bustling life of a large family the likes of which hadn't been seen in several generations. A whole flock of boys and girls, each one more brilliant than the last, and the pride and joy of the whole kingdom.

The thought made Ria smile, and her spirits lifted. The snow thickened as they approached the camp, making it difficult to tell the exact time of day. Perhaps it was best that Artem had stayed away. The road was still easy to travel, but if the snow kept up like this, it might be impassable in a few hours.

As they passed the miserable sentinels on the edge of camp, they were greeted by Captain Talen, his black curls turned white by clinging snowflakes.

"Your Highness," he said urgently. "The Ardanian prince is here. He arrived not an hour ago."

Ria's insides flipped. "Prince Artem is *here*? Are you sure?"

"Yes, Your Highness. Captain Salvin has detained him in the command tent."

Ria's fingers tingled, and her breath grew shallow. Artem was here. In the camp. He'd left the city, but instead of coming to their place of rendezvous, he'd somehow circled around past her soldiers and brazenly entered the camp outside of her knowledge. *Her* camp.

She frowned at the command tent looming in the shadowy distance and motioned to Eldar to help her dismount. "Captain Salvin is there, you say?"

"Yes, Your Highness. It didn't seem right to make him wait out of doors as we didn't know how long you would be."

"You could have kept him in the privy; I wouldn't have minded," Ria grumbled. "Lead the way, Talen. Biren, with me, please."

For all her brave words, Ria approached the majestic striped tent with foreboding in each hurried step. What did Artem mean by this display? She tried to calm her racing thoughts. She couldn't allow him to control the conversation. Whatever his purpose in surprising her, she must keep control over her tongue.

But she wasn't prepared for what she saw when she entered the tent. For there was Artem, sitting in Merek's chair, leaning back in a relaxed posture as though this were his tent and she were the guest. Three Ardanians stood near him, two of them armed guards who watched Captain Salvin and his men with tense postures. The third was the pale man, Domar. The sight of him sent a chill down Ria's spine. The last time they'd met had been in a humble farmhouse when he'd tried to abduct her, and she would never forget his reptilian coldness.

Artem, on the other hand, looked as comfortable as if he were at home in Rellana entertaining a host of sycophants. As Ria entered, throwing back her hood and shaking the snow to the ground, he stood and moved gracefully to greet her.

"Ah, here she is!" His smile was warm and his eyes bright. His handsome face was clean-shaven in spite of the cold—like most Ardanians, she'd never known him to wear a beard. But she didn't find him as attractive as she once had. Indeed, the way his shrewd eyes looked over her incited instant umbrage.

"How dare you?" she demanded.

"It's a pleasure to see you as well, Ria dear." He leaned forward as if to kiss her cheek, but before she knew what she was doing, her hand shot out and slapped his face.

She wasn't sure who was more shocked. He froze, and Biren gasped at her side. Ria shrank a little with mortification. There was a moment's pause as the room stilled, then the two Ardanian guards drew their swords and stepped forward. Instantly, a large arm pushed Ria roughly to the side, and she found her view blocked by Captains Eldar and Talen, standing between her and the prince with their own weapons drawn.

"I take it that you're upset that I missed our little meeting this afternoon."

"You might say that." The truth was that it made her skin crawl to see him there in Merek's tent, sitting in Merek's chair. The thought of him trying to touch her was too much. But she couldn't say those things, for they would only delight him. Trying to bury those feelings, she placed a hand on Talen's shoulder and slipped between the two men to face Artem again.

"Stand down, Captains," she said, pleased that her voice sounded calm. "Artem, tell your soldiers to stand down so we can have a civilized conversation."

"You call that civilized?" Artem asked, and Ria had a flash of guilty pleasure at seeing the red outline of her hand on his pale cheek. Behaving like a slighted wench was hardly the way to get the upper hand over a cunning enemy, but it came with a certain satisfaction.

"That was nothing. Certainly not what you deserve after trying to have me abducted."

"Abducted? I don't know what you're talking about." Artem's eyes narrowed.

"Do you not? Ask your man Domar. This is not the first time we've met."

The pale man stepped forward and bowed respect-fully to Ria. "My apologies, Your Highness. That unfortunate incident was merely an effort to avoid a full conflict. Taking you prisoner seemed a preferable way of getting the leverage we wanted without having to engage in a long campaign."

"There, you see?" Artem said, shooting an annoyed glance at Domar. "It wasn't personal. And you can't hold me responsible, for this is the first I've learned of it."

"Many of my soldiers died, Artem, and I'm quite fond of my soldiers." Ria kept her gaze on Domar, unsettled by his lifeless eyes.

Artem glanced back and forth between the two of them. "You've already met Domar, then? He's a long-time friend, a cousin of sorts."

"Ours was not a civilized introduction," Ria said, and Domar sneered as he bowed to Ria. "A cousin, you say? Why didn't I meet him at court?"

"Oh no, his bloodline isn't of the kind that would make him welcome at court. But that's for the best as he's invaluable at managing business of a more...delicate nature."

"Such as invading an ally and starting a war?"

Artem's lips parted in a mischievous smile. "Oh yes, he's particularly suited to that little task. Come, you must be tired. Let's sit and have something warm to drink. Is there any proper wine in this camp? This man wouldn't even produce a weak ale when I asked him." He nodded to the glowering Captain Salvin.

Ria chafed again at his presumptuous attitude. She didn't move. "I don't recall inviting you here, Artem. Indeed, I spent the better part of the afternoon waiting for you at the Hoggen bridge as we agreed."

"Yes, I do apologize for that. It was incredibly rude, but I think you'll forgive me when you hear my proposal."

"Your proposal?"

"More an invitation, really."

"Keep it brief. I'm soaked through from my long ride in the snow."

"A party. I know how you love a party! You and your betrothed will be my special guests. It's a pity he isn't here. I can't wait to meet him."

Ria stole a glance at Eldar. She'd forgotten about their planned deception.

Artem saw her look and laughed heartily.

"Oh come, Ria! You can't really think I would believe that this old codger has won your hand. But I do wonder, where is he? The *real* General Strong." All levity dropped from his tone. His gleaming teeth suddenly seemed predatory.

Ria suppressed a shiver. "I won't be attending any party, Artem. Surely you can't expect me to deliver myself up as a hostage that easily."

"Not a hostage, a guest! There will be dancing and food and blazing fires to warm you through. Then, we can discuss the matter of you abdicating the throne to me."

"Me—what? Are you mad?"

"No, but your father is," Artem said flatly. "My condolences, by the way."

"What do you know about my father?"

This time Artem switched to his native tongue and with it came a sense of intimacy, as if they were the only two in the tent. "I admire your efforts, Ria, I really do. But it's time to stop pretending that Rahm has a king and give her one who is truly suited to rule."

"Rahm has a leader," Ria answered in Ardanian, feeling short of breath.

"Who…you?" Artem laughed again, but when he

spoke it was not with scorn but compassion, which made it worse. "Ria, darling, you can't be serious. It's valiant of you to try, but you know that you're not fit to rule this kingdom."

"Why? Because I'm a woman?" Indignation made her words hot against her tongue.

"Because you've asked half a dozen questions since you entered this tent and none of them have been the right one. The question you should have asked is, 'Why was this man not dead the moment he set foot in my camp?'"

He stepped closer, and Ria's cheeks warmed at his nearness and the uncomfortable truth of his words. He smelled of perfumed soap and clean linen, with a faint trace of sour wine.

"You're not a leader, Ria," Artem said kindly, his accent caressing the vowels of her name with warmth. "You're too soft and emotional. That makes you a wonderful companion but incapable of making the hard decisions required to rule. And so, your enemy can come straight into the heart of your camp unchallenged, bending everyone to his will because they sense that he is a ruler they can follow. Now, the question you should be asking yourself is, 'How quickly can I put this man on my throne?'"

He was distressingly close, but Ria resisted the urge to back away. She held his gaze. She sensed Biren shifting uncomfortably nearby but didn't take her eyes from Artem's.

She replied in Rahmish. "If you imagine I would ever think that thought in a thousand lifetimes, you do not know me at all."

Artem smiled and stepped away, the intimate moment broken. "You needn't decide right away, of course. Take some time. Come to my soiree. We'll discuss it further, and I will lay out for you my plan for this kingdom. I think you'll find I can be very persuasive."

"Never. We can meet on neutral ground as we arranged. I'm not such a fool as to give myself into your control so readily."

Artem sighed in exasperation. "I don't want you dead, Ria! Why would I? I would still have to conquer your armies to get to the throne, and there's nothing like a dead maiden to give men reason to fight. You would become a martyr, inspiring each of your soldiers to personally bring me to justice. What a lot of bother! It would be much simpler to just surrender the throne to me and be done with it. Save all those lives, even as you drain the fight out of them."

Ria's fingers clenched under the long sleeves of her cloak. "I can't decide whether to be repulsed by your arrogance or impressed at your efficiency. But the answer is no. Now, I'll ask Captain Salvin to escort you out."

Artem nodded as if he'd expected her response. "Of course. I won't trespass on any more of your time. After all, you do have a burial to arrange." He bowed to Ria with a flourish and gestured to his men to follow him.

"Whose burial?"

Artem turned back with a gleam in his eye. "Did I not mention it? How careless of me. Your betrothed, of course."

Her stomach leaped into her heart at his words. "What do you mean?"

Artem's voice turned hard. All playful pretense was gone. "I know about the men hiding in the forest. As we speak, a thousand of my soldiers have surrounded them and are slaughtering them at will. Your beloved general will die unless I give the command otherwise. Domar is ready to put a stop to it at my word. All I ask is that you accept my invitation."

Panic washed over her. Talen and Eldar tensed at her side. He knew. He knew about Merek. About the troops. About their plan to attack the city. She suddenly felt like a fool for ever thinking they could outwit him. Her mind raced, looking for a way out of the trap he'd laid.

"It's a pity," Artem said in the silence, "for such a good man to die. Say yes, and he'll live."

"I'll come," she said in a rush. "Don't hurt him. Please."

"Wonderful!" Artem clapped, grinning again. "It will be magnificent. And please, do bring him along. I can't wait to meet the man who has such a hold over you." He nodded to Domar, and the man slipped out of the tent without a word.

"If he doesn't return to me alive and whole," Ria said fiercely, "I will burn that city to the ground to find you."

Artem raised an eyebrow. "You see? Too emotional. Oh, this will be a lark! Three days. I shall send you the details."

"Ten." It was all happening so fast. She needed time to think. To plan a response. "I need time to find something suitable to wear."

"That's more like it! Five. You could come in trousers and you would be ravishing as always." His knowing wink left Ria blushing in his wake.

NINE

"What news of Captain Firl?"

"Two companies are on their way, sir. They should be here within the hour."

Not soon enough.

"And Captain Orri?

"No sign of him, sir."

Merek stepped over the Ardanian soldier who had just fallen by his blade. The forest floor was littered with corpses, their bodies still warm enough that the swirling snowflakes melted before they landed. Merek paused to drive his sword through the heart of a wounded enemy reaching for his fallen weapon. They would be taking no prisoners tonight.

Merek knelt next to a Rahmish soldier whose mail had been shredded across his chest and shoulder. The young man made a ragged sucking noise amplified by the stillness around them. His eyes were open and afraid, and his gaze locked on Merek with the desperation of one unprepared to die. Merek knew by the sound of his breathing that the soldier wouldn't live another hour. In the fading light, the young man's chest was an indistinguishable mess of flesh and bone, the blood leaking steadily out with each beat of his heart.

"Shhh, don't try to speak," Merek said as the soldier rasped out a sound like he was trying to form words. Merek laid a hand on the young man's bare head, his hair wet and cold with matted sweat. "You've served your king well. Be at peace."

The soldier's eyes flickered briefly with gratitude, but then filled with panic again. *How terrifying to drown in your own blood.* Merek had seen death in many forms on the battlefield, and very few seemed an enviable way to die. The dampness of the ground seeped through his clothing where he knelt, and he felt an urgency to find Captain Orri and see how he was faring. But he was loath to leave the poor young man alone with his fear.

"Sir!" Borth approached in a low crouch, breathing heavily. He too wore the forest greens and browns of the north and would have been nearly indistinguishable from his surroundings if he hadn't been moving so quickly through the undergrowth. They were unprotected without mail or armor, but blending in with their surroundings had proven to be an asset as they attacked the Ardanian soldiers unawares.

"Captain Falbrook says he's found Captain Orri. He's been taken along with some of the other officers."

"Where have they been taken?"

"A clearing just on the other side of this hill. They're alive, for now."

Merek signaled for the others to follow him. The heavy forest canopy protected them from much of the falling snow, but as they approached the area Borth spoke of, the canopy fell away. Snow clung to the ground and the undergrowth, settling on the grassy floor of the clearing where Captain Orri and a dozen officers knelt.

Ardanian soldiers surrounded them with weapons drawn, but no one moved. Instead, there was an air of expectation.

"Falbrook and the others are concealed awaiting your orders," Borth whispered.

Silently, Merek ran a hand over a slender arrow and drew his bow. It was near dark, but the snow reflected whatever light was left in the sky, illuminating the scene.

An Ardanian soldier with white hair stepped forward and looked at the Rahmish prisoners.

"Who is General Strong?" he called out in clear, accented Rahmish.

Merek cursed inwardly. The prince knew about the ruse, and he wanted Merek.

None of the prisoners responded.

"One of you is he. Who is it?"

The white-haired Ardanian barked an order and soldiers entered the clearing carrying three bodies. They threw them to the ground, but at this distance, Merek couldn't identify them.

"Is General Strong here?" the leader asked, gesturing to the dead men. "No? Then we must kill you all just to be sure."

"That won't be necessary," a voice rang out. "I am General Strong." Captain Orri pushed himself awkwardly to his feet, his hands bound behind him.

The Ardanian captain glanced him over and wiped his nose. Then he muttered some instructions in his native tongue, and two soldiers grabbed Orri and pushed him back down to the ground. They held him tightly as the other men raised their swords over the remaining Rahmish officers.

With only a breath of a moment to spare, blinking back the snow building up on his eyelashes, Merek loosed his arrow. It flew straight into the neck of the nearest soldier, and immediately was answered by five more finding their mark in other soldiers.

The Ardanians cried out at the sudden onslaught of arrows, realizing all at once how exposed they were against the stark whiteness of the snow. Some ducked in confusion when their comrades fell next to them, but others set about their bloody work with a vengeance. Merek focused on these first, trying to stop the butchery. Together, he and the other archers brought them down in moments.

But Orri was no longer there. Merek glimpsed two soldiers driving a bound man before his view was obstructed by the surviving Ardanians scattering to the bushes to find the archers. Praying that Stefan's men were clever enough to escape, Merek chased after Orri.

He plowed recklessly through the undergrowth, leaping over fallen logs and fallen men. The sounds of battle faded as his own heavy breathing filled his ears. Orri had taken his place. He wouldn't let him die for it.

All at once, he came out of the brush onto a road. Snow fell silently all around, filling the tracks recently left by a small group moving in haste. If he'd been a few minutes later, he would have missed them entirely. Orienting himself quickly, he pursued Orri and his captors.

The snow muffled his footsteps with an odd squeaking sound and collected on his boots, slowing his progress as he ran. The trees rose up on either side of him, shadowy sentinels contrasted with a dusting of white snow. The falling snow obscured his vision and muted sound, making him feel as if he were the only living being in a world of shadows and white. At last, snatches of muffled voices came to him on the wind, and he slowed. Ahead, shapes formed in the dimness.

Merek moved off the road to approach under cover of trees. The shapes resolved into soldiers, three of them standing guard over Captain Orri who sat in the snow tied to a tree. He was alive and appeared unharmed, but the signs of battle were clear in his weariness and bloodied armor.

Merek didn't speak Ardanian, so he could only guess as to what instructions the white-haired captain gave before mounting his horse and starting back down the road.

Making a quick decision, Merek slunk further into the forest and moved quickly back the way he'd come. He had only a few minutes to get into position. When he'd rounded the bend and the other soldiers were lost from view, he stopped and nocked an arrow. Calming his breath, he waited only a moment before the white-haired Ardanian appeared before him, passing just a few feet from where Merek was hidden.

The man and his horse were both well-shielded by armor, and Merek couldn't afford to miss. There was only a sliver of a second when he would be able to—

There.

He released the arrow and it flew straight into the

soldier's gloved hand, piercing through to the horse's neck on the other side.

The man let out a choked sound of pain, and the horse screamed and reared back. Merek leaped out of the bushes and sprang for the horse's thrashing head, but the rider—showing incredible skill—managed to not only keep his seat, but also swung his shield at Merek to ward him off.

Merek ducked out of the way and grabbed the man's shield arm before he could right himself. The rider couldn't keep his balance with so many forces trying to unseat him, and with a look of panic, he toppled off the terrified animal.

His hand was still pinned to the stallion's neck, and he gave a guttural cry as he hung awkwardly against the moving animal. The horse stumbled and screamed, trying to shake free of the weight on his neck. Merek ran and caught his head, pulling him to stop, then plunged his long knife into the horse's throat and pulled, severing his windpipe.

The Ardanian reached for his knife with his good hand, swiping at Merek while he was exposed. But Merek sidled out of reach and wrestled the knife out of the man's grip. He tossed the knife away, grasped the arrow shaft, and snapped it, freeing the pinned hand. The man groaned and let out a stream of angry curses that Merek didn't understand. He slumped against the dead horse, tucking his wounded hand close to his chest.

Merek didn't feel as much compassion for the Ardanian as he had the horse who now lay still on the road, its blood steaming red against the snow. He crouched down and pointed his knife—still wet with the horse's blood—at the man's face.

"How did you know about the men in the forest?"

The captain looked at him blankly and didn't respond.

Merek tried again. "Why did the prince not meet with the princess? What does he want with General Strong?"

The captain shook his head and said something in Ardanian. Merek looked him over, then prodded each leg in turn with his boot until the man flinched. Merek pressed against the offending knee until the Ardanian choked out a pained gasp, his eyes filling with tears.

"I know you understand me. What does the prince want? Does he plan to kill the general?"

The man resolutely held his tongue.

"Have you ever seen a man eaten by a pack of wolves?" Merek asked coldly. "It's winter, and they're hungry. If the battle doesn't draw them, this horse will. How long do you think it will take before they find you? If you're lucky, they'll go for the throat first. But if you're not, how much of you will it take to fill their bellies before you die?"

The Ardanian captain shot a hateful look at Merek.

"He wants General Strong," he said begrudgingly in accented Rahmish, "but killing him is up to the princess."

"What do you mean?"

"I hold him under guard," the man said, wincing as he tried to shift his weight. "If the princess agrees to my lord's request, he lives. If not, he dies."

"What request is that?"

The captain shrugged. "What does any man want from a beautiful woman?"

In a flash of angry desperation, Merek stabbed his knife into the man's shoulder, in the soft unprotected place next to his shoulder plate. The officer bellowed and tried to fight back, but moving only drove the blade in deeper. A torrent of Ardanian curses spilled out of the man's mouth.

"Where is Ria? Did Artem take her?"

A look of uncertainty flashed in the man's eyes. "Who are…you?" he panted.

Merek caught his mistake too late. "Where is the princess? Is she in danger?"

The man's eyes hardened. "*You* are General Strong."

"Tell me where the princess is."

"Why?" he gasped in defiance, even as his face contorted with pain.

"Because this wound might not cost you your life if a surgeon tends to it soon. If you refuse to answer, I will leave you for the wolves. But if you answer me truthfully, I will spare your life."

"I'm dead anyway. The prince will not ransom my life. He will kill me merely for speaking to you."

The sound of drums caught Merek's attention. Firl's men weren't far.

This didn't comfort the Ardanian. His voice held a new edge. "I do not know where she is. I was to hold the general, that is all. You must believe me."

Knowing that help was at hand, Merek was seized with an overwhelming desire to leave the forest in search of Ria, to learn for himself if she were in danger or not. But Orri was still a prisoner, and Firl's arrival might put him at greater risk if his captors felt threatened.

Merek wiped his knife clean on the snow and stood.

"You promised you would not leave me here to die," the Ardanian said resentfully.

"And I won't," Merek replied. "Help will come soon; I swear it."

He turned and ran back to Orri, marveling at how the snow had already mostly filled the horse's tracks. With as much blood as he was losing, the Ardanian captain didn't have long before the snow would chill his body beyond rescue.

As he neared the place where Orri was guarded, Merek slowed and raised his bow, an arrow nocked and ready to fire. The crunching squeak of his boots announced his arrival, and the Ardanian soldiers became alert. With the swirling curtain of snow obscuring the air, it wasn't until he spoke that they fully recognized the threat.

"Orri!" Merek called out. "Do you speak their tongue well enough to translate for me?"

"Yes, sir!" came the sharp reply.

The Ardanian soldiers moved closer to their prisoner, looking warily in the shadows off the road.

"Good. Tell them that the sound of drums they hear is their death. If they stay here, they will be overrun by Rahmish soldiers in only a few minutes' time."

He paused and waited for Orri to relay the message. The soldiers didn't move.

"Tell them that their commander is bleeding in the snow not far from here. If they reach him first, he will be spared from either becoming a prisoner to the Rahmish or a feast for the wolves."

As if on cue, the mournful cry of a wolf sounded in the distance. The soldiers looked at each other uncertainly, but they still raised their swords, their feet firmly planted before the tree where Orri was bound.

"If they do not leave now, I will be forced to kill them. Because *I* am General Strong, and I will not allow them to hold my captain for even a moment longer."

This got the Ardanians' attention, even more so when Merek loosed the arrow into the tree between them.

They jumped, startled, and began a hasty conversation in their native language. Orri interrupted with increasing insistence until, with a nod to Merek, the Ardanians lowered their weapons, mounted their horses, and rode away.

Merek wished for a horse himself, as Orri didn't look strong enough to walk. He slumped against the tree, half buried in a layer of snow.

As Merek cut his bonds, Orri asked weakly, "My men? My officers? Did you save them?"

"The archers shot true."

Orri sighed gratefully. Merek helped him to his feet and looked him over. His clothing was wet where the snow had melted, and his skin was frighteningly pale, looking all the more ghastly with blood dried from battle.

"That was a brave thing you did to save your men, Captain Orri."

Orri looked at him in surprise. "Thank you, sir, but I didn't do it for my men."

"No?"

"It's an honor to serve my king," Orri said simply. "By my life or my death."

They were common enough words from a soldier. But the way he said them, and the sincerity of his gaze, pierced Merek to the core. Because he realized at once that Orri was not speaking of Sindal. He meant Merek. This man was ready to die for *him* because he thought he was going to someday be king.

Merek burned with shame. He was a fraud. It was one thing to indulge Ria in her dream of an unlikely marriage, knowing that someday she would come to the realization that he had—it was impossible while her father retained his murderous grudge against him. But it seemed a harmless wish. Now, he chided himself for being a fool. A good man had sacrificed himself because he thought Merek would be the next king.

"Do you think you can walk? We must get you moving to get your blood flowing."

In answer, Orri began walking stiffly, beating his arms against his body to increase circulation. They moved off the road and trekked into the forest, heading in the direction of the drums. They spoke little, trying not to impede their senses as they tracked their men. With night coming on and the snow increasing, the going was slow.

Orri's words rang in Merek's mind. He felt like he should apologize for the deception that nearly cost Orri his life, but he couldn't bring himself to say the words. If he said it out loud, the dream would end. But maybe, if he pretended a little longer, he would find a way.

In that moment, he realized that he wanted to be king. It was no longer just the price of marrying the woman he loved. He, Merek Strong, *wanted* to be king.

Because when a soldier laid down his life in the name of his king, that king should be a man who would just as willingly lay down his own life for that soldier. He shouldn't be a man who spent his days in idleness and paid other men to run his wars. He should be a man who fought and bled and died right alongside his people—a man who earned their sacrifice not only once but over and over again. He should be a man who knew as well as any of his people the pang of hunger and want, the despair of toiling to feed your family only to find that a great storm at the wrong time, or bandits, or death had made it all for naught.

Only a man like that was worth dying for.

Feeling a rush of purpose, Merek suddenly longed to tell Ria. He stopped in his tracks. Ria. She might be in danger, and here he was plowing through a forest looking for a battle that would probably be over before he found it.

Orri stopped with him. "What is it, sir?"

"The princess may be in danger. The Ardanian said she was safe, but I don't trust him or his prince."

"Then my men and I will come with you. If there's a plot against her, it will likely pose a threat to you as well."

Merek thought to object, to insist that hers was the only life worth saving, but he stopped himself. Maybe it *was* just an idle dream, but if he were ever going to be king, he needed to start acting like it.

Dear Lotta,

I write to you now in the middle of a snowstorm. It's likely mere rain for you, but here closer to the mountains it is a relentless snow that threatens to collapse the tent which covers my head. In another time and place, such a storm would be cause for celebration. A time to sip hot drinks and listen to fascinating stories told by a traveler who is stranded in our hall until it passes. Instead, I find myself sitting alone in the dark next to a smoking brazier that is hardly adequate to ward off the cold, let alone ward off the despair that surrounds me.

I can't speak of details, but if you were here, I would unburden my soul to you, and you would somehow make it better. Instead, I sit here and wait restlessly for hour upon hour. Why is it that we women must always be the ones who wait? I tried to join the rescue party, but the snowstorm and the lateness of the hour made a convincing argument that I should stay. Now I wish I hadn't listened. I feel as if I will go mad with worry and no useful way to occupy my mind.

I wish you were here to distract me or at least that I had a fresh long letter to pore over. It's been some time since I've heard from you. Indeed, I have received no word from Albon in any form.

Here, Ria paused and lifted her pen. "Sergeant Rorden, has the general received any communications from Albon recently?"

The young officer looked up from where he slouched in a chair against the large table.

"Not that I can think of, Your Highness."

His eyes were bleary, and a day's growth of stubble shadowed his features. Biren sat next to him, dark shadows under her eyes and her lips tinged purple with cold. Rorden held her hands, warming them with his own, but she seemed not to notice. Ria had tried to send her to bed, but she had refused, claiming that she would not rest until they heard word of Strong.

Talen had also remained in the command tent, anxiously worrying a hole in the tabletop with his knife as he waited.

"And you, Captain Talen?"

"I've had no word from Albon since shortly after I arrived," Talen answered.

"That's curious, isn't it?"

"Not at this time of year." He shook his head. "I'm sure once this storm passes, we'll have a deluge of messengers who waited it out in towns along the way."

Ria nodded, but something about it didn't seem right. The weather had been cold but clear earlier, certainly conducive to travel.

She finished her letter to Lotta, and then, warmed to her task, penned one to Galinn and to Captain Drenall for good measure. Galinn had hinted in his last communication that perhaps it might be time to formalize her assumption of her father's duties. The idea made her uncomfortable, but with a resigned kind of dread that told her it was inevitable.

There was one aspect of the prospect that was very tempting. As queen, Ria could marry whomever she chose. As things currently stood, she was stymied about how to bring it to pass. If only Merek's gallantry wouldn't oppose marrying her now. It would cause an uproar, undoubtedly, but then the deed would be done, and her father would be forced to accept it. And if he didn't, well, Merek would have an army at his command, wouldn't he?

That was a vexing thought. Especially because it also gave her a guilty thrill of pleasure. Of course, she would never embroil her kingdom in a civil war, but the thought of Merek exercising his considerable might and resources for her sake—well, it was the stuff of every woman's daydreams.

But first Merek had to survive whatever awful trap had been laid for him. She cursed Artem, and for the hundredth time replayed their conversation, wishing she'd said things just so instead of acting like a cowering wench trying to please her master.

Ria stood as voices sounded outside the tent. Rorden, Talen, and Biren followed. The flap opened to admit Captain Eldar.

"What news of the general, Captain?" Ria asked tensely.

"The general is well, Your Highness," Eldar said with the closest thing to a smile Ria had ever seen on the man's wooden face.

Ria exhaled. "You're sure? You saw him for yourself?"

"He sent me ahead to assure you of his safety. He's returning with the remainder of Captain Orri's forces, but they'll be slower in coming due to the storm and the number of wounded. It seems he was never in as much danger as Prince Artem would have had you believe."

Rorden sighed, and Biren slumped with relief against him, letting out a slight sob.

Ria was overwhelmed by conflicting feelings of relief and foolishness. Artem had deceived her, cunningly manipulating her into agreeing to something she never would have agreed to if she weren't acting out of fear.

Glancing sheepishly at Captain Eldar, she asked, "Did you tell him of our surprise visit from the prince?"

"I did, Your Highness. He was most concerned for your welfare, as you can imagine."

"Thank you, Captain," Ria said, inwardly grimacing. Merek would never have allowed himself to be tricked in such a manner. How would she explain to him why she'd responded to Artem's threat with such emotion?

"Your Highness," Captain Eldar said uncertainly, stepping closer. "I hope I'm not speaking out of turn, but I feel after our conversation yesterday that I would be remiss if I didn't tell you that I think you made the right decision. The loyalty and fidelity you've shown to the general was...well..." He cleared his throat. "I fear I may have misjudged you."

Ria managed a smile. "Thank you, Captain," she said again, and this time, she meant it.

Ten

Sore, tired, and soaked through from cooling sweat on the inside and melted snow on the outside, Merek thought the camp had never looked more inviting. Snow softened all the harsh edges and made it glow with reflected starlight, giving an illusion of pristine cleanliness. That wouldn't last. Captain Eldar and his men had passed this way before, and the main road was already a churned up soup. Heedless of the mud, Merek urged his horse forward, anxious to reach his tent which glowed with firelight from the inside.

Ria was there, waiting for him. Captain Eldar had brought word of her safety just as Merek and Orri were preparing to leave the battlefield to rush to her aid. This halted their plans, freeing him instead to focus on gathering their wounded for the cold march back to camp. But there was still a part of him that wouldn't rest until he could see Ria for himself and know that she was well. It was unfortunate that he couldn't clean up before she saw him. It made him cringe for her to see him weakened by exhaustion and bloodied by battle.

The guards at the command tent hurried forward to assist him as he approached, one acting as groom at this late hour, and the other opening the tent door as he dismounted.

To his disappointment, only Rorden and Captains Eldar and Talen waited inside.

"Where's Ria?" he blurted.

"I encouraged the princess to retire." Captain Eldar explained. "We didn't know how long you might be, and she needed rest after the arduous day she'd had."

"She did make me swear that I would notify her as soon as you arrived," Rorden said with a tired smile. "Shall I send word?"

"No. No, let her sleep," Merek replied, though the restless part of him protested, urged him to go to her himself. Instead, he removed his damp gloves and wet cloak. Rorden jumped to assist him, taking his quiver and bow as Merek pulled them over his head.

His shirt was damp with sweat and blood. Stripping it off, he moved to the washstand and scrubbed his hands and forearms, face and neck in the cold water. In the dim light of the tent, the water looked a cloudy gray, but it felt good to rinse away some of the grime of battle.

"Tell me what happened," he ordered as he washed.

Captain Talen cleared his throat. "There were only four of them: the prince, two soldiers, and one other man."

"Domar," Rorden clarified.

"Captain Salvin said they'd been waiting as much as an hour before we returned," Eldar added.

"So the troops the prince sent must have left the city first. It would have been easy enough for four riders to slip away unnoticed while our spies were busy warning Orri's men about the troops coming for them," Merek said. "And Salvin didn't challenge them in any way?"

Talen frowned, his tone sour with distaste. "Salvin was in another part of the camp at the time. By the time I got word and came to see for myself, the prince was already here, acting for all the world as if he owned the place and Salvin were the usurper."

"And you came because...?" Merek regarded Talen suspiciously.

"Just hoping to be of use."

I wonder, Merek thought darkly, reaching for the clean shirt that Rorden held for him.

"Where was Salvin?"

"Sir?"

"You say he was in another part of the camp. I want to know where he was and whom he was with. What business was so pressing that he allowed the Ardanian prince to enter my camp unmolested on his watch?"

"Yes sir." Eldar said. "Though I expect it was less than reputable. He seemed reluctant to discuss it when I pressed him."

"You mean he was visiting a tavern or a whore." Soldiers weren't allowed in the taverns while on duty, but Captain Salvin was known for having a thirsty tongue. As for the whore, in his time Danvir had banned brothels from setting up their tents in Rahmish army camps, which meant that they operated on the fringes under the guise of other trades. But Merek expected better of his first captains.

Eldar again cleared his throat. "That is my suspicion, sir."

"I want to see him in the morning. Whatever story he gives, verify it." Merek nodded to Rorden. "Be thorough. If it was a tavern, which one? How many pints did they serve last night? Smell the very tumbler he drank from. It it was a whore, find out her name, how long she's been in camp, even how she cleansed herself when her work was finished. At the very least, his captaincy is at risk."

Captain Eldar leaned against the table, watching Merek closely. "Sir, am I to understand that you don't trust Salvin? That you suspect him of conspiring with the prince?"

"I suspect everyone," Merek snapped. "The Ardanians knew where Orri was hiding. They knew I wasn't with the princess. Someone can't be trusted."

Rorden and Eldar glanced uncomfortably at each other. He saw the unasked question in their eyes. *Do you suspect me?* The truth was, they were among the few he thought he could trust. Artem thought Merek was with Orri's troops. That meant he didn't know about Stefan's men, so whoever he got his information from, it wasn't someone who knew about the climbers. Which ruled out Rorden and Eldar.

But not Talen.

"A spy could be anywhere," Rorden observed. "It might not even be a soldier. A camp like this has thousands of eyes and ears. It might be a cook. A blacksmith. A tanner."

Merek slumped into a chair and rubbed his eyes wearily. His mind felt foggy. The prince had played them all skillfully. "Tell me more about the prince. What does he want? Why this charade of a party?"

"He claims to have good will for the princess," Rorden said, his brow furrowed. "I know it sounds unbelievable, but he seemed sincere. That was the only time he didn't seem to be acting a part. I think he truly doesn't wish her harm."

"But he won't hesitate to harm her if that's what it takes to get what he wants," Eldar interjected gruffly. "I know his kind, sir, and you can't trust him."

"I have no intention of trusting him, but I wish I could see inside his head, understand his next move. He's wasting his troops in half-hearted efforts instead of mounting any serious campaign to move inward. What does it mean? What's he planning?"

"He wants the princess to abdicate the throne on his behalf."

"Abdicate?" Merek straightened. It was an arrogant prospect but made a kind of sense. If Artem could wear Ria down with an extended campaign over the winter, posing enough of a threat to incite panic, she might give in with minimal casualties on both sides and the kingdom still intact.

If she were a coward.

"She'll never agree. He doesn't know her at all if he thinks he can intimidate her that easily."

Merek frowned at the glance that passed between the other men.

"Except," Rorden began uncertainly. "The princess wasn't...herself...when he was here. She seemed...shaken. Unsure of herself." He looked to Eldar and Talen for corroboration.

Talen shook his head. "I never thought she was one to be intimidated. It was like he'd put out a fire and she didn't know how to find a spark among the embers."

"She did refuse him soundly," Rorden offered.

"But then agreed to meet with him," Eldar countered.

"Only because she thought your life was at stake," Talen added.

Merek spat a bitter curse. What sort of a mess had he created by leaving her to face the prince alone? The resolve he'd felt on the battlefield came back to him. This wasn't a time for caution. It was a time for action. He knew what he needed to do.

He yawned. But first, sleep.

"Thank you Eldar, Rorden. We'll discuss this in the morning. Get some rest. You've earned it, both of you. Talen, a word."

Talen waited, expressionless, as the other men left the tent. When they were alone, Merek motioned him to sit.

"I aim to marry her, Talen."

Talen nodded briefly. "I know."

"No, you don't. I didn't know myself until just a few hours ago. Our betrothal is a farce, but tomorrow I intend to ask her properly to be my wife."

Talen looked at him in surprise. "Why are you telling me this?"

"Because I need to know what you plan to do. If moving forward with a wedding will prompt you to denounce us, I must know your intent now. Sindal's opposition cannot touch us here, but yours can."

"I see," Talen said gravely. "And if I told you that I have no intention of stopping your wedding?"

"Then why are you here? What do you hope to learn

by lingering in the camp instead of returning to Albon where you belong?"

Talen's dark eyes were open and honest. "In truth, I hope to convince the princess to return with me to Albon."

"Why?"

"There are troubling things going on at court. The longer the king stays in his tower, the more his enemies organize against her and her allies."

"Meaning you?"

Talen glanced down sheepishly. "I would hope that she considers me one of her allies, yes."

"It may be a bit hard to count you as such with the constant threat that you may expose her as a traitor."

"That's not fair," Talen objected. "I swore that I wouldn't act without informing you both. Have I given you any indication that I—"

"What did you know of our plans to attack the city today?"

Talen paled. "Very little. In fact, I was surprised to learn that you weren't with the princess tonight. I assure you, Strong, I'm not your enemy."

"You heard Eldar and Rorden. The enemy could be anywhere."

"If I meant you harm, I wouldn't waste time spying for the Ardanians," Talen retorted.

He had a point. Merek rubbed his eyes and stifled a yawn. "I would like to trust you Talen, as I once did."

"And I you."

It wasn't the most secure of truces, but it would have to do. After Talen left, Merek lay on his cot in the quiet of the empty tent and watched the shadows of firelight dancing against the ceiling. Exhaustion settled heavily behind his eyelids, but his mind refused to calm. He breathed deeply, but jumbled images from the battle and anxious thoughts of Ria kept sleep at bay. At last his thoughts blurred, and he sensed sleep waiting just on the horizon.

"Praise St. Lucia and all her twelve children."

Jerking back to consciousness, Merek opened his bleary eyes just as Ria threw herself upon him, pressing her lips against his. Was he dreaming? The weight and smell of her felt real enough, and he responded with an instant fervor that burned away any thoughts of sleep. He kissed her with the desperation that comes with fear: tasting her, breathing in her smell of perfumed soap mixed with traces of campfire smoke. He threaded his fingers through her hair, drawing her closer, pressing her body against his, her warmth chasing away the cold night.

When at last he pulled away, she let out a small moan of disappointment.

"You torture me, Strong," she breathed, settling on the cot beside him. "Does this mean that you missed me too?"

"Missed you?" Merek traced her jawline with his thumb. "I was furious when I heard that Artem had ambushed you like that. I was ready to hunt him down and—" He couldn't give voice to the murderous thoughts he'd had. Not while they still simmered so close to the surface.

"Shh...don't speak of it now. Fear and love are both powerful emotions. Let's forget the one for a moment and think only on the other." She nestled against him, and he noticed for the first time that she was still dressed in the same clothes she'd worn the previous day. Despite Eldar's best intentions, she hadn't yet slept that night either.

He held her for a few quiet moments, feeling a measure of calm for the first time in many hours.

When Ria broke the silence, her voice was tinged with regret. "I'm afraid I did a foolish thing in agreeing to meet Artem in the city. I hope you can forgive me."

"There's nothing to forgive. You warned me that he would have spies in the camp, but I underestimated how much he knew. We played right into his hands, and I'm equally to blame." He reached for her hand resting on his chest and kissed her fingertips gently. "In any case, it may yet be an opportunity. Getting our first look inside the city may tell us what we need to plan an even stronger assault."

Ria looked up at him, her head on his shoulder. "I don't want to talk of assaults tonight. You're safe, and that's all that matters."

Feeling her breath against his ear made it difficult to concentrate. Perhaps he should wait for morning—sleep on his decision before acting. But the emotions stirring within him wouldn't be stilled. He'd already made his choice. With a rightness that he felt as surely as he felt the blood coursing through his veins, he knew that he shouldn't waste one more moment.

"Ria, my beloved, I've decided that you are right. The future queen and king, together as husband and wife, would be a stronger force for Artem to contend with than a princess alone."

Her breath stilled. "What are you saying?"

"I'm saying that I will marry you. Now. Today if you wish. I'll be your husband and face our enemy as the future king, as you wish me to."

To his surprise, she drew back. "No, not like this." She pulled away from him and sat up.

"Not like what?" He raised up on one elbow.

"Not because of him. I don't want you to marry me because of Artem. I don't want you to agree because he pushed you into it. He thinks he has such hold over me. I will not allow him to have any hold over you." Her voice was firm. The tender moment was past.

Resigned, Merek sat up. Ria was still close enough to touch but felt miles away.

"I thought this was what you wanted."

"What I don't want is for you to marry me only as a way to gain leverage over Artem."

Merek stifled a short ironic laugh. "I thought marriage to you was all about leverage and political maneuvering."

He meant to lighten the mood, but he was answered by a faint sigh. "I don't know what I think anymore," Ria said softly. "Artem got into my head tonight, and I can't seem to get him out. Everything comes back to him, and I find myself questioning every emotion. Every decision. Wondering if he's manipulated me into thinking and feeling as I do."

Merek felt an unfamiliar pang of jealousy. He didn't want another man filling her head. His timing was all wrong. They were both tired and strained from the rigors of the night. He should have waited until morning when they could discuss it in daylight, when she could make room in her thoughts for him instead of the prince.

But it was so blasted hard to get any privacy in this camp, and there were certain things he simply didn't want to discuss publicly.

Whatever else, he couldn't end the night without ensuring that she understood what was in his heart. In one last gesture of sincerity, he moved off the cot and knelt before her on the cold, hard earth so he could better look into her eyes. Her hands rested in her lap, and he gently stroked them, marveling at her soft and supple skin.

"Ria, if you don't want to marry me now, I won't pressure you. I'll always honor your choice. But I realized something tonight; I've been selfish. I haven't been willing to take what you offer me because it would mean giving up my simple life. This," he gestured around the tent, "this is a life I know. I'm comfortable with it. I belong. The thought of someday becoming king terrifies me, makes me feel like a fraud. Or rather, it did until tonight. But something happened out there while I was fighting with Orri, and everything changed. I'm ready now. I'm ready to leave behind my old life. I'm ready to marry you, and I'm ready to serve our people at your side."

Ria didn't reply immediately. When she did, there was a smile in her voice. "I always knew I liked Captain Orri." She reached out and fingered his earlobe, her touch sending a pleasant tingle down his spine. "And what about my father?"

"I'm not trying to steal his throne."

"I know you're not, but he expressly forbade our marriage. What do you plan to do about that?"

"I plan to marry you. Here, in this camp. With or

without your father. We can't wait for him to emerge from that tower a whole man. We must act the best we can and hope that all will be well."

"Even if it means committing treason?"

He wasn't sure if she was serious or not. "There's more at stake here than your father's petty grudge. You know it, and I know it. If he condemns me as a traitor, I will fight him as a patriot. I don't think it will come to that, but if it does, I will not submit to his arrest again."

He paused, hesitating to ask the question he dreaded to put into words. "If it comes to that, will you stand by me?"

It was a hard thing to ask. He knew it. But he also knew that he couldn't marry her without knowing where her allegiance lay.

The silence grew long between them. At last, Ria spoke.

"You sound like a king," she said simply.

She slid off the cot and curled up in his lap in one graceful motion. She kissed him gently, a kiss full of promise and longing. "Yes, I will stand by you. Always. Now kiss me one last time before I leave you. Enjoy the solitude because soon you'll have a new bride to entertain during these long winter nights. And I assure you, I will be very demanding."

THE CLOUDLESS SKY REVEALED STARS SO RADIANT THAT they seemed scrubbed fresh from the storm. Reflecting the starlight, the deep snow seemed to glow with its own light, lighting Ria's path back to her tent. In the east toward Endvar, a cold gray light bathed the horizon, indicating that the sky pondered dawn, but the rest of the night was inky black.

Ria entered her tent and found Biren sitting slumped in a chair, blinking wearily as though she had just awakened.

"Have you waited for me all this time?" Ria asked in dismay.

"No, my lady, I just didn't feel like sleeping." Biren straightened and busied herself at the small table. She quickly closed the small chest which held Ria's jewelry and slid the hair brush into place next to it.

"You're as protective as Lotta," Ria chided, but she softened it with a smile. "I was going to let you sleep until morning, but I'm glad you're awake. If I have to contain myself much longer, I'm afraid I will burst into a thousand bubbles of glee."

Biren left her distracted work and stood, all attention focused on Ria. "My lady?"

"We need to plan a wedding, and quickly too; we have only two days."

"Two days?" Biren looked at her blankly. "You mean Strong agreed?"

"Yes! We are to be wed! Right here in camp! In the snow and the mud and with a whole army in attendance." They were the most delicious words she'd ever spoken.

Biren, however, was appalled. "Here? But your father is in Albon. I thought you wished to be married at the Hall."

Ria's joy dimmed at the mention of her father. "There are many things I wished that cannot be. If my father were well, I wouldn't be here in the first place." How would her father react when he learned of the wedding? There would come a reckoning as surely as night follows day, but she couldn't face the awful truth of it now. Not with her head filled with Merek and Artem and war. If they succeeded in driving out the Ardanians, and her father returned to sense, and she and Merek had to stand before him and face his wrath, she would count that day blessed. Because as it was, she couldn't be certain they would even survive the week.

"My lady, I know this may not be the best time to speak of last night, but Prince Artem—"

"Ugh! May we not go even ten minutes together without speaking of that man?"

"Forgive me, I only—"

"It's bad enough that I must live with the knowledge that my future husband only consents to the wedding because of him. I would like to pretend at least for a time that there is more than mere strategy behind his choice. For these next few days I don't wish to speak of Artem or hear his name. I shall have to endure it enough in Merek's tent, but in this tent I want to speak of nothing but the wedding. Is that understood?"

Biren's eyes widened at her sharp tone. Ria regretted her maid's hurt expression, but it passed quickly and Biren nodded.

"Good. Now, let's see if I have anything suitable to wear. What do you think, the wine or the cobalt?" Ria opened her nearest trunk, digging through the carefully packed gowns to find the ones she was looking for.

Biren, to her credit, didn't even flinch at her rough treatment of the fine garments. "It's unfortunate we don't have time to send for wedding silk in Albon."

"White would look stunning against Merek's uniform," Ria agreed. "But under the circumstances, we'll have to make do. What of this?" She pulled from the depths of the trunk a gown of shimmering gold. Trimmed in lace and pearls, it looked almost garish in the humble tent. It was a dress for parties and sparkling chandeliers, and as such hadn't yet seen the light of day in the army camp.

"Dazzling," Biren said.

"But a little too much, don't you think? We're at war, and many of these men have suffered greatly. Would it be a mockery to indulge in such frivolity?"

"It's a wedding. I'm sure they'll forgive any frivolity, perhaps welcome it."

But Ria couldn't help but think of her conversation with Captain Eldar the day before. If there were other men who felt as he did about their commander, the last thing she wanted to do was flaunt her vanity. The gold was out of the question.

"What is this?" In the depths of the trunk, Ria spied a roll of fabric that didn't look like any gown she owned. Her fingers closed around its delicate softness as she pulled it up to the light.

Biren gasped. "My lady, I swear to you I did not pack that in your trunk."

The fabric flowed over Ria's fingers and puddled in her lap with the smoothness of water. Deep emerald green—the last time she'd seen it was when she admired it in the hands of her father. It was the gift from Merek; the peace offering he'd given her father before the king had turned against him.

"Never fear, Biren. I do not suspect you of thievery,

but search these trunks. I don't know what else my poor father may have hidden in them."

As it turned out, there were additional stowaways: a slender white flute and a delicate gold ring set with blood red garnets. Ria recognized it as one that had belonged to her mother. She slipped it on her finger and held it up to the light.

"It's an omen, Biren. A sign that the father I know—not the madman who locked himself in a tower—blesses this union. There will be reconciliation and celebration; I'm certain of it," she said fiercely. "Gather all the tailors in the camp, starting with the one who created the general's uniform. We have two days to turn this unexpected providence into a wedding gown fit for the future queen of Rahm."

Eleven

Night fell earlier in the Dimm Forest than Aiya was used to. The days were far too short, and their progress rebuilding the wall much too slow. She'd been joined by Dan on that first day and by Veln and Marga on the next. Now, one week later, most of the villagers came every day to spend at least a few hours sorting, hauling, or placing stone. Fathers, mothers, older children, even some of the elderly set about digging away the frozen mud to pry out the embedded stone. Children who were too young to work helped care for the littlest ones, and during the busiest part of the day the building site became as noisy as a city market.

But now, as the late afternoon light began to dim, most of the women had already gone home. The few who remained loaded tools into a wagon or hoisted young children onto their backs for the return to the village, where they would work late into the evening doing the chores they'd neglected during the day.

Aiya didn't envy the tiring work that lay before them,

with hungry children and animals clamoring for attention, but she wished to join them all the same. She was weary and wanted somewhere to go where the conversation might help her forget her exhaustion. Bruises peppered her thighs and forearms, and her back protested savagely when she straightened. It would be a comfort to go home to someone with whom she could share her pain and frustration.

Dan had taken to keeping watch with the night guard and sleeping at the guardhouse during the day. It was an ideal arrangement since there was only one cot, but it meant that Aiya spent her long dark nights alone. In those empty hours she missed Imar more than ever and wondered what news of Endvar's fall her brother had received while in Branvik. She wished she could get word to him that she was well and hoped he wasn't distressed for worrying about her.

Watching the women of Haldin sharing one another's burdens with tired smiles made her think fondly of her secret visits with Hala. Behni and Hala had likely returned to Khourin by now. What might their friendship have been if she and Hala hadn't had so many secrets between them?

As Aiya delivered her last load to the wall, the man working there straightened. He smiled at her a little too warmly, revealing a missing tooth, and hurried to take the stone from her hands.

"You've come to the right place. I have just the spot for it right here." He made a slight whistling sound with every 's'. Turning the stone on its side, he hefted it into a v-shaped area that did indeed seem perfectly suited to the stone's shape. The stone made a dull cracking sound as he set it in place. It didn't fit, a slight bulge on one side making it too big.

"Oh," Aiya said in disappointment. "I guess not, then."

"Nonsense! It will fit, it just needs a little help."

He tried to wriggle it into place, straining with the effort. Aiya joined in, watchful of her fingers. But the more they worked the stone into place, the more the neighboring stone shifted out of its spot.

"Perhaps another stone will work better," Aiya suggested when they both paused to catch their breath.

"Try lifting this one instead of sliding it." a familiar voice sounded above her.

Dan jumped down from the wall and reached around Aiya to grab the neighboring stone, lifting it while Aiya and the other man wrestled the new one into place. His arm brushed against her side as she worked, and Aiya felt a flutter of pleasure at his nearness. What had gotten into her? She must indeed be feeling lonely.

It worked. The top stone slid into place, and Dan released his hold on the other so that all three stones locked into place. The man gave a hoot of triumph, and Aiya grinned.

"Beautiful!" the villager said, and then blushed as he caught Aiya's eye.

Dan looked at the two of them, nodded curtly, and turned on his heel without another word.

Aiya watched him go and tried to feign interest in the villager's excited chatter. By the time she extricated herself, Dan was visiting with a soldier, and Aiya hesitated to interrupt. Instead, she helped load the last of the tools for the return trip to the village.

"Just what is your relationship with the sergeant?"

Aiya was surprised by the bold question. The woman who had asked it wore a dark brown headscarf and blew into her chapped hands impatiently to warm them as she waited for Aiya's answer. Aiya had seen her before, but they'd never spoken, so for those to be her first words to Aiya was shockingly rude.

"I only ask because my cousin, Rolan, he favors you." She nodded in the direction of the friendly villager with the whistling smile. "Not sure why he'd take to a foreigner after all these years, but you know men!"

"Excuse me?"

"Oh, he's a fine catch. He's got two wee ones, though. I don't suppose you're any good with children." She eyed Aiya critically. "But he won't go pushing in where he's not wanted, so I told him I'd find out if there's an understanding between you and the sergeant." She sniffed, and in her expression Aiya read a mountain of disapproval.

"There is no understanding," Aiya said, affronted.

"But you're both unmarried?" the woman pried.

Aiya glanced over the woman's shoulder and was horrified to see Dan approaching. The wagon driver hailed him, and he stopped mere feet from where Aiya stood. Aiya wished the woman would pitch her voice lower, but she didn't seem concerned with being overheard.

"I do not see how that concerns you," Aiya said quietly, feeling heat in her face.

The woman smiled carelessly, but she looked disappointed. "Of course, no woman of sense would want a man with only one arm. Not a proper man at all. Rolan, though, he works harder than most and fares well for it. You'd do well to consider him."

Aiya opened her mouth to protest, but the woman was gone before she could form the words, leaving with another loud sniff of disapproval.

Indignation robbed Aiya of speech. She kept her eyes fixed on Dan, watching for any sign that he'd heard the woman's rude comments about him. He didn't acknowledge Aiya, and she knew there was nothing she could say to make it better if he *had* overheard their conversation, so she retreated as quickly as she could to the path that led to the guardhouse.

"Miss Aiya!" Rolan caught up to her before she'd gone far. "Might I walk you home?"

Aiya couldn't look at his kind face without thinking of his prying cousin. "I'm afraid I would be poor company. Thank you, but I'd rather be alone with my thoughts tonight."

"I see. Only it's nearly dark and these woods can be dangerous with bandits about."

The truth was, Rolan did seem like a nice man, and Aiya didn't care to walk in the woods alone. But that was precisely why she couldn't accept his invitation. It wasn't fair to encourage his feelings when she knew that she could never return them. She knew enough of life and love to know that.

"It's not far. I'm sure I can manage. Good night." With that, she stepped into the trees.

She had lingered too long, and the forest was darkening fast. It hadn't snowed in days, and the crusted footprints that remained marked the trail in the dimness. The forest was inhospitable enough during the daylight, full of thick undergrowth and false trails by which an unwary traveler could easily get lost.

But at night, it was downright unnerving.

The towering trees closed in on her, creaking mournfully in a wind she couldn't feel. Shadows shifted in the brush, startling her and causing her to keep a suspicious eye on either side. Never before had she longed with such fervor for the wide open skies of Khourin. The guardhouse wasn't far, but in the twilight it seemed she would never reach it.

A woman's scream split the night, and Aiya froze, holding her breath. Another scream. It came from behind her, back at the gap in the wall. An icy chill crept up her neck. Aiya's first instinct was to flee, but that meant running into the darkness. She didn't want to be alone if there were bandits about. She wanted to be with people. Making a quick decision, she turned around.

Two shadows stepped out of the undergrowth and onto the path. Aiya's stomach clenched with fear. Despite the low light, she knew immediately from their postures that they were not friendly. She turned and sprinted away. The men chased after her, calling out in a language she didn't understand.

Aiya's bulky clothing made running awkward, and the thick undergrowth slowed her, but she ran as she'd never run before. Soon she lost the path but forged ahead anyway, stumbling at a reckless pace over the uneven ground.

In the streets of Endvar, or on the rooftops of her homeland, she would have had no trouble losing these men. Their size alone would have given her an advantage. But the forest slowed her, whereas they seemed comfortable with its treacherous footing. They didn't try to be stealthy, and their crashing through the undergrowth told her they were perilously close. If only she had a rooftop to climb to escape.

Or a tree...

In the last of the fading light, Aiya spotted a fallen tree resting precariously against another, a tall giant of the forest. The angle of the fallen tree was steep, but if she could use it to get to the larger tree's branches, she might find safety in the forest canopy. It was the only chance she had, and she was tiring, moist with sweat beneath her warm layers.

She leaped onto the trunk and ran up the length of the fallen snag. The mossy bark was slick with ice, but she reached the giant tree and heaved herself up onto one of the limbs. She scrambled higher up several more branches, working her way around to the opposite side of the tree. When she thought she'd gone far enough, she risked a glance downward and saw that one of the bandits had reached the tree. He was climbing too.

Aiya cursed. She'd hoped that he would be daunted, but clearly he was as comfortable in the trees as he was racing through the forest. With Aiya's smaller size, she might be able to climb higher than he could, but it would be risky. One wrong move would mean plummeting to her death. And he was closing fast.

There had to be another way.

The trees grew thickly together, their branches overlapping with those of their neighbors. Trying to pretend she was climbing walls and drainpipes in Khourin, Aiya stopped moving upward and began sidling outward on the limb. The forest floor was lost in the darkness beneath her, and she resisted the urge to look down, knowing it was best to focus her eyes ahead. Her heart pounded in her ears as the limb bent with her weight. *Just a little further.*

Shouts sounded below. Aiya tried to ignore their urgent calls and focused instead on the lower branch of the nearest tree. It was unnerving to feel the limb she was on tipping her toward the ground, but learning how to fall correctly was one of the first lessons of climbing.

Now. As the branch bowed low, Aiya released her hold and dropped, arms splayed out to catch the branch of the neighboring tree. But the limb refused to hold her weight, and she fell, scrabbling for a secure hold. Branches whipped her violently. Layer after layer, they slipped through her hands. She panicked, desperately trying to catch hold of something. The sharp needles sliced her skin, and she closed her eyes against the barrage of branches lashing her face.

At last, she struck a limb, knocking the breath from her lungs. Although it bowed dangerously low with her weight, it held in her grasp. Quivering and panting, she opened her eyes. She was still a dangerous distance from the ground. She lowered herself onto a thicker limb below her, then crawled closer to the trunk and paused, catching her breath. In the dim light, she could just make out the bandit in the tree opposite her climbing down at a fast pace. It would take him a few precious minutes to reach her, and by then she would be long gone.

But wait..what was that? Over the pounding of her heart and gasping breath, there was something else. Men grunting with effort, the sound of weapons striking. On the forest floor below, she could just make out a bandit fighting a plainly dressed villager.

She gasped. *Not* a villager! It was Dan, fighting left-handed against the Fehr bandit with his long handled axe.

He'll get himself killed, she thought in despair, as the other bandit dropped to the ground and engaged in the fight. She was both relieved and irritated that Dan had come; grateful that he was distracting her pursuers, but filled with fear that he couldn't defeat them. She started to climb down the tree, then stopped, watching the contest.

He fought like she'd never seen before. It reminded her of the way he'd fought Hala, but then he'd had the benefit of two arms. This. This should not be. He swung his sword as deftly as if he'd been born to it in his left hand. Gone was the awkwardness she'd seen earlier. In its place was a powerful ferocity that left her speechless.

He dispatched the first bandit quickly, and when the other man saw his companion fall, he faltered. His weapon was a large quarterstaff, and he clearly doubted his own abilities against the one-armed soldier dressed like a peasant. After a moment's indecision, he bolted, and Dan gave chase.

Trembling with relief, Aiya lowered herself down the tree. She wasn't in any hurry now and had to be careful with her footing. By the time she dropped to the earth below, Dan had returned, his sword dark with blood.

Words struggled to form in her throat. "You came. How?"

Dan wiped his sword clean before sheathing it and looking her over with concern. "Are you hurt? I saw you fall. I thought—"

"No, I didn't fall. I jumped. It looks much the same." She gave a half smile and found that her face hurt a great deal. She must look as if she'd battled one of the strange forest creatures with the sharp spines that she'd been warned about.

"Jumped? From the top of a tree?" he asked incredulously.

"It was either that or find out what two Fehr bandits do with a Khouri woman half their size once they catch her. But how did you know to come?"

Dan's eyes were bright from the heat of battle, but he avoided meeting her gaze. "When the bandits attacked, I searched for you, knowing you didn't have time to get safely back to the guardhouse. They are either more desperate or more bold, coming before nightfall like this."

"You searched for me?"

"I heard you scream, and it led me here, but I didn't see you in the tree until you fell." He shuddered at the memory.

Aiya wanted him to reach out to her. To hold her. She wanted to relax against him and feel safe in a way that she hadn't for many years. But that was not for her to do. All she needed was a sign from him, one touch, and she would tell him how she felt. But instead, he searched the fallen Fehr bandit and shouldered the axe.

"It probably belongs to someone we know."

Cold with disappointment, Aiya followed him back through the forest, but not in the direction of the guardhouse. They came out of the trees to find a small house with lights in the window and figures herding pigs and sheep back into their enclosures. The bandits had been here too.

"This is Marga and Halth's place," Dan explained. "I'm going to ask if you can stay here instead."

"No, you can't! I can't impose on them! I will be well enough at the guardhouse."

Dan turned and looked her squarely in the eye for the first time. "It's not safe for you there. Why were those men following you? I don't like it. It may have been a coincidence. Or someone may have known you would be there."

The thought sent a shiver down her spine. Suddenly, she very much wanted to stay in the warmly lit cottage. "But what about you?"

Dan shrugged. "I'll be fine. I'm only there during the day. No one will bother me."

He turned and walked across the yard before she could argue further. They welcomed her readily, the women ushering her inside and fussing over her scrapes and bruises. In truth, there was something wonderfully comforting about being surrounded by the hustle and bustle of an active family—even one that was burdened with worries of bandits and the unspoken fear of how they would make it through winter if the raids didn't stop soon.

Twelve

Yulda moved with the crowd of spectators down the hillside. Soldiers and civilians milled about excitedly as if it were a holiday. And why not? Shouldn't a royal wedding be a holiday?

The flowing mass of people slowed to a standstill, blocking her way, but unlike the families and small units of soldiers, Yulda only had to worry about herself. She squeezed her way through the crowd a little further until she wedged herself between two women with a gaggle of children between them. Here she had a good view of the proceedings below.

Not that there was much to see. A simple canopy had been erected in the center of the meadow, strung with garlands of evergreen boughs. There stood the priest, a paunchy man of middling years who looked as if he'd wandered onto a theater stage and couldn't quite remember his lines. Yulda smirked as she thought of how the priests in the fine Albon churches would fume when they learned of what was happening today. A royal wedding taking place in the humble field of an army camp? Such sacrilege!

All the camp was abuzz with the news, speculation running like wildfire about why the hasty wedding. The less imaginative tales proposed an unexpected pregnancy, but Yulda scoffed at that. The princess was young and beautiful and had the frustrating ability to command the attention of every man, no matter his age or station. But the general didn't seem to be the sort of man who would forget himself like that.

Unless, of course, the child wasn't his and he was marrying her quickly to divert knowledge of the true father. Now *that* would be worthy of gossip.

Yulda scanned the canopy and found Rorden dressed in his nicest uniform and looking even more handsome than usual. Next to him was the lovely princess's maid, who wore a simple gown of pale blue with very little ornamentation. She seemed thinner than when she'd first come to camp but still managed to make it look elegant. Rorden shot her a covert glance, and she smiled weakly.

Yulda frowned. *What is it with men who see only a pretty face?* She knew she wasn't pretty, not like the maid or the princess. But Manni, the surgeon, had said she had wit and that was better than beauty. He said he wouldn't have taken her on without it, and he wouldn't have kept her on if she didn't work harder than any soldier.

Unfortunately, most men didn't appreciate hard work and cleverness when there was a pretty face to distract them. Even the general himself—a man of uncommon wisdom—had chosen to marry a spoiled princess a dozen years younger than himself. Was there no justice in this world?

But—Yulda smiled to herself—she had a secret. The general needed *her*. When Rorden had come to her and said she was needed to lead a troop of men back into the city through the tunnels, she'd sworn and thrown a heavy pestle at his head. However later, in the general's tent, when Strong looked at her in his calm way with his penetrating gray eyes that really seemed to *see* her, she'd agreed. And now, she knew things that almost no one else in camp knew. Dangerous things. Things that would get people killed. Even Captain Eldar, whose troops she would be leading through the tunnels, had only a vague idea of how they would be getting into the city. She alone knew the truth.

A collective murmur rose from the crowd. The princess's carriage was approaching. A carriage! While the rest of them walked! It's not as though she were wearing a fine gown that she didn't want to spoil. Yulda had heard some of the women in camp talking about it. There'd been no time to have a proper wedding gown made, nor even to send word to Albon for a suitable substitute, so the princess was going to be married in a hastily constructed garment of dubious origin.

General Strong emerged from the carriage first, then turned to take the Princess Honoria's hand and escort her down the steps. Yulda was unimpressed. All that fuss over a dress, and then it was covered by a heavy fur cloak anyway.

As the general and the princess approached the canopy, Yulda fidgeted. The day was chilly, but not as cold as a few days earlier when they'd had snow, though patches of it still remained. The rest of the ground was soft, and the princess stepped gingerly, avoiding the droppings left by the meadow's previous residents.

The priest's voice came to Yulda on snatches in the breeze, but most of the ceremony was lost to her. Far more interesting was the smell of bacon that drifted over from the direction of the camp. Bacon! Where had they managed to find bacon? She supposed it wasn't as fine as the wedding of a princess should dictate, but it smelled like a king's feast to her after weeks of turnip soup and shriveled apples. Too bad she wouldn't get to taste it. Even if she'd been invited to the private celebration, she and Captain Eldar planned to leave as soon as the ceremony ended. There was no time to waste if they were to be in place in time.

Yulda wished Aiya and Dan could join her. She missed her friends and would have enjoyed their company. Because of the secretive nature of her mission, she was required to speak as little as possible to Captain Eldar and his men, lest she share a clue to their route or final destination. Not that it was hard. It was much easier keeping people at a distance than trying to impress them by pretending to be interesting.

The crowd let out a whoop and a roar of applause, and Yulda realized it was over. The general and princess were kissing. Despite her ambivalence about the wedding, she watched the kiss with a kind of detached envy.

What would it like to be kissed? *Really* kissed. She didn't count the panicked kiss she'd given Rorden in Lord Bolen's kitchen when they were about to be discovered by Master Domar. Nor did she count the awkward smashing of lips a stablehand had given her one morning before sunrise when they were the only two in the yard. She meant *this,* a real kiss. She watched the way the general lifted the princess's chin with one hand while the other slipped around her waist and held the small of her back. Tender-like. As if they were the only ones in the world.

Yulda sighed.

She hadn't realized it until the woman next to her chuckled.

"Aye. It's about like that, isn't it?"

"I don't know what you mean." Yulda ducked her head to hide her blushing cheeks.

The older woman winked. "I've six grandkids and a husband of my own, and I'm still dreaming of the day when he holds me like that."

She laughed cheerily and moved past Yulda into the crowd before Yulda's protest could fully form on her tongue.

Yulda watched her go. The wedding was over. It was time to get to work.

Thirteen

An anguished cry brought Aiya roughly out of her sleep. Her first thought was of Imar, and she momentarily imagined herself back in the rooms they'd shared in Endvar. In a heartbeat she remembered where she was and sat up, looking for Dan. Clouds dimmed the moon and stars, but the snow that covered the ground glowed faintly, highlighting a dark figure moving away from the small rock hollow where they'd sheltered for the night.

Aiya let him go. She knew from her own experience that she couldn't give him the comfort he sought. It had been years since the darkness had brought demons to torment her, but she remembered well those haunting nights that seemed to last forever. Dawn couldn't come soon enough.

She was still awake when Dan returned. He moved quietly, but she sensed him crawling into his blanket all the same. She waited until he stilled, then said gently, "It might help if you speak of it. The more you bury it, the more its power grows."

Silence. Had she spoken too softly? Was his mind so far away from her that he couldn't hear her at all?

She pushed herself up on one elbow and tried to make out his form in the dark. He lay unblinking, staring into nothingness. Aiya crawled out of her bedroll and moved to his side, but before she could touch him, a rustle sounded not far from the wide entrance of the grotto.

Dan sprang into action. He jumped to his feet in a crouch, pushing Aiya aside as he planted himself between her and the entrance. Aiya squeaked in surprise, falling to the ground and scraping her elbow against a rock.

"Shh! There's someone there," Dan spoke in a hoarse whisper.

Aiya's heart raced. She listened, but heard nothing over the blood pounding in her ears.

"I think it was just the horses," she whispered. She reached out and touched Dan's shoulder. It was taut with tension.

"Stay here, out of sight."

He was gone only a few moments, but it was long enough for Aiya to marvel at how quickly he'd moved to place himself between her and danger. It filled her with awe and emboldened her. When he returned, his tone was apologetic.

"It was nothing. Just the horses, as you said. Are you alright? I'm sorry if I frightened you."

He reached out his one hand to her and Aiya grasped it, her heart pounding.

"I'm not frightened with you. I could never be."

Her own daring surprised her.

Dan stiffened. "You should be frightened. I frighten myself sometimes."

"Tell me," Aiya insisted. "Tell me what dreams haunt you in the night. Name them. Steal their power."

"I can't," he hissed, pulling his hand away. "Not to you. I can't burden you with...no. I won't."

He grabbed his blanket and moved to the entrance of the grotto. There he sat, a stoic silhouette against the pale snow, his shape made bulky by the blanket around his shoulders. Clearly he had no intention of sleeping. Aiya wondered how many nights he'd spent like this. How did he find the strength to keep going every day after fighting such exhausting battles each night?

Aiya wrapped her own blanket around her shoulders and moved to the entrance. She sat against him, her back leaning against his. At first he sat rigidly, but after a time, he relaxed into her. She couldn't see his face, but she felt his warmth against her back. It was easier to speak that way.

"You know that I lost a husband before I came to your country," Aiya began. "I didn't tell you that I also lost a daughter. My own kinsmen came to my home and murdered them in front of me. Only my brother and I survived, and we had to flee with nothing but the clothes on our backs." She paused, but he gave no response. She wasn't sure he even listened. But it felt good to say the words, so she went on.

"I know a little about nightmares. I know of the terror that descends when the sun goes down. Seeing things in shadows that aren't there. Hearing footsteps or the sound of breaking glass..." She trailed off, the memories fresh again in her mind.

When Dan spoke, she felt it as a rumble against her back. "They came for us, not long after you left. We tried to hide, to run, but they had lanterns and dogs—mean things that would tear a man's throat out. A few of the Ardanians thought it was great sport to let the dogs off their chains to chase us in the tunnels. The wounded fell first, giving the rest of us a chance to escape while the dogs fed."

Aiya shivered and pulled the blanket tighter around her.

"Jax fell behind. I turned back to help, but the dogs got to him. They went for his face, until a soldier plunged his sword into his stomach and ripped it open, like opening a sack of grain. Do you know how long it takes a man to die when he's being eaten from the inside out?"

In the dark, Aiya could too easily picture herself being back in the nightmarish tunnels and felt as if she were going to be sick. Wetting her lips, she asked, "And you saw this? How did they not find you too?"

"They did. They found us all. But they'd come into the tunnels looking for survivors. They needed some of us alive. I was one of the lucky ones," he said with bitter irony.

Aiya wished to comfort him in some way, but his pain seemed unreachable. All she could do was listen. She leaned her head back and rested it in the hollow between his shoulder blades.

They'd left Haldin the day before, laden with gifts of gratitude and two sturdy farm horses to make the journey back to the army camp. Now Aiya questioned the wisdom of that decision. Dan had been more himself in the forest village. Turning toward Endvar brought a resurgence of the gloom he'd shouldered when they'd first left the camp.

"I'm very sorry about Jax and the others, but is it selfish of me to be glad you survived? For days I feared that you were lost. When I heard that you were the soldier who returned with Captain Strong, I could scarcely believe it. It was as if all the grief were instantly changed to joy, and as I had before staggered under the weight, now I couldn't keep my feet on the earth." So easily these words flew from her tongue under cover of darkness!

"Was that before or after you learned that I returned half the man I was before?"

"Nonsense. I don't know of anyone who could have faced down those bandits the way you did. You don't need two arms when you already have the courage and strength of two men."

He grunted. "If only I could believe that."

"Why shouldn't you? I've known men of strength and men of character. Rarely have I met a man with both."

"But how can you say those things when you've seen me at my weakest?"

Aiya moved around to sit by his left side, hooking her right arm in his and resting her head on his shoulder. He shifted slightly to accommodate her weight. "How can anyone truly know another's strength until they've seen them at their weakest? When we cannot pretend to be anything else than what we really are, that is when we discover our true strength."

Dan said nothing more for a long time, but he

squeezed her hand, and Aiya felt an inner warmth that stayed with her long after she fell asleep.

THE FOLLOWING DAY DAN WAS CALM AND GOOD-humored, but Aiya sensed the agitation settling in again as the light faded. She sat by his side that night as he unburdened himself by sharing details of his capture and imprisonment. As she listened, she wished the dark of winter didn't last so long.

"I think your cousin is dead," he said unexpectedly.

"What's that?"

"There was a man, a Khouri man. Every few days he came to look us over and then picked one to go with him. Those who left never came back, but we heard their screams. We all vowed that if we were chosen, we wouldn't scream. We wouldn't torment those left behind. But they always did."

A long silence followed this statement. Aiya felt his terror as thick as a shroud.

"Why do you say my cousin is dead? The Khouri man?"

Dan didn't answer right away. When he did, his voice sounded hollow.

"He picked me."

Aiya drew a quick breath.

"That last time, he chose me. But another man had come with him, and he disagreed with his choice. I couldn't understand their argument, but I saw that they hated each other. The angrier the Khouri man got, the more the other man smiled. Finally, the guards took the

Khouri man away instead. They forgot all about me. We didn't see the Khouri man again. The next morning, the pale man ordered us all taken to the city wall to be killed by our own army."

He fell silent, and Aiya didn't press him to continue, but she wondered; could it be true? She'd assumed that Behni and Hala had returned to Khourin. What would become of Hala and the children if Behni was dead?

Exhaustion finally got the better of Dan in the early morning hours, but he slept fitfully, waking frequently with Aiya at his side, holding his hand.

In the morning, Aiya felt as if she'd drunk a whole barrel of forest grog the night before. Her movements were slow and painful, and her head pounded incessantly. But the night took its toll in other ways as well. The horrors of Dan's tales clung to her even in daylight. By the time the third day waned, she too searched the darkening shadows anxiously, starting at unexpected sounds or movement.

Whether Dan had seen how worn Aiya was becoming or had said all he needed to about those days, the next night he chose not to speak of them. Instead, he asked her questions about her own past, and she found herself telling him what it was like to make a new life in the thrilling and frightening city of Endvar.

"You really must see more of the country someday," Dan said. They sat together in a small makeshift shelter of evergreen boughs like the one he'd made on their first night, his arm draped comfortably over her shoulder. "Endvar is a fine city, but Albon is the crown jewel of Rahm. It's said that all the poor wear shoes and have full bellies."

Aiya snorted her disbelief.

"It's an exaggeration, of course, but I've seen myself that there's a difference. King Danvir's ideals of educating commoners and teaching all a trade were best implemented in his own city. In the further reaches of the kingdom, not all have caught the vision. But in Albon, there's a sense of purpose and industry that drives the heart of the whole country."

It all sounded like a fairy story to Aiya, but she didn't want to argue with him. "I should like to see it myself. Will you take me?"

She felt Dan shift against her. He looked down at her, and the light from the campfire brightened his eyes.

"If you'd like," he said, "perhaps I shall."

Fourteen

Ria decided she rather liked sharing her bed with a husband. The winter cold didn't seem so invasive with his warmth near her. And in the deep hours of the night when Merek wrapped one arm around her and Ria curled up close to him, a feeling of perfect contentment melted away the dirty reality of camp life. Then, she felt like the luckiest woman in the world.

Unfortunately, she couldn't enjoy that feeling for long. Well before dawn, Merek would inevitably awaken and return to the command tent, their shared pallet bed growing cold in his absence. Ria would awaken hours later, alone in the cold gray light of morning, cursing the war and what it required of a new bride.

On the morning of Artem's party, Ria didn't rush to the command tent as she had on other mornings. Instead, she sat in her tent in front of the looking glass, trying to determine if Artem would be able to read her emotions. Nervousness, that was to be expected. Dread of seeing Artem, that was also understandable.

But the need, that deep yearning—*that* she must find a way to hide. Only married a few days and already she wondered how she'd gotten along without Merek before. She'd sought strength in their union, but instead she only felt more vulnerable. She felt incomplete without him, missing him keenly when he wasn't around. But worst of all was the fear. If she'd feared for him the night Artem threatened his life, that was nothing compared to how she felt now. More than anyone she'd ever loved, she feared losing *him.* It was astonishing how marriage seemed to have intensified her love for him almost overnight.

Fortunately, there'd been no skirmishes while both armies marked the calendar to Artem's gathering. Just the thought of sending Merek to battle made her feel weak.

And how do you think the other soldiers' wives feel? she chided herself, raising a taunting eyebrow at her reflection. "Your first experience with mature love has proven how childish you really are," she muttered. Selfish, even. And that was something a queen of Rahm could never be.

Biren moved quietly about her work, laying out the lovely gown of emerald green trimmed in white and gold. It was the same gown that Ria had worn to be wed, constructed furiously by Merek's tailor who had earned her undying gratitude for his masterpiece. The man's seamstresses had found a jeweler in the market that had a "not completely useless" inventory of beads and gems. They'd not slept the night before the wedding, instead spending the hours sewing a remarkable cascade of tiny pearls and gold beads to enhance the fitted bodice. The full skirt fell away from her hips in artful tucks that accentuated her waistline to perfection. Lotta would have said the wide curving neckline was impractical for a winter wedding, but Ria thought the advantage to her figure was worth the extra cold.

The tailor had despaired that there'd been no time for anything else, until Ria had assured him that he would have many opportunities to prove his talents in the future. A position at court was his if he wished it, but this gown would not be altered. It would stand forever the way it was when she wore it under the canopy three days earlier.

She ran her hand over the smooth silk and traced the beadwork, thinking warmly of Merek's expression when he'd seen her in the gown. "I can't do it. Bring me the gold one instead."

"Are you certain, my lady? You said yourself that you promised the prince a new gown."

"Then he'll have to be disappointed. It feels like a desecration to wear my wedding dress before that devil. I won't give him the satisfaction."

"He doesn't have to know you were wed in it."

"Oh, he will know; you can be sure of that. He'll know what I wore and what we ate and at what point in the evening we retired. If he had had a way of posting a spy inside my tent to get a report on the wedding night, he would have done that too. The man has no scruples." Ria couldn't resist glancing over Biren's shoulder as if she expected to find a figure hidden in shadow, but the room was empty save for the two women.

Biren, too, looked nervous as she moved to retrieve the gold gown from Ria's trunk. She shook it gently to loosen the wrinkles—no time to air it properly before wearing—and slipped it over Ria's shift. As she worked the stays, Ria sensed the tension in her movements.

"Biren, don't be afraid. We will be safe; I swear it," Ria said with more conviction than she felt. "Artem has promised it, and Strong guarantees it. We won't be harmed. This is a diplomatic meeting, not a hostile conflict. I wouldn't be going if I thought there was any real danger."

Biren didn't respond. Indeed, she struggled even to meet Ria's eyes in the looking glass as she set to work styling her hair.

"My lady," a soldier called at the tent door. "There's a message from the general. He requests your presence in the command tent."

Ria watched Biren with concern. "Come, Biren. Out with it. You look as though Death himself is whispering in your ear. What's the trouble?"

Biren glanced at the tent door and licked her lips as if gathering great courage. "I don't think it's wise for me to attend you tonight, my lady."

"My lady?" the soldier's muffled voice called again. "May I tell him when I can expect you?"

Ria didn't take her eyes off her maid. "Tell the general that I'm sleeping soundly, and if he wants to come rouse me himself, he's welcome to do it."

When the guard's footsteps receded, Ria attempted a smile. "You're a fine and courageous companion, Biren. I have no doubt that you will act with grace and poise in the presence of the enemy.

Don't let this fear overcome the steadiness of your heart."

A look of anguish crossed Biren's features, and a sound like a sob choked in her throat. "Forgive me, my lady. I cannot. I would gladly face danger for you. Surely you know this. It's not for myself that I fear but for you."

"What do you mean?" Ria tried to keep her tone light, but she felt a cold dread creeping through her middle. "Why should you fear for me?"

"Please don't be angry. I should have spoken to you sooner, but there's been so much going on with the wedding—"

"Tell me now, Biren. It cannot be worse than I'm imagining." Ria had never seen Biren so discomposed.

Biren went to her own trunk and slipped her hand beneath the layers of garments. She withdrew something hidden, wrapped in a scarf. "Whatever evil you may face, I couldn't bear if it came at my hand."

As the cloth fell away, Ria stiffened. Biren held a packet of letters addressed in a graceful hand that Ria immediately recognized.

"What is this?" Ria's spine went rigid.

Biren struggled to meet her eyes. "He's been writing me this past year. Ever since we passed through Rellana on our return from your foreign tour. It seemed so innocent. He seemed so lonely—"

The words sickened Ria. "Oh, Biren. What have you done?"

"I didn't mean any harm. I thought he cared for me—"

"Cared for you? The man is a lying bastard! The only person he loves is himself. Everything he does is for his own gain!"

"I know!" Biren cried, her eyes wide with pain. "I see him now for what he really is. I was a fool and never meant to put anyone in danger—"

"*You* told him about the soldiers hidden in the woods?"

Biren shrank from her anger. "I don't know! I never meant to. You must believe me! He has spies here, people working in camp who would pass letters to Rezon."

Ria remembered the Ardanian soldier who had helped her escape from the enemy camp when she and Brandel had been captured. No wonder he had claimed to know Biren so well. Her face warmed with anger.

"How could you, Biren? You who knew what he was?"

Biren looked away helplessly, wiping at her nose with a trembling hand. "I can't say how it happened. He was always kind to me. I thought maybe you misunderstood him. At first it seemed he just needed a friend, someone to help him through his lonely marriage. By the time I learned that he was behind the attack on Endvar, I was so confused and didn't know what to do. He seemed so genuine. He seemed to really need me. I know, it sounds pitiful now."

"Pitiful? Soldiers died! Merek was almost captured!" Ria wanted to shout but checked her anger. After all, didn't she carry Brandel's blood on her hands? Lowering her voice, she asked, "Why didn't you tell me earlier?"

"I thought...I thought you might be jealous." Biren's complexion reddened. "And then I realized what a fool I'd been, and I was so ashamed. I didn't know how to say the words. But I can't go there today; I can't. I can't face him because I can't risk putting you in danger. Whatever he has planned for me, I know it will only hurt you."

"Noble words, Biren," Ria said icily, "but if you truly cared about me you would have told me long before now. Guard!"

In seconds, a soldier entered the tent looking alert.

"What is your name, soldier?"

"Corporal Osten, Your Highness."

"Osten, place Biren under guard."

"My lady!" Biren flushed darker. "Please! I swear I meant no harm!"

"No more. You will tell your tale to Strong. You've done far more damage than I can bear to hear alone."

"SERGEANT! AIYA! YOU ARE MOST WELCOME! THIS SNOW made me fear we wouldn't see you again until spring."

"These are strange times, sir, for nature to be working against us in this way." Dan saluted Merek comfortably with his left hand, with a confidence that he hadn't worn when he'd left some weeks before.

"Ten years I've lived in Endvar and never seen snow like this." Aiya, too, seemed changed. She was still dressed as a lad, but her eyes held bright promise, and her smile seemed less guarded.

Merek ushered them both into his tent and ordered a serving maid to bring steaming porridge and biscuits. His joy at seeing them was fueled by gratitude. Gratitude that, thanks to their efforts, Stefan's men were positioned to attack the northern gate in the event they needed an escape route out of the city. And gratitude that their timely arrival allowed him to think about something else at the moment than contingencies for the day ahead.

Ria's safety was his greatest concern. Despite all they'd done to prepare, there was still so much that could go wrong. Perhaps Eldar's men hadn't reached the tunnels in time or had met with resistance. Even if they were safely in place, they were a small enough force that they couldn't hope to overwhelm the Ardanians. If combat became necessary, it would require a wild push to get Ria to safety with disastrous losses on Eldar's side. Their best hope was to avoid conflict altogether.

In spite of all the risks, Merek was glad they were going. He was anxious to see the city for himself and gain a sense of how troops were operating within its walls. This farce of a diplomatic meeting might just provide the opportunity he needed to plan an assault on the city directly. He needed an insider's perspective, and with any luck he would have it before the night was over.

But there were too many hours of waiting ahead. It was barely daylight, and they wouldn't depart for Endvar until the afternoon. Dan and Aiya's arrival was a godsend. Hearing news from home improved his mood considerably. He didn't even mind when the messenger returned with Ria's rebuff, though her words drew startled glances from his guests.

"We were married three days past," he explained, which solicited a barrage of congratulatory wishes and tales of how the villagers in Haldin received the news of his betrothal.

"Your mother and Marga will be sorry to have missed it," Aiya said, "but your mother didn't seem surprised as did the others. I think she will understand."

This brought a smile, though Merek didn't need such reassurance. His marriage was only three days old, and already he knew it was the most perfect decision he had ever made. The intensity of his feelings for his new bride scared him sometimes, and it took great effort to set them aside and think strategically. But never did he wonder if they'd acted too hastily. Indeed, if anything, he regretted that they hadn't wed sooner.

When Ria arrived at the command tent, she was resplendent in a gown of shimmering gold. Pearls dripped like snowflakes in her brown hair and rested in tiers against her throat. Only her boots looked out of place, more suited to navigating the crusted snow than the fine slippers that should have accompanied such a brilliant gown. Merek wondered if he would ever get accustomed to thinking of her as his wife without feeling a sense of awe.

But Ria was not in the mood to be admired.

"Clear the tent!" she demanded.

"Ria?"

"Now!"

Merek nodded to the servants, and they retreated obediently.

"Give us a moment," he said apologetically to Aiya and Dan, "but stay close. I wish to hear the rest of your tale."

Rorden moved as if to follow them.

"Rorden, you stay. You need to hear this," Ria said darkly. "Bring her in, Osten."

A soldier entered the tent with Biren at his side. It took only a moment to see that his posture was stiff and defensive as if guarding against a threat.

"Biren?" Rorden asked warily.

"Tell them," Ria said. Merek had never heard her speak to the young woman in such a cold way.

Biren looked up at him, her freckled face pale with pink splotches on her cheeks. Then she looked at the floor as if she couldn't bear to lift her eyes. She clutched a packet of letters.

"I've been writing to Prince Artem this past year."

"*What?*" Rorden choked.

"Rorden!" Merek warned. "Let her speak."

Biren glanced at Rorden and looked away. She kept her voice calm, but the trembling of her hands showed that it was only through great effort.

"I thought he was looking for companionship, but he was playing on my sympathies to get information about my mistress."

Merek chanced a look at Ria. Her eyes held barely disguised rage. "What information did you offer?" he asked.

"Nothing! At least, not that I meant to. I suppose I probably shared more than I should have. I didn't know that he was behind the attack on Endvar. Our letters were more of a personal nature."

"Meaning?"

"He spoke of his father. His brother. His marriage. How unhappy he was. In turn, I shared things in confidence—"

"What sort of things?"

Biren looked down at the floor. "My own childhood. My service to the princess. My hopes for the future."

"Did any of these things divulge information that could have compromised the princess's safety?" Merek asked, keeping his voice measured despite feeling anxious to uncover the full nature of her betrayal. This was grave news to receive mere hours before meeting their enemy.

Rorden fidgeted close by.

"I didn't think so at the time," Biren said, meeting his eyes with a pleading expression. "But when Artem didn't appear at the designated meeting place, I remembered sharing information about the camp. Innocent things, humorous little stories and such. But if taken together with whatever his other spies had fed him, I might have given him more information than I'd planned."

"Such as?"

"Captain Eldar teaching my mistress defensive lessons. How I hoped to return to Albon before midwinter. Nothing intentionally duplicitous because I thought he was trustworthy. You can read his letters for yourself, but I don't have copies of my own replies."

"Why tell us this now?"

Biren glanced at Ria, and regret echoed painfully in her voice. "The night that he came here, I realized what a fool I'd been. When I saw him in the tent, he didn't even acknowledge me. Always everything had been about my mistress. I knew that whatever he had planned, it would only do her harm. I wanted to tell her Highness then, but there never seemed to be the right time. With the wedding and afterward—"

"Are you in love with him?" Rorden demanded, and Merek cringed at the anguish in his voice.

"Rorden—" Merek began, but Biren hastened to answer.

"No!" She said desperately, looking at Rorden. "Not

really. I felt needed. Wanted. Special. But it was a lie. How could I love a lie?"

Finally, Ria spoke. Her voice was hard, but her dark eyes were wounded. "She can't come with us today."

"No, of course not. Rorden, take the letters. You and Eldar will scour them for information and intent."

Biren flushed as she handed the letters to Rorden, and he too looked as if the act pained him.

Merek tried to keep his voice dispassionate. It would do no good to rail at the girl. "Biren, is there anything else you haven't shared? Anything we need to be aware of before we go to the city today?"

With a desperate look at her mistress, Biren answered, "Nothing. I haven't written to him since the night he came to the camp. He, too, has been silent. It is over."

"And the others in the prince's employ?"

"I know of two. A farrier named Ren and a girl who works in the armory. Ana, I think, is her name."

"The silversmith's daughter?" Rorden blurted in surprise.

"Do you know her?" Merek asked.

Rorden colored. "Only a bit."

"Corporal," Merek said, addressing the soldier who'd watched the exchange. "Sergeant Dan is waiting outside. Take him and discreetly find these two individuals. I don't want them catching wind of what's happened here and disappearing before we can find them."

Osten looked to Ria for confirmation. "Go," she agreed. "Biren will be under our watch."

He stepped out of the tent, and Biren sank to a chair, looking defeated and worn. Rorden watched her with such a dark look that Merek felt a twinge of sympathy for the young woman.

"Do you believe she's telling the truth?" he asked Ria quietly.

Ria looked at Biren with a mixture of hatred and sorrow. "How can I say? I thought I knew her. I thought that she…Merek, I'm so sorry."

"You? You have no fault here."

"My own maid was conspiring with our enemy under my very nose, and I didn't know. How can I not feel responsible? When I think of what almost happened to you—"

"It's done, Ria. And if her story is true, she wasn't exactly conspiring. She was foolish and secretive but didn't have ill intent."

"I can never trust her again."

"No. No, you cannot."

Ria's shoulders shrank a little. "Never mind that now. I'll deal with Biren later. We need to focus on meeting Artem today. I have no other attendants here who could fill her place, and without a lady to attend me, Artem may provide his own out of courtesy."

"I'm sure he would be more than happy to oblige," Merek said with exasperation.

"Unless you bring your own attendant after all."

They turned. Neither had realized Aiya had entered the tent.

She didn't waste time apologizing for intruding. "Bring someone who hasn't been targeted by the Ardanian prince, someone completely unknown to him."

Merek understood first.

"You suggest yourself?"

Aiya nodded.

"You can't mean that," Rorden objected, joining them. "You would go back into that city where you barely escaped with your life?"

"I want to help. I'm finished with cowering. In the forest Dan reminded me how to fight, and I'm not afraid to do this." Aiya turned to Ria. "Your Highness, it has been some time since I've acted a noble part, and never here in this country. If I might be permitted to spend an hour with your maid, it would be useful to ask her some questions."

Ria took in Aiya's appearance with her filthy boyish clothing. "You are a Khouri woman attending a Rahmish princess. There will be questions, and you will be under far greater scrutiny than a Rahmish maid," she said dubiously. "And Biren is taller than you. Her gowns will not fit."

Aiya smiled. "Do not worry, I know a few tricks to fix that. You spent time in my country, did you not? It's not unreasonable to think that you agreed to bring back the daughter of a rich minister or count to train in your court. Perhaps the niece of the ambassador?"

Ria fingered the pearls at her neck thoughtfully. "You're known in the camp. His spies will spot the trick."

"His spies won't have time to send word," Merek interjected. "By the time they inform the prince of her true identity, she'll be far away from him."

"I still don't think this is wise," Rorden protested.

Ria raised a hand to silence him, holding Aiya's gaze. "Your knowledge of our language is too good for one only recently come to Rahm. If you speak, the lie will be obvious."

"Leave it to me. I 'member how hard speak Rahmish," Aiya said with a thick Khouri accent.

Merek nodded to Ria. "With an accent like that, the prince will have to reconsider her usefulness. She won't be a target for his schemes."

Ria seemed satisfied. "Well, Aiya, it seems that we have work to do. A bath first, I think." Ria kissed Merek's cheek in parting, and in her brief touch, he sensed the desperate fear that she struggled to keep at bay. A part of him yearned to take her far away and shield her from any threat of danger or evil. But that wasn't his place. Instead, he would stand with her and either conquer or fall together.

These were dark thoughts to have today of all days.

Four hours more.

FIFTEEN

"It's true, then? You are coming with us?" Aiya asked, her words clipped short with irritation.

Dan hesitated briefly but didn't take his eyes off his warped reflection in the tarnished brass plate. The rough scrape of blade against stubble continued rhythmically.

Aiya's worry colored her tone, but she couldn't help it. "You might be able to pass for an Ardanian without a beard, but having only one arm is going to attract attention."

"And you think you'll be less obvious with your dark skin?"

"Why didn't you tell them no?"

"Why didn't you?"

"That isn't an answer."

"Are you scolding me now?" Still he didn't take his eyes off his reflection.

"You can't go into the tunnels, not after what happened there," Aiya pleaded. "You know this as well as

I. I have half a mind to go tell General Strong myself. To tell him about the nightmares, what they did to you."

"I'll do what needs to be done. The general needs someone to contact Captain Eldar in the tunnels, and I'm the only one besides Rorden who has been there."

"So let them send Rorden!"

Dan gingerly felt at his neck for missed patches, then wiped the long razor clean and ran the dirty rag over his face. "Apparently he's met the prince. He'll notice if Rorden is missing. At least I'm not going into the enemy's lair—" He turned, and his words died on his lips as he took in Aiya's appearance.

Aiya blushed at his expression. "What's the matter? After all the time we've spent together, did you forget I was a woman?"

"Forget? Never. But you don't have to bludgeon me with it, do you?"

Aiya smiled weakly. "I think I did a fine job with the gown myself, but the princess just sniffed and said, 'Not bad. The bodice works nicely, but that hemline is a disgrace. Let's hope your pretty face is distraction enough to pull it off.'"

Dan snorted. "Trust me, the prince won't spare a glance for your hemline."

"Then you prefer it over the trousers?" The borrowed gown she wore felt heavy and clumsy. It wasn't made of the thin silks common in her country, nor was it the simple linen of a shopkeeper as she'd worn in Endvar. It was layer upon layer of shining plum-colored taffeta that made her feel ill at ease with the stares and whistles she received while walking through the camp.

Dan muttered a curse under his breath and shook his

head. "That dress makes you look like something out of a dream...a really good dream like the kind they say men have as they lay down their lives to die." He reached for his discarded uniform coat and draped it around his right shoulder before slipping his left arm through the sleeve.

"Oh." It was the strangest compliment she'd ever received, but in Dan's way, she suspected it was also the most sincere. She watched him fumble with the buttons of his coat and stepped closer to help him.

"I can manage," he grumbled, glancing at a soldier who stared openly at Aiya as he passed.

"Haven't you noticed? I'm a maid now with official dressing duties."

"For a princess, not a one-armed soldier." But Dan dropped his hand and allowed Aiya to fasten the coat. She took her time, enjoying the opportunity to be near him and the blush that crept up his neck at her touch.

"I don't care a snitch for the princess," Aiya said softly, "but the one-armed soldier is another matter." She focused on the brass buttons, enjoying his scent of lye soap and leather. His pulse throbbed subtly in a vein on his neck.

"There you are!"

Dan started. Aiya dropped her hands. Rorden waved a roll of parchment at them as he approached.

"Stop mooning at her Dan, and kiss her already," he said.

Dan reddened but was quick with a retort. "And give you the satisfaction? Not on your life."

Rorden's smile was strained and lacked his typical effortless humor, but Aiya thought it promising that he could smile at all after the scene in the general's tent. He'd clearly been shaken by Biren's betrayal.

"Here are the maps you asked for," Rorden said, tapping the roll against his hand. "They don't have the markings of the sewers you and your men explored last summer."

Of course. Those would have all been lost when Endvar fell.

"It doesn't matter," Dan said. "I remember well enough. I just want to see which would fall on a likely route for the procession."

"Why?" Aiya asked. "I thought they didn't join with the tunnels."

"They don't, but it'll be a fine way for me to slip away without drawing notice."

As they followed Rorden to a nearby tent where they could view the maps in private, Aiya longed to ask after his welfare. But she didn't think he would appreciate discussing it in front of Dan, so she held her tongue. If all went well, there would be time for that later. And if not, then after tonight it would hardly matter.

"YOU'VE BEEN IGNORING ME."

Merek stopped pacing and turned. He hadn't heard Talen approach, so consumed he'd been by his own thoughts. Feeling stifled in the command tent, he'd decided to stretch his legs and seek a moment of quiet on the banks of the frozen pond. He didn't realize he'd been followed.

"I've been a little busy."

"I know. I'll only be a moment." Talen's boots crunched against the frozen ground as he came to stand next to him, looking out over the dull gray ice.

Merek felt momentarily chagrined. He *had* been ignoring Talen. Every time he saw him, Merek was reminded of Ria's folly and how tenuous his own situation was. He couldn't risk being distracted, so it was much easier to just ignore Talen altogether.

"Take me with you to the city today," Talen said.

"No."

"Strong…"

"No. How can I be sure you don't have ill intent toward the princess? I can't afford to take that risk."

"Listen to you. You sound like Grammel."

Merek glared at him. "Easy enough for you to say."

"There's nothing easy about it. You think I enjoyed arresting you? You think I wanted to see you suffer?"

Merek watched the path of an eagle arc across the sky. "No," he conceded. "I don't think that."

"Then listen to me. Grammel's jealousy made him suspicious. If he'd seen clearly, he would have known that your heart was true. I ask you not to make that mistake of me."

Merek turned to face him. "I don't hold you at fault for Grammel's actions, but your presence in this camp gives me no ease. Especially when I just learned that Ria's own maid, whose heart was as true as any, has betrayed her to the enemy."

Talen paled. "Lady Biren?"

"It was unintentionally done but is a stark reminder that even our friends may not be as trustworthy as we think."

Talen was silent a moment, then he reached into his coat and withdrew a folded piece of vellum. Merek's heart skipped a beat at the sight of the familiar seal.

"I have no need of this," Talen said. "I came to the camp looking for answers, and now that I've found them, I want you to have it."

Merek took the vellum and opened it to reassure himself it was indeed the forged pardon. Then he tucked it away in his own coat.

"You're afraid for the princess; I understand." Talen gestured placatingly. "But think. Since I arrived in camp, have I done anything to deserve your suspicion? Anything at all? And you can't deny I've had ample opportunity."

"It's too dangerous for unnecessary risks."

"Yes, it is. Very dangerous. That's why you need as many skilled hands and loyal soldiers at your side as possible."

"Loyal?" Merek asked pointedly. "Just how loyal?"

Talen sighed and ran a hand through his curly hair. When he looked at Merek, his expression was open and frank. "The truth is, I understand now what I didn't before. The future of Rahm rests on your shoulders. What you and the princess do today may determine our course for generations, and I can think of no one more worthy of that honor. I was wrong to doubt you."

Unexpectedly, Talen knelt before him on the frozen ground in a posture of fealty, his head bowed. "I pledge my sword to you not only as my friend, which earns the right, but also as my future king, which demands it."

It took a moment for Merek to find his voice. He was both deeply moved and alarmed at the same time.

"Get up, Talen. No need to make a scene," he said gruffly, then gripped his friend's hand warmly and smiled. "If you think you can keep your feet, you may join Orri's men today."

Sixteen

Merek nudged the embroidered drapes aside to reveal the world outside the rocking carriage. It was disconcerting to be trapped inside a box instead of facing his enemy on horseback with sword drawn. No matter how comfortable the velvet cushioned seats were, he still felt cornered.

Gray paving stones rumbled beneath the carriage wheels. Hundreds of Ardanian soldiers lined the streets, keeping the people of Endvar at a distance from the princess and her guard. The citizenry watched with somber faces, men and women wrapped in mufflers and hats to keep away the winter chill, shuffling to get a better look at the carriage. But there were no smiles, no excited cheering. This was no parade.

If anything, it echoed a funeral procession.

"I thought I would die here," he murmured.

Ria looked at him sharply.

"Not in a tragic way," he hastened to add. "I simply

thought I would live out the rest of my days here in Endvar, protecting Danvir's Wall."

"How very much has changed in such a short time," Ria mused, slipping her hand comfortably into the crook of his arm. "Now your life shall run its course in the warm embrace of Thorodan Hall, and you'll die as an old man surrounded by your children and grandchildren instead of all this cold stone."

"I don't mind the stone. It's beautiful in its own way. But," he squeezed her hand reassuringly, "I'll be happy to make Thorodan Hall my new home."

The idea that there might be something more than this—the conflict to win back Endvar—was hard to make space for in his head. Any future together was so fraught with its own challenges that he couldn't envision the happy scene she described. But it made her smile, as he knew it would.

Rorden and Aiya sat on the opposite bench, blanketed by furs to keep them from freezing in the wintry air. They seemed oblivious to their companions, so engaged they were in a whispered conversation of their own. Aiya was radiant in her borrowed gown, and Rorden had adopted that preening air he always had around beautiful women. Merek stifled a smile and turned his gaze back to the window.

In his mind, he reviewed their careful plans of the last few days. Guided by the girl Yulda, Captain Eldar and his company should even now be hidden in the tunnels underneath the city to provide rescue in the event that Prince Artem's intentions proved to be hostile. Judging by the large number of soldiers Merek saw in the streets, they would have to act quickly, lest they be overwhelmed by the enemy force.

Stefan and his men were also in place, prepared to secure the north gate for an escape route, but only as a last resort. Merek still hoped that their skills could be put to use reclaiming the city, and revealing them now would negate their advantage.

"You shouldn't gawk at the citizens," Ria's teasing voice broke into his thoughts. "Don't you know that we royals must keep ourselves aloof and disinterested when we travel through a city?"

"Is that right?" Merek scoffed. "I seem to remember hearing a tale about a princess who climbed into the driver's seat while riding through this very city, precisely so she could have a better view of the crowd and they of her. Is that what you'd call 'aloof'?"

Ria's lips twitched in a smile. "What an outlandish rumor! I really don't know where you hear such ridiculous stories. You of all people should know that I'm nothing if not prudent and restrained, a model of perfect self-control."

Merek snorted.

Ria arched a graceful eyebrow in mock disdain. "You doubt me? You clearly underestimate how much restraint I exercise when we're alone, Strong, lest the entire camp be privy to things that are not meant for their ears."

Merek reddened, and her eyes sparkled with triumph. After all this time, she still had the ability to make him feel like a tongue-tied schoolboy. It was maddening.

If they'd been alone, he would have kissed her for it.

He turned his attention back to the window. They

were approaching the last underpass before the street curved upward to Lord Ogmun's grand estate. The carriage slowed perceptibly.

"Why are we slowing?" Ria asked, all humor lost from her tone. "Is something wrong?"

She reached for the window, but Merek stopped her with a hand on her arm. "Don't attract attention. The Ardanians must not think anything is amiss."

She looked at him sharply, and he saw the question in her eyes. But she withdrew her hand, for which he was grateful. It meant that for all she was used to getting her way, she was also learning to trust him.

· · ✳ · ·

Dan hooked his legs over the edge of the hole and looked down into the impenetrable darkness.

And hesitated.

He didn't have time for this. The carriage had slowed as planned, presumably to navigate the icy slope with caution. But in truth, the delay was to buy Dan a few precious seconds with which to slip away into the drain while the other soldiers reformed their lines without him. All under cover of the wide stone bridge so that the Ardanians didn't notice the disturbance.

But Dan hadn't counted on the fear. It gripped him like a vise around his throat, making it difficult to breathe.

Jump, you fool! he shouted in his head. But his body wouldn't obey. *Three, two—*

Before he reached one, some hidden strength surged inside him, and he pushed off from the edge of the hole, dropping into the blackness. He landed awkwardly in a shallow puddle, falling to one knee. Overhead, another soldier replaced the metal grate. The soldier wished him well with a faint oath that included calling him a 'cursed fool.'

Dan couldn't disagree.

Footsteps marched overhead, and Dan closed his eyes, trying to adjust to the dimness and ease the choking feeling of panic that threatened to overwhelm him. His pulse raced, and his breathing was shallow and fast. When all was quiet overhead, he opened his eyes. Trickling water echoed in the tunnel and faintly glimmered in the weak light from above. The tunnel yawned before him—dark, but not as hopelessly black as before. He picked his way along the water's edge, his boots crunching on ice where the shallower depths had frozen.

He and Jax had searched these sewers the previous summer, and although the stench was worse then, they'd welcomed the cool respite from the heat above. Now, he shivered in the cold air and missed his discarded uniform coat. He moved uphill, knowing that this would bring him deeper into the wealthier district. His only companions were the large rats that fed on the piles of detritus floating in the water, then skittered out of the way as he approached, disappearing into shadowy holes invisible to his eyes. One particularly large one bared its teeth and hissed at him, until he hissed back and threw a rock in its direction.

Rats didn't bother him. But when he heard a dog bark overhead, the sound echoing menacingly through the cavern, he was nearly undone. Images of Jax flashed through his mind, and he swore he heard the beasts coming for him. They'd found him. They wanted his blood. They would kill him this time. He heard it in their snarling, smelled it on their breath, saw it in the shadows the lanterns cast on the tunnel walls of great snapping jaws and tearing fangs that would rip through his flesh and—

Dan blinked. His vision cleared. He found himself on the floor of the sewer tunnel, back against a wall, his sword abandoned on the ground and his left arm thrust over his head protectively. All was quiet. There were no dogs nor soldiers. He was the only idiot down there in the muck.

Trembling, he reached for his sword and sheathed it. He didn't know how much time he'd lost cowering like a simpleton, but his face burned with shame, and he blessed his good fortune that no one had witnessed his humiliation.

Each time he reached a new grate, he paused, listening. At the third one, he found his opportunity. The alley above was silent and vacant, save for a lone dog which sniffed at the gutter running into the drain. Dan cringed and waited for the skinny animal to pass before pushing the grate up and sliding it open.

Two hands would have made a quieter job of it, but he would have to trust that if any curious eyes spied him from a window overlooking the street, they wouldn't suspect him for a Rahmish soldier. Without a beard, he looked Ardanian enough to keep the Rahmish at bay, no matter what Aiya said.

Thinking of Aiya stirred the unease in his belly as he crawled out onto the icy stone street. He remembered all too well the look of panic she'd tried to disguise when they'd seen her murderous cousin in the square, and here she was going right back into danger. What was she thinking?

You might ask yourself the same thing. How many times must you nearly lose your life in this city before you stay away for good? Yulda had once accused him of trying to be a hero. Is that what this was? He didn't feel very heroic with his boots caked with sewage and the cold sweat of fear on his back.

It was a relief to be out under the open sky in daylight again. A high wall edged one side of the alley: the back side of some noble estate. Dan moved quickly toward the road to get his bearings.

He hoped to leave Endvar when this was all over. In fact, he'd almost decided to quit the army for good. He didn't think General Strong would mind that he was two years short of finishing his service. He'd almost asked, but something had stopped him. It was all well and good to imagine making a fresh start with Aiya when it was just the two of them sharing a tender moment in the northern forest. But returning to the army camp had reminded Dan that a woman like her deserved so much more than to be bound to a cripple for the rest of her life.

Dusk was just beginning to descend as Dan approached Lord Bolen's estate. The princess's carriage had already passed this way, and the crowd was breaking up. Dan shuffled his way through the grim-faced citizens who looked at him askance and gave him room to pass. The lower classes never before would have been seen in this part of the city in such number, but now that the nobles had been executed or imprisoned, it seemed the old rules of conduct had been discarded.

Dan merged with the flow of the people, letting them carry him past Lord Bolen's gate. The heavy wooden doors hung open, unguarded. One was scratched and scarred by fire, while the other looked as though someone had taken an axe to it. Dan's momentary glance was enough to see that the courtyard was empty. This was a good sign. If Lord Bolen's estate was no longer being used to house soldiers—and why would it with the guard complex better suited to that purpose?—it would be far easier to sneak into the kitchen and, from there, the tunnels.

Dan doubled back and moved with the thinning crowd past the estate. But this time, he slipped through the entrance and ducked out of sight behind the broken gates.

Not very subtle, he thought to himself. *If anyone is watching you, they'll surely know you're up to something.*

But there was nothing for it. He had to get into the tunnels, and he had to do it soon. As he looked over the quiet courtyard and judged the distance between him and the great house, he paused. For there, coming from the nearest chimney, smoke rose lazily into the air. Lord Bolen's estate wasn't abandoned after all.

SEVENTEEN

Lord Ogmun's estate glowed from a distance. While the rest of the city was dim and quiet, the place where Artem resided was afire both figuratively and literally. Torches lined the exterior of the stone walls, and as they passed through the outer gates, the grounds exploded in an array of light. Braziers, lanterns, and thick candles mounted on pillars in a variety of colors created a veritable tunnel of light as the carriage passed the still fountains and sleeping gardens to the inner courtyard. Ria would have been impressed by the display if she could have felt anything but tense dread.

"He knows how to make a statement; I'll give him that," Merek said drily beside her.

Ria offered a strained smile. Merek watched out the window as the carriage drew to a halt and their escort filed in rows around them. His gray eyes were keen and sharp, but other than that he showed no sign of being agitated. She wished she had his strength of nerve.

As if sensing her thoughts, Merek squeezed her gloved hand briefly. Then, the door opened and a uniformed Ardanian was assisting her from the carriage. There would be no more private moments with her husband. The drama had begun.

The late afternoon air made Ria catch her breath and had the blessed effect of clearing her head, so that by the time she mounted the polished stone steps—her golden skirts whispering faintly against the black stone—she'd straightened her spine and resisted the urge to lean against Merek for strength. He stayed at her elbow, but his posture was one of deference. He may be her husband, but she was the blood heir to the throne.

Rorden and Aiya followed behind, and as they passed the line of stiff Ardanian servants—with one or two Rahmish, Ria noted—she was conscious of the sensation that they were all looking to her as clearly as Merek's troops looked to him on the battlefield. She was the commander here, in this battle of words and diplomacy, refusals and acquiesces. If she failed, Rahm could just as surely fall as to a conquering army.

Hoping her smile looked more confident than it felt, Ria swept into Lord Ogmun's grand ballroom to face down her enemy.

LORD BOLEN'S KITCHEN HAD BEEN RANSACKED. DRAWERS lay cast aside, their contents scattered on the floor. Cupboard doors hung open, their insides empty and forlorn. A shadow of a figure darted away into the far passage as Dan slipped through the back door. A child.

Curious, Dan followed, one hand on his knife. The hallway was empty, but a low hum of voices sounded at the end of it. He slipped cautiously to the shadows near the front entrance and peered inside.

The main hall was dark and poorly lit. A small group of people sheltered under draperies and tapestries strung around the room for privacy. In the large fireplace that stood at shoulder height a fire blazed. Its fuel appeared to be broken tables, chairs, and carved bedsteads. The child Dan had startled in the kitchen was speaking to a young man who looked in Dan's direction.

He was discovered.

Dan ambled into the room, hoping to look non-threatening. Two men stood and met him before he'd crossed the distance to the refugees. One was gray-haired with a tangled beard matted with old food. The other had a heavy build and large hands that looked as if they could break Dan's neck with a mere twist. The young man who'd spoken to the child joined them.

"Good day to you," Dan greeted genially.

"You're not welcome here, stranger. Go find another home to loot," the youngest of the three snarled.

"Better yet, go back to Ardania where you belong," the large one spat.

"I'm Rahmish," Dan insisted.

"Yeah? You don't look it."

"I know. Keeps me out of trouble, but I'm no friend to the Ardanians, believe me. Used to be a soldier in the Wall Guard before the Ardanians took my arm."

At this, the other men looked at each other uncertainly.

"What brings you here?" the younger one said, his voice less hostile but still not quite friendly.

"Food, like you. Maybe a warm place to spend the night."

"There's no food left, and we haven't got blankets to spare. Go back to wherever you've been hiding these past months. We've got our hands full caring for our own."

The older man laid a hand on the younger man's arm. "I've got an extra blanket, Kaz. It won't hurt me to share it."

The younger man looked as if he wanted to protest, but a meaningful look passed between the two of them, and he shrugged. "So be it. Now we're taking in cripples? As if we weren't starving fast enough on our own," he muttered as he stalked away. The big man followed with a long last glare at Dan.

The older man smiled, revealing broken teeth behind the matted beard. "Pay him no heed. Kaz has lost more than most, but he'll do right by you, he will. We're not doing half so bad as others in this city."

"How did you come to be here? Last time I was in this place it was full of Ardanian soldiers. Where have they gone?"

The old man looked at him as if he were daft. "Where they've all gone, of course. Out fighting and conquering our blessed Rahm. Thousands of Ardanian soldiers spilling like poison over our land."

"And they just left the city empty?"

"Not empty, what with all those troops marching through every day. Ten thousand they've got camped just outside the eastern gate, sending reinforcements to the battlefront. Our poor army never had a chance."

Now it was Dan's turn to be confused. "Reinforcements? There hasn't even been a proper battle in days, and the Ardanians have never shown that kind of strength."

The old man peered at him. "Just where have you been, son? I know what I've seen and I've seen those soldiers coming through here on their way to battle. I've heard their bloody tales of our own soldiers fleeing at the sight of 'em."

Dan almost scoffed at this, until he remembered that he wasn't supposed to know the things he did. He was supposed to be as ignorant of what was going on outside of Endvar as this old man. "So the soldiers just let you lot move in here?"

"They cleaned it out of anything useful first. Kaz wasn't lying when he said there was no food left, but it's dry and warm. Lots of these folks lost their homes in the fires of the early days and have nowhere else to go. Lost my own son then. He was a solider, like you. A peacekeeper. Cut down by the first wave before we figured out there was no sense fightin' 'em. Come, let me introduce you to his wife and children."

"Thank you, but I can't stay. There's someone I'm trying to find, but it looks like she isn't here." Dan feigned a look of disappointment. "I'll just be on my way then. Thank you for your kindness, and if I can't find her, I might be back for that blanket."

The old man offered a clumsy salute and chuckled as Dan left him. Dan hurried back to the kitchen, anxious to avoid Kaz and his beefy companion. He was relieved that no soldiers would challenge his way in or out of the tunnels, but he couldn't make sense of it. Where were all the soldiers the old man had seen passing through the city? If the Ardanians had a force that large, they would have pushed more aggressively against the general's troops.

Unless they weren't joining the Ardanians facing the general. What if those troops were merely a diversion? What if there was a larger force amassing somewhere hidden to attack the Rahmish troops when least expected? A chill ran through Dan, and he froze in place.

What if they were using the tunnels?

Again, the constricted feeling seized him. His heart pounded so hard in his chest he couldn't breathe. Were Captain Eldar's men lying slaughtered in the tunnels right now, waiting for him to discover them? Dan leaned against the wall, panting. He closed his eyes, but the images came unbidden into his mind. Not just images, but pain. His body ached as surely as if the Ardanians were beating him there in Lord Bolen's kitchen.

Dan pushed himself shakily to the larder. He felt cold. Stripped and bound with cords, the icy stone burned his skin.

No. That was only a memory. He wasn't a prisoner anymore. He shook his head, trying to clear it, but still the pain haunted him.

What he saw in the larder finally brought him back to his senses. It had been pillaged just as thoroughly as the kitchen. Whole shelves were left empty, while the leavings of broken crockery and shredded burlap littered others. What gave Dan pause, however, was the large barrel that marked the entrance to the tunnel. It was no longer there. Instead, splinters of wood dusted the floor in front of a gaping black hole. The entire barrel front had been ripped from the wall, leaving the tunnel entrance exposed.

Dan lit a candle stub slowly, his hands trembling. The small light did little to illuminate the tunnel entrance. *You're a right bundle of nerves*, he chided himself. *What would Aiya say if she could see you now?*

Voices sounded in the hallway outside the kitchen. Soon they would be upon him. Shielding the faint flame from draft, Dan took a deep breath and stepped into the darkness.

Eighteen

Music wafted from a small ensemble on a platform in a corner of the ballroom, and dozens of dancing couples turned as one to watch Ria and Merek enter. Ria spared not a glance for them, her eyes fixed on Artem. He stood on the near side of the ballroom in a relaxed posture with his hands clasped behind his back. He wore an Ardanian formal long coat in deep blue, the color accentuating his fairness and making his skin and hair shine in the light from hundreds of candles around the room. His eyes lit up as she approached, and he bowed respectfully.

"I had hoped to dazzle you with my hospitality," he said in the slight accent of his homeland, "but I see that I failed to account for your own brilliance. You transcend the sun, my dear."

Ria offered him her hand in greeting, feeling as if she were acting out a familiar script. "All these candles and lanterns must have cost a fortune. Shall my poor people in this city now go without light through the rest of winter because of your extravagance?"

"Not at all," Artem said, his teeth gleaming. "This city is mine now, and I care for its people, both Rahmish and Ardanian alike. Aid flows freely from Ardania for all in need."

Ria raised a skeptical eyebrow. "Indeed? How generous you are." Then, switching to Rahmish she added, "I must ask you to speak in Rahmish tonight, Artem. I'm afraid my husband doesn't speak your tongue."

At the mention of Merek, Artem's eyes flickered over her shoulder. "Ah, yes, how thoughtless of me. My apologies, General, I mean no disrespect."

Merek bowed his head stiffly in return. "I doubt that very much, Your Highness."

Artem's smile widened, and he looked over Merek appraisingly. "General Strong, at last we meet. I feel as if I'm greeting a brother."

"Do you?"

"Certainly. We're quite the kindred souls. Dazzled by the same woman. Fighting over the same city. It must be excruciating to watch me steal her right under your nose."

"Not at all. You and I both know that you won't hold Endvar for long."

Artem laughed, moving closer to Ria and taking her arm. "I don't know about that. She's quite warmed to me. I think you'll find by the time I'm through she will have quite forgotten you."

"Surrender isn't the same as loyalty, Your Highness,

but a man like you has probably never learned the difference."

"Why should I? If I get what I want, it makes no difference to me whether I've had to rough her up a bit first."

Ria resisted the urge to shrink from Artem's touch.

"Then you may control her, but you'll never win her heart. There's only one way to do that."

"And how is that?" Artem's impish tone held an edge.

"You must be willing to die for her. Only if you're willing to lose everything for her will she give you everything in return."

Merek spoke calmly enough, but Ria recognized the look in his eye. She'd seen it before when he'd protected her against Domar's men, a hard, calculating coldness. She hurried to interrupt. "You mustn't be too hard on Artem, Strong. He doesn't have as much experience as you engendering loyalty and devotion in those who follow him."

"I dare say there aren't many men alive with as much experience as the general." Artem smirked, but Merek nodded as if it were a compliment.

How were they ever going to survive this night?

"The prince needs a distraction, my lady," a soft voice whispered in Ria's ear.

It took a moment for Ria to realize that Aiya had spoken in Khouri, so surprised she was that the woman had dared to impose herself at such a moment. Before Ria could respond, however, Artem had stepped forward with undisguised interest.

"And who is this lovely creature attending you? I

don't believe we've met," he said silkily, all tension gone from his tone.

"No, you haven't." Ria was both irritated and grateful for the interference as Artem took Aiya's hand. As quickly as that, Merek was all but forgotten. "Miss Firah is the niece of Lord Melo, and has been with me only a few months."

"My, my, what happened to dear Biren? I do hope she hasn't fallen out of favor."

"Do you?" Ria couldn't quite keep the sting out of her voice. "I'm touched by your concern. I simply thought this might be a fine opportunity for Miss Firah."

Artem looked over Aiya appreciatively. "A fine opportunity indeed," he murmured. Aiya performed a curtsy of such deference that Ria couldn't help but admire her grace. In return, Artem took Aiya by the hand and brushed his lips ever so gently against her skin.

Aiya was all smiles and coy glances through her long, dark lashes. "Your Majesty is very kind," she said with a heavy accent.

"Nonsense. Your kindness is in gracing us tonight with your beauty," Artem said in fluent Khouri. "I do hope to see more of it before this evening is through."

Aiya blushed and curtsied again. Ria pressed her lips together in irritation.

Artem's hand brushed Aiya's cheek before he turned away and led the company to the high table.

"You were supposed to avoid attracting his attention," Ria whispered angrily when his back was turned. "Instead, you came just shy of accepting an invitation into his bed!"

Aiya's response was tight. "I did what any lowly noble

would do when flattered by a man like him. He's less likely to question my presence if I give him what he expects."

Ria narrowed her eyes. "Well let's hope he doesn't expect more than you can give."

Aiya looked at her and Ria saw in her dark eyes an unexpected intensity. "Do not concern yourself about me, my lady. I know his kind well enough and will perform my part. Be certain that you do the same."

A FEAST OF SUMPTUOUS MEATS, GLAZED FRUIT, AND mulled wine lay before them, but Merek couldn't eat. Ria sat across the table, and he felt the distance between them as a taut line stretched to fraying. To his left, at the head of the table, sat Artem, his handsome face arranged in a permanent sneer. To Merek's right was the dangerous man who had first been introduced to him as Master Domar. Merek had been effectively flanked by his enemies.

"Are the oysters not to your liking, General?" Artem asked pleasantly. "These were brought specially from Khourin, a rare treat for our honored guests." A large ring glittered from his left hand as he plucked another from his plate, and Merek recognized it as Lord Ogmun's. The ring of the Lord of Endvar. His insides roiled.

"No, Your Highness. I'm afraid I have little appetite tonight. I'm not in the habit of breaking bread with my enemies."

Artem chuckled, shaking his head. "Ah, General, you

have no imagination. Don't think of me as your enemy then. Think of us as...if not friends, then at least confederates."

"Only a fool would suggest such a thing."

Ria shot him a look of warning, but Merek thought he was showing remarkable restraint. If he hadn't been required to surrender his sword before entering the hall, he would have been sorely tempted to use it and end this whole charade at once.

Artem didn't seem to mind the slight. He pushed his plate out of the way and shook the silken folds of his sleeves to rest his forearms on the table.

"Then from one fool to another, I invite you to consider this prospect: A thriving Rahm united under the rule of a powerful king and strengthened with the might of an army led by a man distinguished like none other in an age. A man akin to Danvir himself, who will continue his legacy of peace so that Rahm may prosper."

The conversations at their end of the table ceased. Ria stilled, and Orri and Talen watched intently from their seats between Ardanian officers.

"You suggest that you and I form an alliance?" Merek asked.

"Yes. Together we will take Rahm into a new age of prosperity. I have plans for this beautiful land, but to reach such unparalleled heights, I'll need a mighty army that is unrivaled among all the six kingdoms."

"What makes you think we want anything to do with you and your plans?"

"You will. I've learned much of you, General Strong, and I'm impressed. Your skill is unmatched in any Rahmish or Ardanian commander living today. But I also know that you're not a man who seeks power for power's sake. Or is it untrue that you denied King Sindal's request when he wished to appoint you as general instead of your predecessor?"

"A lust for power isn't a requirement in a ruler. Show me a king who loves his people more than himself, and I'll show you a kingdom that will prosper for generations."

"You see, Artem," Ria interjected, "it has always been a hallmark of Thorodan rule to see your reign as a service, not a way of exalting yourself. It's a sacred obligation that you will account for someday before God, and as such, one must be willing to sacrifice all for the good of the people."

"How quaint!" Artem said warmly. "What a lovely inscription for a mausoleum! But it sounds like a rather dour existence with all that worry of the final judgment weighing you down. No wonder it drove your father mad!"

Ria's smile cooled. "I did say sacrifice *all*. Not all men who imagine themselves worthy of the honor are suited to the task, which made my selection of a husband particularly challenging, as you well know. There was far more to consider than simply how he might enjoy the feeling of a crown upon his head."

"It's unfortunate you wasted such time abroad when General Strong was so close to home."

"Not at all. Spending time with the nobility of other lands offered me a perspective I couldn't have gained otherwise. I wouldn't have learned to value Strong's qualities if I hadn't first learned how unsuitable my other prospects were."

Artem's smile widened. "I agree that the general has many fine qualities which make him particularly suited to leading armies to victory in war. But that is only one part of a king's duties."

"Some would say that's the most important duty of a king," Merek said. "A king who cannot keep his people safe is a poor king indeed."

Artem dismissed this with a wave of his hand, Lord Ogmun's ring flashing in the candlelight. "But what about in times of peace? The king whose mind is full of war will struggle with the messy decisions that come with peace. So leave that to me. You weren't bred for it as I was, General. You weren't weaned on court intrigue and raised with a mind for political maneuvering. I can see even in your expression that it's distasteful to you. Can you deny that you would rather face me on the battlefield than as my dinner guest?"

Merek grunted. He hated that Artem was right. "I won't deny it. But fortunately the greatest burden to rule falls to our future queen who will more than make up for any of my deficiencies."

"Thank you, Strong," Ria said with a tip of her cup in Merek's direction. She sipped her wine carefully with her eye on the prince. "I'm curious, Artem, what role you expect me to play in this little imaginative drama. Am I merely to tend the hearth while you two have all the fun?"

"Oh no, not at all." Artem turned his attention fully to Ria now, looking unpleasantly as though she were to be his dessert. His voice was thick with velvet innuendo. "You'll be having a great deal of fun yourself. Remember what revelry we used to have together? I have a special place for your many talents, and I look forward to uncovering those that have not yet fully...blossomed." He reached out and stroked Ria's hand tenderly.

Ria blushed and pulled her hand away. Merek instinctively gripped his table knife, but a hand stopped him.

"What my lord means," Domar said evenly, "is that Your Highness would be a valuable asset at court, as an advisor or an ambassador even."

"An advisor? In my own court?" The color in Ria's cheeks heightened. "That is *my* home you're speaking of, Artem. I am heir to the throne of Rahm and will be her queen, nothing less."

"That can be arranged too, if you wish."

Merek stood before he half knew what he was doing. But Ria was quicker.

"Strong! How perfect of you!" she said before he could utter a word. "You've read my mind. This lovely music has got me wishing to move my feet." She smiled, but he could hear the urgency in her voice. She was rattled, but not by Artem's offensive proposal. Suddenly Merek felt ashamed to have acted so transparently.

"I'm at your service, of course," he said lamely, as she rounded the table to take him by the arm. Artem scowled momentarily, until he spied Aiya.

"What an excellent idea. Miss Firah, shall we acquaint ourselves better?"

Ria steered Merek away from the table and out onto the dance floor before Aiya had even offered a reply.

"You know I don't dance," Merek said through clenched teeth.

"I know that you claim not to dance," Ria whispered

fiercely, "but you can't possibly have spent all that time in my father's court and not have learned."

"That was years ago, and even Sindal realized I was a lost cause and stopped tormenting me to join him."

Ria swung around to face him and raised her right hand up to meet his left, palms touching. "Then let's just hope your feet remember more than you think."

NINETEEN

The square grate that marked the hole in the floor of the guard complex cellar was gray against the black of the tunnel ceiling. Yulda sat on the dirt floor and watched the hole darken as night descended. That gray square was the only sign of daylight she'd seen for two days.

"I thought I might find you here," a deep voice sounded out of the shadows next to her. Captain Eldar's haggard face looked like something out of a child's nighttime terror in the low lamplight. "I believe I told you to stay away from here. If you give us away, we're all dead men."

"Not a sound, Captain. Not a scurry of man nor beast. It's as silent as a graveyard up there."

Her words hung in the air between them. She fixed her eyes on Eldar. "What do you think happened up there? Where did they all go?"

The captain regarded her for a moment. "These are weighty questions for someone who wants no part of this fight."

Yulda sniffed at having her own words thrown back at her. "I'm curious, that's all."

"You're a strange one, miss. Come. We've received word from General Strong. The meeting with the prince has commenced. We're to be on alert in case our services our needed tonight."

"Received word? How?"

"He sent a man to find us. The general and the princess are in the city as we speak."

Yulda scrambled to her feet. "What man?"

There were only two men she knew of still living who had been in the tunnels, and she knew who would have been her first choice. But last she knew, Dan was far away in the north.

"Why does it matter?" Captain Eldar asked, but she'd already grabbed her lamp and brushed past him down the corridor. With any luck, she would soon be free of this underground tomb.

AIYA KNEW IMMEDIATELY THAT THE ARDANIAN PRINCE WAS a dangerous man. The intent look of his eye roving over her, the grip of his hand on her back—this was a man who was used to getting what he wanted. He commanded her attention completely. He *owned* her as they moved across the floor. All she needed to do was be light on her feet, and he moved her where he wanted her to go. The rest of the ballroom retreated as she saw nothing but him, heard nothing but his voice murmuring in her ear, and felt nothing but his arms and hips pressed against her.

That made Aiya's task almost too simple. Lust was such an uncomplicated desire. It was a pity that she wasn't there to rob him, for he would have been such an easy target.

"Are you enjoying yourself in your first visit to my city?" Artem spoke fluently in Khouri, though his accent betrayed his homeland as surely as his shining yellow hair.

"Yes, my lord. Though this is not my first visit. I passed through this summer on my way to Albon. I confess that I preferred it then to winter."

"Why do I not remember you with the princess's company when she last came to Rellana?" Artem asked, his eyes narrowed. "You're not a woman who would be easily overlooked."

"I didn't travel with the princess, my lord. My father brought me separately. He had business with my uncle and wished to see me to Albon himself."

"I'm surprised he could bear to let you go. I'm certain I wouldn't have." He pulled her even closer, his breath hot against her neck as he bent to kiss it.

Aiya swallowed, resisting the urge to pull away. "But an opportunity to be trained in the Rahmish court is a distinctive privilege, don't you think?"

"Indeed. And how do you like your training? Is the princess good to you?"

"Of course."

"Because if she ever says even one cross word, you would be welcome at my court in a heartbeat. I believe I could find a much better use for you than she can."

Aiya affected an embarrassed laugh. "You flatter me,

my lord. Your invitation is most gracious, but I have much more than my own comfort to think of. My father and uncle would be devastated if I flouted their hopes for me in such a way."

"Pity," Artem said with a smile. "But perhaps there will come a time when you think differently."

They glided around the outer edges of the dance floor, passing through pockets of cool night air that flowed into the room from the open balcony doors.

After a time, the prince tried again. "May I confess something to you, Miss Firah?"

"If you wish, my lord."

"I'm worried about your mistress. We've been dear friends for years, and I fear that the strain of her father's madness is too much for her. Don't you think she looks peaked? I'm shocked at how much she has changed since we last met."

Aiya shot a glance at the princess dancing with the general in the center of the floor. She was changed, that was certain. Months of wintering in an army camp had taken its toll. Her hair had lost some of its luster, and her skin was more dull than when Aiya had first met her. But most of the change was for the better. She seemed more aware, more confident, and less inclined to the youthful immaturity she'd displayed on that first meeting.

"I don't know her as well as you, my lord, and the Rahmish tongue is a challenge, so she doesn't seek my confidence. But I can truthfully say that she grows in my esteem the longer I'm acquainted with her."

"Hmm." This displeased the prince, but Aiya had no wish to become a tool for his schemes. She had only to provide distraction enough to diffuse tensions as the evening wore on: keep things light and uneventful so they could all leave the city in one piece.

Aiya wondered if Dan had been successful in meeting with Captain Eldar. Thinking of him alone in the tunnels filled her with unease, and she suppressed a shudder.

"You're far away, I can see it in your eyes," Artem murmured. "Did I upset you?"

"No. Forgive me, my lord." Aiya quickly brought her attention back to the prince. "I was thinking of home, that is all. It's been so long since I've conversed with anyone in Khouri that it has made me feel quite homesick."

"What about your uncle? Surely it's a comfort to have family at court with you."

Aiya cursed her own carelessness and answered with, "Do you know my uncle, Your Highness?"

"I've not had the pleasure of meeting him, no."

"There are few people who would find comfort in his company."

Artem's eyes sparkled mischievously. "I see. Then I may have some entertainment for you. I must introduce you to someone." He turned her deftly toward a quiet corner of the ballroom where no other couples danced. A few servants stood at attention in the shadows of the dark pillars, quiet and unobtrusive. "There's a Khouri man in my employ who may help you feel at home here, though he's been away from your country for some time. I'm sure you will have much to talk of."

Aiya tensed. Dan had said Behni was dead. She wouldn't have risked coming to the city if she thought there was any chance that she would meet him.

Panicked, she searched around her, but the room

swirled too quickly to make out any faces. And then, the prince turned her to an abrupt stop, and she stood before a dark-skinned man whose features she did indeed recognize.

But it was not Behni.

It was Imar.

Aiya smothered her instinct to cry out in recognition. Imar, too, knew better. If he was surprised to see her, he did not show it. Indeed, he showed no emotion at all as he bowed stiffly. A new kind of dread pricked the corners of Aiya's mind. How had Imar come to be there?

"Master Imar, Miss Firah is attending the Rahmish princess tonight. She misses home, and I thought she might appreciate visiting with a fellow countryman."

"Miss Firah, did you say?" Imar said, speaking smoothly. "Welcome to the house of Prince Artem."

"Thank you, sir." Aiya knew him well enough to see the confusion beneath his mask of polite disinterest.

"Then I'll leave you to share stories of your homeland." Artem reached out with a slender hand and traced the line of her collarbone. "But do not go far, Firah. I'm sure I'll want you again."

She tried not to shiver under his touch, but instead affected an obsequious bow, then turned her attention to her brother.

THE COUPLES NEAREST MEREK AND RIA EDGED ASIDE TO make room for them on the dance floor: Ardanians, mostly, with a few Rahmish mixed in. They watched the royal couple with great interest, and Merek faltered under the attention.

"This is a really bad idea," he muttered as he pulled Ria close, smelling the clean scent of her hair and skin.

"I thought it was preferable to you threatening the life of our host. You mustn't let him goad you so."

"It's one thing for him to threaten me, but I will not stand by while he threatens you." The fire in Merek's belly flared as he thought of Artem's insults.

"It's just his way. He finds your source of pain and uses it against you. Don't rise to his challenge. That's what he wants."

"So I'm meant to look an impotent fool who won't defend his own wife?"

"No. You ignore the meaningless threats and strike back when and where it matters most."

Merek sighed. "I'm not cut out for this, Ria. Give me an enemy I can face with weapon in hand. But this..."

"Don't say that." Ria looked at him sharply. "Don't listen to him. Do not doubt yourself because of what he said."

"I didn't mean—" Merek couldn't deny that Artem's argument made a kind of sense. It was one of the reasons he'd resisted Ria's proposal for so long, and if he'd heard it from Sindal, he wouldn't have disagreed. But Artem was no Sindal, and his words had lies at their heart, no matter how much they may have been twisted to sound like truth.

"Nothing he says can shake my resolve," Merek said firmly. "If anything, every time he opens his mouth it's only strengthened."

Ria relaxed. She spun away from Merek with a flourish, then reeled back in with such speed that he grasped her tightly against his chest. They lingered that way for a long moment, Ria breathing slightly with the exertion, a smile teasing her lips. "You see. You can be quite a fine dancer when you forget for a moment how much you hate it."

Merek wished he could hold her like that forever. To savor her scent, the alluring line of her neck, and the feel of her pressed against him. But it was over too soon. The music ended, the other couples offered a polite applause, and Artem was at his elbow with his hand extended to Ria.

"Shall I show you how it's done, Strong?"

TWENTY

"What are you doing here?" Imar hissed quietly, his thin mouth barely parting.

"I might ask you the same, dear brother. How long have been in the prince's employ?"

Imar's dark eyes sharpened at the accusation. "Not long," he said curtly. "When I heard of the attack on Endvar I abandoned my business in Branvik and returned to find that I'd lost everything while I was away."

"Behni burned the shop."

"It's not for the shop that I've grieved," Imar snapped. "When I could find no trace of you anywhere in the city, I offered my services to the prince, hoping to learn of your fate."

"Does he know?" Aiya asked, alarmed. "Did you tell him you had a sister in the city?" If the prince knew about Imar's sister, he might guess who Miss Firah really was. She glanced toward the dance floor and saw Domar watching her. She lifted her eyes and tried to lighten her expression. It was difficult with the anxiety brewing within her.

Imar cleared his throat in an offended manner. "I'm not a fool. Of course he doesn't know. I made discreet inquiries but never spoke of you directly. I'd nearly given up hope, and then you arrive tonight dressed like a Rahmish noblewoman and attracting attention like sweet wine draws summer bees at a picnic."

Aiya smiled at his churlish tone. "I've missed you, Imar. I took comfort imagining you safe far from here, untouched by war and intrigue."

"While you are caught in the thick of it."

"Don't criticize me. Their cause is just, and more to the point, they're my friends. I'll help them if I can."

"Well, you have chosen more wisely than I, I'm afraid."

"Why?" Aiya asked with alarm. "Is the prince cruel to you?"

"Me? No. Not that he isn't cruel, but I'm not the sort to incite his interest." Imar paused as a servant shouldered past them carrying a tub laden with soiled dishes from the banquet table.

Imar stepped nearer to Aiya and his face fell into shadow cast from the nearest pillar. He spoke so softly that Aiya could barely catch his words. "The prince is out of his league. I suspect he shall not hold the city for long."

"Why? What do you know?"

"I'm not part of the prince's inner circle, you understand. He would have my head if he suspected what I knew, but one does not simply forget how men like this work."

Aiya understood. Working for her uncle had given

them both a singular education that would forever color the way they viewed the world.

"And what do you know?" she urged.

"I know that he's exhausted his forces. That one strong push from the Rahmish and the defenses will fall. The city has been all but abandoned by the Ardanians."

"Abandoned? We saw thousands of soldiers as we passed through the city today."

"A farce. Like the thousands of tents that make up the army camp on the Ardanian side of the border. If one watches carefully, it is always the same soldiers tending the same fires strategically placed to look as though they are part of a large host. The soldiers you saw today were the same. Moved to different parts of the city after you passed and rearranged so that you might not notice the same faces."

"I can't believe it. Why would the citizens not rise up and revolt against the prince?"

"They make a big show of bringing troops through the city so that it looks as if thousands of reinforcements are passing through. The people haven't realized that it's all just a sham. I don't know how the prince thinks he can win this war, but from what I've seen, he—"

Imar broke off and Aiya followed his gaze to see Domar approaching.

"Miss Firah, I'm afraid this gentleman has quite monopolized your attention. I do hope he's not becoming a nuisance."

"Not at all," Aiya insisted demurely. "I was merely asking if we might take some air together as the dance has warmed me excessively."

"I'm afraid the prince wouldn't approve. It seems

you're quite a favorite of his. He won't like it if you wander." Domar's eyes glinted unpleasantly. He offered his arm, and Aiya instinctively recoiled. "Come, let us return before you're missed."

Aiya resented being treated like the prince's property, but she smiled graciously as if she were honored by the attention.

She nodded to Imar, wishing she could warn him to leave this place and find safety. But their private moment was gone. With another smooth bow, Imar said, "If you should have need of my services again, Miss Firah, you need only ask. I shall be at your disposal." Then he was gone, slipping out the servant's entrance before Aiya could say another word.

ARTEM MOVED LIKE A PREDATOR STALKING ITS PREY. His grip was firm and insistent, as if at any moment Ria was his for the taking, but he was merely prolonging the delay for his own enjoyment. There was a time Ria had found dancing with him in this way exhilarating. But now, it was exhausting.

She didn't move as easily in his arms as she once had. There was no longer the flowing harmony she remembered from their courting days. Instead, she felt a kind of dissonance as they moved past the dancing couples arrayed in Ardanian finery. A hesitation when there should have been action. Resistance where there had once been submission.

No one else seemed to notice the battle of wills between them as they danced. The other couples moved to give them a respectful distance while offering sidelong glances of admiration.

Take a good look, Ria thought with an inward grimace. *This is the last time he shall ever touch me like this.*

But with Artem, she was pleasant and attentive. She didn't even lose her temper when he criticized Merek.

"Really, Ria, such a bore! I wonder how you can stand to be in his company for two minutes together."

"Don't be peevish; Artem, it doesn't suit you. You're just jealous, as well you should be. He's in every way a perfect contrast to you, my dear. And therefore, he makes me perfectly happy."

Artem coughed out a small, skeptical laugh. "You mean he's old, dull, and humorless?" His hand tightened on hers painfully.

"On the contrary. He's full of honor and integrity and inspires me to be someone I'm proud of, with a thriving wit that keeps me on my toes." She turned away from him in a small spin, twisting her hand from his grasp.

"Honor...integrity...hardly an enticement to warm your bed."

"You know nothing of what it takes to warm my bed, Artem. I suspect that's what pricks you so. Though it's none of your business, rest assured that the future of the royal line is in *very* good hands."

Artem frowned, and his pace quickened aggressively, his leg pushing against hers as they moved with an insistence that communicated domination more than desire. The room warmed around her, and Ria felt herself becoming flushed.

"You mistake my intent, Ria," he murmured, his voice taking on the bewitching quality she knew so well. "I'm not your husband's rival for anything except your father's crown, and in that, I trust that you'll see that I'm the strongest contender." He pulled her in so close that it forced her breath out of her lungs.

"We will never yield," Ria gasped.

"He will if you tell him to," Artem said softly, his breath warm on her cheek. "He'll do exactly as you say. You know it. I know it. Give me the throne and this little war will be over. You two may be free to do whatever you wish. Stay on in my court if you desire. I meant what I said earlier about Strong continuing on as general of my armies. You would both be welcome. Or you may retire to the country and live a quiet life for all I care. I won't interfere. I wish for nothing but your happiness."

"My happiness and my throne," Ria corrected, pushing against his chest. He didn't release her.

"Yes, that too. But it's not such a bad prospect. Your people will prosper under the rule of a man fit to lead them while you enjoy all the honors and comfort you deserve. That's the extent of my desire for you, and I think you will find it more than generous. After all, there are other ways of getting what I want."

He released her at last in one smooth motion, spinning her away from him, her slippers shushing against the floor as she moved. Ria breathed deeply and straightened her spine as she prepared to meet him again.

MEREK STOOD ON THE EDGE OF THE ROOM WITH HIS officers, watching Ria dance with Artem. With her height and presence they were evenly matched, and they moved with the practiced rhythm of experience. If she hadn't been Merek's wife, he would have thought they made a lovely couple, flowing smoothly across the polished black floor. Ria's gold dress was luminescent in the candlelight, and all else in the room seemed dim and shadowy by comparison. Watching them together made his hands sweat.

"What does that man want with Aiya?" Rorden asked, interrupting Merek's dark thoughts. He gestured to where Aiya stood in a distant corner, conversing with a man in the shadows. A foreign man.

Merek cursed under his breath.

"What's that, sir?"

"Imar! It's Aiya's brother! How did he get here?"

"Aiya's brother?" Rorden started. "Is she discovered then?"

"Best get her away from there, now!"

Rorden moved quickly, skirting around the edge of the ballroom to avoid the dancing couples. Before he reached her, however, Domar appeared at Aiya's side and took her arm. This was not an improvement.

Rorden blocked their path and offered Domar a stiff bow. Domar didn't release Aiya immediately, and his expression was stern. Perhaps Merek should intervene, though he would prefer not to cause a scene. They were trying to avoid a conflict, after all.

"General Strong, sir," a voice sounded from behind him.

Reluctantly, Merek turned away from the ballroom to face Captain Orri.

"Yes?"

"He's returned." Orri spoke so quietly that Merek could scarcely catch his words.

Now? Dan's timing couldn't be worse.

"Talen, be mindful of her Highness," he instructed. With one last parting glance at Ria and Artem, Merek slipped behind the line of soldiers and followed Orri into the dimly lit corridor.

"He found Captain Eldar's men, but there's more he wished to tell you himself," Orri murmured as they walked. Carpets of deep blue and gold muffled their footfalls, and soon the music and voices of the great hall dimmed as Orri led Merek to a polished staircase at the end of the corridor. They stepped down a half flight of stairs to a wide landing where stood a long window that opened out onto the ground floor.

There, in the shadowy darkness, sat Dan. And someone else. It took a moment for Merek to recognize the young woman he'd dispatched to lead Captain Eldar's men to the tunnels.

"What's this about, Dan?"

Dan jumped to his feet and gestured to the girl. "Don't worry about it, sir. I'll take care of her. But I thought you should know that Yulda here claims that the barracks at the guard complex are completely deserted."

Merek looked at Yulda, who shivered slightly in the night air leaking through the open window. "How do you know this?"

"I spent two days watching the cellar, and there was no sign of life. Two days! Captain Eldar wouldn't let me investigate lest I risk discovery, but tell me—what kind of an army doesn't need to eat for two days?"

"There are rumors of large numbers of troops passing

through the city, supposedly to join the Ardanian forces outside," Dan said.

"We haven't seen such reinforcements," Orri observed.

"Aye, sir. I thought they might have been using the tunnels to gather somewhere, but Captain Eldar says no. It's been as quiet as a grave down there."

Laughter sounded overhead, and Dan paused, shrinking further into the shadows of the courtyard. Footsteps sounded high above them in the stairwell, echoing off the stone walls.

"Stay close, Dan," Merek said quietly, a plan forming in his mind. "We may have need of you yet."

The footsteps drifted away on an upper floor, followed by another burst of distant laughter. Dan and Yulda slipped into the shadows, hinges creaking as they closed the window.

"What do you think, sir?" Orri asked as they returned to the hall.

Merek wasn't sure what to make of Dan's information. Was this a trap? Or an opportunity? "Make ready your men, Orri. I think it's time we make our exit."

"Agreed, sir."

They entered the ballroom and found Rorden heading straight for Merek, looking greatly agitated. He spoke quietly but couldn't contain his excitement.

"Sir, you'll never believe what Aiya has just learned."

TWENTY-ONE

Hot anger made Ria scarcely aware of the other dancers on the floor. Dancing was supposed to be a pleasurable activity, but Ria couldn't relax. Artem offended her with every touch. Every word. His very presence in this great house was unforgivable, and the more he talked of how much better the Rahmish people would be with him leading them, the more his words stoked her wrath. As much as she tried to hide her distaste, Artem sensed it like a hound on the trail and smiled knowingly.

"You don't seem to be enjoying yourself as I'd hoped, my dear. Please, let's talk of something amusing. Tell me all about your wedding."

"I'm sure you already know all about it."

"I confess I may have heard an account or two. What else could I do when you failed to invite me? Such bad manners. I did invite you to mine, after all."

"I heard vaguely of your marriage while I was at court in Branvik. That hardly constitutes an invitation." Ria scanned the room for Merek and felt a rush of worry when she couldn't find him. Captain Talen and the other Rahmish soldiers stood where she'd last seen him, but Merek was no longer there. "But there's no harm done as I assure you I held little interest in attending."

"How unfortunate! You missed a grand time!" Artem said with a chuckle. "My father enraged and threatening to banish me unless I broke the marriage agreement, Idan siding with him and hoping he would follow through with it; it was all very dramatic."

"Your father didn't care for your bride?" she asked distractedly, still searching for Merek.

"Oh, he was never much fond of the Delth. He thought it was just shy of treason when I married one."

Ria stumbled, pulling her hand away and stopping in place. Now she was genuinely interested. "You jest, surely."

Artem's eyes shone with mirth. "Not at all! Did you not know? It caused such an uproar in my family that I was certain all the kingdoms knew, in spite of my father's efforts to contain the scandal. Surely you noticed she's not Ardanian."

Ria thought back to her one brief meeting of the new princess. She hadn't looked like the Ardanian nobility that Ria knew, but she'd assumed she came from an outlying area. The young woman hadn't uttered a single word in Ria's presence to give herself away.

"But they're barbarians," Ria hissed. "Savages. They have no proper civilization and honor no treaties. Why would you ever take one to be your wife?"

Artem deftly snatched her hands and began pulling her through the dance again. He held her closer than he had before so that his voice was a gentle hum running through the undercurrent of noise in the room. "Oh, I find that they can honor treaties well enough with the right leverage, and unchecked barbarism can be a wonderful weapon to have on your side in a war. Don't you agree?"

"This is uncommonly low, even for you." Ria's head swam with the implications of Artem's words. A question burned on her tongue but she didn't want to give him the satisfaction of hearing her fear. *Are you raising a Delth army to bring against Rahm?* Instead, she said, "I hope your new bride makes you as miserable as you deserve."

"Not at all. She gives me exactly what I require, and in turn she receives greater luxuries than she could ever imagine. Do you know, it was months before I could convince her to sleep in a bed rather than on the floor. She comes from a family of quite some prominence in Dell, but even they didn't have proper beds. I can't count the mornings I nearly stepped on her when I rose." He laughed in a conspiratorial fashion, but Ria couldn't smile in return.

As a new bride of only a few days, it sickened her to hear Artem sharing such personal details about the woman he'd married. Ria held no love for the Delth, but she was certain the quiet woman she met would have been mortified to hear her husband speak so.

"Your father would have been right to banish you for such an act. Someday you will risk too much, Artem."

"And yet here we are, you and I together, with all your beautiful kingdom between us. That's worth any risk and any price." Artem fingered a loose tendril of hair that brushed against her neck in a move that was frighteningly intimate. Her pulse quickened.

"Surely even you wouldn't dare bring the Delth to my borders."

Artem simply shook his head and said gravely. "My dear, you know better than to think I won't do whatever it takes to get what I want."

Ria felt as if her feet were dragging and couldn't quite keep up. If Artem could command a Delth army, it didn't matter that he didn't have his brother's support.

"And you surely must know that I will stop you at whatever cost."

"Whatever cost? You mean you'll consider my proposal? Because that is the only way to stop the war that is coming. I know you, Ria. You won't let your people fall under the Delth just to spite me."

Ria cocked her head at Artem in one last effort to gain the upper hand. "I'm not convinced the Delth are even a threat. There are rumors that a plague swept through their lands years ago and they are only a fraction of their former strength."

"I suppose you could take that chance, but I never thought you were much of a gambler. The plague wasn't as serious as all that. Those who survived are as ruthless and bloodthirsty as their forebears. It won't take much to convince them to go to war."

Desperation crept into Ria's heart. *Calm down. This is what he does. He finds your sore spot and squeezes.*

The strains of music rose to their final conclusion. With conviction, she said, "It's nice to see you finally revealed as the thug you truly are, Artem. Your threat is duly noted, but you will not have my throne. Bring your army of savages. Strong has defeated them once. He'll do so again."

Artem's smile cooled. "You place so much faith in this man. How devastating it would be if he was not all that you think him to be."

The last chord ended in a tremulous crescendo, and Ria broke from Artem's grasp, sweeping into a graceful final bow. He bowed to her in return, his eyes narrowing as they flickered to Merek, who had appeared at her side the instant the dance ended. His hand at her back felt steady and sure. Palpable relief washed over her.

"It's been a most instructive evening," Merek said, addressing Artem. "But I'm afraid that the princess and I have had our fill of dancing."

"You're leaving already? What a shame."

"We wish to return to camp before ice forms on the roads."

"Of course. It would be horrible if anything happened to your lovely wife. Horses can be so unpredictable in the dark, after all."

Merek's expression darkened at the veiled threat.

"Thank you for understanding," Ria said graciously, taking Merek's arm, "and thank you for your hospitality. It's been most welcome to enjoy a fine meal under a proper roof."

"Not at all," Artem said with a lingering kiss on her cheek. "Please, think on my proposal. It is more generous than you know."

Orri's men formed a guard around them as they made their way toward the entrance hall.

"I have grave news," Ria whispered to Merek as they walked. "Artem has made an alliance with the Delth and threatens to use them to strengthen his numbers if we do not concede."

"He's bluffing," Merek said dismissively. "If he had command of the Delth armies, he would have used them already and not wasted his own troops on a lengthy winter campaign."

Ria considered this. "Perhaps he really does want to seek an alliance with us. Perhaps—"

She stopped abruptly as Domar passed them in the company of two rough-looking men.

"We'll speak of this later," Merek said in a low voice. "There's more you should know."

The outer doors of the entrance hall stood open to the night, and the cool air felt wonderfully refreshing against Ria's flushed cheeks. She breathed deeply. As unpleasant as it had been, she was glad they'd come. Now that she understood Artem's game, she would be better able to counter it. But they would need to act fast before he brought an army of monsters down upon them.

Aiya draped Ria's heavy cloak about her shoulders but paused as she reached for her winter boots, poised in perfect stillness in a half crouch. Ria followed her gaze and saw that the Khouri woman was watching Artem and Domar back in the great hall, her expression one of great intensity.

"Please tell me you're not pining for another dance, Miss Firah."

Aiya roused herself and brought Ria's boot to her foot. "The prince has received some news which makes him very happy."

Startled, Ria glanced at Artem again. "How do you know this?"

"I watch them speak and can read their words."

"You *what?*"

Aiya glanced at Ria and colored slightly. "It was a useful skill in my former life, my lady." She shrugged, tying the laces tightly and reaching for the other boot.

"I cannot tell what to make of you, Aiya. Are you a great boon sent by the saints? Or you are going to murder us all in our sleep?"

The Khouri woman didn't smile. "Your husband trusts me," she said stiffly.

Ria sighed. "Let's hope he's right to do so."

Aiya finished the second boot and tucked Ria's slippers under her arm. She looked back at the great hall. "Something has changed, my lady," she said tensely. "I think we should leave immediately."

MEREK FOUND RIA WAITING FOR HIM BY THE LARGE OPEN doors. She was as anxious to leave as he was, though the evening had been more valuable than he'd anticipated. With a word through Sergeant Dan, Captain Eldar would soon be poised to attack the city after midnight while Merek would prepare his troops for battle as soon as they reached the camp. Now that they knew the Ardanian's numbers were not what they'd been led to believe, they wouldn't hesitate to risk an all-out battle to take back Endvar. The city would be theirs before long. His optimism made him feel indulgent.

He paused to kiss Ria's temple. "You were marvelous."

"Oh, how I hate that man!" she said vehemently,

glancing back at the ballroom. The strains of music continued uninterrupted.

"Then let's be rid of him." Merek led her outside to their waiting carriage.

But as they stepped out into the night, his heart skipped a beat. He tightened his grip on Ria's arm and thrust her behind him. Surrounding their carriage were not Orri's men, but Ardanian soldiers, their swords and clubs drawn.

Ria gasped. "What is this?"

"Oh dear. It appears we have a problem."

Merek turned to see Artem silhouetted in the light from the open doorway, his posture confident and carefree.

Anger burned hot and quick in Merek's chest. "What is this trickery? You gave an oath that we wouldn't be harmed."

"No, that's not quite how I remember it." Artem stepped forward, and the light falling upon his features from the flickering torches on the staircase was warm and playful. "Ria is free to leave as she wishes. But you, General, are another matter. I made no such oath on your behalf, and it turns out that I'm not quite finished with you."

"There's nothing you can say that I want to hear. Make it quick."

"Oh no, I think you should come inside and have a drink or two. We may be some time yet."

Ria dropped Merek's arm and pushed past Orri and Talen until she was face-to-face with the Ardanian prince. She stood nearly at his height, and he drew back slightly at the force behind her words. "No more of your schemes, Artem. I'm tired. I'm leaving now, and I am bringing my husband with me. Call off your soldiers, and let us pass."

Artem grinned tauntingly, and at his signal, the Ardanian soldiers advanced, hemming them in on the stairs. Orri's soldiers looked at him, their stances guarded and ready to fight at his command.

"Hold," Orri warned.

The Ardanian soldiers stopped short of seizing the Rahmish guests, but the threat was clear.

"Look around you, Ria. You're in no position to be making demands. You may leave, but the general and I have unfinished business. Never fear. I'll return him to you when we are through."

Merek could only imagine the nature of the unfinished business, but of one thing he was certain. He recognized the look in Artem's eye. It was the inhuman look of a man who enjoyed watching others suffer. Merek had seen it on the battlefield when a man lost his grip on humanity and enjoyed the brutality of death instead of suffering it out of duty. But Artem was something more. His intelligence coupled with such viciousness was a ghastly combination.

Artem held his gaze and smiled. The mask of pleasantness was gone. This was the smile of a ruthless killer.

In a way, it was a relief to finally have him exposed for what he truly was.

"Go, Ria," Merek said at last.

"Don't be absurd. I'm not going anywhere without you."

"Go back to camp. I'll join you soon."

She whirled to face him. "I will not leave you. You don't know what he is capable of."

He took her hands and drew her close. "I know well enough, and that's why you must go. He's promised your safety. You will be all right."

"And you? Can you promise me the same for you?"

Seeing the fear in her eyes squeezed his heart painfully. He couldn't lie to her, no matter how much he was tempted. No trite reassurances would do either of them any good, so he quietly spoke the truth. "Ria, I can't bear for you to stay in this place another minute. Please, for my sake, look to your own safety."

She held his gaze a long moment. "You want me to go?"

"I do. Trust me, it's for the best."

She pressed her lips together and swallowed. "If you do not follow within the hour, I will send an army to fetch you."

This seemed to satisfy Artem, and at his command the Ardanian soldiers backed away, making room for Orri's men to resume control of the carriage.

As Merek escorted Ria down the steps, Rorden whispered at his side, "Sir, let me send word to Captain Eldar now."

Merek didn't need to ask what he meant.

"No. Hold to our plan. The princess must be safely out of the city before he acts."

"But sir, that may not be enough time..."

"I will take that risk. She must be safe, is that understood?"

Rorden nodded, his face pale. "May I stay with you, sir?"

Merek smiled in spite of himself. It was a noble gesture, but he didn't think viewing Rorden's mournful face would do him any good with whatever was to come. Not to mention that he would only be a burden if Merek needed to attempt an escape. "No, but thank you. Stay with the princess. Make sure she's safe. That's all that I ask."

Rorden nodded and saluted Merek grimly, then held out a hand to Aiya. Her expression was inscrutable, as if she wanted to speak, but under Artem's watchful eye she merely curtsied and entered the carriage.

Ria waited, watching Merek with eyes luminescent with anguish. His heart filled with words he couldn't utter, so he said nothing. She reached out one soft hand to his face, and he caught it and pressed it to his lips. Never had he wanted to flee a fight more than in this moment, but he wouldn't embroil Ria in a bloody battle to save himself.

"Forgive me," he said simply.

Her eyes shone with tears of frustration, and when she blinked, they spilled over onto her smooth cheeks. But her voice was strong when she spoke. "You're a stubborn fool, Merek Strong, and I hate that I love you so much." For a moment, her lips met his and then she was gone, leaving behind the salty taste of her sorrow.

Twenty-Two

Ria wanted to scream or weep or even just stomp her feet like she had as a child when life wasn't fair. Instead, she sat unmoving in the dark carriage, feeling Merek's absence as a tangible thing in the space beside her.

Aiya and Rorden were silent too. After a few minutes, Rorden offered a tentative, "There's still reason to hope. This is the legendary Captain Strong, after all. I wouldn't be surprised if—"

"Shut it, Rorden," Ria snapped.

In the abashed silence that followed, a muffled snicker sounded in the darkness and something bumped against Ria's legs. Startled, she cried out as a dark shape crawled out from underneath her bench. Rorden swore and lunged for the shadowed figure while Ria groped hastily for her hidden knife.

"Stop!" Aiya cried. "Rorden, it's—"

Rorden pulled back the figure's hood to reveal a filthy

young woman with short cropped hair. And she was laughing.

"I'm sorry, but it's about time someone put Rorden in his place. I would have said it myself if you hadn't, my lady."

Ria stared at the insolent girl. How dare she have the impudence to laugh when Ria's heart was being torn out of her?

"Who are you?" she demanded.

"My lady, please forgive the child," Aiya spoke in her calm way. "She does not mean to offend."

Ria rounded on the Khouri woman. "But why is she here in my carriage? Do you know her? Is this your doing?"

The girl stifled another laugh and settled into Merek's empty place. "Dan said I could hide here. I was supposed to stay out of sight, but there's a great draft on the floor, and I'm half frozen. I thought the general was supposed to be returning with you, but since he's not, may I sit here instead?"

Her careless words pierced Ria afresh, and she couldn't properly breathe.

"Yulda," Aiya said shortly. "Hold your tongue."

Yulda's eyes widened, and with a glance at Ria, she bit off a retort. She shrank into the corner of the carriage and went quiet. In another life, Ria would have felt sorry for the wretched creature, but she had no room for compassion in the swirling mass of fear, hatred, and anger that surged within her.

"Yulda was employed by the general in leading the soldiers to the tunnels," Rorden explained quietly.

Ria sat up straight, a strangled cry escaping her

throat. "Of course! What a fool I am! Rorden, how do I contact Captain Eldar? He must raid Ogmun's estate at once."

Rorden shook his head solemnly. "I'm afraid that's impossible. General Strong already issued orders to have him attack after midnight."

"Then we must change the order. Midnight is too far away. They must attack at once." A new feeling swelled within her, and she seized it. Hope.

To her frustration, Rorden didn't echo her enthusiasm. "General Strong forbade me from doing anything until you were safely out of the city. He didn't want to endanger you. But I swear to you that the moment you're out of danger, Captain Orri and I will launch a rescue."

"That's not good enough. Merek may be dead by then." *Curse him for being so gallant.* Ria glanced at the young woman beside her, and a wild notion struck her. "Rorden, avert your eyes. Yulda, I need your dress."

"I beg your pardon?"

"Hurry, girl! Aiya, help me with mine. Rorden, turn away!"

They all looked at her with baffled expressions as she threw off her cloak and gloves.

"You want my dress?" Yulda squeaked, with a horrified look at Rorden.

"Yes, quickly now. Don't worry, you won't be left in your underthings. I'll give you mine instead. Would you like to play princess for a night?"

Ria reached around to unfasten her stays, but the rocking of the carriage made it difficult. "Aiya, please! Every moment we waste is one Merek can't afford."

For a moment, she feared that the rest of the group

would refuse to help. But Aiya—bless her!—finally roused herself from her state of shock and began loosening Ria's bodice with quick fingers.

"Rorden, be a good boy," Aiya warned.

"You can't be serious!" he complained, but he turned his head to the curtained window. "This is madness, Your Highness."

"No, madness is leaving my husband behind alone when there's a company of soldiers hidden in the depths of the city as we speak." Ria grabbed the back of the seat to keep from pitching onto the floor with the jostling of the carriage and Aiya's tugging.

The cold air bit at her exposed skin as the gown slipped from her shoulders. Hastily, she grabbed Yulda's woolen dress, and cringed as she slipped it over her head. Not only was it thin and strained across her shoulders, but it stank of unearthly odors that made her eyes water. The girl's cloak wasn't much better, and she tried not to think about what biting pests may have infested it as she drew the hood over her head. At least the cloak added some small measure of warmth and disguised the ill-fitting dress well.

Yulda's eyes grew wide and reverent as Aiya helped her into Ria's gown. It was comically ill-suited to her narrow shoulders, and her dirty undershift was exposed at the neckline, but Ria's cloak covered it all. With the hood up, one almost might not notice the imposter at a glance.

"Sit up straight, and keep the hood low. Avoid speaking or looking directly at anyone. The gate is guarded, and Ardanian soldiers hold the road outside. If they should question you, speak firmly, but they will most likely let you pass unimpeded."

"Most likely?" Yulda squeaked.

"Aiya, perhaps you should do the speaking for her. Try to divert attention from the grieving princess."

"On the contrary, if you aim to do what I think, I insist on going with you."

Ria frowned. "Rorden will be companion enough. He knows his way into the tunnels, and his sword will be useful."

The Khouri woman glanced at Rorden, and something passed between them. Rorden spoke apologetically.

"I agree with Aiya. She's far more resourceful than you give her credit for. You may have need of her."

Ria was less certain of this, but they didn't have much time to debate. Besides, she hadn't fully decided what she was going to do. Somehow she needed to get word to Eldar immediately, but the details were still cloudy in her mind.

"Very well, then. Yulda," she said kindly, "pretend to be asleep or crying if you must. When you arrive at camp, explain everything to Captains Orri and Firl. I've stayed behind to arrange the general's rescue. Tell them to prepare troops to storm the city immediately. Do you understand?"

"Yes, Your Highness," Yulda said uncertainly.

"And Yulda, if you do this for me, you can keep the gown."

The girl's choked gasp almost made Ria smile.

She looked out the window. All was dark in the city, with not a candle or a fire to be seen lighting the windows. Whatever Artem said of aid, this was either a city reduced to poverty or one hiding in fear. But the darkness would make her escape easier, and for that she was grateful.

Soon the carriage slowed as it descended a hill. At the bottom, they would pass beneath a large bridge, the same location where the carriage had slowed on their arrival to allow Sergeant Dan to slip away.

"Are you ready?" Ria asked Rorden and Aiya. They nodded in unison, Rorden's eyes shining with excitement. For all he'd tried to dissuade her, he was glad of the change in plans, which gave her confidence. He was just as desperate to save Merek as she was, and she was glad to have him with her.

As for Aiya, she wasn't so sure.

Merek watched Ria's carriage only for a moment before turning to face his enemy. He couldn't afford to pine for her now that she was on her way to safety. The prince was of far greater concern.

Artem stood at the top of the staircase, feet apart, looking like a hero out of an epic tale. With Merek below on the flagstones, the height advantage made it difficult for him to feel anything but subservient.

"Come, Strong," Artem said cheerfully. "We have much to do before the night is over."

Ardanian soldiers followed as Merek climbed the stairs to the entrance, but they didn't touch him. At this point, his purpose was to stay alive long enough for Eldar's men to find him, preferably still whole enough to be worth the rescue. Midnight was a long way off.

Merek followed Artem into the great hall. He paused as they entered, disoriented by the sudden change. The dancing couples, the musicians, and most of the servants were gone. The feasting tables and chairs remained, but even those were being cleared away at a startling rate. They didn't linger in the hall but continued to a narrow corridor that ended in a small room filled with books where a fire already blazed in the hearth.

Prince Artem settled himself behind the desk, gesturing for Merek to sit on one of the soft upholstered chairs opposite. With a wary glance at the soldiers near him, Merek did as he was bidden. Artem clasped his hands together and looked at him intently.

"Now, General Strong, you must tell me the name of your tailor."

An expectant pause followed. Merek wondered if he'd heard him correctly.

"Excuse me?"

"Your tailor in Albon. I also want to know which cobblers you would recommend, and who in the city prepares the best roasted drakeling."

Merek was dumbfounded. "You're looking for a cook?"

"Among other things," Artem said, picking up a piece of paper from the desk. "I have a list, but it's quite lengthy. Would you like some refreshment while we go over it?"

Merek couldn't decide if the prince was insane or simply trying to make him look a fool. "It seems premature to be putting together your household when you have yet to gain the throne."

"A mere formality," Artem disregarded.

"The princess has soundly refused you, and you don't have the strength of arms to conquer it by force. Even if you kill me, there's an army double the size of yours standing between you and Albon, with thousands more stationed around the kingdom ready to respond to your threat. That is far more than a formality."

Artem replaced the list and regarded Merek with eyes that were confident and intelligent. "A very astute observation, General. Unless, of course, I managed to draw your forces away for an extended campaign in the borders of the kingdom while another army swept in and took the capital while your back was turned."

Silence.

The horrific implication of these words settled on Merek with agonizing slowness.

Artem grinned malevolently. "Oh, I do love these moments! I confess it's a guilty pleasure, but I just can't help myself. Why send you to your death full of righteous indignation that your cause will be won when I can send you tormented with the knowledge that you've lost everything? Do forgive the indulgence."

Merek jumped to his feet, blood rushing to his head. "You threatened Ria with an army of Delth. You promised her that she could avoid war if she conceded."

"Another diversion. Albon is burning as we speak, and when we're finished here, then my men will tear you limb from limb. So, I repeat, General Strong," he said, raising a quill pen, "would you care for some refreshment?"

· · ✳ · ·

RIA JUMPED OUT OF THE CARRIAGE BEFORE IT HAD FULLY stopped rolling and stumbled as her boots hit the uneven stone. She quickly moved aside to make room for Rorden and Aiya.

"Rorden, grab a lantern from the carriage," she ordered.

"No light, my lady," Aiya said.

"But how will we see? There's no moon tonight."

"Precisely. The darkness will hide us well."

Ria didn't like the sound of that but could say no more as Rorden rapped on the carriage door, and it started moving again. Mere seconds had passed since they'd signaled the driver to stop.

They moved out of the way of the soldiers marching in the wake of the carriage, Ria keeping her head low to avoid recognition. Soldiers glanced at them curiously, but only one broke rank and called to them.

"Is something wrong, Aiya?" Sergeant Dan asked with concern. "What are you—" He jogged over to join them and swore softly as he recognized Ria.

"Come with us, Dan," Aiya said urgently. "We must get into the tunnels quickly."

"What's going on here?" Captain Talen called as he brought up the rear on horseback.

"Shall we ask the Ardanians to join us too?" Ria huffed in exasperation. "Could you at least *try* to be discreet, Captain?"

"Your Highness!" Talen shot a panicked look at the retreating carriage. "What is the meaning of this?"

"Do not be alarmed. We're going to rescue Strong."

"But it's too dangerous for you—"

"Can you really tell me that I'm in any greater danger

now than I was sitting in a carriage that Prince Artem could have seized at any time?"

Talen didn't respond.

"Strong may have wanted me out of the city, but I'm not convinced that the carriage is the safest way. I want him out of the city alive, and you and I both know that is most likely to happen if we don't waste any more time arguing under this bridge."

Talen was conflicted; she could see that even in the dim light from the fading carriage lanterns. Protect his friend or protect his future queen? Follow orders, or follow his own loyal heart?

"Barrus!" Talen called to a soldier in the back of the line before the last of the troops passed out of sight. "Take my horse. Don't tell anyone except Captain Orri what has happened here."

Ria felt a wave of satisfaction watching the soldiers march away in the wake of the carriage. Until Talen looked expectantly at her and asked, "Well, Your Highness, we're now stranded with you. What do you propose?"

For a moment, the weight of what she'd done robbed her of speech.

"I suggest we get off the main road," Dan volunteered.

"Yes," Ria agreed. She hesitated when Dan moved further under the bridge to a metal grate set into the street. "Are you mad?" she demanded when she realized his intent. But Talen had already opened the grate and was asking Dan how far they would have to jump.

"Not far," Dan said reassuringly. "And it won't take long to get to Lord Bolen's from there."

Ria had no time to argue because voices down the street signaled that someone was approaching.

"Quickly, my lady," Talen urged.

Dan and Rorden dropped into the hole first while Talen stayed above to help the women. Ria had a fleeting glimpse of Aiya's face—her amused expression looking unexpectedly smug—before she too dropped into the darkness.

TWENTY-THREE

It was difficult to think of drapers and tailors and leatherworkers when one was jittery with the need to fight. The only thing that kept Merek focused was knowing that he might be saving these people's lives. For what future, he couldn't be sure, but it was something.

He included Lotta and Pedr on the list, as well as the cobbler, Jes, with his son, Finn. And while Artem wrote, Merek chastised himself for not guessing the prince's true purpose sooner. The recent silence from Albon that they'd attributed to poor weather. The Ardanian army's failure to launch a full push into Rahm. Suddenly everything took on new meaning. Endvar was merely a diversion; the true prize had been Albon all along.

He couldn't sit and instead moved fitfully about the room. The prince didn't seem to mind, though the guards kept a close watch on Merek's movements. He wasn't armed, but that didn't stop him from imagining a dozen different ways he could kill the prince before the list was complete.

"My thanks, Strong," Artem said as he stood and stretched. "This will save me a great deal of frustration when I get settled in my new home."

"What if I reconsider your offer?" Merek asked, desperate to save his people at whatever cost. He was the only one in Endvar who knew that Albon had been invaded. Somehow he needed to live long enough to get word to his captains and launch a counterattack. "What if I support you as king of Rahm and agree to lead your armies?"

Artem waved his hand dismissively. "And spend the rest of my life waiting for a knife in my back? I think not." He stood before Merek, and there was something like respect in his eyes. And envy. "I've seen your character, General Strong, and I know you would not be so easily bought. Men who are greedy and ambitious are easy to control. But men like you who are motivated by principles are the most dangerous because I can never truly be your master. Now, shall we?" He indicated the door which led back to the great hall.

As they moved down the corridor, Artem said pleasantly, "If it makes you feel any better, I'm only killing you now because you would have made a magnificent king. I'd hoped you wouldn't, but I should have known not to argue with Ria's discerning taste."

"You say that as if you regret my death."

"Oh, I do! Such a waste! But I can't have you raising up a revolution now, can I? Unfortunately, you would be quite effective at it. This will be ever so much cleaner. The army loses its commander, Ria loses her husband, and in her grief she abdicates without argument. I expect to be crowned before the end of the month—once I clean up the mess the Delth have made so we can have a proper celebration."

The prince's flippant tone made Merek's blood boil. He spoke as if a violent war were merely an inconvenience. "And Ria? What do you plan to do with her?"

"That I haven't fully decided," Artem admitted. "A great deal will depend on her, I suppose. If she opposes me, it might be amusing to keep her close, see what it takes to win her to my side. A lot depends on how she reacts to me sending her your head in a box."

They entered the great hall, and Merek's heart sank. In the center of the room, where Merek and Ria had danced together earlier in the evening, stood a long table whose rough surface held many dark stains. Iron shackles were chained to each corner. Domar stood near a rack of tools placed conveniently close to the table. It wasn't hard to guess their purpose. Looking at their barbed and serrated edges, the blood drained from Merek's face, and he was suddenly glad he hadn't eaten much at dinner.

"Thank you, Domar! Highly efficient, as usual," Artem called out cheerfully, advancing into the room. "Well, Strong, shall we get started?"

Merek tackled him from behind.

Rough hands grabbed Ria before she hit the ground. Her awkward, interrupted fall as Rorden tried to catch her made her think she might have done better on her own.

"Alright, my lady?"

"Yes, thank you," Ria said shakily.

Once Aiya and Talen joined them, Dan led them deeper underground. The darkness was unnerving. Ria couldn't see her companions, let alone the route they were taking. Aiya caught her by the arm and spoke to her in a soothing voice. It was proof of how skittish Ria was that she wasn't affronted by the intimate contact. Instead, she clutched the smaller woman gratefully.

"You are very brave, my lady," Aiya said, the musical lilt of her accent gentle on Ria's ears. "Far braver than I expected."

"Yes, well, it's surprising what idiotic things we do for the men we love."

Aiya chuckled warmly. "That is very true." She spoke with such fervor that Ria wondered for a moment what story lay behind her words. Then Ria cringed as cold water splashed over the tops of her boots. She tried not to imagine what the water would look like in daylight.

Their voices echoed through the sewer, so the group kept their conversation at a minimum, but there were some things Ria had to know.

"When did the general give the order to attack? He was adamantly against it when we discussed it in camp."

Talen and Rorden explained the information that had been discovered through the evening, the most valuable of which had come from Aiya's own brother.

"Your brother is working for Prince Artem?"

"It was a shock to me as well, Your Highness."

"How do we know he can be trusted? What if he deliberately fed us false information to reveal our hand?"

"My brother has twice lost everything for my sake. His allegiance may not lie with kings and countries, but he would never do anything to endanger me."

Aiya's words held an undercurrent of warmth that filled Ria with unexpected remorse. And a twinge of envy. Once she could speak with such confidence about her own father, but she'd lost that, and in its place was a void that she tried very hard to ignore. Until something like Aiya's comment drew attention to its emptiness.

One thing was certain, she couldn't afford to lose anyone else she loved. No matter the cost, she must find a way to save Merek.

The first casualty was her dignity. By the time they reached their exit—which required clambering awkwardly on Dan's back and getting pulled to the street by Talen and Rorden from above—Ria understood that wearing the filthy servant girl's clothing was not the worst of her humiliation for the night. Aiya seemed to take it all in stride. No, she almost seemed to be enjoying herself. It was both impressive and irritating, so Ria carefully packed her wounded pride away until later when she might have the luxury of tending to it properly.

"Lord Bolen's is just down the street from here," Dan whispered, panting slightly from having just climbed onto the road himself. "Lord Ogmun's is further to the east."

"East? Which way is east?" Ria demanded, her sense of direction hopelessly handicapped by the darkness.

"To the left, my lady," Talen said patiently.

"Very well. Dan, I trust that you can find your way.

Tell Captain Eldar to attack Lord Ogmun's estate without delay. Rorden, you will signal Captain Falbrook to seize the north gate for our escape. We'll find each other again at Ogmun's. Let us pray that we are not too late." The men nodded in assent and slipped away into the night.

MEREK KNOCKED THE PRINCE TO THE FLOOR, STEALING HIS sword from the scabbard at his hip as he fell. He spared little thought for Artem—who cried out in annoyance and scurried out of the way—because three soldiers were upon him instantly. Alas, the prince's sword was light and flimsy, more of a ceremonial weapon than one meant to do any real harm. It reverberated painfully with each strike against the soldiers' blades, and Merek had trouble getting any real strength behind his thrusts.

One soldier cried out and dropped his sword as Merek sliced his hand. Merek used the distraction to dodge around a pillar, trying to get nearer to an exit. The door through which they had entered was still open, but that corridor only led to Ogmun's study. He needed to reach one of the other doors which were now being systematically sealed off by soldiers. Dozens more moved to intercept him, and even as his faulty sword failed to fully penetrate the gut of one opponent, another soldier struck his left thigh.

Grunting with pain, Merek paused, panting. He watched the circle of soldiers closing in on him, looking for a weak spot where he could break through. It was no use. Blood flowed freely from his leg, and already his trousers were damp down to his boot tops.

"Good show, General!" The fair prince was on his feet again and moved through the wall of soldiers to glare at Merek. "I hope you feel better after that completely unnecessary display."

"I only wish I'd stabbed you through the heart while I had the chance. Though this poor excuse for a sword might not have had the strength." He threw the stolen weapon at the prince's feet in disgust.

Artem picked it up and whipped it through the air a few times. In a quick motion, he pressed it against Merek's neck. "Should we test it? What do you say, Strong, should we end the drama right now?"

"You like drama?" Merek said, his voice tight as he tried to avoid moving his throat. The blade pricked his skin, burning as it drew blood. "Give me a proper sword, and I'll show you drama."

"You hear that, Domar? He aims to be our entertainment for the evening," Artem said fiercely, his breath hot on Merek's face. "I have a better idea." He nodded at the nearest soldiers. "Strip him," he commanded.

The pain in Merek's leg made it difficult to stand as his blood leaked onto the floor. He almost welcomed the support as multiple pairs of hands seized him from behind.

TWENTY-FOUR

Stefan watched from the trees where he and his men were hidden. They preferred to sit in the lower branches of the great firs because in the darkness there was no way they would be discovered. No one ever thought to look up.

"They should have let us attack tonight," Gyll said at his side.

"While the future king and queen are dining with their enemy?"

"Of course. Perfect distraction. They'd least expect it."

"Because it'd be daft," Stefan chided.

Gyll was a fearsome fighter, but he was a bit too impetuous for Stefan's taste. Which is probably what made him such a good climber.

"Ah, there's our friend again," Gyll whispered. "You think he knows we watch him like this every night? You think he can feel our eyes on him, following his every move? Thinking about how to kill him most quietly?"

The thought prickled the hairs on Stefan's neck.

"Why do you say it's the same guard?"

"Because it is," Gyll said matter-of-factly. "I call him Mossback and the other one Tunbridge."

Stefan just looked at him.

"You know, after—"

"I jolly well recognize the names, but why are you calling two Ardanian soldiers the names of our friends at home?"

Gyll shrugged. "Easy to remember."

"What makes you think they're the same guards every night?"

Another shrug, barely visible in the darkness. "I've watched them enough now, I can tell. Mossback always takes his time over there near that spot. There must be something very interesting on the other side of that wall. Tunbridge has got a cold and spits over the wall every few minutes, which got him in trouble one night. Lots of bellowing from below. It was funnier than watching old Morton—"

"Sir!" A hoarse whisper brought them both to attention. Gyll's brother, Gersil, stepped out of the undergrowth below. "There's a light in the church tower!" The younger man could barely contain his excitement. Stefan didn't share his enthusiasm. If they were being signaled, it meant that things had gone wrong with the princess's meeting.

"Very well. Gyll, it appears that you'll get your wish after all."

Within a few short minutes, all six of Stefan's climbers gathered on the forest floor at the edge of the trees.

"Are you ready?" Stefan asked.

"More than ready sir," Gyll said eagerly.

Stefan nodded. "Gyll and Gersil, you'll attack from the east. Ryken and Garth from the west."

"So we're taking Mossback and they have Tunbridge?"

Gersil snickered.

Stefan ignored him. "Borth and Mahl, I want you to scout out the guards on the ground. You have the element of surprise, but if there are more than two, don't attack without Ryken and Garth to back you up. Remember, you don't have reinforcements to help, so you must keep absolutely silent. Don't leave any alive to sound the alarm."

The men nodded. Stefan wished that Merek was with them, or that he'd learned to climb as Merek had suggested. But Stefan had never possessed the same reckless confidence that came so naturally to his friend. Just the thought of trying to climb that height made his head swim.

Unfortunately, that meant he was stuck on the ground just watching and praying these boys could handle themselves. He'd never thought of himself as a coward, but the feeling he had watching his men settle their nerves and begin climbing felt uncannily similar.

COLD.

Merek couldn't remember a time when he'd been so cold. He was vaguely aware that it was probably due to the loss of blood more than the loss of clothing, but that knowledge certainly didn't help. He'd resisted the soldiers as they'd stripped him, but all it had earned him was a painful lump on the back of his head and a boot to the groin. Now, as he lay shackled to the table, he knew his only hope was to stay alive long enough for Eldar's attack.

"Artem, let us just end it now," Domar spoke in a quiet tone nearby. "What harm is there in giving him the dignity of a quick death?"

"You surprise me, Domar. I never thought I'd see the day when you lost your nerve."

Artem busied himself at the table, his back to Merek. They were speaking in Rahmish, as if to ensure he heard their plans for him.

"I haven't lost my nerve," Domar said heatedly, "but I hate to see what happens when things don't...go well. I don't like what it does to you."

"Then help me make sure things go well. Stick this in the fire, will you?"

Artem passed something to Domar that Merek couldn't see, then he turned to face Merek lying on the wooden table. He looked him over, his brow furrowed intently. "So much blood," he tsked. "Can you feel it? Can you feel your life draining away? We'll have to fix that, won't we? Can't risk leaking it all out prematurely, not when we'll need it for...other things."

Merek didn't answer. He *could* feel it, and that scared him. He felt so exposed, lying on the splintery slab like a beast prepared for the butcher, his ankles and wrists painfully bound. He tensed as Artem touched his leg, the pain from his wound causing it to throb from hip to knee.

"He's strong, Domar," Artem said. "So much stronger

than the others. I think he will do very well."

Merek caught only a glimpse of the white hot iron before Artem plunged it into his leg.

When the north gate opened, the sound of the crossbar being lifted and the door swinging on its hinges resonated so loudly in the stillness that Stefan jumped in surprise. It opened only a crack, and Mahl's smiling face greeted Stefan as he slipped through.

"Nicely done." All six of his men stood before him with no visible wounds. At their feet were four Ardanian soldiers.

"Get these bodies away from here. I don't know how long we'll have to hold this gate, but we need to be prepared to hold it most of the night. Put out those torches. I don't want to announce to the whole city that we aren't Ardanians."

A shadowy figure darted down the street, and Stefan tensed. He drew his sword and signaled Ryken and Garth to hide in an alleyway. The figure had disappeared, but it had clearly been moving in their direction.

Several quiet moments passed, then a sound drew Stefan's ear, followed by a relieved sigh.

"Captain Falbrook!" Rorden greeted as he stepped out of the shadows, breathing heavily from his run. "There's been a change of plans. I need you and your men to come with me."

"We've been tasked with holding this gate, Sergeant. Your signal means a rescue mission is underway, correct?"

"The gate will have to hold itself, sir. You *are* the rescue mission."

"IN ALL MY LIFE I NEVER IMAGINED MYSELF IN A SITUATION like this."

"I understand, my lady. In the tales it's always the princess who needs rescuing, isn't it?"

"Well, yes. But I particularly meant sitting here in a rubbish heap."

Aiya chuckled. "It is not my first time."

Ria looked at her incredulously. "You must have a very singular history, Aiya." The woman's features were difficult to distinguish in the shadow of the wall where they hid out of sight, but a flash of white teeth told Ria she was smiling.

"It's not so interesting to me, but I suppose to a princess it must seem remarkable."

Ria rested her head against the stone wall and sighed. "You speak as though you resent me, but right now I don't feel like being a princess is much of an advantage."

Aiya said nothing, for which Ria was grateful. She didn't want meaningless platitudes or insincere encouragement.

They quieted as someone approached from around the back side of the wall. Ria recognized Captain Talen and hurried to her feet.

"We're here, Talen!" she whispered. "What did you find?"

"Strong is alive."

Ria exhaled in a rush. "You're sure? Did you see him?"

"No. But I…" Talen shifted uncomfortably. "I heard him."

"Heard? What do you mean?"

Aiya let out a soft oath in her native tongue.

All at once Ria understood, and she felt weak. "Where is he?"

"He's being held in the hall. There are balconies on one side of the building and one of the doors must have been left open."

"Balconies?" Aiya asked, interested. "How far above the ground are they?"

"Perhaps twenty feet?"

Ria shivered and hugged herself, but it was not the cold which troubled her. "What now, Captain? How do we get him out of there?"

"For now, we wait. Eldar should be here soon. There's nothing we can do without more men."

"Wait? While he is subjected to—"

She broke off as another shadow joined them.

"The climbers have been signaled," Rorden said quietly. "Our escape route will be secure by the time Captain Eldar arrives."

Ria shook her head firmly. "We can't wait for Eldar. We must act now!"

"How?" Talen shot back. "We simply do not have the force. I would give my life for Strong, Your Highness, but that would do nothing to save his, and that's all I could hope for if I storm the palace alone."

"Who said you would be alone?"

"Your Highness—"

"Don't patronize me, Talen. I will walk into that hall and fight for him myself if you refuse."

"With all due respect," he said, his tone growing increasingly impatient, "you would get yourself killed faster than my old nursemaid. Trust me when I say it's best to wait."

Ria knew he was right, and thinking of her shoulder injury reminded her how little accustomed she was to handling true pain, not to mention her weakness at the sight of blood. "Then I've failed him after all. What a poor rescuer I've turned out to be!"

"Not at all, my lady," Rorden said kindly, his hand on her shoulder. She knew he meant to comfort her, but the gesture seemed infuriatingly condescending.

"If you hadn't acted with such courage, Eldar would not be on his way right now with his company," Talen said. "The general will be saved because of you, but we must be patient a little longer."

"No," Ria said, fear gripping her heart as a new thought occurred to her. "Eldar won't be able to save him either. As soon as Artem gets word that the soldiers are here, he will kill him outright. He will not risk Merek's survival, especially now. Don't you see?" She shrugged off Rorden's hand. "If we don't try to save him now, he's dead either way."

Talen rubbed his forehead in frustration. "I wish there was another way, but there simply isn't. If you command it, I'll try. But you must prepare yourself for the likelihood that I won't succeed."

"There may be another way," Aiya said quietly from the shadows. The others turned to her expectantly. "We don't need to fight the prince's soldiers. We'll save that for Captain Eldar. All we need to do is steal the general back. What we need is an expert thief."

TWENTY-FIVE

"Care for a pastry?"

Merek blinked to clear his vision. Artem stood over him, eating a berry tart, his teeth stained purple by the juice. He licked his lips and proffered it to Merek. The scent of burning flesh still lingered in the air.

Nauseated, Merek turned his head away.

"No? So be it. Your bleeding has stopped, so that's fortunate. Unnecessary bleeding really gets in the way. Are you sure you don't want dessert while you wait? These preserves taste surprisingly fresh."

He waved it under Merek's nose, and the sweet sickly scent was too strong for his already weakened stomach. He turned and retched, straining against the manacles to lift his head. Warm vomit spread down his side and splashed onto the stone floor. He coughed and spit the vile taste from his mouth.

Artem just laughed, a low dark sound. "What do you

think, Domar? Should we start with a leg vein? Or go straight to the chest?"

"I told you what I think." Domar appeared on the other side of the table. He looked at Merek with revulsion. "This is your game, not mine. I would rather just kill him at once and go to bed."

"And miss such an opportunity?"

"You know I don't subscribe to those Delth superstitions. What you did to those soldiers..." he trailed off, shaking his head in disgust.

"You think keeping them trapped in the tunnels was somehow better? At least they got to see the sun one last time before they died."

Merek stopped coughing and strained to listen. His head pounded and waves of nausea washed over him, but he pushed it aside, trying to guess Artem's purpose. He'd spent enough time fighting the Delth in his youth to know that anything stemming from one of their barbarous rituals would leave him forever maimed, if he even survived it at all.

"It's not the soldiers that concern me," Domar said in exasperation. "It's how much *you* suffer when they disappoint you, when they die before you're finished with your childish ritual. I wish you would just leave it alone!"

"Childish?" Artem's eyes flashed angrily. "Is that what you think?"

"What else should I think? I know as much about how to kill a man as anyone, and the idea of consuming a person's strength before he dies is laughable."

"It is an art," Artem breathed, "practiced for generations by the Delth. I've seen it myself."

"What I've seen is a form of butchery that no man can survive. What if he's no different?"

There was a wild look in Artem's eye as he looked down at Merek. He placed a hand on his chest, touching him reverently. "You shall see, Domar," he murmured softly. "You shall see."

Domar made a small noise of disgust before he turned away, conceding the argument.

Somehow Merek needed to delay what was coming.

"What makes you think the Delth will listen to you?" Merek said, his voice sounding weak in his own ears. That worried him almost as much as the long hook that the prince was examining in the light. "When you go to Albon and proclaim yourself the new king, how do you know they won't unleash their bloodlust on you?"

Artem ignored the question, prodding Merek's skin with a frown of concentration. First his leg, then an arm, then his neck. His eyes shone with greed. Merek had never felt so vulnerable in his life, and he pulled against the shackles reflexively.

"Now, now," Artem said pleasantly, but his jaw tensed. "You'll need to relax for this to work."

Artem produced a gleaming long knife and pressed it experimentally against the inside of Merek's left elbow. A sharp pain shot through his arm and Merek jerked his arm away, causing the blade to slip.

Artem's expression darkened, and he swore in Ardanian. "Domar! Fetch the Khouri. He needs a tonic, but a mild one. We don't want to rob him of his senses. What would be the fun in that?" he added with an angry glare.

Warm blood trickled down his arm, and Merek tensed as Artem raised the knife and brought it down hard on the table near his arm. Merek flinched and Artem humphed in satisfaction, then stalked away. Merek relaxed, listening to Domar's footsteps receding at the far end of the hall. He knew it was dangerous to anger Artem, but anything he could do to delay his bloody dissection was worth the risk.

Merek closed his eyes and hoped Imar would be difficult to find. How much time had passed since he'd said goodbye to Ria? It felt like an eternity. Had she reached the city gates yet? For a moment he indulged himself thinking about her safe and out of Artem's reach. She would be worried, he knew, but at least she didn't—

Pain erupted as Artem grabbed his right toe with cold iron pliers and snapped it, breaking it in one motion. Merek shot up, the shackles cutting into his wrists. But that was nothing compared to the pain of the freshly broken toe, followed by another, and another, and another as Artem moved systematically from biggest to smallest down his foot.

Merek bellowed and kicked out uselessly, but Artem calmly moved on to the other foot. When he was finished, Merek lay panting on the table, hot tears of pain squeezing out of the corners of his eyes.

"It's most fascinating how much pain is localized in one small digit. I'm always curious: Is the pain magnified ten times? Or does it reach a certain threshold and plateau?" Artem moved toward his head and leered down at him.

In answer, Merek spat out the most vile curse he could think of, though his slurred speech robbed it of its potency. Pain fogged his mind, and he feared he might lose consciousness again.

"Ah, that's good," Artem said with satisfaction. "Hold on to that hatred. It will make it most rewarding for me when you are sobbing like a child. Not long now. Not long."

. . ✳ . .

"If you plan your climb to work around that protrusion, you'll be glad you did. It doesn't look like much from here, but it'll be a lot bigger once you get close to it."

"And don't grip the stone too tightly. Keep your hands nice and loose or you'll wear out your arms faster."

"Make sure your feet are planted before you move your hands. Better to go slowly than to have to make a lot of adjustments."

Aiya smiled and thanked the young men politely. It's true she hadn't climbed a wall like this in years, but she was younger than they when she'd first learned, so it seemed laughable that these forest climbers were giving her suggestions. To them, she was clearly both a novice and a novelty. They all had something to say and hovered around her like anxious old women dispensing marriage advice to a new bride.

Aiya adjusted the rope that held up a pair of thin trousers she'd found in a mending pile near the laundry. They were too large for her, but there was no way she could have gotten even a few feet off the ground in the slippery taffeta gown. Unfortunately, the only shirts in the pile were missing functioning buttons, and Aiya couldn't fasten them with a rope as easily as she had the trousers. So, she'd taken her knife to the maid's gown, brutally cutting off the heavy skirt just below the hips, keeping the tight bodice for a blouse. For a moment, she thought the princess was going to choke on her own fury when she saw what Aiya had done. But then the young woman had shaken her head and, with a small chortle, simply said, "You are without question the worst lady's maid I've ever known."

Now Aiya stood at the wall, partially hidden by large evergreen shrubs, planning a path in her mind as others quietly moved into position. There were three large balconies on this wall, with two climbers stationed beneath each one. The balconies didn't appear to be guarded, but each would ascend on opposite sides just to be cautious.

Aiya looked at her partner, Gyll, who looked barely old enough for the stubble which sprinkled his chin. He stood about thirty feet away, and in the darkness, she could barely make out his form against the wall until he moved. He stepped up to balance on top of the foundation stones and looked at her expectantly. It was time.

Soldiers moved about the courtyard, extinguishing the lights of dozens of candles, lanterns, and braziers that had burned to welcome the Rahmish guests. Ria, Talen, and Rorden watched them from the shadows of a tall stand of arborvitae that lined the gardens.

"Do not enter the building," Talen whispered to Ria. "Draw the prince outside, if you can. It will be much easier to escape if we stay out in the open. Do you have a weapon of any kind?"

"I left my knife in the pocket of my gown, but that's a small loss since I'm not very skilled."

Talen nodded as if he'd expected as much. "Take this," he said, handing her a large, heavy knife in a leather sheath. "Slip it into your boot. It may buy you a few precious seconds."

"They're climbing," Rorden said softly. Ria followed his gaze but struggled to make out the dark forms on the wall of the keep. Only after watching for several long moments did she catch enough movement to distinguish one shadow from another.

She shivered with cold and nervous anticipation. When the climbers were in position on the three balconies, she would emerge from the shadows and command an audience with Prince Artem. After that, she couldn't even begin to guess what might happen.

TWENTY-SIX

Aiya was out of practice. In her youth, she could have mastered a wall like this easily, but it had been years since she'd done this kind of climbing. Her forearms burned, but she resisted the temptation to move more quickly, knowing that the stone courtyard below would be unforgiving if she misstepped.

She paid no attention to the other climbers moving soundlessly not far away. The stone was cold under her fingers, its roughness scraping her hands and feet. The chilly breeze numbed her, and soon she could scarcely feel her fingers and toes. Once, her hand slipped, and she felt a surge of panic, but her bare feet held firm. After a pause to collect her wits, she continued. She might have been out of practice, but there were some things one never forgot. Calming herself when panic pushed her into recklessness was the most critical.

Voices sounded from down below, and she paused. Her arms ached, and her feet felt like blocks of ice, but she waited for the people below to pass, urging them on silently in her mind. As long as she stayed still, there was no reason for them to suspect she was there. But she couldn't stay too much longer, or her muscles would be in danger of giving out. As it was, her arms were shaking by the time they passed.

At last, she reached the height of the balcony. Gyll had already arrived and stealthily crept toward her around the rectangle of light that spilled from the glass doors onto the balcony floor. By the time he reached her, Aiya had firmly planted her feet on the base of the stone balustrade and was pulling herself over.

"Well done, miss," Gyll whispered.

Together, they crouched to the glass doors that opened into the pillared arcade surrounding the great hall. The banquet table had been laid out with an array of sweets, pastries and puddings heaped high with cream as white as the tablecloth. It partially blocked her view of a man chained to a large table. She knew without seeing his face that it must be Strong.

The prince sat at the feasting table, eating a thick golden sauce with a spoon. He seemed unconcerned, and for a moment she worried that they were too late, that Artem had already killed Strong. But then a side door opened, and she realized he was simply waiting.

Aiya's breath caught as Imar entered the room. She'd neglected to ask him what sort of work he did for the prince. Artem must have learned of some of his lesser known talents.

Aiya swore.

Gyll looked at her questioningly.

"That man is my brother. We cannot attack while he is there."

"Then pray he leaves before the princess arrives."

"Can we get word to the others to spare him?" Aiya was frantic. She knew Imar well enough to know that he would take no pleasure in helping the prince. He didn't deserve to die just because he was in the wrong place at the wrong time, and their rescue force couldn't afford to be distracted fighting a man who was not their enemy.

Gyll was quiet for a moment. "There may be a way," he said. "I'll signal to them to let me take the lead. If we go in first, and you can get to your brother in time, perhaps you can warn him."

It was the best Aiya could hope for. She scanned the room for soldiers. She counted fourteen milling about in the hall, clustered on the edges to avoid the prince and his ghastly prey. That was a considerable force but still less of a threat than the five bowmen who could kill Imar before the soldiers even knew they were there. She would have to move quickly to protect her brother.

SIXTY-FOUR. SIXTY-FOUR PETALS ON THE ROSE PATTERN engraved in the ceiling of Lord Ogmun's great hall. If there were twelve rows of six roses each—was it twelve? Or fourteen? Merek counted again in his desperate attempt to focus his mind on something—anything—that would keep him from surrendering to the fear and the pain. He must stay awake, no matter the sweet temptation of unconsciousness that nipped the edges of his mind.

Voices and footsteps sounded as if from a great distance, and Imar's face appeared in Merek's vision. Immediately, he felt ashamed. It was one thing to be stripped and broken in front of one's enemies. It was another thing entirely to appear like that to someone whom he had known for years. He would have once even considered Imar a friend.

But as Imar looked down at him impassively, his face showed no warmth of recognition. "You want to take away this man's ability to fight? Haven't these shackles already done that for you?"

"I need you to force him to relax," Artem's voice called from the direction of the dessert table. "I can't work with his resistance. One false move and he'll bleed out before I'm done. You see that cut on his arm? Sloppy. But I still want him awake. I want him to feel everything."

A familiar sound, as if from a memory, drew Merek's attention away from the conversation. It was the mournful call of an owl, sounding very near. After a long silence, it sounded again, this time at a slight distance. Awareness rushed through him. The first call was not the same as the second. Just a slight difference, but clear to one born and bred in the forest.

Imar didn't seem to notice.

"Imar," Merek whispered quietly. He wished he had water to rinse out the bile that burned his throat. "Don't do this."

Imar's lips scarcely moved as he replied. "I can end it all now if you wish. That is all I can do."

"No! Help is coming. I just need time."

A look of pity flickered in Imar's eyes. He turned back

to the prince. "I can do what you ask, but it will be difficult. I will need to administer it slowly, monitoring him closely as it takes effect so that I don't give him too much."

Heavy footsteps and then Artem's face appeared next to Imar's. "How long will it take?" he asked crossly.

"An hour. Perhaps less. Has he eaten since he emptied his stomach?" Imar asked with a glance at the table where Merek's vomit stank. Artem shook his head. "Then it should be faster."

Artem scowled. "I suppose we could always break his fingers while we wait."

Down at the other end of the hall, a door opened. Artem swore and let out a violent stream of Ardanian. Whatever response he received, however, made him look up with interest.

"I want him ready when I return," he ordered Imar as he left.

As soon as his back was turned, Imar pressed a vial against Merek's teeth and in a quick, practiced motion, dumped the contents into his mouth then clamped his nose shut so that he swallowed reflexively. Merek choked on the bitter fluid, but it was down before he could spit it out.

He glared at Imar, who nodded in satisfaction.

"The prince will be back soon. I'd suggest you rest while you can."

"Why did he leave?'

"The guards say there is a woman here to see him. Someone claiming to be the princess."

Merek's head snapped up. "The princess?"

"The guard wasn't certain if it was her. She is dressed like a servant, but she has two soldiers with her."

Merek felt a rush of panic. Surely Ria wouldn't be so foolish as to return. What could she be thinking?

"Can you free me while he's gone?" he begged.

Imar shook his head slightly. "I dare not. Not with well over a dozen soldiers watching me."

Merek growled in frustration, pulling against the manacles even though they rubbed his skin painfully. "How long until your tonic takes effect?" he asked, trying to calculate how much time he had before he was useless to aid in his own escape.

"It should have already begun."

"I don't feel any different."

"Your pain, has it changed?"

Merek suddenly realized that for several minutes he hadn't thought about the pain in his toes. The fresh cut in his arm had subsided to a dull ache. Even his leg wound was more bearable. "What did you give me?"

"Not what the prince requested. You will remain alert, but the pain should be more controlled. It will not last long enough, though," Imar said regretfully.

"Do you know what the prince plans to do with me?"

Imar opened his mouth to answer, but a rough voice called out in Ardanian and Imar closed it again.

More than a dozen soldiers? Even if he could escape the chains, Merek was unarmed and hopelessly outnumbered. Escape was futile. But the owl's cry...

· · ✳ · ·

"Let's go," Gyll said as the prince exited the hall. The princess's message had been delivered. Aiya slipped through the door without a sound, hoping the other climbers would honor Gyll's signal and give her a moment to secure Imar's safety.

Then she could think of nothing else, for an Ardanian soldier stood immediately to her left, hidden just out of sight until she stepped inside. He was just as shocked to see her, but she recovered faster and jumped out of reach before he could grab her. Gyll was there in a flash, and while he grappled with the man, Aiya raced to the table in the center of the room. The other Ardanian soldiers called to each other in alarm.

So much for a quiet entrance.

Arrows flew overhead, and Imar ducked as Aiya reached him. She barely spared a glance for the general, angling her body between her brother and the archers.

Imar cursed freely in Khouri. "Aiya, what are you doing here?"

"Get low," she urged. "Beneath the table." She crouched beside him. "We have only a few minutes to free Captain Strong. Will you help me?" she asked, glancing out from the table as two Ardanians rushed the archers, swords raised. Arrows sprouted from their torsos like pins in a cushion, and they stopped, dropping to the floor.

"Help you? I gave up this life ten years ago," Imar spat, "and so did you."

"Yet here you are dealing in deadly poisons for a tyrant with more power than our uncle could have ever dreamed. You said yourself you chose the wrong side.

Come, save a good man who doesn't deserve to die. You've done far worse for less worthy reasons."

Aiya didn't wait for Imar's answer. She crept out from beneath the table. Eight of the soldiers had been dropped by the archers, but the smarter ones had moved to safety behind pillars or chairs. Gyll and his companions crept through the room, trying to flush them out. With a wary eye toward the remaining soldiers, Aiya turned her attention to the prisoner.

Strong blinked in astonishment when she appeared near his head, his eyes bleary and unfocused. "Aiya!" he exclaimed as she grabbed the nearest manacle.

"You know me? That is good. He hasn't stolen your mind then." Aiya hurried to the rack of hideous torture implements and searched through them in earnest. Imar joined her after a moment, and together they began trying various instruments on the manacles.

"Is my wife here? Did Ria return?"

Aiya glanced at Strong, and her hands faltered momentarily. Her hesitation told him all he needed to know.

He cursed softly. "Get me out of these as fast as you can."

"Patience," Aiya replied with gritted teeth. She couldn't think about the princess who would not have time to escape if the prince suspected a trap. She could only think of the lock, could only envision its inner workings as she probed it gently with a steel needle. Where the needle was too short or thin, a long flat hook from the nearby table proved to be effective. So close. If she could just—

A terrific crash sounded from the far side of the room

as several Ardanian soldiers overturned the feasting table to shelter behind it. Aiya and Imar froze, exchanging a look of dread. They looked to the door through which the prince had exited only a few minutes before.

In desperation, Aiya thrust the needle in again.

"We have no time!" Imar whispered in Khouri. "Likely the whole city heard that. They'll be upon us any moment!"

Aiya exhaled in triumph as she released the catch and the lock slid free.

Three soldiers nearby cried out as the shackle came loose and gave up their cover to rush the table. Arrows flew from the darkness of the colonnade, but only one soldier fell.

"Imar..." Aiya warned as she rushed to the next lock.

Imar snatched a long blade and threw it deftly, hitting an Ardanian soldier in the throat. Before the first man fell, Imar grabbed a heavy chain from the rack and whipped it out toward the other soldier, who paused to assess this new threat.

Aiya worked feverishly at the lock, ignoring the sounds of death around her, and it came free faster than the first.

Strong sat up and rubbed his red, swollen wrists. "Find me a sword."

Right. A sword.

"Gyll!" Aiya cried as she loosed the last of the manacles, but the young man had already searched the hall for Strong's things and rushed forward with a bundle of clothing. "Gyll, I could kiss you!" Aiya said gratefully, and the young man blushed.

"No boots," Strong said.

Aiya stepped away and turned to Imar. Three Ardanian soldiers lay at his feet. Imar dropped the chain next to the bodies, a dark scowl on his face.

"What have you done, Aiya?"

She ignored the question. "Can you find us a way out?"

Imar roused himself from his dark reverie. "Come with me."

TWENTY-SEVEN

Ria felt a momentarily thrum of satisfaction at Artem's surprised expression. Whomever he had expected to find waiting for him in the courtyard, it wasn't her. He took in her strange clothing and the soldiers at her side, and his eyes glinted unpleasantly. Talen and Stefan were with her, but Rorden remained hidden in the garden to scout out their escape. The closer Artem approached, the more tension she felt from the captains.

Artem's smile held no warmth. "You miss me already? I'm flattered. What on earth are you wearing?"

"I've considered your proposal, Artem," Ria said, "and I've decided to accept, with the condition that General Strong returns with me now."

Artem folded his arms and regarded her with a calculating expression. "I'm afraid you're too late. I have what I want. What else can you offer?"

Ria paused. "You asked for my support and easy

access to the throne. I'm telling you that I will concede if you release Strong. How is that not what you wanted?"

"I told you, I have other ways. You're useless to me now, Ria. Unless you can think of an offer I can't refuse, I see no reason why this conversation should continue." He nodded to the soldiers flanking him, and they moved in closer, coming between Ria and her guard.

"Your Highness..." Talen growled a low warning.

She swallowed. "You want me to beg? Is that it?"

"That might be amusing, but no. Your husband is dead, and you are interrupting my dessert."

"You lie," Ria said fiercely, closing the distance between them. "You think I don't know why you're so anxious to return? You think I haven't seen you like this before? I know well this distraction when nothing I say or do can take your mind off the victim you have hidden away. What it tells me now is that Strong is still alive."

Artem's eyes flickered with surprise. He hadn't known that she knew about the young women he'd toyed with in their courting days. He narrowed his eyes and grew very still. "Very well. You have my attention."

Ria squared her shoulders and lifted her chin. How much time had passed since Artem appeared? It couldn't have been more than a few minutes. Was that long enough for Aiya to free Merek?

"My people will not bow to you as long as I oppose you. I offer you my solidarity. I will call my armies back. We will work out a peaceful exchange of power. Just give me back my husband. Immediately. Because if Strong dies, I will fight you to the bitter end, rallying my people from every quarter of the land to drive you out of here on your knees."

Artem merely yawned.

"Useless," he sneered.

"My lord!" a soldier called urgently from the top of the stairs.

Artem held out a sharp hand, and the man's words ceased.

Artem took a step forward and reached out to stroke Ria's neck, sending a shiver down her spine. Then his grip turned firm, wrapping his fingers around her neck and gently squeezing his thumb against the base of her throat. Talen cried out, and Ria heard swords being drawn, but Artem ignored him, leaning in close, his voice as soft and intimate as a lover's.

"This kingdom is already mine. Albon is burning as we speak. There will be no one to oppose me when I march there and crown myself Rahm's next king. No General Strong. No princess. No mad king locked in a tower. And here you are, delivering yourself up into my hands. Your guard is hopelessly outnumbered and will soon become table scraps. So what shall I do with you?"

Ria smelled the remnant of something sweet on his breath. There was a bestial hunger in his eyes that sickened her, but she held his gaze and focused on breathing, vaguely aware of the sounds of a scuffle behind her as Talen and Stefan tried to fight through the Ardanian soldiers to come to her aid. The pressure on her windpipe was painfully strong. She dared not speak, and her right hand flexed, longing for the knife in her boot.

"I have an idea," Artem announced, suddenly releasing her throat and seizing her arm painfully. "Let's reunite you with your dear husband. Let your tears be the image that he takes to his grave. Then you will have the honor of watching him die."

· · ✳ · ·

WITH A REVERBERATING THUD, THE DOOR TO THE GREAT hall opened. The sharp-eyed Domar stood frozen in the entrance, shocked at what he saw. Merek was the first to move, leaping from the table to his feet. Clothed now in trousers and shirt, he left the boots and coat behind. Imar's tonic was a marvel. Minutes before he couldn't have stood, but now he walked—shakily, it was true— toward the entrance. But the boots...he paled just thinking of shoving his broken toes into them.

"This way!" Aiya called after him. " We must hurry!"

Domar barked a short command, and Ardanian soldiers rushed into the hall. Immediately, a volley of arrows came from somewhere behind Merek, dropping the first few Ardanians. He hefted the blade Gyll had brought him. The weight of it was unfamiliar in his hand, but it was forged well and had been recently sharpened. His left leg protested when he shifted his weight into a wide stance prepared to engage the enemy.

"My captain!" Aiya urged, motioning him toward a side door. "Imar has a way out."

"I won't leave her, Aiya."

"She only came back for you. The longer you stay, the more you put her in danger."

Merek hesitated, eyeing the exit behind her. In the end, Gyll made his decision for him. The young man, quiver empty, charged at the oncoming soldiers with the courage of ten men, his sword held out before him and a bellow of 'For the king!' coming out of his throat. Outnumbered, he was quickly surrounded by the Ardanians, and Merek sprang to his rescue, even as Gyll fell beneath their blades.

"You've forgotten yourself, Artem! I'm not some common whore to be dragged about at your pleasure," Ria spat, trying to jerk her arm out of the prince's grasp. But he was surprisingly strong and his grip held.

"Which will make this so much more fun," he agreed nastily. "Don't tarry, my dear. This promises to be an unforgettable night."

Do not enter the building, Talen had warned.

Desperately, Ria fought against Artem. The old pain in her shoulder flared dully as he yanked her toward the stairs, but still she pulled back, digging her heels against the flagstones. Relentlessly, he pulled her forward, and she struggled to keep her feet.

If she could just get to her knife…

The next time she stumbled, she dropped to the ground and bit off a yelp as her shoulder protested. Her fingers brushed the top of her boots. *Just…there.* Artem growled and struck her hard across the face. She stifled a whimper, but it was enough. In her right hand she now held Talen's knife tucked against her skirts.

And yet, she hesitated. Could she really stab Artem? Her anger and fear were potent, and her face stung from his blow, but still she trembled at the thought. Captain Eldar's training flashed through her mind, but that seemed a far cry from actually driving her blade into

Artem's skin and muscle. She risked a backward glance but couldn't make out Talen and Stefan in the melee behind her, and there was no sign yet of Eldar's men.

If she didn't get away from Artem soon, she risked complicating Merek's rescue.

Or worse, requiring a rescue of her own.

The knife slipped in her sweaty fingers. She tightened her grip.

Movement at the top of the stairs caught her attention. Behind the Ardanian soldiers, another man stepped into view. He was short and stocky, and the right arm of his plain coat dangled uselessly at his side. Ria's heart leaped as he raised his left hand in a quiet salute before slipping back into the shadows.

"I'll go no further." She jerked to a stop, and this time, the power in her tone made Artem pause. "You really thought I would give myself to you so readily? You misjudged me, as you always did. Strong is not the only one you should have feared." A shout from the entrance drew Artem's attention as a mass of Rahmish soldiers poured down the steps. He blinked in surprise and didn't notice Ria's knife until—with a grunt and a heavy thrust —she plunged it into his side.

"COME, AIYA! THERE'S NOTHING MORE YOU CAN DO HERE." Imar tugged at her elbow, but she shook off his hand.

"I came to save him, not watch him get cut down by the enemy," Aiya snapped. The sounds of battle rang in her ears as men fought for their lives. Inwardly, she cursed Strong. Things had been going so well—much better than she'd hoped—but now instead of fleeing, he was embroiled in a battle where he and the band of climbers were outnumbered and surrounded. Two had fallen already, and Strong was flagging.

A dull roar from the entrance hall drew her attention. Rahmish soldiers!

"Where are you, Dan?" she breathed, trembling slightly. They overwhelmed the Ardanians from the rear, but the doorway to the great hall was so clogged with enemy soldiers that there was no way they would make it to Strong and his men in time.

"Come with me, Aiya. There's nothing you can do here," Imar repeated urgently.

He was right. She was no warrior. She was only a simple thief.

"Perhaps not. But you can."

Imar's eyes narrowed. "This is not our war."

"It is *my* war, and the man I love is fighting for his life. If you do not help him, I will."

His eyes flickered to Strong, and she realized her mistake. He knew nothing of Dan and his indomitable courage. But she held her tongue, waiting for his decision.

"Promise me you will run," Imar said, his jaw set and determined. She nodded, and with a heavy sigh, he stripped his outer coat and shook his arms to loosen them up.

Then, he *pounced*.

That was the only word for it. He leaped for the nearest Ardanian soldier, burying his knife deep in the man's neck before the man could react. Before that man dropped, Imar sprang for another one, moving with feline grace. This one was felled with a quick twist to his head while Imar used the man's own sword against his nearest companion.

Aiya felt a surge of pride as the path cleared between Imar and Strong. He fought in his shirtsleeves and loose trousers, lacking the menacing anonymity of Hala's black costume, but he was no less deadly. His movements were more focused, like the tension in a tightly wound spring. Soon the Ardanians nearest him turned away from the battle in the center of the room, closing ranks against this new threat.

Imar stood perfectly still, watching them. When they moved against him, he slid to the floor, scrambling over a fallen corpse and coming up behind one of his attackers with a discarded arrow in hand. The man had no time to react before Imar plunged the arrow deep through his ear, then threw the body onto the sword of an oncoming attacker, even as Imar used the momentum to launch himself forward and strike another soldier in the face with a high kick. As that soldier staggered backward, Imar grabbed a knife from his belt and sliced his throat. The man's companions paused, wary of advancing. Imar stared them down, and after a long moment, they moved aside, making room for him to pass unchallenged.

RIA FELT AS IF TIME HAD STOPPED. ARTEM RELEASED HER with a grunt, but she didn't run. She stood there, her eyes wide with shock, looking at the knife protruding from his flesh. Her angle had been awkward, and she hadn't been able to get enough force behind her thrust to drive it in more than a couple of inches. Even that had been a horrifying sensation. She shuddered and swayed on her feet, but someone was at her side before she fell.

Talen threw his body in front of hers, forming a shield between her and the Ardanian soldiers.

Soldiers. With a jolt, Ria suddenly became aware that she was in great danger. As Artem's soldiers swarmed him in a defensive formation, Talen pushed her toward the arborvitae lining the garden. Stefan lingered in the courtyard, covering their escape with his bow as Ria and Talen stumbled into the shadows.

Ria yelped when she saw the shaft protruding from Talen's shoulder blade.

"What should I do?" she asked, her hands fluttering uselessly.

Talen breathed heavily, his features twisted in pain.

"You? Nothing," Stefan said, ducking low and joining them in a crouch. He grasped the shaft of the arrow, and snapped it in one quick motion. Talen let out a low sound with his teeth clenched, panting with the exertion of holding back a scream.

"I'm so sorry," Ria said, though it felt wholly inadequate.

"A surgeon will tend to the rest," Stefan said brusquely. "We can't stay here."

"Where's Rorden?" Talen asked, his voice strained.

"Here, sir." Rorden crept out of the shadows behind Ria. "The prince is gone; his soldiers are looking for you."

"We need to get you to safety, Your Highness," Talen said. "Our best hope is to find Captain Eldar. We need more strength than just the three of us."

"And just let Artem escape?" A chill ran through Ria at

the thought, and she instinctively glanced over Rorden's shoulder into the layered shadows of the garden.

"You have a better idea?" Stefan demanded. "We aren't even supposed to be here, let alone hunting a prince."

Ria bristled at his acerbic tone, but he was right. "Captain Eldar, then. How do we reach him? His men attacked from *inside* the building." She'd assumed that the Rahmish soldiers would attack the courtyard first. On the one hand, she was grateful that they came to Merek's aid so quickly. Unfortunately, that also meant that her party was cut off from their strength, surrounded by the enemy.

"There may be a way," Talen said, moving stiffly as he got to his feet. "Follow me."

TWENTY-EIGHT

Dan had barely raised his sword against an Ardanian before two more Rahmish soldiers drove the guard down the steps. Dan paused, watching the scene unfold in the courtyard. Captain Eldar had assumed the princess would be in the keep, and Dan had led the troops through the same unguarded side window he and Yulda had used earlier in the evening to report to General Strong during the party. But as it turned out, the princess and the devil—that's how he thought of the man who had tortured his friends and cost him his arm—were outside in the courtyard, surrounded by Ardanians.

Dan directed men to the courtyard, and soon the Ardanians were hopelessly outnumbered, confused by the sudden insurgence of enemy soldiers. They dispersed as the Rahmish advanced, and in the confusion, Dan saw Captain Talen leading the princess out of harm's way.

The devil shouted to his men angrily, then ducked as an arrow flew past his head. Dan chortled and wished for his own crossbow. He hadn't yet figured out how to work one one-handed, but he would happily learn now if it meant using the devil prince as target practice.

Just inside, Rahmish soldiers fought their way through the entrance hall to the feasting room. A cry drew Dan's attention, and he turned to dispatch an Ardanian before the man could deliver a death blow to a Rahmish soldier. Dan glanced into the building where the Rahmish colors outnumbered the Ardanians two to one. He wanted to join them in fighting to save Strong. He had even hoped to lead the charge. But all that changed once he'd seen the prince in the courtyard. Memories of his fallen friends gave him new purpose. He would not rest until he saw the devil dead or in chains.

MEREK LEANED ON HIS SWORD, BREATHING HEAVILY. HE wiped the sweat from his brow and grimaced at the blood that came away on the back of his hand. He couldn't remember if it was his or not. His head pounded, his throat ached for water, and he wasn't sure how long he'd been fighting. He didn't think it had been more than a few minutes, but his weariness spoke of hours. He must have lost more blood from his leg wound than he'd realized.

A sound behind him caught his attention, and he turned just in time to raise his blade against Domar. The man was fresh, as yet unbloodied from the fight. Despite Merek's size advantage, he struggled to do more than parry Domar's blows. Domar attacked with the efficiency of a mercenary, even dispassionately. He was moderately skilled, but wouldn't have been a serious threat if Merek hadn't been so weakened.

The smooth stone floor was cold against Merek's pained feet, but the throbbing of his toes was nothing compared to his leg. With each movement he felt as if his thigh muscles were tearing, and he compensated by protecting that side from Domar's thrusts.

What are your motives, Domar? Merek found himself thinking. One couldn't help but learn something about an opponent in a life-and-death contest, but Domar betrayed nothing. He was calculating and ruthless, but there was no fire behind his eyes. Merek thought briefly of the argument between Domar and Artem, the only time the man had shown any emotion that Merek had seen. *What is it that you fight for, Domar?*

Merek twisted to avoid a quick slice, and his leg buckled beneath him, his sword dropping as he tried to catch his balance. Domar took advantage of his stumble, not to strike with his sword, but to reach forward with his heavy boot and stomp on Merek's nearest foot.

Blinding pain erupted in his broken toes, sending him down on one knee. Spots appeared in his vision, and for a moment, he could scarcely make out Domar with his sword raised high.

And then someone was there, between him and Domar, brandishing something that looked like an iron poker and a long knife. Imar's billowing shirt the color of aged parchment was streaked and splattered with the blood of his enemies. Merek paused, momentarily stunned by the incongruity of the quiet shopkeeper turned fierce warrior.

He had only a moment to catch his breath before

another soldier was upon him, but the reprieve had steadied him, and he dispatched the Ardanian with a thrust between his ribs. He turned his attention back to Imar's fight. Domar had fled, and the soldiers who remained shied away from engaging the Khouri warrior. Beyond the doors, Merek saw the familiar crimson of Rahmish uniforms overpowering the Ardanian slate.

It is done. A wave of exhaustion hit Merek so hard he had to lean upon his sword to stop from swaying.

"You fought like a lion," a calm voice said beside him. "I should think you are in need of rest now."

Merek turned to see Imar wiping his long knife on the hem of his blood-stained shirt. "Considering your sister's many talents, I suppose I should have guessed long ago that you are no more a mere shopkeeper than I. Thank you, Imar. You saved my life."

"It was a life worth saving, my lord," Imar replied, bowing his head in respect. "But I'm serious about needing rest. The tonic will wear off soon, especially after all that exertion."

Merek grimaced. He couldn't walk without limping, but it wasn't time to think about rest. "Not yet."

He looked around the room with a sorrowful eye. The sounds of the dying echoed piteously in the vast hall. Merek looked for Gyll, but the boy was dead. His brother sat at his side, pale from a grave wound of his own that soaked the front of his shirt.

"He needs a surgeon," Borth said, his brow creased with worry.

"And you?" Merek asked, noticing the bloodied cloth tied about his arm.

Borth shrugged.

"Where is Captain Falbrook?"

"With the princess, sir."

"And that would be...?"

Borth looked chagrined. "I'm not sure. They were to draw away the prince. Beyond that, I can't say."

Merek gritted his teeth. "Finish up in here. Dispatch any Ardanians whose wounds are fatal. Kill any that offer resistance. Leave the rest."

"No prisoners?"

"There's an army between us and safety. We'll need every sword we can get."

Borth nodded and glanced at Merek's bare feet. "Would you like my shoes, sir?"

Merek looked at Borth's climbing shoes, the soft supple leather wrapped around his feet in such a way that the toes were unrestricted. Merek's aching feet cried out for protection from the stones.

"Brilliant. Thank you, Borth. You're welcome to my boots if you can find them in this mess."

THE DEVIL HAD ESCAPED.

Somehow, he'd disappeared when Dan's back was turned. Dan cursed and ran down the steps to the courtyard, skirting around a pocket of fighting soldiers. He turned his back to the light spilling from the open door, trying to adjust his vision to the shadows.

How had they let him get away? He'd been right there! But now there was nothing but an overturned brazier and a broken planter. Dan growled in frustration.

If the demon gets away after all this...

He paused, trying to think. Where would he run? Rahmish soldiers in the keep, soldiers in the city, but an army of Ardanians camped just outside the gate. Dan scanned the courtyard for the stables and ran.

. . ✴ . .

IT WAS ODD FOR THE WOUNDED TALEN TO BE LEADING out, placing himself in the greatest danger, but Ria didn't argue. The sounds of fighting in the courtyard were lessening as Ardanian soldiers scattered in the night. Twice, lone soldiers stumbled upon them as they ran through the dark gardens, and Ria turned away and covered her ears to mask the wretched sounds of death, her eyes squeezed shut. She felt ridiculous, but this was no time to worry about her pride. By the time they slipped out into the open courtyard, running full tilt for the stables on the far side, Ria trembled with nerves.

They paused under the stable eaves, leaning against the wall to catch their breath. Ria's lungs burned, and she coughed from exertion.

The others looked at her with a mixture of pity and concern, and she stifled the urge to cough again, her eyes watering with the effort.

"There," Talen said with satisfaction, gesturing to a gathering of troops passing through a glass door on the ground floor. "Those are Eldar's men. Are you ready to run?"

Ria looked at the distance and groaned inwardly. If Talen could run with an arrow in his shoulder, surely she could do it without complaint. But she was so winded. "Just give me another moment."

A movement near the corner of the stables caught Ria's eye. A faint lightness in the shadows.

"Artem!" she whispered, clutching Rorden's arm. "He's there."

Rorden looked uncertainly at Talen. "Should we go after him?"

Talen shook his head with a glance at Ria.

"You can't just let him get away!" Ria cried. "The man deserves to pay for his crimes!" *Not to mention that I will forever be jumping at shadows if he goes free.*

· · ✳ · ·

Dan burst through the door of the stable, his hand on his sword. A solitary lantern burned from the rafter, casting a mellow light over the snuffling beasts housed in their stalls. All else was quiet.

No prince.

Dan cursed. He'd guessed wrong.

All at once, the door at the other end of the building opened, and the devil himself slipped in. Dan froze, but the tall prince barely spared him a glance.

"You! Help me!" He stripped off his deep blue coat and Dan started at the sight of blood on his white shirt. Which soldier had managed that? He'd have to buy him a drink.

"Are you deaf, man? Does it look like I can manage this on my own?" The prince sneered as he tore open his shirt to examine the wound.

Dan didn't move. Did the devil not recognize him? He thought Dan was one of his own soldiers. Dan felt a flush of indignation that the monster could have forgotten him so callously. But that was soon replaced with opportunity. As long as he didn't speak and betray his accent, the devil might not realize his mistake.

Dan's heart beat rapidly with the close proximity of the man he'd so often dreamed of killing. The wound on his side wasn't deep.

Unfortunately.

"Give me your shirt," the devil growled at him, holding his own shirt against the wound. He brushed against Dan as he reached for a length of rope. Dan's fingers itched to draw his sword, but he didn't want to risk alerting his enemy with the scraping sound of sliding steel.

A shovel leaned against the nearest stall. Moving slowly, Dan reached for it. But just as he raised it to strike, the devil turned. He cried out and dodged, Dan's blow glancing uselessly off his shoulder. The prince was surprisingly fast, but Dan was faster. His next swing took the monster in the knees, knocking him to the ground.

Dan raised the shovel to strike again. No, it shouldn't be done like this. The man should feel Dan's steel parting his organs as his life bled out onto the filthy stable floor. Dan threw the shovel aside, and the devil scrambled, trying to draw his own sword awkwardly while gathering his feet beneath him.

Dan never gave him the chance.

"I agree with the princess."

Unexpectedly, it was Stefan who came to Ria's

support. "Talen, take her to safety. Rorden and I will go after the prince."

Talen looked for a moment as if he too would dearly love to join them, but before he could speak, a muffled yell startled Ria, followed by a crash from inside the stable.

The men looked at each other in surprise, and Ria seized her opportunity. She darted out from behind them and ran to the stable door. Throwing it open, she stepped inside and froze.

Her companions followed behind and stopped in the doorway. They, too, stood shocked into momentary silence at what they saw.

On the floor of the stable lay one very filthy prince. A Rahmish soldier sat on his back, one knee pinning Artem's head against the mucky floor, and his left hand brandishing a knife against his throat.

"Sergeant Dan!" Ria cried in delight. "What...? How did you...?"

"This cur was trying to slip away, Your Highness. I wasn't about to let that happen."

"Well done, Dan! Talen, Stefan, bind him."

They were eager to oblige. The captains pulled Artem to his feet while Rorden found a length of rope hanging on the wall.

Artem smirked. "Bind me all you like; it won't save your people. You've already lost everything, you just don't know it yet. The Delth have taken Albon on my command. There will be nothing left by the time you return."

Fear clenched Ria's heart, but she kept her voice calm. She wouldn't let him manipulate her again. "If that's true, then I'll just have to take extra satisfaction in the delightful experience of seeing you in chains. Believe me, I plan to enjoy it immensely."

Artem's eyes narrowed. "What are you going to do, Ria? Torture me? Execute me? Prove that you have the strength it takes to rule? Show the world that you can be as ruthless as any man?"

"That would feel like victory to you, wouldn't it?" Ria shot back. "But I have no intention of ruling like a man, and I have no intention of killing you. I'm sure I can find a dark hole deep enough for even *your* treachery where you can rot for the next thirty years."

Artem glared at Ria murderously, but the effect was lost as he shuffled awkwardly toward the door, his hands and feet now tightly bound. "You know that Idan won't stand for it. He'll never agree to you keeping me prisoner. Would you really start your reign by flouting our fathers' treaty so recklessly?"

"Don't presume to know my mind, Artem. You should have learned by now that you will only make yourself a fool."

And with that, Ria turned her back on him and walked out into the night.

THE FLOOR OF THE GREAT HALL WAS LITTERED WITH bodies: some dead, many more wounded. Merek paused beside a cluster of Rahmish soldiers who moved aside for him, their faces grave. On the floor lay Captain Eldar, his hair matted black with blood where his skull had been crushed. Merek crouched beside him, grief settling like a stone in his heart. It was an ancient pain that was as familiar as breathing, so long it had been his companion through a lifetime of watching friends die in battle.

Eldar's eyes were unfocused, tracking without seeing. Merek placed his hand on his chest, feeling it rise and fall weakly.

"She's here! The princess!"

The cry came from outside in the courtyard. Merek stirred and straightened, moving toward the door.

The entrance hall had been cleared of the dying, so Merek blessedly left their grisly cries behind as he shouldered his way out of the hall. "Close these doors behind me," he ordered as he passed. There were things in that room he did not wish Ria to see.

An excited murmur rose through the crowd of Rahmish soldiers gathered in the entrance hall. All at once the mass of men parted and Ria was there. Wide-eyed and disheveled, but beaming a joyous grin, she rushed forward and grasped him fiercely, nearly toppling him in her enthusiasm. He gripped her tightly, burying his face in her hair. All the pain and anxiety of the night melted away with her warmth in his arms.

"Are you well?" Ria asked, pulling away to search his face.

"Well enough," Merek said, and he meant it. Nothing else mattered now that she was here.

She took in his appearance with a critical eye, and he was conscious of the stench of sweat, blood, and vomit clinging to him.

"It's done," he said, putting a stop to her questions. She would learn the truth eventually, but now was not the time. He looked her over and noticed her clothing, the ill-fitting, filthy garb of a servant. "What are you wearing?" he blurted.

A smile pulled at the corner of her mouth, that lovely mouth that he would have kissed if they'd been alone. "It seems we both have stories to share. But first, what shall we do with *him*?" she asked, and for the first time, Merek looked over her shoulder.

Dan and Rorden stood with Prince Artem between them, shirtless and bleeding, his face and hair soiled, his hands and feet bound with rope. Blood oozed from a wound in his side. Talen and Stefan stood close behind, weapons drawn, watching the prince with expressions of wary triumph.

"Dan!" Aiya called out in dismay, pushing her way through the crowd with Imar at her heels. She stopped in her tracks when she saw Artem.

His face twisted into a snarl, and he spoke to her in Khouri, the foreign words lost to Merek. But she answered him in Rahmish so all could understand her.

"I'm afraid you have it wrong, Your Highness. My name is not Firah, it is Aiya. The only pleasure I have in seeing you again is seeing these bonds and knowing that the man I love bested you despite having only one arm to your two." And then, she boldly walked forward, threw her arms around Dan's neck, and kissed him full on the mouth.

A few laughs and whoops from the crowd grew into a mighty cheer. Dan's face reddened, but he kissed her back warmly.

Ria murmured, "Well, I'd say that was a long time in coming, wouldn't you?"

Merek gave them a moment, then squeezed Ria's

hand and stepped forward. The crowd quieted to an excited hum.

"Thank you, Dan. And thank you, Aiya, for all you've done this night. Now, as for you," he said, moving within arm's length of the prince. "What shall we do with the shining prince who has been wallowing in," he sniffed, "what is that, horse offal?"

Artem's eyes flashed. "Do with me what you want. It won't save your people. Every minute you waste here, one more home burns. One more child watches his father die and his mother brutalized while he—"

Merek's fist struck Artem's mouth with a satisfying crunch. Artem's head snapped back with the force of the blow, and Merek swayed as his leg threatened to give out. But he regained his balance and barked at Talen. "Gag him. If I have to hear one more word, I will strangle him myself. Tie him to that pillar while we decide what to do with him."

Talen and the others got to work with zeal, and Merek heard a few congratulatory calls from the soldiers. There was a general celebratory air among them, and for a moment, Merek allowed himself to smile.

Then Ria pulled him aside, her brows drawn together in concern.

"What he said about burning homes and dead children…"

Merek sighed. "Artem claims that an army of Delth have taken Albon."

"Do you believe him?"

"There's a chance it's all a ruse, like everything else the prince has done. But I fear it may be credible. The recent silence from Albon. The half-hearted campaign here. Even inviting you here this evening was likely another tactic to divert our attention while his secret army moved against the capital."

Ria nodded. "I've puzzled over why Artem was ready to let you go one minute and then changed his mind the next. He must have received word of Albon's fall just as we were leaving. He couldn't play his hand until he knew Albon was secure, but once he knew the city had fallen, he was free to do as he wished."

It was a perfect trap, and they'd played into his hands like unwitting fools. "Then we have no time to spare. Let's kill the prince and be on our way."

"Kill him?" Ria asked sharply.

"We cannot take him prisoner. Our march will be swift and he will require an immense watch. We cannot risk him getting free."

"No, we cannot," Ria agreed. "But to kill him? He's a prince of Ardania. He deserves a trial and fair opportunity for his brother to redeem him."

Merek looked at her closely, and the memory of Ria and Artem dancing together flashed into his mind. "Are you sure it's King Idan who concerns you? Not your own feelings for Artem?"

Ria hesitated as she considered the question. "He's my enemy. I know that, and he deserves to account for his crimes. But it must be done in the right way, not as a vengeful execution done in haste. By terms of the treaty between our two nations, we must give Idan a chance to answer for him."

Merek frowned. He cared very little for treaties and still longed to end it all right there. He glanced at Artem, who did look pitiful sitting against the pillar, the gag in his mouth stained with blood from Merek's blow. Still, he felt no compassion for the man.

"A trial, then. But King Idan had better be prepared to—"

A quick movement caught Merek's eye, and he looked away from Ria just in time to see Domar dart from behind a pillar. He moved so quickly that Merek could do little more than let out a choked cry before Domar raised his sword high above his head and brought it down fiercely, severing Artem's neck from his shoulders.

Twenty-Nine

Ria awoke with a sob in her throat, images of Artem's death fresh in her mind. In an instant, Merek was there, holding her until the shaking stopped and her breathing calmed. His warm body next to hers, together with the soft feather mattress, might have felt luxurious if not for the gruesome memory fresh as daylight in her mind.

As it was, she had trouble finding her voice and lay quiet long after she'd calmed. There were no words adequate for what she'd seen, and she had not the strength to try. Merek didn't press her. He simply held her, offering her comfort through his presence.

It did help. Although Ria couldn't forget the horrible image, she was able to gently nudge it aside and make space in her mind for something else. Slowly, she became more aware of her surroundings. Sunlight illuminated the heavy golden drapes, turning the bed curtains a pale yellow. They were in the same bedchamber at Lord Ogmun's that she'd slept in when last she was in Endvar. At that time, she and Merek had just finished the wall tour, and she was fretting because Merek hadn't come to see her since they'd parted company. How foolish she'd been to not recognize the first stirrings of love!

The memory lifted the cloud of darkness over her mind briefly, and she burrowed closer to Merek. When she spoke, her voice didn't even tremble.

"Did you kill him?"

The words sounded cold and harsh after the long silence.

"Not yet," Merek's voice rumbled near her ear. "He's locked away and heavily guarded. It seemed it could wait."

"Did he say why?" The thick sound of Domar's sword striking Artem's neck reverberated in her ears. She tried to push it away. She had very little memory of what happened after Artem's head toppled into his lap because blackness had claimed her shortly thereafter. But the look of surprise on his face haunted her, frozen into her mind.

"He refused to speak to anyone but you," Merek said, "but you needn't see him if you'd rather not."

"I want to," Ria said with effort, her throat dry. She wanted to know why Domar had done it. Why had he killed his prince who had trusted him so completely? There was something going on she didn't understand, an important piece that she was missing.

A heavy knock sounded at the door, accompanied by a gruff voice asking for the general. Merek groaned mildly and threw back the bed clothes. He sat up slowly, as if each movement caused him great pain. She knew now that was indeed the truth of it, and it pained her to watch him walk to the door.

When he'd dismissed the soldier, Merek returned to the bed and sat stiffly next to her, reaching out a hand to stroke her loose hair.

"Please don't leave me," she pleaded suddenly. "I can't bear to be alone with my thoughts." Thoughts of what she'd seen. Thoughts of how close she'd come to losing Merek. Thoughts of what Artem had done to him in her absence. All were dark and oppressive with a heavy weight so real it pressed against her chest and made it difficult to breathe.

Merek kissed her gently. "I'll send Aiya to wait on you. If you want to speak with Domar, I'll postpone his execution, but we cannot afford to delay long. Firl has broken through the Ardanian defenses. The city is nearly ours. It's time we turn our attention to Albon."

As it turned out, Aiya was waiting just outside the door and came in as Merek left. She carried a tray of food, but it was the warm mug of scented tea that she pressed into Ria's hands first.

"This is from my homeland," she said. "It's a tea for mourning and consolation. It's said to make your memories sweeter and dull your grief."

Ria's eyes pricked with tears at her words. The tea was mildly sweet with a faint aroma of cloves.

Aiya watched her drink and nodded in satisfaction. "Personally, I think it's about as effective as chicken dung, but it's tradition, and we Khouris love our traditions."

Ria snorted and blinked back her tears. The tea was

soothing, but even more comforting was the near smile Aiya had coaxed from her.

"I'm ashamed to show my face today after last night. Was my behavior so awful?"

"You mean fainting after witnessing a gruesome beheading? It was perfectly princessy of you. I would have been disappointed if you hadn't." Aiya's dark eyes glinted with conspiratorial humor.

Ria couldn't bring herself to return it.

Aiya sat on the bed beside her. She was far more comfortable with Ria than Biren had ever been, despite Biren's years of service. Ria suspected that was because Aiya had never viewed Ria as her superior. She was surprised to find that she didn't mind.

"In truth," Aiya continued quite seriously, "the whole thing was awful. The Prince Artem I knew was evil and deserved justice, but that doesn't mean that he didn't once have good in him. Do not feel ashamed to mourn what he was to you."

"I thought I wanted him to die," Ria admitted. "But once Merek was safe, and we were out of danger, it seemed so wasteful. My...sensitivity to blood doesn't help. It was all I could do to not faint just being in that room with the signs of battle smeared on the walls and the floor." She shuddered with the memory. Why did she feel like she had to justify herself to this woman?

Because Aiya is stronger than you, she realized. She saved Merek when Ria could not. She didn't faint when Artem died so brutally. And here she was, composed and reaching out to comfort Ria, who still hadn't managed to get out of bed.

Enough. This wasn't helping. It was time to go to

work, no matter how much she wanted to hide from the world. She reached for a biscuit and was surprised to discover that she was hungry.

Aiya smiled. "I took the liberty of selecting a few gowns for you to choose from. Lady Ogmun was tall like you, and her taste was very fine. But I suppose I'm biased, since many of these fabrics came from my own shop."

"No Ardanian silk, please!" Ria insisted. "Is there anything made from plain Rahmish linen?"

Aiya frowned her disapproval. Then her eyes brightened, and she held out a pale blue gown with long layers of translucent fabric that filtered the light as it moved. "This is not Ardanian silk. It's from Khourin and is far superior to anything you'll find in Ardania. It's not quite the season for it, but in a few weeks the days will start warming, so it's not wholly inadequate."

Ria was impressed that Aiya had been so thorough. "Did you sleep at all last night, Aiya?"

Unexpectedly, Aiya colored. "My night was restful enough, thank you."

"Ah, yes," Ria said knowingly, a blush warming her own cheeks. "Dan."

Aiya didn't meet her eyes. "Please do not suspect us of anything improper. After the excitement of the day, Dan simply wished for companionship. We're both of an age where we are not slaves to youthful passion."

"Of course. I wouldn't have suspected either of you of dishonorable behavior," Ria said generously, though in truth she was slightly disappointed. "In any case, I'm very happy for you both. Dan is an honorable man."

"He is," Aiya said, pausing to pour water from the ceramic ewer on the washstand into the basin. "My first husband was very much like your Prince Artem," she said thoughtfully, "except not so cruel. But he was charming and clever, and I was swept away into a thrilling life of passion that ended in tragedy and despair."

Ria said nothing, her interest piqued at the disclosure. She quietly washed her face and neck, the cool water brisk and refreshing.

"Dan has the same kind of adventurous spirit but controls it with a sense of duty that Tupin lacked. I expect that life with him shall not be dull."

"Shall you have a future together, then?" Ria asked, reaching for the towel Aiya held. Only when Aiya hesitated did Ria realize that she'd been too forward. "Forgive me, I do not mean to pry. Of course, it's none of my business."

"Not at all. It's simply too soon to speak of such things. Dan is still recovering, and it would be wise if he avoided making any...commitments until he's whole again."

"Recovering?" Ria said, eyeing her reflection in the looking glass and the shadows under her eyes. "He seems to have recovered well enough already. I'll never forget the sight of him sitting on Artem, like a child wrestling a piglet." A laugh nearly bubbled to the surface, but the humorous memory immediately shifted to Artem's final bloody moments. She cringed.

Aiya watched her. As if guessing where her thoughts had gone, she said, "Dan appears well, it's true, but sometimes the wounds we can't see take the longest to heal."

Ria thought this over and murmured, "I believe it."

A dark silence fell briefly until Aiya jumped forward,

snatching a brush and reaching for Ria's hair with brisk efficiency.

"So there you have it. I'm quite content to leave things as they are for the time being. Though," she added with a sly smile, "just between you and me, if things continue as they are headed, the sooner we find a priest, the better."

Ria chuckled, and it felt so good that her mirth erupted into a full hearty laugh. Aiya joined her, and together they purged away some of the gloom in Ria's heart, leaving her considerably cheerier.

An hour later, she emerged from the room dressed respectably in her borrowed gown (she preferred to think of it that way even though there was no longer any Lady Ogmun to return it to) and her hair twisted into a modest, yet romantic bun of Khouri origin that made it look even fuller than it was and softened the lines of her face. Aiya was no Biren, but under the circumstances she suited Ria quite well, even if she did favor the diet and fashions of her homeland.

Aiya directed Ria down a narrow stone staircase rather than the wide one that would have taken them through the entrance hall. Ria appreciated her choice, and she appreciated even further that Aiya felt no need to comment on it

The great hall was bathed in sunlight which poured through the southern balcony doors and illuminated the polished stone floor. Ria couldn't help but covertly look for signs from the night's conflict, but there were none that she could see. The freshly scrubbed floor gleamed, and the simple table and chairs where Merek met with his first captains didn't bear signs of violence. Ria breathed easier as she approached the table and even managed a small smile as Merek and his officers stood.

"Please, continue. I do not wish to interrupt," Ria said.

Merek gave her a brief nod, and in it she detected a slight release of tension. He'd been worried for her, but whatever he saw in her manner now put him at ease. Ria was relieved. The last thing she wanted to do while her people were fighting for their lives was distract those who were coming to their aid with her own dramatic sensibilities. She was ashamed that her weakness had been so publicly displayed, but she didn't flinch as she met the men's eyes, and in their respectful bows she sensed nothing like the derision that she felt for herself.

Ria listened as Merek and his captains discussed the fight going on outside the walls and which companies of men could leave for Albon without delay. With Artem dead, the Ardanian troops were surrendering, and there was much discussion about whether or not to keep them as prisoners. It would be dangerous to split the Rahmish forces, and some of the captains advocated letting them return to their homeland so that all Rahmish troops could be free to go to Albon.

Just as Captain Firl suggested keeping only senior officers as prisoners, the large doors opened, and all fell still. Domar shuffled into the room, manacles at his hands and feet, clanking as he walked.

Ria stood, her heart pounding. He was dressed in the same black formal wear he'd worn the previous evening, though now it was quite wilted. She wondered if he had Artem's blood on him, and the thought made her swoon, so she steadied herself with a hand on the table. She couldn't afford to think such thoughts now.

Merek joined her, and the other officers came forward as well, but Domar ignored them all. He only had eyes for Ria. For the first time, as she looked into those eyes, they held a measure of emotion. They looked almost...sad. She tried to find her voice but found she knew not what to say to this man. And so, she waited.

"You asked to speak to the princess," Merek said severely beside her. "Now, speak. There is a noose waiting for you otherwise."

"Your Highness," Domar began in Ardanian, but Merek stopped him.

"Rahmish, please. You're skilled enough in our language."

Domar shot him a look of irritation and addressed Ria in Rahmish. "I had hoped to speak these words in private. I know that we are not friends, and you have every reason to doubt me, but I swear to you that I took no pleasure in the events of last night."

Into Ria's mind flashed a memory of Domar with his sword raised. She swallowed hard. "Explain yourself."

With a furtive glance at Merek, Domar continued, "You knew Artem better than most and surely can understand why I did what I did. In spite of my great love for him, he needed to be stopped. I know that you wished for him to be exiled from your land. I overheard your protests, and that's when I knew I must act. The only way to stop the spread of his evil was to end his life."

"This is ironic coming from you," Merek growled, "the man who orchestrated the evil to come upon this land in the first place. Why would you suddenly care about the lives of the Rahmish when you've been spilling our blood for many months now? This is a pitiful excuse to spare your life."

"Then take my life!" Domar spat with heat. "I killed a friend last night, a man I loved like a brother. I'll have to live with that knowledge for the rest of my life! I will be haunted by my betrayal until my dying breath. Why should I care if that comes sooner rather than later? But the princess knows, I can see it in her eyes, that to love Artem was also to hate him. For all my crimes against her people, she owes me a great debt for having the courage to do what she could not."

Ria didn't flinch from his piercing gaze, even as her insides twisted from his words. When she didn't speak right away, he continued, this time in Ardanian for her ears alone.

"I have no quarrel with you or your people. I never have. The man who did is dead. Will you not offer me the same mercy you were willing to give him?"

One of the guards struck him with a fist in the gut.

"Rahmish," Merek barked as Domar gasped for breath.

Ria turned away from his plea, needing a moment to think. Merek's expression was hard. She'd never seen him so ruthless. He'd been angry, he'd been stubborn, but she'd never seen him truly murderous. If she wasn't completely certain of his loyalty, the sight of it would have been frightening.

A hazy connection came together in her mind, and she grasped for it, rounding on Domar. "Artem said you were perfectly loyal to him. He trusted you completely, and he wasn't a man to whom trust came easily."

"And for that I will pay a heavy price."

"But if you questioned the worthiness of his actions, why did you not act sooner? If you believed death was truly the only way to stop him, why not kill him months ago? Surely you had ample opportunity."

Domar hesitated, but the connection was coming clearer as Ria fitted new pieces, and she went on excitedly.

"You wanted to see how far he could go. You wanted to see if he could take the throne. It was only when he failed that you intervened—No! Not even then. It was only when you thought I might release him, when you thought I might send him home to Ardania."

Merek cursed softly next to her, and she knew he'd made the same realization.

"You are loyal as Artem claimed, but your loyalty didn't belong to him, did it?"

Domar's expression clouded over. "I do not know what you mean."

"How long has Idan known about Artem's plans?"

"You're mistaken. My king knows nothing. We've worked tirelessly to ensure that knowledge of our activities didn't come to his attention. Even now, he believes that it is a revolutionary movement within Rahm which has closed your borders and—"

"Count Orlin knew of your connection to Artem, and he too was quick to defend Idan against any complicity. But if Orlin knew, surely Artem's own brother knew as well."

"I have no dealings with the crown. Idan's father made sure of that. Artem fostered our relationship in secret because he knew I'd been wronged and would never side with Idan against him."

"How better to redeem yourself to the king than offering up his troublesome brother as a sacrifice?"

Domar's face paled.

"If this is true," Merek said gravely, "then King Idan has deliberately broken our treaty and waged war against us."

"No!" Domar insisted. "He didn't know...he didn't—"

"What was the condition?" Ria asked angrily. "You would be pardoned? You would receive a title and lands? But only if Artem doesn't come home alive."

"And if he had gained the throne," Merek added, "what then? A knife in the dark, and then you hand it over to his brother?"

Domar said nothing for a long moment. When he spoke, his voice was calm and emotionless. "I can command Artem's troops to retreat. Let me live, and we'll be gone before the sun sets tonight. Then your troops will be free to go to Albon where I'm afraid they are desperately needed."

Ria looked at Merek, who scowled. She spoke quietly so only he could hear. "Taking Domar's life will do nothing to address our grievance against Idan. If anything, it gives him what he wishes because we've cleaned up his mess."

Merek rubbed the back of his neck and shook his head. "He's still a dangerous enemy responsible for killing untold Rahmish citizens, but while he lives, Idan knows we have proof of his complicity. I suppose it's wise to wait to execute him until Idan has responded to our demands."

"Agreed. As far as I'm concerned, this marks a dissolution of the treaty. If Idan's reparations are acceptable, I will consider it the first step in creating a new understanding between our nations."

Merek nodded. "If not, I'll send an army to his doorstep to bring him to his knees. Is that acceptable to you?"

"Almost," she answered, meeting Domar's eyes. "We will also send Artem's remains back to Rellana so that Idan can see the face of his cowardice."

As Domar was dragged from the room, Merek staggered slightly, and Ria jumped to support him.

"You should be resting," she chided. "When was the last time that dressing was changed?"

Merek just grunted and waved her away, limping as he moved back to his chair. A look of pain creased his features as he sat with a heavy thump.

"Excuse me, gentlemen." Ria stepped forward and addressed Merek's officers. "Thank you for your attention this morning. I'm sure the general will ask for more of your time this afternoon, but for now you are excused."

"Ria—" Merek started to protest, but Ria overrode him.

"Who here wants to see the general turn septic from an untended wound and die of blood poisoning?" Ria asked loudly. When none of the officers responded, she nodded curtly. "Good. Then make yourselves scarce for an hour or so, please, so my husband has no other excuses to keep the surgeon away."

Some of the men chuckled. It was a sign of how much pain he was in that Merek just sighed and nodded their dismissal. As they departed, Ria crouched beside his chair.

"I'm not keeping the surgeon away intentionally," Merek growled. "I merely instructed him to tend to the gravely wounded first and save as many as he can. I can wait."

"Well, I can't," Ria said fiercely. "I'll do it myself if I must. Where is Aiya?"

DAN CAUGHT UP WITH AIYA JUST AS SHE WAS LEAVING Strong's bedroom, her arms laden with a basin of cloudy water and soiled bandages whose stench made her wrinkle her nose.

"Can I have a word, Aiya?"

"Of course. Follow me to the kitchens so I can get rid of this lot."

Aiya was quickly learning the layout of the stone keep, and passed through the hallways as confidently as the servants who'd been kept on to tend to the royal couple during their stay. She wondered at that decision initially, knowing that a servant of an enemy could be as dangerous as the enemy himself, but these were all Rahmish servants who seemed genuinely relieved at the change in power. Artem hadn't been the sort to engender loyalty.

"How is General Strong?" Dan asked as they descended a tight staircase into the back kitchen.

"He's lucky Prince Artem cauterized the wound so quickly. He should have lost the leg otherwise, but I think he'll recover."

"And the princess? Did she manage to keep her breakfast?"

"She did," Aiya said with a glance at the kitchen staff as they entered the room. She placed her load on a sturdy cupboard then followed Dan out the back door to the kitchen courtyard that was warm with sunlight. "She only has to keep it clean, nothing too serious. And she's anxious to tend to him herself, so she is motivated."

"Of course she is. Can't risk her husband falling in love with his beautiful nurse, can she?" Dan said playfully.

Aiya grimaced. She knew he meant it as a compliment, but it only highlighted her own foolishness. How wrong she'd been to think that Strong would have been a suitable match for her! Yet she still admired him greatly, and it gave her no pleasure to see him so vulnerable. The sooner the princess began nursing him herself, the better.

"Don't be ridiculous," she said lightly, hoping Dan wouldn't sense her discomfort.

"Why not? It worked for me."

"Surely not. Please tell me you didn't fall in love with me while I was playing nurse. That is simply too droll."

Dan laughed, but there was a nervous edge to it. After an awkward pause, he declared, "I went to see General Strong this morning about quitting the army."

Aiya started. "Quitting? Why?"

They stepped further into the garden as a man passed carrying two squawking chickens, leaving a trail of feathers in his wake.

"I just thought that maybe, after everything that's happened," Dan said, looking at her shyly, "maybe I would stay here with you. Help you rebuild your shop and get back on your feet now that Endvar is safe again."

"Oh." His words hit her like a bucket of cold water, and she felt seized by a strong desire to run.

"I don't mean that…you don't have to—" Dan's fair complexion brightened. "I just want to help you get back to your old life, and I'd like to be a part of that life, if you'll allow. But I won't impose on you. Don't feel as if you have to—"

"You've got it all wrong," Aiya said, smiling at his discomfort. Dan didn't have the easy charm Tupin did, so his words of affection meant so much more for their simplicity. "It's not you I object to. It's the idea of rebuilding my life here. I don't want my old life back. I don't want to be a shopkeeper whose days bleed into each other like so much dyed cloth. Your offer is generous, but it feels like death to my soul."

Dan blinked at her. "Then what do you want?"

"I don't know," she said honestly, "but I think I shall start by leaving this place. I've always wanted to see more of this country, and I seem to remember a certain sergeant promised to take me to Albon someday."

"Then…shall I ask General Strong not to discharge me after all?"

"Oh yes!" She laughed at his expression of open relief. "Don't quit the army for my sake. You are far too good at it and should shrivel with boredom."

"Strong did mention that he might have a special use for me," Dan said, a hopeful gleam in his eye. "And he promised that it wouldn't involve tunnels and sewers. But I couldn't accept if it meant leaving you in the ashes of your old life."

"Accept, and I will come with you. Who knows?

Perhaps the princess will have need of another maid," Aiya teased.

"Not likely!" Dan snorted. "I think you've shocked her enough for one lifetime."

And with a spring in his step, he took her by the hand, and they returned to the keep.

Thirty

The inn at Valdirk was nothing like Ria remembered from when she'd taken refuge there the previous summer. The road was piled with refuse as she approached, and the innyard swarmed with people who looked as though they hadn't had a proper meal or a bath in weeks. Ria stared at a woman wearing an elegant gown that now hung limp and filthy as she knelt on the bare ground picking chicken feed out of the mud. The woman licked the feed off her fingers, gagging involuntarily as she tried to swallow.

Corporal Osten swore softly next to Ria. "Who are they?"

"If I'm not mistaken, they are our people," Ria said grimly as she dismounted. "Refugees from Albon who fled when the Delth attacked."

This was confirmed a moment later when Tatti, the gap-toothed innkeeper, appeared on the steps of the inn. Her disheveled hair formed a halo around her head, and dark circles under her eyes gave her a haggard look.

"Blimey! I didn't expect royal visitors today! My apologies, Your Highness, but as you can see, my inn is overrun. All these people fleeing the war and having no place to go and not a gold coin between them..." She trailed off hopelessly as she looked around at the spectacle.

"Never fear, Tatti," Ria said reassuringly. "We're not here to invade your establishment. The army is making camp just outside Valdirk as we speak. I simply wished to pay my respects, but I see you have more important concerns. How may I help?"

Tatti's shoulders sagged. "I don't have enough beds, and our winter stores are almost gone. But I can't turn them away. They have so little as it is and nowhere else to go. It's not so bad on a day like today with the sun shining, but when it rains I can't keep even the wee ones out of the wet." Her voice broke a little, and she swayed on her feet.

Ria eyed her sympathetically. Tatti was nearly spent. If she carried her burden much longer, she would crumple under the weight of it.

"Osten, inform the general that I need a company of men immediately. We'll tend to shelters and sanitation first." Ria thought back to the previous summer when she'd witnessed Lord Renick's efforts after the Nardin's flooding left his people homeless. It would have been useful to have his experience. But Lord Renick wasn't here. Ria would have to do her best without him.

"Where is your well, Tatti?"

As she followed the innkeeper through the mess of too many people sharing too small of a space, her mind lingered on Lord Renick's people. How had they fared against the invading Delth? Merek had sent a battalion to Lorin when they left Endvar, but it would be some time before they learned the fate of the town.

For a moment, Ria felt a surge of desperate anger that there would be no justice for her people. Domar had robbed them of their chance to make Artem answer for his crimes, and the truth of it sat sourly in her stomach, making her feel as if Artem had triumphed after all.

No. No more of this. She would not give in to one more moment wasted on that man. Her people needed her.

RIA DIDN'T RETURN TO CAMP THAT NIGHT. SHE SENT WORD to Merek that refugees from Albon were gathering in Valdirk, and he heard in her message a sense of relief that she'd found a purpose. In the days since they'd left Endvar, Ria had been withdrawn and pensive with worries of her father always close to the surface. Perhaps an opportunity to help her people directly would ease her fretful gloom.

Merek should have guessed that she would take on this new challenge with gusto. When he searched for her early the next morning, he found her, pitchfork in hand, spreading straw under a canopy. Her eyes brightened as she saw him.

"You have impeccable timing, Strong! Take this."

Without offering an explanation, she handed him the pitchfork and hurried to the other side of the innyard where a group of soldiers were carrying a large watering trough.

"Not here, gentlemen. Behind the smokehouse, please. There's a platform there and Tatti is hanging drapes for privacy."

No sooner had she finished than she hailed a farmer who had just approached the inn driving a team of horses with a large wagon. The pitchfork in Merek's hand seemed forgotten. Shaking his head with bemusement, he rested it against the wall of the inn.

"You're here for the Grym and Lundgren families?" Ria asked the farmer.

"Yes, m'lady. Though I don't know that they'll much care for sleeping in the hayloft."

"They'll not mind a bit. You and your good wife can help when the baby comes, can't you?"

The farmer nodded. "I've delivered three of my own. Not including the animals, of course."

Ria smiled gratefully, but Merek saw beneath her smile a heavy weariness. When the farmer left with his precious cargo—two bedraggled families and a woman heavy with child—Merek took advantage of the lull in her attention.

"You haven't slept," he observed.

Ria blinked up at the gray sky in surprise. "Is it morning already? I suppose I haven't had the time. These poor people are half frozen without proper shelter. Tatti has done what she can, but her inn can do little more than serve as an infirmary. We spent much of the night going to each home in the village to find who has room to spare. There are still so many more without shelter, and I've sent soldiers to the neighboring farms to—"

"Ria," Merek interrupted with a smile. "I've come to fetch you. We leave within the hour."

"Oh. Of course. Forgive me, I…" She looked around the innyard helplessly.

"Your Highness!" Osten called as he jogged toward them. "They're coming."

Ria glanced at Merek apologetically. "This should only take a moment."

Merek fell into step beside her as she followed Osten to the road, though his stride was shortened with pain. He still wore Borth's climbing shoes, which at least made walking possible, but the leg wound would take time to heal. The surgeon recommended rest, but there was little enough of that these days.

"Tatti says some of the villagers have refused to help," Ria explained as they walked.

Out on the road, a small crowd of men and women stood, bundled against the cold in their heavy coats and shawls. They bobbed their heads awkwardly as Ria approached, but the look in their eyes was anything but deferential.

Merek leaned against a fencepost to relieve the throbbing in his leg, curious how the drama would unfold.

"Friends," Ria greeted with warmth. "Thank you for coming to speak with me. I'm sure you know what I must ask of you."

"We know it," one of the men said, his voice as cold as the late winter dawn creeping across the frosted ground. "But we can't do it. We can barely feed our little ones as it is. We're not gonna watch them starve so some rich man from Albon can fill his belly."

Ria nodded with understanding. "I see. But what if that man from Albon were your brother? Or your son? What if he were your neighbor right here in Valdirk?

Because that's what is coming if we do not stop the Delth. If they come and burn your homes, where will you go? To whom will you look for rescue?"

The people looked fearfully at each other. A woman in a blue shawl spoke. "All the more reason we need to see to our own. The others must go somewhere else. We can't take them in, not if the enemy is coming."

"The Delth *will* be stopped," Ria said firmly, catching Merek's eye. "You can be assured of that. But think for a moment of who will give their lives to save yours and your children. A small village like Valdirk cannot have more than half a dozen sons serving as soldiers in our army. Where do you think the largest number of soldiers come from?"

The question hung in the air uncomfortably. The crowd shifted, unwilling to meet her eyes.

When Ria continued, her voice was hard with truth. "The sons of Albon and Endvar will lay down their lives to save your children. You may not have much food now as last year's harvest dwindles in your cellars. But you *will* look forward to another harvest because others will give their lives to preserve yours. Even now, as you count the last of your root vegetables and huddle in front of your fires, they are polishing their saddles and sharpening their swords, uncertain who will live out the days to come. Parents and wives and children will bury their sons and husbands and fathers so that *you* can hold yours one more time. What thanks can you offer but to share what little you have as they flee the terror that would come for you if not for their sacrifice?"

Merek felt a thrill at her words. No one in the crowd dared break the guilty silence.

After a moment, she added more gently. "I know this is a hard thing I ask. It's an easy thing to share of our abundance but much harder when we're already in want ourselves. But *that* is what it means to be Rahmish."

The first man lifted his head, his expression softer now. "I guess we can help 'em if they don't mind living just this side of starving."

Ria's expression relaxed into a smile. "They will bless you as the angels you are. Thank you."

As the crowd dispersed, Merek shook his head. "I don't know how you do it."

"Do what?" she asked distractedly.

He snorted. "Come, it's getting late."

Ria looked back at Tatti's inn and hesitated. When she spoke, it was with regret in her voice. "They need me, Merek. I can't simply leave them."

Merek felt a wave of disappointment. He hadn't realized how much he'd counted on having her by his side when he reached Albon. But he nodded and said, "I'll ask the campmaster to bring your things. It's probably for the best. You'll be safer here."

"And you? Will you be safe?" She looked at him critically.

They had discussed this in Endvar, but she still looked for reassurance. In truth, he was in no condition to go to battle. He couldn't even ride a horse yet. "I'll conduct the campaign from a safe distance. I'm not so reckless as you think."

"Hmm." She squinted up at him and frowned. "I wonder."

The ache in Merek's leg told him he'd been standing too long. He offered Ria his arm and she walked with him to the edge of the village. There the army spread before them, a bustling scene of organized chaos as they readied for departure.

As they came out of the cover of trees, the sun warmed Merek's face, though the breeze was chilly against his skin. The further south the army moved, the more signs of spring appeared around them. Bare trees were beginning to swell with buds, and wild crocuses emerged shyly in fields where the army had not trod.

With a yawn, Ria nestled against him. He wrapped his arms around her and held her as close as he dared without taking too much weight on his weak leg. He held her that way for a long moment, thinking moodily of his cold bed the previous night and wondering how long it would be before she warmed it again.

"Do you think there's any chance my father may still be alive?"

The frank question demanded an equally honest reply.

"It's difficult to say. Initially, with a sufficient force, the tower would be easy to defend. But a focused attack would eventually overwhelm them. Unless Martin convinced Sindal to escape the tower, you must prepare yourself for the worst."

He felt Ria's sigh more than heard it, in the slight way her shoulders sank against him.

"But what *is* the worst? I keep praying that this threat has brought my father back to his senses, awakened that which was lost. But if it hasn't, is it really worse to fall to a conquering enemy than to spend the last years of his life in madness and decay, turning against all those who love him? If he has fallen, I'm not certain that it wouldn't be for the best, though it feels like heartless betrayal to say so."

"It's a messy business," he said in a low voice. "Of course we both wish for his safety, but we must also be prepared for the possibility that if Sindal lives, he may not consider either one of us his allies."

"What pains me the most is not knowing whether his death or his survival will bring me the greatest grief," Ria said somberly. "If you hear even the faintest rumor that he is alive—"

"I'll send word immediately. A single messenger on a fast horse can reach Valdirk in a few days. But are you sure you want to stay?"

Ria didn't answer for a long moment. "I'm not ready. When I close my eyes at night, all I see is death."

There was nothing Merek could say in reply, so he simply tightened his embrace.

After a long moment of silence, she spoke firmly. "I'll come soon. As soon as I'm certain these people will be well cared for. Perhaps I may even learn something about my father from them. But if I stay in that camp one more day with my hands idle and my mind tortured with worry, I fear that *I* will start to go mad."

"And who will care for you while I'm gone?"

She looked at him with bloodshot eyes. Blinked slowly.

"While you are saving all these people, who will be looking out for you? Making sure that you have rest and food when you need it? I know you, Ria. The greater their need, the more likely that you'll neglect your own and suffer for it."

She looked him up and down critically. "That's rich

coming from you. Always so protective of me, yet never of yourself."

"It's my right to protect you."

"And I you." She slipped her arm around his waist and leaned her head against his chest. "Send Biren to me. She'll look after me."

Merek hesitated. "Are you sure?"

"Artem is dead. He has no claim on her any longer, and I believe she never intended me harm."

"But to trust her..."

"I didn't say I trust her—not as I once did—but she is very capable, and our circumstances are dire."

Her last word rang in Merek's head as they both grew silent. Their moment together ended all too quickly. With the last of the wagons loaded, the army was prepared to move out. Ria raised her face to his, her lips brushing his with a softness that sent a tingle down his spine.

"This is hardly the wedding tour I imagined," she said mournfully. "When my father married my mother, they spent a month on the coast with no one but each other for company. Though of course, Danvir was alive then, and my father didn't yet have the duties of king."

She didn't need to say what they both guessed, that it would not be the same for them. *Queen and king.* The thought gave Merek an unpleasant mixture of dread and awe, so he pushed it away to the edge of his mind. One thing was certain. Whether Sindal was alive or dead, everything would change when they reached Albon.

THIRTY-ONE

"I haven't seen you much around camp these days. Cleaning the general's boots must keep you busy," Yulda teased, peering up at Rorden from underneath the wide brim of her hat. It was an improvement over the scarf she used to wear, especially now that her hair was long enough to curl around her face in soft waves. Rorden could almost believe she was a young woman instead of a bristling shrew.

"I'd rather clean his boots than carry bedpans. Or has Manni promoted you to the laundry now?"

Yulda laughed. It was a sign of her increasing confidence that she didn't blush with indignation. "Enough with the bedpans, you clod. Do you want to hear my news or not?"

"News? What news is that?" Yulda wasn't the type to fritter her time away trading gossip with the other women in camp. If she had news that she thought he'd want to hear, he probably did.

Yulda glanced back at the surgeon's tent and grew

serious. "I only have a bit of time, but at the apothecary's yesterday, I heard some things. Some fancy folk talking and ignoring the likes of me. Near as I can tell, it sounds like Lord Hegrin is trying to scrape up support to challenge Princess Honoria."

Rorden frowned. "Challenge how?"

Yulda shook her head. "Not sure. I think Lord Hegrin wants allies before he risks too much. The men I overheard didn't sound convinced, so maybe nothing will come of it. But I thought the general might want to know, in case he wants to slip a little something in Lord Hegrin's food before he goes too far. I've learned a few things if he needs some suggestions."

"Yulda! Strong doesn't operate that way."

Yulda shrugged and smiled in a way that would have been coy on another girl. Except Yulda was never coy. "How should I know? I'm not the one who cleans his boots." Then she turned on her heel and slipped back to the surgeon's tent before Rorden could thank her.

Curse Hegrin and his scheming. Life had gotten increasingly complicated since they'd arrived at Albon. Encamped on the outskirts of the city, the army had become not only a refuge for the suffering Albon citizens but also a broiling tempest of political intrigue for the crafty nobility who sought to turn tragedy into personal gain.

Hegrin was the worst of the lot, which was ironic since he didn't even need the army's protection. He had his own estate in Berseth where he could have retreated but instead stayed to stir up trouble. Rorden spent as much time shielding General Strong from Hegrin's dramatics as he did fulfilling his assigned duties.

Rorden shook his head as he skirted around a wide mud hole. They'd won the fight for Endvar. They were winning the fight for Albon. Why did it feel like they were still fighting a war on so many fronts? Was it the unrest of war and a mad king that brought out the worst in people?

Of one thing Rorden was certain; Lord Hegrin had no idea who he was challenging. If he thought either the princess or the general would yield to him, he was sorely mistaken. But still, Strong didn't need any more distractions right now. Not when they were so close to driving out the Delth and securing Albon for good.

"Rorden! There you are." Captain Talen hailed him from an intersection as a supply wagon rattled past. "Have you heard the news?"

"Which news is that?" Rorden asked, thinking immediately of Lord Hegrin.

"Word just came from Endvar. The prisoner Domar has escaped."

"What?" Rorden stopped in his tracks.

"He just vanished. They don't know how it happened."

"You're sure?" Rorden felt a flush of alarm. This was sinister news indeed.

"Unfortunately. Two guards dead and a horse missing. He was surely long over the border before it was discovered."

"He must have had help."

"Undoubtedly. Firl will have to answer to this. Strong is furious."

Rorden's lips tugged in a smile. "On the positive side,

I should enjoy seeing Captain Firl humbled, wouldn't you?"

Talen's eyes twinkled. "You didn't hear it from me, but if Firl's sizable opinion of himself managed to shrink to mortal levels, he might be more tolerable company."

Rorden snorted. "At least Captain Firl means well. I think Lord Hegrin would be happy to see the whole kingdom in ruins as long as he gets the biggest piece of the rubble."

"Is Hegrin causing trouble again?" Talen sighed.

"No more than usual. There's a rumor in camp that he hopes to challenge the princess, but it'll amount to no more than a headache for the general and Hegrin looking like a fool. With the war in Albon almost won, the people are eager to see the princess on the throne."

As they approached the command tent, Talen paused. "If you want help with Hegrin, let me know. I know something of his activities in Albon before the attack, and I suspect it's not by chance that he managed to escape the city largely unscathed, with his household and possessions intact. I think, between the two of us, we can convince him to skulk back to the shadows where he belongs."

Rorden perked up. The promise of a scintillating story attracted his attention like a hungry man drawn to a savory meal. It was hard to believe that this was the same man whom Rorden had so despised after Strong's arrest. That felt like a lifetime ago.

"That would be a great weight off my mind and one less thing to trouble Strong about. With word that Domar has escaped, he'll be troubled enough for one day."

· · ✶ · ·

Ria peered in vain at the dark trees hemming in the road on either side, little more than textured shadows looming in the weak light cast by the carriage lanterns. They'd driven all night, and Ria thought she would have been more comfortable tumbling down a landslide for all the battering she'd received from the rocking carriage. Sleep had been nothing more than light dozing punctuated by panicked gasps of wakefulness when an unexpected lurch nearly tossed her from her seat.

Ria and her company of soldiers had spent a month in Valdirk caring for the refugees who'd found their way from Albon half-starved and with barely a thread of blanket between them. She hadn't intended to stay so long, but once word had gotten out that she was providing refuge in Valdirk, the numbers had increased until the village had tripled in size. The challenges of caring for them had tripled as well.

It was good for Ria to do something useful, but hearing their stories of suffering had made her feel increasingly restless, wondering about the suffering in Albon. With an increasing sense of trepidation, she needed to know for herself how her father had fared in the invasion. None of the refugees could tell her anything of his fate. Nothing reliable anyway, and nothing that gave her any hope.

"I heard the king and his guards fled to the country."

"They trapped him. Trapped him in the tower and that's where he stayed, watching his city burn."

"The tower was just a ruse. He's in hiding, waiting for

his armies to return so he can lead them and take back the city."

"No way could he have survived. The Delth overran the city like rats. If he was alive, you would know. Best you don't know what really happened."

The haunted pain in the eyes of the man who'd said these last bitter words reflected Ria's worst fears. Dread was her companion every waking moment of every day, kept at bay only by ministering to the victims of Albon's war. Still, it lurked in the corners of her mind and settled heavily on her chest at night when she couldn't sleep.

Then Merek's last letter had arrived with disturbing news that Domar had escaped from Endvar. It included a plea that she restrict her movements to Valdirk and keep guards with her at all times.

She could take no more.

Ria had ordered her carriage and trunk prepared immediately, leaving her soldiers behind to continue her work. She wouldn't sit in Valdirk for one more moment, letting fear wear her down until she jumped at every noise and saw enemies in every shadow. If nothing else, at least she would be able to face the truth of her father's fate instead of playing out her worst fears endlessly in her mind.

Domar has escaped. In the thick darkness of the carriage, she turned the words over in her mind. Should she have let Merek execute him in Endvar before they left the city? Was he coming for her now? She didn't think so. Artem was dead. There was no need to keep his personal vendetta alive. Surely Domar had fled Rahm at the first opportunity and would likely never be heard of in either their country or his own.

Yet still the nightmares tortured her sleep, when she got any sleep at all. Looking out at the black shapes of trees passing in the night, she told herself that he couldn't be there, watching her, waiting to ambush her on a lonely road in the middle of the night.

When Biren spoke, Ria started.

"It will be good to be home, don't you think, my lady? No matter what we find when we get there."

"You're awake, too?" Ria kept her voice light, trying not to betray the tension she felt. "I'm afraid I did us both a disservice by insisting we travel through the night." She breathed deeply to calm herself. Of course Domar wasn't out there lurking in the forest. She was becoming as paranoid as—

"Not at all. If it's not impertinent to say so, I think I'm well accustomed to expecting the unexpected when traveling with you."

Ria smiled weakly, wondering at the turn her life had taken these past months. And then she stopped because thinking of those distant days filled her with pain and longing. She missed Merek. She missed him deeply. But more than that, she missed the carefree innocence she'd had then. Before she'd caught sight of that monstrosity her father had built in his madness. Before her father had turned against her. Before she'd faced the horrors of war and seen good men die in the face of one man's insatiable greed.

Stop this, Ria, she thought. *You had to grow up someday, didn't you? Time to put the princess away and become the queen you were born to be, especially if...*

"My lady?" Biren's quiet voice was a welcome interruption. "If it isn't too presumptuous, I want to thank you for giving me an opportunity to prove myself to you again. I always knew that yours was not a cruel nature, but I never expected such generous forgiveness."

Ria didn't answer. Had she forgiven Biren? These past weeks working together had been...unusual. Though strained at first, Biren had been eager to prove her loyalty, and the work to be done was so relentless that Ria didn't have the luxury of nursing her wounded pride.

But things hadn't returned to what they were before. Though Biren treated her much as she ever had, Ria didn't view her maid in quite the same way. Biren no longer seemed an extension of herself, but rather a woman with passions and dreams that Ria could only guess at. It was an intriguing shift, but one that didn't easily lend itself to servitude.

Yet, hadn't her love for Lotta transformed her from merely a servant to...what exactly? Not her equal, but certainly not a servant. In some ways even her superior. Whatever was taking place between her and Biren, she knew that the woman's days as her maid were numbered.

The silence in the carriage grew long. Biren was expecting a reply.

"Don't thank me. Thank the war. If we were safe in Albon right now, I would have already dismissed you from my service. But you've been a fine help, and I'm grateful to have had you with me."

"Do you still wish to dismiss me from your service when we return to Albon?" Biren asked pensively.

Instead of answering, Ria countered with a question of her own. "What do *you* want?"

"My lady?"

"Would you be happy remaining in my service?"

"Of course! That's all I wish for!"

"Is it? You've had the attention of a powerful man who made you feel important. That is not easily shaken. Are you certain you want to continue a life of servitude?"

"It's a great honor to serve you, my lady! I've never been dissatisfied—"

"But I'm dissatisfied now! Can't you see that? I don't want to spend the rest of my life wondering if you are pining for a future you couldn't have because of me. A future with Rorden or—"

"There is no future with Rorden. That's lost to me now."

"Then someone else. Or some*thing* else. What is it that you would do if you were not bound to me? What do you wish for?"

"I—" Biren stopped. Ria sensed a shifting in the darkness, some agitated movement not caused by the rocking carriage. When Biren continued, her voice held a mixture of pain and wonder. "I cannot say, but I'm humbled that you would ask."

"Then think on it. Take as long as you need. And when you've decided, I will do what I can to help you."

It felt like farewell, but also a bit like healing. The carriage lurched as they ascended a hill, and Ria strained to make out the landscape around them. The trees which had pressed in so close suddenly retreated, and they advanced into a wide meadow, gray and colorless in the first emerging light of day.

Ria's heart leaped with excitement as she recognized where they were. "Signal the driver to stop at the next bend."

As they crested the hill, the driver slowed, and Ria

hurried to let herself out of the carriage, not bothering to wait for assistance.

"Your Highness?" Corporal Osten was at her elbow in an instant, but she ignored him, hurrying through the wet grass toward the overlook.

"Douse the lanterns, please!" When they were extinguished, she paused, waiting for her eyes to adjust to the darkness. Waiting for her first view of Albon.

Against the starry sky, her golden city emerged black and lifeless. Very few lights glowed in the shadowed buildings, and none of the sentinel fires were lit along the walls. In the far distance, her father's tower stood unchanged, but it didn't bring her comfort. What had she hoped to see? A banner telling her where to find him? Near the tower, the shadows of Thorodan Hall looked wrong, somehow, but perhaps that was because of the darkness.

She hoped desperately it was only because of the darkness.

Disappointed, her eyes left the horizon and rested on the many points of light just visible through the trees of the foreground. There, in the wide valley before Albon, camped Merek and his army. He wasn't expecting her, but she hoped he would be as pleased to see her as she was to see him.

Thirty-Two

Aiya moved slowly through the dark room of sleeping bodies huddled close together for warmth. Most of them didn't have blankets or cloaks, and the nights were still frightfully cold despite the warming of the days toward spring. She and Dan had found this pocket of survivors on their third week searching Albon.

Strong's troops were making headway against the Delth, or so Rorden said. But to Aiya, nothing much seemed to have changed. Individual Delth gangs controlled neighborhoods and were just as likely to fight amongst themselves as they were to kill or capture any Rahmish citizens they happened upon. Whatever success Strong's captains were having might as well have been in a different city for all the good it did these people hiding in the dark.

Aiya found Finn laying next to a little boy who looked remarkably similar to him, his eyes bleary with interrupted sleep. Finn whispered to him, rubbing his back soothingly. As she approached, he glanced up.

"Are you coming back?" Finn whispered plaintively.

"Of course! And when I return, I'll have some friends with me who will help move you to safety." Her joy at being reunited with the boy had changed to sorrow at his distressing state. She didn't know if his parents were dead or missing because he refused to speak of them. His younger brother didn't speak at all. Weeks of terror and starvation had taken a heavy toll.

She bent to kiss Finn's forehead, then used the opportunity to slip him a shriveled plum. "This is a lucky plum," she whispered. "My friend found it in the king's own orchard, missed during the last harvest. Make a wish before you take your first bite, and it will bring you blessed fortune."

Finn managed a lopsided smile. "We both will." He patted his brother who was breathing steadily, on the very edges of sleep.

Aiya moved quietly to the open window—the pane of glass long since missing—and used the wooden frame to pull herself out and up onto the roof. From there, she carefully moved across two neighboring buildings, crowded close enough she barely had to leap, and shimmied down a side drain until she dropped to her feet a full block from the building where the refugees slept. If she was spotted, she hoped not to lead any enemies to the poor defenseless survivors.

Scores of refugees had flocked to the army as they'd approached the city under General Strong's banner. Weary and withered from exposure, most had fled with only the clothes on their backs. These were the lucky ones. Inside the city, the tales of suffering were much more grim. The Delth didn't seem to care if there was a stone left standing when they were through, and the wanton destruction had left many casualties.

Had Artem foreseen this kind of destruction when he made his treaty with the Delth? Aiya had no understanding of these wild people. They seemed to be ruled entirely by appetite, with a brutal social hierarchy that mimicked beasts asserting power through strength and violence.

Aiya slipped through the streets as quietly as the first lightening of the dawn seeped over the city, painting everything a dull gray. She skirted around a public square where the remnants of a grand statue now lay as a mournful memorial to what the city had once been. The massive figure had toppled into a great basin covered in fine carvings and was now stained with blood and excrement. Aiya couldn't tell if the figure was a man or a woman from this distance, as it lay face down in the basin, making it appear as if it were drowning. It unnerved her—as it did each time she saw it—yet she couldn't quite bring herself to look away as she passed.

Which is why she didn't notice the Delth man hidden in the shadows until he reached for her.

Her instincts flared, and she ducked just in time. His arm knocked the porter's cap from her head, and he gave a guttural cry of surprise as her hair and face were revealed. His beard was wild and unkempt, and he wore the pelt of a fox on his head: the creature's face brooding over his brow, its feet dangling down to his shoulders. He smelled as if he hadn't bathed in months, and Aiya's nose wrinkled with his sharp scent.

She scurried away, but he recovered from his surprise quickly, his boots scuffling against the broken stones as he chased her. Aiya scrambled over a pile of rubble from a nearby building, the timbers blackened with fire. As long as she could avoid attracting the attention of any more Delth, she should be able to outpace this man. They didn't move quickly even when they were not weighed down with drink, and in the early hours of the day, they would all be slower with the previous night's ale.

Through the gaps in the crumbling outer wall of a building, she spied a staircase in the dimness. Jumping off the rubble to the ground, she slipped inside. The Delth man called to her in a mocking tone. She couldn't understand his language, but it was clear he thought he had the advantage.

A common mistake.

The building had once been a residence, as evidenced by the piles of domestic detritus that littered the floor. Aiya picked her way carefully to the stairs, not worrying whether or not the Delth man saw her. It would be a small matter to reach an upper story window, and from there, she would have access to the roof and freedom. She had yet to see a Delth who could climb as she did, and her confidence in escape surged.

The stairs groaned beneath her weight but held firm. At the top, a chest of drawers leaned precariously against the wall, partially blocking access to the landing. She squeezed through the gap on her hands and knees, satisfied that the large Delth man would have to move the entire chest out of the way to pass.

The second story was largely intact, the walls and floors scarred with signs of violence, but whole. She slipped through the first room at a run and glimpsed briefly the remains of a sitting room now covered in dust and debris.

Through another door, she passed a bedroom and from there spied her escape. A window, with a table and basin beneath it. One easy leap and she would be out and away.

She braced herself against the table and paused, her heart pounding. The basin held water, filthy like the rest of the room, but a few drops of water on the dirty table arrested her flight.

Someone was here. Someone who didn't want to be discovered.

Aiya cursed inwardly, scanning the room for possible hiding places. There, a large cupboard. Or the way the quilt on the bed draped to the floor. Should she warn whoever was hiding? If she fled, the Delth man would likely discover them while searching for Aiya, and their lives would be on her head.

Abandoning the window, Aiya retraced her steps. She had no choice but to lead her pursuer away. Mere seconds had passed since she'd crawled through the gap next to the leaning chest of drawers, and the Delth man was just now climbing the stairs.

With a heave, Aiya threw her shoulder against the chest, leveraging her legs against the nearest wall and pushing with all her might. Leaving a deep gouge in the wall plaster, the chest moved and toppled down the stairs with Aiya close behind.

The Delth man bellowed as the heavy chest of

drawers tumbled toward him. Aiya leaped over the side of the broken balustrade to the floor below. When she hit, a small rock beneath her rolled, and her ankle rolled with it.

She gasped, landing hard on her knee. Hobbling to her feet, she winced as she stepped over a broken stool. A loud crash sounded behind her, and she turned to see the chest lying in a splintered heap at the foot of the stairs. The Delth man leaped over it, the limbs of his fox headdress dangling comically. His eyes were black with rage.

Cursing, Aiya limped outside to the empty street. This wasn't the first time she'd injured that ankle, and the healing process had left it stronger. With each step, the pain subsided, and soon she could jog, though her pace wasn't as quick as before. The Delth man lumbered after her disturbingly close.

Down two more streets Aiya ran, wishing for the safety of the rooftops. At least her pursuer couldn't catch breath enough to alert any of his companions, and she blessed the predawn silence.

Rounding a corner, she risked a glance back at the Delth man and didn't see the man in her path until she ran into him.

She yelped and jumped back, but this man was no threat. Dan stepped around her and raised a crossbow, firing as the Delth man came around the corner. His shot was true, and the man stumbled. Passing the crossbow to Aiya without a word, Dan drew his sword to deliver the fatal blow.

It all happened so fast that Aiya was still breathing heavily when Dan returned to claim his crossbow.

"Picking up stray admirers again, are we?"

Aiya stifled a relieved laugh. "Always so threatened by any competition, Dan. One might think you're jealous."

"Competition? I didn't realize you favored animal skins. I'll have to remember that the next time Imar roasts squirrel for dinner."

Aiya groaned. "Please don't. It's bad enough the people in this city are near starving. Must we wear our kills as trophies like these barbarians?" She started down the street with only a slight hitch in her step, but Dan immediately noticed it.

"Did our fox friend give you some trouble?"

"Nothing to worry about. I'm fine, truly. But I think I discovered more refugees hiding in a house four streets over."

"Of course you did," Dan sighed. "And did you know these ones by name too?"

Aiya shot him a look. Dan had taken to Finn immediately, though not without a healthy dose of exasperation. "I didn't see them, but they were there. I want to go back later and see if we can help."

"It'll have to be much later. Captain Orri wants us to raid the tower today. His troops are ready to attack, and he fears that if they wait much longer, Captain Salvin's men will flush the Delth out of the eastern district, and they'll strengthen the numbers at the Hall."

"But we aren't ready to assault the tower," Aiya protested. "We need more time." They'd scarcely begun exploring the area around the tower in recent days, trying to identify how the Delth were using the fortress.

"If you weren't so busy trying to save every other

citizen in the city, maybe we would already have found the king." He said it good-naturedly, and Aiya didn't bother to point out that it was his idea to smuggle food and supplies into areas occupied by the Delth when they found survivors.

Aiya had never been more proud of Dan than when he'd insisted they rescue a Rahmish girl being kept by a gang of Delth. In his report to General Strong, he'd asked Aiya to write, "I trust that our actions are pleasing to you, sir, and if our current sovereign's heart approaches the same noble depths as yours, I trust he will approve our delaying his rescue in order to save this innocent maid."

But the more time they spent in the city, the more they realized there would be no end to the distress until the Delth were driven out for good. For every citizen they saved, a dozen more were still left suffering. Now, even the king was running out of time.

When they reached the abandoned tavern where Captain Orri conferred with his lower captains, the activity in the room was frenetic. Messenger boys leaped out of the way of stalking soldiers, hurrying to deliver orders to Orri's men waiting in the streets nearby.

"At last!" Orri growled as they entered. "Where have you two been? I thought we'd have to attack without you."

"Sir," Aiya said, ducking out of the way of a soldier carrying an armload of spears. "You cannot mean to attack the tower today. We don't know what sort of force awaits us inside. It would be best to watch the area a little longer—"

"Salvin is advancing faster than we planned. He's

clearing the east quarter, driving all those Delth here. If we want to secure the tower without threat of additional enemy troops, it must be now. Otherwise, we'll be facing the enemy on two fronts." Orri's tone was measured, but there was a sheen to his brow that betrayed his stress.

Aiya looked to Dan. His face was grim, but he nodded. "We'll do it, sir, but we need a sow."

"A what?"

"A sow. Preferably a fat one."

Orri blinked. "I don't understand what—"

"He means to use it as a distraction," a smoothly accented voice said behind them as Imar peeled himself away from the shadows and joined them.

Orri's expression cleared in understanding. "I can't give you a sow. Maybe a couple of chickens, but that's the most I can do. Our stores are depleted as it is, and if we don't drive these Delth out soon—"

"Which is exactly why the sow will draw away the soldiers from the tower," Imar said. "We could simply kill them, but that would risk raising an alarm, and we still have to escape with your king, who may be weak or injured. We could try another distraction—say, a fire in the stables—but they care not for any skin but their own. They would likely just let it burn. But a fat sow loose in the king's garden? Their empty bellies will not let them resist. None will dare risk staying behind and missing out."

Aiya was taken aback at the forcefulness in Imar's tone. Gone was the placating shop owner of Endvar. He'd joined them for Aiya's sake, not because he felt any loyalty to the Rahmish people. He spoke now with dispassionate logic, daring the captain to disagree with him.

She glanced back at Captain Orri and was surprised to find him watching her.

"What do you say, Miss Aiya? Is this distraction worth robbing my men of their last taste of pork?"

"A sow is a small price to pay for a king's safety." Heat rose in her cheeks at the deference with which he spoke. She'd been elevated in his eyes since Strong's rescue, but she still wasn't used to being given such respect.

Orri nodded to a clerk nearby. "See that it's done. We attack within the hour. That's all the time I can give you without risking an all-out slaughter. Salvin has wound up his men so far that he can't rein them in now. They'll push the Delth back with no thought of the mess they're creating for us. Save King Sindal, if you can. Salvin has given us little room for error now." Disgust leaked out in his tone, and Orri turned his back in dismissal.

"Captain Salvin sounds like a man who doesn't deserve the title," Imar grumbled when they reached the outside.

"I don't know," Dan shrugged. "When you've tasted despair as you watch your comrades die, and then the battle turns in your favor, it's a rare soldier who can avoid getting swept away in the push toward victory."

"Then you must not have very disciplined soldiers in your Rahmish army," Imar said.

Dan grunted, but didn't argue, for which Aiya was grateful. After nearly a month of working together, the two men still seemed uneasy, sizing each other up and coming away with a list of unsurpassable offenses. Dan, who accepted Aiya's duplicitous past without hesitation, seemed less keen to trust Imar. And Imar couldn't quite look past Dan's missing arm to give him the credibility due a seasoned soldier. The fact that they both agreed on a plan to get into the tower was surprising enough. Aiya dared not comment on it and led the two men in silence through the broken streets.

THIRTY-THREE

The low rumble of soldiers on horseback vibrated deep in Merek's chest. Usually he felt a thrill when troops were on the move because he was the one leading them. But now…

It was a hard thing to be left behind day after day as other men went off to fight your battles without you.

He got up stiffly from his chair and scowled as he caught Rorden's glance. His leg was healing well, but Rorden still watched him like he suspected he was hiding his true pain. And if he was, what of it? No amount of fussing over him was going to make it heal any faster.

Merek was only paying slight attention to the discussion. Spread out on the table were maps of Albon with markers indicating the areas still held by the Delth. The enemy forces were being driven back and congregating at the royal estate. Captain Alrek was amassing troops to come to Orri's aid to ensure that victory was swift and complete. Everything was going according to plan, but still Merek felt no satisfaction. Only irritation.

"Sir?"

Merek glanced up and realized all the men were watching him expectantly.

"What shall I tell Captain Firl?" Rorden repeated.

Tell him to do a better job of keeping track of his prisoners. "What is there to say? Firl needs to be patient. We can't bring the Ardanian prisoners here just yet. The city is nearly ours, but it will take time to restore order. He'll need to keep them in Endvar."

"Yes sir. Do you want Captain Audon to secure the prison, or would you prefer to leave that under Captain Talen's charge?"

Why did he care about the prison? Orri was attacking Thorodan Hall this very day—possibly at this exact moment—and he was expected to care about who established control over the prison? But details like these were all that remained for him and those who had been left behind.

"Talen," he said sharply. "Do you wish to secure the prison yourself?"

"To be frank, sir, I'd rather be with Orri if it's all the same to you."

There were a few grunts of assent. Of course he'd rather be with Orri. Every person sitting at that table would rather be with Orri leading the final charge against the Delth. Talen wasn't technically under his command, and had no troops of his own, so he didn't have to answer to Merek at all. The significance that he still deferred to him was not lost on Merek.

"Audon, take your men and clean out the prison. Talen, you may ride with Alrek if you wish."

The look of gratitude that flashed across Talen's face only spiked Merek's annoyance.

He dismissed his captains and paused to pour a tumbler of water. What would Orri find when he attacked the Hall? How much of the estate would be left standing when the fighting was ended? Was Sindal being kept a prisoner in the tower, or had he been executed by the Delth? Had Drenall helped him escape before the Delth advanced to the royal estate?

All these questions simmered unpleasantly under Merek's skin. The cool water soothed his parched throat but didn't ease his turmoil.

Rorden watched him for a moment before offering quietly, "One word from you, sir, and I'll request your horse."

"What's that?" Merek asked distractedly, drumming his fingers against the smooth tumbler.

"I can't help but notice that you're not yourself, sir. It must be eating at you to not be riding into the city today."

Merek glared at Rorden. Knowing his feelings were so transparent to his aide didn't make him feel any better. Instead, he felt churlish. "Do you wish to join Orri too?"

Rorden shrugged. "If all goes well, this will be the last major battle. The people will be celebrating in the streets tonight. It's hard not to want to be there."

"It's not the celebrating I care for."

"Of course not, sir. I only meant that if you feel inclined, we could go. What's to stop us from saddling our horses and slipping quietly into the city? Just you and me. No troops. No banners. We'll stick to safe areas to avoid conflict so that even the princess can't object, and we'll be there in time for the surrender."

For a moment, Merek thought back to a dark night nearly a year ago when, dressed in simple forester's garb, he'd climbed the wall outside of Haldin and surprised Stefan. He missed the freedom and anonymity he'd enjoyed then. Could he manage to leave the camp without drawing attention? It hardly seemed likely. But the glimmer of hope seized him and wouldn't let him go. To do something—anything!—would be better than sitting in this stinking camp on this fateful day.

"Very well. No banners. No crests. Do you know where I put my old captain's uniform?"

Rorden grinned with anticipation and jumped into motion. He didn't like missing the action any more than Merek did.

While Rorden sent for his horse, Merek searched his trunks for his old uniform. As he freshened it up with a brush, the familiar motion and blue fabric filled him with nostalgia. He told himself it was poetic to ride to Albon's aid in this, of all uniforms. He tried to ignore the gnawing feeling that such secrecy was not the way of a man who would someday be king.

Raised voices sounded outside with a whinny of horses. Rorden had been faster than Merek expected. But the voice that drifted through the tent door was not Rorden's.

Merek turned in disbelief just as his wife stepped into the tent.

"Ria!"

She looked tired and worn but beamed when she saw him. His heart skipped a beat at the sight of her glorious smile. Then it sank as he realized he wouldn't be going anywhere.

"You look like a child caught stealing sweets under Cook's nose," Ria taunted. "Am I interrupting something?" Her clothing was rumpled, and her hair had the relaxed look of many hours without attention, but she still walked with a grace that attuned his senses to her every movement.

"Whatever it is can wait," he said with a smile, gathering her into his arms.

She kissed him, but he sensed her distraction and knew she was troubled.

"What brings you here, Ria? I told you I would send for you when it was safe to return."

"They're weary of me in Valdirk," she said flippantly. "Besides, I hear that Albon shall be ours before the day is through." Her sharp eyes lingered on the sight of his old uniform. "What is this? Revisiting old memories?"

Merek felt the shame of his deception creep up his neck. Before he could answer, Rorden appeared at the door.

"The horses are ready, sir—" he began, but broke off as he saw Ria.

"Horses?" Her eyes narrowed. "My dear Strong, please tell me you weren't thinking of riding into battle today. Not after promising me that you would stay out of it."

"Not battle," Merek said sheepishly. "But I wish to be close at hand once Thorodan Hall is seized. Orri and Alrek will soon have the Delth on the run. There will be no real danger by the time we get there."

To his surprise, instead of being angry, Ria's eyes

sparkled with excitement. "Fantastic! Rorden, have a horse prepared for me as well."

Rorden's complexion paled. "My lady?"

"If there is no danger, then I will ride at your side," Ria said, addressing Merek. "We shall enter the city together as liberators."

"That wasn't exactly—"

"But this old uniform won't do. You must be as splendid as possible. Where is your cape?"

"We were hoping not to attract attention," Merek objected.

"Oh, but that's where you're wrong. Attention is exactly what we want. Rorden, a horse! And send Biren in with a change of clothes for me. Don't look so glum, Merek. She'll have me primped in far less time than it will take for you to put on that heap of metal." She gestured to his gleaming armor that hadn't been worn in weeks. She threw off her heavy traveling cloak and tossed it casually on his cot before moving behind his privacy screen.

"Ria, it's one thing for me to enter the city unnoticed. Our safety will be guaranteed by the fact that we won't attract attention. But you? Everyone in the city will know who you are!"

"Exactly! What better way to declare our victory than by inspiring our people that their day of deliverance has arrived?" She peeked around the corner of the screen, one eyebrow arched saucily. "Now, are you going to come help me with these stays or shall I have to wait for Biren? That would be a disappointment for us both, I'm sure."

"Why must everything be a spectacle for you?" Merek

grumbled as he obeyed, but he didn't altogether dislike his assignment as he reached to unfasten her gown. His lips brushed her neck, and she leaned against him for a moment, sighing contentedly.

"We need a spectacle because the people need to see us behaving as their future queen and king. When they see us ride into the city today, this is what they will remember for years to come. They will speak of it to their children and their grandchildren." She turned to face him, and her eyes were bright with passion. "For their sakes, we must make it a memory worth cherishing, one that will sear away the horror of war and leave only the light of hope."

THIRTY-FOUR

Aiya scanned the slope where heavily pruned fruit trees stood like bleak sentinels against the gray morning sky. These marked the beginning of the king's garden, or what was left of it. Aiya didn't care for their mournful, skeletal look, bare as they were without their summer foliage. But it was the tower itself, rising black and formidable beyond the trees, that gave her a creeping sensation at the base of her skull. The unfinished structure brooded over her and Imar as if it were conscious of their intrusion and might betray them at any moment. A single upper window on the near side gaped like a baleful eye, with no light or sound evident from within.

Together, Aiya and Imar crawled up the slope, grateful for the low hanging clouds that kept the dawn sluggish and disguised their approach. This was the back side of the tower, and the massive structure shielded them from view of the larger courtyard and upper windows of the main building.

"Why not build a proper palace?" Imar wondered aloud. "Prince Lahri's summer home for his mistresses is finer than this. It's shameful that the Rahmish have no vision of true beauty."

"When have you ever seen Prince Lahri's summer home?"

Imar smiled. "You're not the only one who deprived the prince of one or two valuables in your youth."

At the top of the slope stood a neglected hedgerow of currant bushes which rose taller than their heads. The day before, they'd begun cutting a passage through the intertwining branches, and now, they immediately set about continuing their work. Although they removed the twisting twigs carefully, it seemed to Aiya as if the whole bush shuddered with each movement. Swollen with buds, the currant bushes were yet leafless and wouldn't hide them from sharp eyes alerted by persistent rustling.

"Cut, don't watch," Imar said.

"I *am* cutting," Aiya replied, resisting the urge to glance up at the tower again. "But I hate working in daylight. I feel as if we're being watched."

"There's nothing alive in that tower. If this Rahmish king is half as intelligent as his daughter, he fled to safety long ago, and we're wasting our time. And if he was too foolish to leave—well, then we're still wasting our time," he added meaningfully.

"We have to know for certain," Aiya said, straining as she cut through a larger branch. The closer they got to the center of the bush, the thicker the branches grew. "If there is any chance he's still alive, Dan has sworn to do whatever it takes to find him."

"Which just shows what a fool Dan is. Why am I the only one who realizes that risking your life to save a mad king is not noble? It's lunacy!"

"I disagree. Loyalty *is* noble." Aiya slipped another branch out of the tangled mass, and it slid down the slope behind her. "It's no more foolish to give your life to save a king whom your people look to as a ruler and protector than it is to risk your life to save your little sister. Such loyalty seems no different to me."

Imar grunted and said no more. They cleared the final branches in silence then crept inside the hollow, grateful that these were currant bushes and not wild roses or something else with wicked thorns.

"I wish you wouldn't give Dan such a hard time," Aiya whispered as they waited. "He's a better man than you think and deserves respect."

"Respect? Or pity? You showed better judgment in your attachment to Captain Strong. I still cannot understand how a crippled half-soldier managed to win your affection after all these years."

"That's not fair. He's so much more than what you say. If you knew half of what Dan has been through—and I'm not just talking about losing his arm—you would be ashamed of your words."

"Tell me then."

"It's not for me to say. But you know that I do not bestow my favor lightly, and that should be enough."

Boots crunched on gravel nearby, and they shrank further into the hedgerow as a hulking Delth man rounded the tower. He took no notice of them, turning to relieve himself against the stones. They waited, motionless, until he finished, yawned noisily, and stalked back out of sight.

Aiya felt Imar relax next to her and ventured another whisper. "As for the other matter, you assume too much about Strong. My feelings for him were not what you think."

Imar gave an amused smile. "You forget that I'm equally skilled in detecting a lie as you are in offering them. I know what I saw."

Aiya's cheeks warmed. "Perhaps there was the beginning of affection, but that has long since passed. Captain Strong—General Strong—is too...irreproachable. Easily admired but less easily known, you see? I could not feel for him what I feel for Dan."

Imar regarded her for a long moment and tilted his chin in an *I care not* attitude. "I wish only to see you settled safely with a man who can care for you as you deserve."

And I wish only to be with a man who doesn't feel a need to see me settled at all, Aiya thought. *One who will not hide me away in a quiet life where I don't belong.*

But she did not say this, for she didn't wish to offend her brother. He meant well, and she would always feel a debt of gratitude for how he'd cared for her in those difficult years when they'd fled Khourin to begin a new life in a strange land. But it wasn't enough anymore. Being with Dan had reminded her that life still held some surprises for her if she would only stir herself from her languor long enough to seize them.

She looked at Imar's profile, with his high brow and pronounced cheekbones. She loved him, but she couldn't live under his stifling watchful eye any longer. For the first time, she wondered if he felt the same way about her.

What might you have done with your life if you hadn't been bound to care for me? she wished to ask, but she was afraid of the resentment her question might raise. Someday, but not now as they crouched in the shadows of a forgotten garden, preparing to save a mad foreign king.

A muffled shriek off to the right caused her to jump. The squealing of the sow was amplified in the early morning stillness, and for a moment, Aiya worried that Dan would bring the whole of the enemy army down upon their heads. The Delth soldier that she and Imar had seen before appeared first. He peered into the trees, and Aiya breathed a silent prayer that Dan was well hidden. Two more Delth men joined the first, looking considerably more rumpled and disheveled. They conversed between themselves, but it wasn't until the sow herself appeared, running at full tilt toward the tower, that they jumped into action.

Two of the men leaped aside, but the other stood his ground as the sow plowed into him. Despite his size, she easily knocked him to the ground. He fell with a heavy grunt and lost his grip on the great pig, who escaped around the far side of the tower. With knives drawn, the Delth chased after her, and soon their crashing pursuit could be heard through the far side of the garden.

"That could have gone better," Imar said drily.

"It worked, didn't it?" Aiya pushed her way out of the hedgerow. Imar followed close behind, and by the time they reached the tower door, a breathless Dan had joined them.

"Did you mean to wake half the city?" Imar sneered.

"I couldn't hold her any longer," Dan said, chagrined, "but at least they took the bait."

Aiya looked past the two men, peering through the open door into the dark interior of the tower. "At least we know the tower's empty."

The smirk died on Imar's face, and he and Dan turned to follow her.

The inside of the tower was even more ghastly than the exterior. The room was warmer but smelled of rotting things, and the walls were so thick that what little light came in through the high slit windows made daylight seem a world away. The shadows felt unnaturally deep, as if something evil had coalesced there and watched them now.

Aiya shivered. The sooner they left this place, the better.

Upstairs they found few signs that anyone had recently inhabited the tower. A table lay overturned in the center of the room, its legs brutally ripped off. Whatever other furniture may have once existed had been removed, or perhaps scavenged for firewood. It didn't appear that the fireplace had held a blaze for some time.

Dan and Imar looked to the next flight of stairs, but Aiya hesitated on the first step, suddenly afraid to climb.

Pull yourself together. You've seen death before. What ails you? Bracing herself, she forced another step and another. Dan and Imar were already at the door, trying to force it open. Imar's frame was too slight, but with a well-placed kick and a great crack of splintered wood, Dan broke the door from its frame.

Then it hit her. The acrid scent of hell rushed down

the stairs from the floor above. Fire. Whatever waited in that room was not only death, but a scene out of her worst nightmares.

Dan moved the broken door aside and whispered a low oath. Imar muttered an ancient Khouri prayer against demons.

Aiya couldn't see beyond the men's backs filling the doorway, but she didn't need to. She smelled death and burning. Loss and horror. She closed her eyes against an image of flesh boiling and blistering in the heat, of white bone under a layer of ash, and when she opened her eyes, Imar was looking at her.

"You shouldn't be here, Aiya," he said gruffly.

"Where else shall I go? Shall I go chase a pig with the Delth?"

Dan stepped forward first—no, he stepped *over* something to enter the room.

Bending low, he examined the form on the floor. A body, Aiya knew without looking.

"There are others," Imar said, following Dan.

Aiya was the last to enter. She forced herself to look only at the charred remains of boots and bone as she stepped over the dead man's legs.

The room was rank with burning. Near the high ceiling, remnants of tapestries fluttered against blackened stone in the draft created by the open door. A large bed sat in the center of the room, its grand posts reduced to charcoal, the bed curtains lost to flame, and the center supports collapsed under their own weight.

Aiya stepped over a mass of metal barely visible in the ash—a candelabra perhaps?—and edged her way around the burned-out shell of a fallen bookcase, covering her nose against the stench. With every step, she kicked up a small cloud of ash. She made her way to one of the broken casement windows: its fragments of glass stained black with smoke.

"Here," Imar said from the far side of the bed. "Another one."

Dan joined him, but Aiya turned her back to the room. She rested her hands against the windowsill and let the crisp morning breeze wash over her, filling her lungs with clean air. She didn't want to hear their murmuring voices discussing the man whose body was only half burned, patches of thin white hair betraying his age. She'd seen death. She'd seen violence. But this was a scene out of the darkest recesses of her own personal hell, and she struggled simply to breathe.

Until Dan's voice rose with interest. "Whoever he is, it was not simply the fire that killed him."

Aiya's attention left her memories and focused on the present. The room was now hazy with stirred up ash, shafts of light from the open windows illuminating the gray dust lingering in the air. "What do you mean?"

"He's right," Imar said. "There's a head wound, a large one. Did he fall, do you think?"

"Then we should have found him on his back."

"Unless someone moved him."

"And would they have turned him over on his face? It doesn't seem likely."

"You think he was struck intentionally?"

"Perhaps," Dan replied. "I don't know how to see things any other way than as a soldier, but it does look like a battle wound."

"If it's a battle wound, then there should be a weapon."

"What about a candelabra?" Aiya offered. "I saw one just over there."

It took only a little searching before Dan found the ornate candelabra, silver by the look of it. "By the blood of the saints, Aiya, I think you're right."

"So they were attacked first," Imar said grimly, "and then the fire was set."

"Not burned alive, then?" Aiya asked hopefully.

"I don't know." Dan frowned. "The other body showed no sign of violence, though a sword lay nearby. He was still alive when they were locked inside and spent his final moments trying to get out."

The image haunted Aiya, and her throat constricted. Air. She needed air. But there was something else that tugged at her mind. Something important that she was forgetting, but she couldn't quite grasp it.

A shout from outside drew her attention back to the window. From that great height, she could see out over the courtyard and past the gates of the royal estate to the streets of the city.

"Captain Orri's troops are here!" she cried.

Hundreds of men in the crimson of the Rahmish army filled the streets, armed with a large battering ram to bring down the gates. Crying out in the guttural sound of their language, the Delth army gathered as a mob in the large courtyard.

"They must know they cannot win this fight," Aiya observed, watching the disorganized Delth preparing to face a sea of Rahmish soldiers.

"Let's hope they don't decide to gain advantage of a better view," Imar said pointedly.

Aiya shied away from the window, suddenly conscious of how precarious their situation had become. In doing so, she stumbled over a pile of debris, and Dan caught her before she fell.

"Thank you—" she began, then gasped and gripped Dan's arm.

Hidden in the shadows, a man leaned against the wall. For just a moment, Aiya thought the spectral shadow was grinning at her, then realized it was yet another corpse. But her composure was undone. She coughed on the rising ash, gagging as she thought of the death she was breathing in; the skin, the hair, the clothing now reduced to ash that filled her nose and throat. Nothing could clear the taste of it from her mouth and lungs.

Dan held her as best he could, his one arm wrapped around her shoulders. "I'm so sorry," he murmured into her hair. "If I had known—"

"Let's leave this place," she said, gasping for air. "There is nothing for us here."

"Not yet," Dan said apologetically. "If none of these bodies belongs to King Sindal, then he may yet be a prisoner of the Delth."

Aiya's heart sank, and she pulled away from Dan, finding her footing again. "Then quickly, please. Do what you need and let's go."

A thunderous boom resonated through the tower, startling them both. Dan rushed to the window. "Orri's men are breaking through the gates. We have little time. If any of the Delth seek refuge in this tower—" The rest of his words were drowned out by another terrific boom. In haste, he joined Imar in examining the third corpse.

Aiya glanced at the blackened door now hanging

from its frame, imagining how hopeless it would be to secure it against invaders. If the Delth tried to force their way through, there would be nothing to reinforce it, no way of pushing back against—

Then the missing piece fell into place, and she looked at Dan with horror.

"Dan! They were locked from the *inside*."

"What's that?" he asked, looking up from his search.

"You say the Delth locked them in, but the door was barred from the inside. Whoever barred it was still inside when they died."

Dan and Imar looked at each other.

"He was not trying to get out. He was guarding the door to make sure no one else could escape," Imar said darkly.

"But who...?"

At once, the two men rushed back to the first corpse they'd found, the one lying against the door just inside the room, a sword at his side. Aiya stayed at the window, watching as Dan and Imar sifted through the ashes, even shifting the body itself looking for some way of identifying him. Was he Delth? Or Rahmish?

Beneath layers of burned leather gloves, two rings appeared, fused to the flesh. Aiya turned away as Imar drew his knife to pry them free just as the boom of the battering ram gave way to an ear-splitting crack. The gates were breached. The sounds of battle and cries of the dying drifted through the windows as Orri's men flooded the courtyard.

"Dan, we must go!" Aiya urged.

He acted as if he hadn't heard her, staring at the rings in his hand as he knelt over the dead man.

Imar stooped to pick up the sword and started down the stairs at a run.

"Now!" Aiya said, tugging on Dan's sleeve. He nodded and clenched his fist around the rings. But still he paused, touching his hand briefly to his bowed head before rising to follow Aiya.

THIRTY-FIVE

As much as Merek hated a spectacle, Ria was right. The energy in camp—which had already been expectant—became almost celebratory as the two of them rode out side by side with an escort of soldiers. Soldiers and refugees alike gathered to see them off, and children pulled away from their parents to follow the procession to the main road.

Ria looked positively regal, despite the fact that the only adornment on her head was the sun glinting like fire in her chestnut hair. She held herself straight and tall in the saddle, and Merek was glad she'd come. He knew there had been ugly whispers among some of the nobility in camp that she wasn't fit to rule. If there were any doubts about whether she were fit for the throne, one only had to watch her confidence and poise to know she was born to this in a way few people ever were.

Inexplicably, however, Ria had taken one look at Merek astride his horse with that ridiculous cape fitted to his shoulders before announcing, "My dear Strong, I believe that you outshine me for once."

"Impossible." Merek snorted dismissively. But as they rode toward Albon, it did seem wherever pockets of individuals gathered to watch them, it was not Ria, but Merek himself who drew their attention.

He was taken aback the first time he heard a voice call, "I see him! He's coming!" The stirrings in the crowd grew at his approach, and the feeling of embarrassment turned to wonder.

"You're quite the attraction, it would seem," Ria mused.

"I can't imagine why," he grumbled. "It is you—not I—who should command their attention."

"Me?" Ria cocked her head. "I'm not the one who saved their city. Besides, they know me well. You, however, are something new. Can you blame them for wanting to see the man who will be their king?"

Merek's stomach tightened as he considered making such public shows a part of his new life. He'd ridden in processions with Sindal in the past, but then he'd been virtually invisible, one officer among many. It was discomfiting to have every eye turned to him.

But even discomfort fades in the face of tragedy. As they advanced further into the city, Merek forgot his embarrassment as the signs of war became more evident. The once bustling city seemed deserted, with beautiful buildings reduced to ruin and rubble. Familiar streets were all but unrecognizable, their buildings burned or left empty shells with paved roads impassible. Once majestic trees were lifeless now, chopped to ragged trunks or scarred by fire.

It pained Merek to see the beauty of Albon reduced to such waste in so short a time. When he'd fought the Delth as a young soldier under King Danvir, their battles had been in villages and towns near the border. He'd seen their ruthlessness, but somehow it was worse to see it on this scale; villages were easily built and twice as easily destroyed, but to see a noble city brought to its knees filled him with a cold anger.

Ria, too, grew quiet the closer they got to Thorodan Hall.

As they approached a wide plaza, a messenger met them with word of Orri's victory in securing the royal estate. The soldiers cheered this, and Ria smiled, but her smile had lost its luster.

"Go on," she said in a low voice for his ears alone. "I'll remain here until you return with word of my home." *Or what's left of it.* The unspoken words hung in the air between them.

"But your father. I thought you were anxious to know—"

"I've been thinking it over," she said, twisting the cuff of her riding glove nervously. "If my father lives, there will be time for reunion and rejoicing. But if not, I don't want to confirm with my own eyes the horrors I've imagined this past month. I want to remember him as he was before. He deserves that much, at least, no matter what he became at the end."

Merek understood. It had been more than twenty years since he'd watched his own father fall to bandits. He couldn't blame Ria for not wanting to live with such memories.

He instructed a dozen soldiers to stay behind and

guard her in his absence. As he left her, he dismissed the urge to turn back. *Pretend I am my father*, she had once told him, nearly a year earlier. He could no better do that now than he could then.

So much was complicated by his love for Ria that hadn't muddied his thinking when it was her father by his side. He would have supported—even encouraged—the king's boldness in conflict, risking his own safety to fulfill his duty to his people. But Ria? Merek abhorred the idea of putting her in any danger.

Yet how could he honor her as a true monarch if he was always trying to insulate her from risk? As he followed the avenue to the royal estate, Merek wondered if it would ever get any easier.

If he would ever learn how to love a queen.

The sounds that reached him as he approached the gates of the royal estate told him long before he rode through them that the fighting was over. There were no battle cries or a discordant chorus of steel, only the moans of the dying and commands to see to their comfort, or dispose of them as the case may be.

Passing through the gates, Merek dismounted to better make his way, appreciating the chance to stretch his leg. The courtyard was littered with the remains of the dead, and Merek was grateful that Ria hadn't accompanied him.

"Where can I find Captain Orri?" Merek addressed two corporals loading corpses into a hand cart.

They looked at him in surprise and quickly straightened into sharp salutes. "General Strong, sir! We didn't expect you. Shall I fetch the captain for you?"

"It's no matter. I don't wish to interrupt your work.

The princess follows behind, and I need you to be quick about it. Tell me where Captain Orri is, and I'll find him myself."

"He's inside, sir."

"And Alrek?"

"Captain Alrek is flushing the last of the Delth rats from the barracks."

And what do you know of the king? Merek wanted to ask, but he didn't dare. He didn't want to hear the ugly truth from a soldier whose name he didn't know.

"Thank you, Corporal. I believe I can find my way well enough."

Half of Thorodan Hall was gone, the roof collapsed and blackened walls leaning precariously on each other. It appeared the fire had started in the kitchens and had consumed one full wing before being extinguished.

But the main structure—the original manor that had been built by Albon the Great himself—still stood proudly amidst the destruction. The entrance doors were gone, but the large, aged timbers that braced the walls and ceiling looked sound. Indeed, as Merek looked up at the building he'd admired since his youth, it seemed to him that it gazed back in defiance. Gaining some comfort from this, Merek mounted the stairs.

Daylight filtered in through the gaping entrance to illuminate the hall. Once polished wood was now gray with filth and ash. Soldiers moved through the empty rooms, clearing the dead with dispassionate efficiency. Most of the dead were Delth, their furs and animal skins making them seem like half-man beasts from a child's nightmares. The illusion was enhanced by embellishments of teeth and hair and bones around their necks, arms, and hands. Merek's stomach turned at the sight of one man's headdress featuring what could have only been a child's hand preserved in some ghastly manner.

"General Strong!" Captain Orri emerged from a dark corridor, his hair limp with sweat and smelling of battle. "Forgive me, sir. I didn't know you had come."

"You've done your work well," Merek said, moving aside as three soldiers passed carrying a Rahmish man whose skull was pocked with splintered pieces of wood.

"I can't decide which is worse," Orri said with disgust. "The butchery these animals committed before we got here or the cowardly way they turned on each other once we did."

"Each other?"

"Yes, sir. In the chaos that followed breaching the gates, they lost all order and fell to attacking each other in an effort to save their own skins. Utterly mad!"

"What news of the king?"

Orri shook his head, and Merek's heart sank. For as much as he'd suspected the truth, a part of him had still hoped.

"Tell me."

"It's best you hear the story from Miss Aiya, sir. She's here somewhere, if you'll follow me."

Orri led Merek up through the gallery toward the private family rooms. It had been years since Merek had been in this part of the house, and it galled him to see personal items treated like so much refuse. A painting of the late queen had been defaced and lay discarded outside the king's bedroom, but it was the small lap harp lying in the debris which drew Merek's attention. His leg complained as he stooped to pick it up, gingerly cradling the limp pieces of wood that dangled loosely from the broken frame. Again, he was grateful Ria wasn't there to see the destruction. She would know the truth soon enough.

Sindal's rooms had been emptied to furnish his room in the tower, but they weren't empty now. Piles of clothing and straw mingled together to form nests where rats foraged for food. A horrible stench permeated the room despite the fresh air wafting down the corridor. Dark stains on the floor and walls mingled with bits of entrails and some foreign matter Merek didn't recognize. Merek's throat tightened as he envisioned himself chained to a table with Artem leering over him. His leg flared painfully in memory.

"Did the Ardanian prince know the devastation he was unleashing on this city?" a quiet voice reflected behind him. Aiya stood in the doorway, so still that Merek hadn't heard her approach. "Even if he gained all he wanted from the princess, what did he think he would find when he came to claim his prize?"

"Men like Artem don't see loss and grief as anything more than opportunity. He would have used it to his advantage and ignored those ravaged by his greed."

Aiya glanced around the room with a look of undisguised revulsion. "Your king is dead, my lord. I am sorry."

Merek nodded. "You found him here?"

"No, sir. In the tower. There was a fire. He and two others were lost. I do not know their names. Dan is searching for someone who can tell us who they are. But this, this is the king's?"

She stepped across the threshold and held out her

hand. In her palm rested a charred ring, streaks of black staining her skin.

Merek took it from her and peered at the familiar markings, now black with soot. "You found this on one of the bodies?"

She nodded. "I'm sorry we couldn't save him. It happened long before we came, probably while we were still in Endvar."

Merek closed his hand over the ring. The marred silver mocked him as a symbol of his failure. After a lifetime of friendship, how could he have let Sindal fall to the Delth? He wanted to be alone, to wrestle with his feelings unrestrained. But for now, he simply sighed. "Thank you, Aiya. You did all you could. I'm very grateful."

Aiya grimaced. "There is more. Dan thinks I shouldn't tell you. He says it will do no good to share the truth and that I should let the king keep his honor in death. But you were his friend, and I think you should know."

Merek's breath stilled. "What is it?"

"You can examine the tower room for yourself, but it appears there was a fight before the fire broke out. At first we assumed it was the Delth who caused the destruction, until we realized that the door was barred from the inside."

Merek was silent as the weight of the words settled over him. As grim as the signs of death were in the room where he stood, the thought that Sindal had been killed by one of his own trusted men was even darker.

But Aiya had spoken of honor. There was more she wasn't saying.

"You believe it was the king?"

Aiya hugged herself as if warding off the cold. "We found the ring on the body nearest the door. His sword was by his side. However the fire started, it would seem that the king condemned himself and the others to burn to death. I am...so sorry."

Merek gripped the ring tightly in a rush of anger against his old friend. How could he end his life in such a way? How could he give up and not fight against the Delth? How could he not stand against them to save his people?

"I will leave it to your discretion how to tell the princess," Aiya said, and with a half bow, she backed out of the room.

Merek's anger immediately gave way to pain. How could he tell Ria the truth? But on the other hand, how could he keep it from her? It was a heavy burden to carry such an ugly secret, and one that he couldn't protect her from forever.

Nor, he realized as he limped out of the room, did he have a right to.

Orri waited for him in the corridor.

"Find the princess a clean room to spend the night. I'm going to the tower."

Thirty-Six

Ria grimaced at the fallen statue that had once stood as a memorial to her grandmother who had started the first common schools in Albon. She'd been told as a girl that it was a beautiful representation of hope, but she had always thought the figure looked rather fierce with her unsmiling mouth and dead eyes. Now, Queen Irpa was nothing more than a trough for human waste, lying as she did in the center of the desecrated fountain.

"We've found her, Your Highness," Osten said at her elbow.

Ria looked past him into the crowd of citizens that swelled at the edges of the plaza. The soldiers had created a buffer around her, preventing the people from approaching too closely, but the fact of the matter was, the citizens of Albon only gave her a passing glance. They were far more interested in each other, anxious to inquire after loved ones and share the stories of those whom they'd lost. It was a peculiar mix of both joyful reunion and solemn grieving.

Osten's pronouncement kindled hope in Ria, and she followed the soldier around the base of the filthy fountain, scanning the crowd for Lotta's familiar face. Men and women looked at her curiously as she approached, and she smiled back in confusion. Where was Lotta? These were the faces of strangers, not her beloved friend. Ria's polite smile slid past a frail old woman, but she sensed the woman watching her so intently that Ria's gaze returned for a closer look.

"Am I that much changed that you don't recognize me?" the woman asked in a voice warm with familiar humor.

"Lotta! Oh!" And it *was* Lotta, Ria could see that now, but she no longer had the soft plumpness of a baker's wife. Instead, her skin sagged in wrinkles that made her look much older, and her eyes held a weighty sorrow unfamiliar on her friend's face.

The soldiers let Lotta pass, and Ria enveloped her in an embrace, cringing at how diminished she was. Yet, ill-fitting clothing and thinning hair notwithstanding, Lotta still carried herself with the poise and grace of a lady, and she would not allow Ria to fuss over her.

"It is good for my heart to see you so well, my dear," Lotta sighed.

"Tell me how you've been. I'd hoped you'd made it out of the city, but when I heard no word of you, I feared the worst."

Lotta's smile faded. "They came before we knew what was happening. With the bulk of the army in Endvar, and the king locked away in his tower, there was little resistance. The Delth could not have chosen a worse time to rouse themselves and come to war."

"On the contrary, it was exactly the time that Artem intended," Ria said bitterly. "He deceived us all, luring the armies to Endvar so that he could take Albon at will."

"Artem!" Lotta's eyes widened. "Prince Artem brought those savages to this land?"

"He's dead now," Ria said flatly. "He gambled everything and lost, and now we get to clean up his mess."

"Oh my," Lotta murmured and gripped Ria's hands. In her expression Ria saw a fresh grief that pricked Ria's heart with fear.

"Lotta, where is Pedr?"

Lotta's shoulders slumped slightly, and her eyes wandered to the crowd. Speaking quietly so that Ria had to strain to hear her above the rising din of the voices around them, she said, "I lost him early on."

Ria stifled a gasp. "How?"

"Pedr wanted to leave the city from the beginning, but there was so much confusion it was hard to know what was best. One day we heard tales of people fleeing to safety, and the next we heard of families who were caught trying to escape and flayed alive in the street. Some people claimed that the army was returning from Endvar, and others spread the tale that a winter storm made the roads impassible. It was hard to know what to do, and I begged him not to be reckless.

"Eventually, when it was clear no help was coming, I agreed to leave. Pedr had heard of a way out of the city, and we had our bags packed and were waiting for first light. The Delth were most active at night, you see, and by then we'd learned that early morning was the quietest time when we might sneak through the city unnoticed."

Lotta glanced at Ria and laughed weakly. "Look at me. Can you imagine an old woman like me trying to sneak anywhere? We're not soldiers or spies. A baker and his wife had little hope of getting far, but we decided to try. We had taken to sleeping in the oven rather than our beds, in case the house was searched during the night. It was warmer too, and the Delth had little enough imagination. They never looked for us there."

Ria tried to imagine her plump friends climbing up into the brick oven and squeezing themselves inside with no light and little air.

"What happened?" she asked, afraid for the answer.

Lotta licked her cracked lips. "They came the night before we were to leave. We slept with our packs, so we could leave at dawn. I was nervous about the winter cold, but Pedr was determined. So determined, in fact, that he left the oven to find another pair of stockings to add to his pack for me. Before he returned, three of the Delth came. The beasts found him upstairs." She shuddered. "I don't know what they did to him, but I heard his screams long after they left as they dragged him through the street."

Ria's throat constricted. "Might he still be alive? Are you certain—"

"I only pray they killed him quickly, and that his suffering was brief," Lotta said firmly. "And I praise the saints that you weren't in the city when they came."

Ria was silent. She couldn't speak to Lotta of the guilt that washed over her. It was a different kind of sorrow to know that she was safe and comfortable while Lotta was haunted by the memories of her husband's screams.

"What do you know of my father?"

"I wouldn't advise you to hope, my dear. Soon after they came, there was fire in the tower. It smoked for two days." As Lotta said these words, she shrank a little, her frame seeming so much older than her years.

Ria reached instinctively to support her, wrapping her arm around her hunched shoulders. "Let's find you somewhere to rest." The wide lip of the fountain was stained with filth. She removed her cloak and draped it over Lotta's shoulders, encouraging her to sit.

Around them, people milled about, humming with excitement. Ria's grief was new, but the suffering of these people had been replaced with hope, and they were invigorated.

Across the plaza, a stirring in the crowd signaled that someone was approaching. A chord of anticipation thrummed through the people until finally they parted to reveal a company of soldiers on horseback with Merek at the head.

Ria felt a slight release of tension. Nothing was more welcome than the sight of him, resplendent in uniform, towering over the crowd. He carried himself with such strength and command that a collective wave of relief passed through the people. A few even cheered their deliverer. But Merek only had eyes for Ria.

He dismounted in the middle of the plaza, and Ria stepped forward to greet him. He made an imposing figure, and if she hadn't known him as she did, she would have been intimidated into silence. Instead, her heart filled with pride. It wouldn't be difficult to turn her people's hearts to him.

Conscious of hundreds of eyes watching, she called out, "General Strong, I speak for the people of this city when I say that we owe you and your soldiers a great debt."

Merek's gray eyes were as hard as flint as he turned to face the crowd. Goodness, he was impressive in his armor.

"Albon is ours," he called, his voice resonating across the plaza. "The Delth have been vanquished, and our borders are secure once more." Merek didn't smile as the crowd roared. He looked weary, and Ria noticed that his hands were stained with soot.

Fire in the tower, Lotta had said.

My father.

Ria's own smile felt suddenly empty. She wished to be alone with Merek, away from the jubilant crowd, to ask the questions that rose in her throat.

"There's much work that needs to be done," Merek continued. "There are many graves to dig, homes that have been destroyed and roads that will need to be rebuilt. Anyone with a strong back will make the work lighter."

This dampened the joy of the crowd. Some looked at each other with stricken expressions. Others murmured with grim resolve. Ria understood how they felt; the complex war of relief, fear, and jubilation battled within her as well. She ached to gain comfort in Merek's arms, but her needs would have to wait. Her people needed her now.

"Good people of Albon," she said, and they quieted

again. "Many of your families and friends who fled the city have received great kindness from our neighbors. I saw with my own eyes how the people of Valdirk opened their homes and gave all they had. We will look to our brothers and sisters across Rahm to help us now, and they will come. It's this generosity of spirit that will rebuild Rahm and usher in a new era of peace."

Merek nodded deferentially and addressed the crowd even as he held Ria's gaze. "That new era begins today with all of you good people here as witnesses."

Ria's breathing grew shallow as, with an apologetic air, Merek dropped to one knee. A collective gasp hissed over the crowd. In the heavy silence that followed, he lifted his gray eyes to hers and held out a ring. It was her father's ring, charred black but still recognizable. It seemed a foreign thing to her now, separate from Sindal's strong fingers. And she knew, with a knowledge that ground into her heart like a silent clap of thunder, that he was dead.

"King Sindal is no more," Merek said without emotion, his private pain kept carefully out of sight. "Long live the queen!"

There was a rustling in the crowd as they took in his words, and then they took up the chant. Haltingly, at first, then growing in volume and fervor until the plaza stones rang with their zeal.

"Long live the queen!"

Ria smiled at their enthusiasm, but inside she felt sick. Had Sindal felt this way when Danvir died and he assumed the throne? She vaguely remembered her father's coronation as a time of feasting and celebration and a lovely new gown for the child princess. She never supposed he could have been hiding such crushing grief and despair behind a mask of gracious composure.

Queen.

It was a wretched way to fulfill one's destiny, and despite always knowing the title would be hers, somehow she hadn't fully considered the darker side of what it meant. She hadn't anticipated the loss that made it possible. She'd never imagined standing before a cheering crowd when all she wished to do was crumple onto the stones and weep.

Ria swallowed painfully and reached a hand toward Merek, taking the ring and raising him up to stand beside her. He squeezed her hand reassuringly as she smiled at the cheering crowd. For the first time in her life, words failed her.

Epilogue

"Finn! Your waistcoat looks as if you've used it to rub down Horace. Get a brush and tidy it. Quickly!"

Finn snatched the waistcoat from Aiya's outstretched hand and grinned sheepishly from behind a heavy forelock of hair that persistently fell into his eyes. She wished he would let her trim it more neatly so that he looked like a respectable young man, but Finn was now taller than she and carried with him a weight that made him seem older than his thirteen years. The things he'd experienced during the war had left him changed, and Aiya was careful to give him space to grow into himself.

Devn bounded down the stairs with his customary cheerful energy, bringing a smile to Aiya's lips. Devn reminded her more of Finn as she'd first known him than Finn himself. Carefree and eager to embrace life, Devn had regained his childhood. Aiya was determined to never give him a reason to lose it again.

"Those don't look like your boots, Dev," she chided him gently.

"I couldn't find mine," Devn explained, looking down at his feet where a pair of Aiya's own boots rested.

"Well, I won't have you running about the royal estate and putting holes in my shoes. Go look on the back step."

"Where's Dan?" Finn asked as he grabbed a cold flat-bread and stuffed it into his mouth.

"He left hours ago. This will be a very busy day for the Royal Guard, so we won't see him much."

"Will he save us a place to watch the queen?"

"Don't forget the king!" Devn added.

"I'll make sure we have a nice view, don't worry. Finn, make sure Dev finds his own boots. I'll meet you boys near the tower garden. Don't be late!"

Aiya kissed each boy on the cheek—and the excitement of the day was such that they forgot to complain—before slipping out the front door of their neat little house and into the street.

They couldn't have chosen a more beautiful day for a coronation. The sun shone warm and filled the air with the scent of lilac blossoms. Everywhere Aiya passed on her way to Thorodan Hall, signs of spring burst from each patch of earth and crevice.

Three months had passed since the Delth had been driven out, and the city was shedding its pallor of mourning in favor of youthful exuberance. There wasn't a street that didn't boast at least one —if not dozens—of new storefronts and homes. Streets had been repaved and trees replanted. Aiya was in awe of the industrious-ness of these Rahmish people who seemed not only content to return Albon to her former glory but also to give her a shiny new gown and slippers in the process.

The bustling traffic in the streets thickened as Aiya approached Thorodan Hall, and she was glad she'd chosen to walk rather than taking Horace and the cart. Otherwise, she couldn't have slipped past the row of carriages waiting for entry into the estate, walking through the gates with little more than a nod from the guards.

If spring had performed its dance all over Albon, it had been positively drunk with pleasure when descending on Thorodan Hall. Blossoming boughs bedecked walls and balconies, lanterns danced in leafy trees, and shrubs and flowers exploded with life in the beds edging the great house. With a coronation today and two days of feasting to follow, Aiya privately suspected that the princess was trying to compensate for her humble wedding. Delaying the ceremony until the height of spring certainly added to the extravagance.

A platform had been erected in front of the entrance steps, and servants were placing large bouquets of flowers along the edges, creating a profusion of plant life that would have seemed garish if it hadn't matched the lighthearted mood of the birds which whistled and sang overhead.

"Lady Aiya!" called a soldier in the green of the Royal Guard.

Aiya didn't know the young man's name, but they all seemed to know her. Ever since Dan had been chosen to replace Captain Drenall as head of the Royal Guard—a remarkable honor which had quickly gained Dan respect and notoriety—most of the soldiers had taken to treating

Aiya as if she were nobility. She'd grown weary of trying to correct them.

"Can I be of service, my lady?" the young man asked solicitously. "Shall I fetch Captain Dan for you?"

"No need. I'm here to answer a summons from the queen. Can you tell me where I might find her?"

The soldier looked toward the great house. "Master Rorden should know. I saw him not five minutes ago in the great hall."

Aiya nodded her thanks and skirted around the platform to climb the steps to the great house. The interior was a buzzing hive of activity as servants and courtiers moved about in rushed attention to the final preparations of the day.

"Aiya! Have you brought the boys with you? I'll put them to work filling woodboxes or polishing silver in the kitchens if you have." Rorden smiled, his dimples hidden by a trimmed beard, and his eyes just as mischievous as ever.

"Master Rorden," she greeted, offering a slight curtsy.

"None of this 'Master' stuff for me," Rorden scoffed. "I still suspect this is Strong's idea of a joke. Stewards are supposed to be old and experienced beyond the years of their lord. I think he appointed me just so he could get a good laugh when Cook gives me a dressing down about the quality of pork she has to work with. Never mind the war and the thousands of people still without homes. Her culinary reputation is at stake!"

Aiya laughed. "And I'm sure you smoothed her feathers in your winning way, just as Strong knew you would. He's fortunate to have you and wise enough to know it."

"Well," Rorden said, slightly mollified at the compliment, "it's still rather stifling, all these people watching and deferring to me."

"I know you too well to believe that." Aiya grinned. "You love to be admired."

"There is that, I suppose. Between you and me, the general is having a much harder time of that than I am. He can't stand all the groveling and hushed reverence when he enters a room. I don't blame him. There are those who won't look you in the eye so you can read their true thoughts but would put a knife in your back if they thought it would be to their advantage. It seems more of that kind survived the war than not."

"Dan says much the same. He's fierce in his loyalty and expects the same from his men in the Guard, but he still has a hard time trusting the royal couple's safety to anyone but himself. I expect we won't see him these three days until all the feasting is done and the guests have gone home. Is it true the Ardanian king himself is expected?"

"Not until summer. The queen didn't want to taint the coronation. This celebration is to be a gift for her people, and his presence would only be a mockery of their suffering."

Aiya nodded. "She's become quite the queen in such a short time, hasn't she? She's actually the reason I'm here. She asked to see me this morning, but I can't imagine why."

At this, Rorden pinked slightly. "That was likely my doing. I've suggested that Yulda be offered a position studying under the royal physician. His health is ailing, and he needs a new apprentice since the war. I thought Yulda would do well."

Aiya detected a warmth in his words that made her smile, but she didn't comment on it. "Why would the queen need me?"

"I suspect Her Majesty is afraid that Yulda's manners might not be suited to royal life. You worked with her in the camp and have been a good friend. If you spoke for her, it would mean a lot."

Aiya left Rorden with a promise to do her best for the young woman and made her way upstairs toward the private family rooms. She hadn't been in this part of the Hall since the early days of reconstruction, and the long corridors were now clean, well-lit and cheery. She stopped at the door to the queen's room where a rigid young soldier stood faithfully outside. But before she could knock, the door opened, and General Strong emerged.

He was conversing with a man dressed in white robes—the priest performing the ceremony, Aiya guessed—and didn't notice her at first. In that brief moment, Aiya caught her breath because before her stood a king. It wasn't simply the ceremonial armor and crimson robes lined with gold. It wasn't the royal crest that draped across his shoulders. No kingly crown yet sat upon his brow. And yet everything about his bearing, from his posture to the intelligent look in his eye as he dismissed the priest, spoke of both wisdom and authority. Aiya found herself bowing low in a deep curtsy, a movement of deference as natural as breathing.

Then he caught sight of her and smiled familiarly and the moment passed, the king giving way to Captain

Strong who used to roam the wilds of Rahm in simple forest garb, showing up shabbier and hungrier than when he'd left.

"My lord."

His gray eyes glinted with humor. "I suppose I can't correct you now. Strange, isn't it? A year ago who would have imagined the scene taking place today?"

"I could call you 'my captain' as once I did, if it makes you feel more comfortable."

"Please do. It sounds much better than 'Your Majesty.' Then I won't forget myself so readily when I'm drowning in a sea of empty-headed sycophants who are anxious to erase any memory of my humble beginnings."

"Will your mother and sister be joining the ceremony today?" Aiya bit off the words 'my lord' which so naturally to her lips. "I should be delighted to see Marga again."

Strong's eyes brightened. "Indeed. I'm anxious to see them myself. I've been told they arrived last night. I offered to let Mor stay here with us, but she said she couldn't leave Marga to manage the children on her own what with the baby—"

"Sir!"

They both turned as Dan's voice rang down the hallway. He strode down the corridor, his boots clicking crisply.

"Forgive me, sir, but Captain Talen is here to report on security. Rorden says if we take up more than thirty seconds of your time, we might as well cancel the entire coronation because we've already fallen so far behind schedule." A hidden smile colored his words.

As captain of the Royal Guard, Dan wore a rich green

uniform tailored well for his stocky build. These past months had seen a return of his former strength with no lingering trace of the damaged soldier who felt a burning need to prove himself. Indeed, his confidence and reputation earned him so much respect that Aiya sometimes had to remind him to put aside the 'captain' at home and just be Dan for her and the boys.

As he respectfully herded the general down the corridor, Dan glanced back at Aiya and gave her a swift wink. Her cheeks warmed pleasantly, and she indulged a private smile before entering the queen's chamber.

Ria sat on a padded stool before a large looking glass as Biren pinned yet another jewel in her hair that already sparkled like sunlight on water. An older woman who held herself like a great lady beamed at her with an expression of motherly approval.

Ria caught Aiya's reflection in the looking glass and greeted her warmly. "Do come in, Aiya! We're nearly finished. Lotta, please inform the general that we'll join him in the reception hall shortly."

"I believe General Strong is meeting with Captain Talen at the moment, Your Highness," Aiya offered.

"Is that right?" Ria glanced up at her maid. "In that case, perhaps Biren should join you, Lotta. And while you're at it, be sure to remind the good captain that he's invited to sit at our table during the feast where I expect he will find a most engaging dinner partner."

At this, Biren blushed prettily. "I think you're far too concerned about my love life, my lady."

"Nonsense," Ria said good-naturedly. "I wouldn't have to be concerned if every eligible bachelor in the court wasn't seeking your attention. I could scarcely converse with Lord Vestri the other day for all his attention to you. It's for the good of Rahm, I assure you."

After Biren and Lotta left, Ria's smile faded. "Thank you, Aiya. That was quite timely. Biren won't mind having a few extra minutes with Talen, so we should be undisturbed for the time being."

She rose from the stool and moved to the window, settling herself carefully on the edge of a padded bench to avoid putting creases in her voluminous robes. Aiya saw weariness behind her cheery disposition and recognized the attempt to hide her preoccupation.

Feeling like she were an intruder in the queen's private thoughts, Aiya was anxious to learn her purpose and excuse herself. "I understand that you wished to ask me some questions about the girl Yulda," she said.

Ria glanced at her. "Yulda? No, I believe I know all I need to about her. Keeping her tongue in check might be a challenge, but Erland will be a thorough teacher, in manners as well as skill. No, there's something else I need from you. Or rather, something that I would like to ask." She glanced down at her hands and smoothed the folds of her skirts.

"Yes, Your Majesty?"

Ria smirked a little. "The truth is, Aiya, for all your fine manners, you've never really honored me as a princess."

Aiya opened her mouth in astonishment, but Ria quickly interrupted her protest.

"Don't mistake me! I don't accuse you of disrespect. But I can sense that to you I'm only a woman playing dress-up with a pretty crown. In truth, I don't mind. I have plenty of subjects to appeal to my vanity when I wish it. What I lack are those who can look past the crown and speak to me as a woman."

Aiya wanted to object, but she sensed that Ria had a greater purpose, so she held her tongue.

Ria looked at her beseechingly. "Merek says that you lost a child some years ago, and that it was quite...tragic. Forgive me if I offend, but I was hoping that you might...well..." She took a deep breath and plunged ahead. "Can you tell me how long I'll feel this way?"

"What way is that?" Aiya asked, though she suspected she already knew. It was important for Ria to find the words herself.

"Like I'm living two lives. The first is what everyone expects of me: hopeful, industrious, and decisive. The other is filled with a dark pain that makes the rest feel false and meaningless. I can't number the days I long to send Biren away and close the bed curtains to hide the world. But each morning I paint on a smile and hope that this will be the day it gets easier. Then at night I dream of my father and awake as troubled as ever."

"What is the nature of your dreams?"

"Memories, sometimes. Usually happy ones, before his mind grew sick. Sometimes it's like a memory, but it's not a true memory, more like a wish. He's healthy and well and we're laughing together as we once did. Then I remember that he's gone, and I try to explain this, but he laughs and tells me not to be foolish because of course he's right there before me. And then he embraces me, and the feeling and smell of him is so real that I'm certain it has all been just a bad dream. His madness, the war, his death...Then I wake, and the hope only makes the pain in my heart more severe. But I don't wish the dreams to end because that's the only time I can hear his voice and see his face."

Aiya hesitated to speak, uncertain of how Ria might wish to be comforted. "Have you spoken to Strong of these dreams?"

A warmth crept into Ria's dark eyes. "Often, and I couldn't ask for a more solicitous husband. But when he lost his father, Merek fled to the army. I'm not sure he wrestles with his grief in quite the same way. Where I look for answers and meaning, he tries to compensate by saving the world. Not a bad trait to have in a king, but it does make me feel a bit needy by comparison."

Aiya knelt before Ria and clasped her hands, recognizing that this gesture of comfort only proved the truth of Ria's earlier words that Aiya didn't revere her in the same way her other subjects did. But Ria didn't shrink from her touch. If anything, she seemed grateful for it.

"Perhaps these dreams are a gift. Perhaps your father wishes to reassure you that he's well and comfortable and you needn't concern yourself about him any longer."

"I do, though. I wonder about his final moments and what happened in that tower room. I dream of it too, and it's…ghastly."

There was nothing Aiya could say to this because the king's end had indeed been horrible. She took a measured breath. "It won't last forever; I promise. You'll think of him every day, but it won't always be with such pain. In the meantime, each day you honor him by becoming the queen he always knew you would be. Beginning with today."

Ria grimaced. "I couldn't do it at first. For three months I couldn't bear to move forward with the coronation. I blamed the reconstruction and the need to divert all resources in caring for the homeless and hungry. But in truth it was because I feared that I wouldn't have the strength to stand before my people without resenting them for making me queen at the cost of my father's life." She paused and laughed lightly, shaking her head. "You see why I can't share these thoughts with just anyone? You must think me an ungrateful coward."

Aiya squeezed her hands. "Forgive me, my lady, but you're wrong about me. Perhaps I do see you differently, but that means that I can speak with great honesty unburnished by gleam of crown when I say that I will be honored to hail you as queen today."

Ria's eyes glistened momentarily, then she blinked and smiled ironically. "Once again, I find myself in your debt, Aiya. How do you always know what to say when I'm floundering? You know, we're in need of an ambassador to Khourin. I would be happy to grant the position to you if I thought you would even consider it."

Aiya laughed. "Never! I'm happy to leave the political intrigue to you. And you know that I could never pull Dan away from the Royal Guard."

"Then we have you well and truly trapped. Excellent. I'll have to thank Merek for his brilliant choice of captain."

A knock at the door brought them both back to the present as Biren and Lotta swept into the room.

"The king awaits you in the reception hall," Lotta said, a thrill of restrained anticipation in her voice.

Ria stood, and Biren hurried to arrange her long skirts behind her. She towered over Aiya as she straightened her shoulders. Only her dark eyes retained a hint of vulnerability. "May I call on you again, Aiya?"

"Of course. I'm at your disposal, Your Majesty," Aiya said with a smile.

Ria smiled back and despite her pain—or because of it—her smile illuminated her face with a beauty born of experience and understanding. Aiya watched the new queen leave the room with her attendants and marveled at the transformative power that love and purpose can bring to a life wounded by sorrow and loss. Then she left to find her boys.

· · ✳ · ·

With the great hall prepped for a large feast to follow the coronation, the private reception had been moved to the library——the second largest room remaining in Thorodan Hall since the war. All furniture had been removed to accommodate the dozens of nobility who'd been issued an invitation, requiring that the guests remain standing as they milled about the room, jostling for position closest to the royal couple.

"Perhaps they'll tire and leave quickly," Merek had said hopefully when he'd learned of this arrangement.

Ria had only laughed.

"Not sooner than you will, I can promise you. It's amazing how stroking a vain man or woman's ego with a private invitation will increase their stamina for social events. It's as though they're in an unspoken contest to outlast each other and prove that they are the most worthy guests deserving of our notice."

As in most matters in this new life of theirs, Ria tried

to hide her amusement at Merek's discomfort. The preening nobility paraded into the reception hall with such airs that the room soon grew hot with their own self-importance. Despite scarcely having room to fan themselves, they seemed in no hurry to leave, especially the more unpleasant ones.

Thankfully, not all of the guests were so tedious. There were a few whose attendance was as welcome as it was disruptive. Captain Falbrook and his wife brought with them a wonderful burst of refreshing earthiness in their homespun clothes and unadorned heads. And Ria was especially pleased to see Sigrid and Marga—the latter beaming with awe and approval, her belly swollen with the new baby to come any day now. Aiya's brother Imar also made an appearance as an honored guest, looking characteristically tidy and composed.

"I wonder if Imar would consider an invitation to serve as an ambassador to his home country," Merek murmured.

"How remarkable! I thought the same thing of his sister not an hour ago." Ria watched the slight man greeting others in the room, his dark eyes calculating behind his stoic expression.

"Aiya?" Merek considered this. "Would she accept, do you think?"

"No. She was very clear on that. I felt as if I were insulting her. I sense that Aiya wishes to stretch her wings without intrusion on her freedom, no matter how well intended."

Merek grunted. "She has certainly earned that right."

"I agree. Ah, the wolf has made an appearance at last," Ria said sourly as Lord Hegrin approached with his son at his side. "Smile, my love, lest he knows how much we despise him."

And so it continued. The sun was high in the sky and cast patches of bright light on the polished wood floors before Rorden finally invited the guests to make their way outside and find their seats for the coronation. As the doors closed upon the last guest, Merek exhaled in relief.

Ria chuckled and scanned the room for the nearest decanter of wine. "You did very well. You didn't even strike Lord Hegrin when he suggested that we allow his family to cover the cost of the festivities, as I know you wished to."

"It was that obvious?"

"Only to me. Come, have some wine. It will calm your nerves." She handed him a glass.

His fingers brushed hers as he took it, but instead of drinking, he reached for her waist with his other hand and pulled her to him, his gray eyes softening. "I don't need wine to calm my nerves. All I need is you by my side, and I can face anything."

Her heart beat quicker at his nearness. "Anything?"

"Anything."

"Even dancing at the feast?"

Merek grimaced. "Even dancing at the feast. Though I fear I'll be revealed as a clumsy oaf in king's robes."

Ria laughed brightly. "You don't give yourself enough credit. You're frightfully imposing, you know. I will dazzle them with my smile and you will awe them with your scowl."

Merek snorted. "*That* at least will be genuine."

She reached up to kiss him softly. "Does this settle your nerves?" she murmured against his lips.

"Hmm. Only if it means you won't stop. Do you think we could bar the door, and they'd all go away?"

As if in answer, a rousing cheer from outside drew their attention to the window. Rorden was addressing the crowd which had swelled to fill the courtyard and spill over into the streets beyond. Lords and ladies and commoners alike crowded into the courtyard dressed in their best, the children waving ribbons and flowers that would later be showered upon the new queen and king as they stood before them as newly crowned monarchs. Every face beamed with jubilation. Ria's heart swelled in her chest.

But next to her, Merek wiped his palms on his robe. She could feel the tension leaking from him. She reached for his hand and squeezed it reassuringly.

"I just pray that I will never give these people any cause to regret offering their allegiance to me today."

"Of course you will," Ria said lightly. "We both will. We'll make mistakes which bring their own regrets. And for as many of our people as think we can do no wrong, there will be others who curse us and think we can do no right."

"That…isn't comforting."

"That is what it means to rule. We'll spend the rest of our lives earning their allegiance over and over again. But as long as we honor them for it, and remember that their loyalty is bought with our service, then they will give it freely."

At that moment, the doors to the library opened and Captain Dan entered.

"It's time, Your Majesties," he announced.

Ria felt a surge of excitement, but Merek only sighed. Ria made a show of straightening his robe on his shoulders and smoothing the fabric with her fingers. Then she stood back and looked him over approvingly. "Well, then. There's only one thing missing. Let's go get our crowns, shall we?"

Don't say goodbye to Wallkeeper just yet!

If you enjoyed *Gleam of Crown*, please consider leaving a review on Amazon or Goodreads. (Or both for you over-achievers!) Thanks for helping get my work into the hands of other readers like you.

If you aren't ready to leave the Wallkeeper world just yet, I have a special treat for you. After finishing Ria and Merek's story, I couldn't stop thinking about some of the untold stories that didn't get time in the spotlight, including the truth behind Domar's betrayal of Artem. I wasn't sure I wanted to commit to another full novel, so for two years it sat in my mind as a "maybe someday" project.

But it wouldn't rest.

Eventually I realized that I could share the important

highlights in an extended epilogue, and I'm delighted to make it available to you now.

Taking place about five months after the coronation, the occasion is a visit from Artem's brother (King Idan of Ardania) who has come to negotiate a new treaty with Ria and Merek. You'll get a peek into how all your favorite characters are growing into their new roles, and will learn how one peripheral character impacted the events in *Gleam of Crown* without Ria and Merek ever realizing it. For years I've kept these connections to myself, and I'm delighted to finally share it with you!

This exclusive epilogue is available to download when you sign up for my newsletter at https://carenhahn.com/crown. As a special perk, you'll also be the first to know about current projects and new releases.

Here's a short excerpt from the epilogue:

Merek crouched beside Orri, peering through a thick elder-berry bush to see the carriage below. It was outfitted with a stunning team of six, all white and wearing ornate livery in lavish purple. A few figures milling around in matching livery must have been servants. But it was the soldiers who caught Merek's attention.

His breathing accelerated and his hand went to his hilt before he realized he'd moved.

Ardanians.

The last time he'd seen that many Ardanians in their distinctive pewter-colored armor had been in battle.

Orri shifted next to him. "Is that King Idan?"

Merek blinked, clearing away the memory of death. He scanned the surrounding area and spotted a man and woman in royal dress. The woman was sitting on a stump while the man paced. Merek felt a twinge of humor at his impatience.

"Let's go meet them."

"My lord?"

Merek still grimaced inwardly at the term. Every time someone used it he felt like they were trying to put him in his place. To remind him who he was supposed to be. Perhaps that's why he now felt so reckless.

"They don't know who we are. We have the advantage."

"But Your Majesty, there are over thirty soldiers down there. And only three of us." Orri was careful to keep his tone respectful, but Merek knew him well enough to hear the undertone as if he'd spoken it aloud. Are you mad?

He grinned. "Come, Orri. A chance to measure our enemy before the battle? Why wouldn't we take it?"

Want more? Download the full prologue at carenhahn. com/crown.

THE HATCHED TRILOGY

**Domesticated dragons.
What could go wrong?**

"Interesting, funny, dragon drama and I can read it in
public - PERFECT!"

"Super fun, great writing, and nice romantic tension"

"witty banter, sweet romance, and daring intrigue"

"highly recommend"

What do a high-octane mommy blogger, a Wild West romance, and a [possibly] possessed antique doll have in common?

You can find them all in my FREE collection of short stories. Visit carenhahn.com to download your copy!

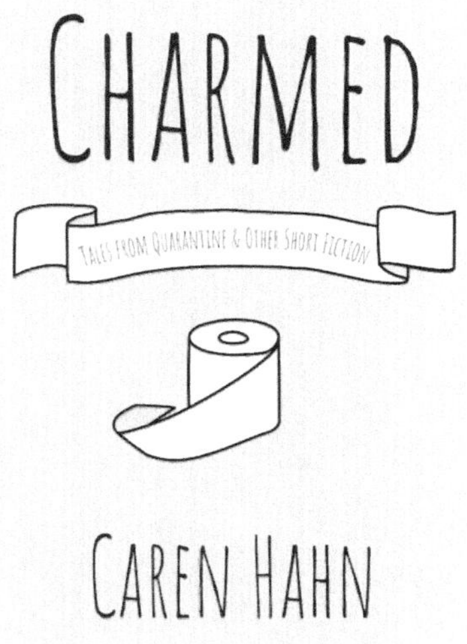

Acknowledgments

Thank you so much for joining me on this adventure! It's been a fantastic experience sharing the *Wallkeeper* trilogy with the world. I can't express enough my appreciation for readers like you who took a chance on a debut author, and then followed Ria, Merek, and Aiya all the way through to the end. Nothing is more rewarding than hearing from new readers who've fallen in love with this story!

Beta readers are a crucial part of any writing process, and I'm grateful to Crystal Brinkerhoff, Rachel Stauffer, Cori Hatch, Carli Schofield, Joan Schofield, Cindy Schofield, Chris Schofield, Jenny Hahn, Julie Whipple, Sara Epling, and Renae Southwick for their early input.

I remember vividly where I was when Cori Hatch called me after reading the first draft. Her enthusiasm for this project still gives me courage even three years later.

A special thanks to Julie and Chandler Whipple who took me rock climbing among the pounding surf of the Northern California coast so I could learn for myself what impossible things I expect from my characters.

Crystal Brinkerhoff was in the trenches with me from the very beginning, and has more recently tried to teach me how to establish a social media presence. (Trust me, that's harder than it sounds.)

Once again, Rachel Pickett deserves a medal for not only polishing things up until they shine, but also for being game when I pushed up the deadline. Because I'm considerate that way.

I couldn't have taken on this challenge without the support of my family. My children endured a global pandemic, social isolation, and remote schooling while their mom was feverishly working on a project whose scope was more ambitious than any of us fully comprehended when I started.

Last of all, my husband, Andrew, continues to be my unfailing support, business partner, and biggest fan. In addition to his amazing design skills, he performs all the mind-numbing technical work of bringing my ideas to life so that I can focus on creating worlds through words. In many ways, Ria and Merek's story is our story, because everything I know about love, cooperation, and loyalty comes from our more than two decades together.

About the Author

CAREN HAHN is a Fantasy and Mystery author specializing in clean, relationship-driven fiction featuring empathetic characters who are exquisitely flawed. She graduated from Brigham Young University where—between courses on Humanities,  English Lit, and Biblical Hebrew—she squeezed in as many Creative Writing classes as she could. Caren lives in the Pacific Northwest with her husband and six children.

Visit carenhahn.com to learn more about her upcoming projects and download a free collection of short stories.

www.ingramcontent.com/pod-product-compliance
Lightning Source LLC
Chambersburg PA
CBHW050855210726
48290CB00004B/1237